SHAKESPEARE FOR EVERYMAN:

Ben Greet in Early Twentieth-Century America

Figure 2. *Ben Greet. 1909*. Photograph by Arnold Genthe.

SHAKESPEARE FOR EVERYMAN:
Ben Greet in Early Twentieth-Century America

Don-John Dugas

Foreword by Simon Callow

Society for Theatre Research
London
2016

First published in 2016
by the Society for Theatre Research
c/o The Theatres Trust, 22 Charing Cross Road, London WC2H 0QL

ISBN 978 0 85430 081 5

General Editor of STR Publications: Marion O'Connor

Volume Editor: Franklin J. Hildy
Volume Designer: Leigh Forbes

Printed and bound by
Henry Ling Ltd., The Dorset Press, Dorchester DT1 1HD

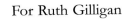
For Ruth Gilligan

CONTENTS

LIST OF FIGURES AND SOURCES

It has proved impossible to locate some of the copyright owners of some of the figures, but if the author or publisher is informed, details will be added at the earliest opportunity.

LIST OF TABLES

Abbreviations of Sources Frequently Cited

Archives

Iowa = Redpath Chautauqua Collection, University of Iowa.

Michigan Love = Letters, Playbills, and Photos to Mrs Lucy Love from Sir Philip Ben Greet, University of Michigan Library (Special Collections Library).

NYPL = Sir Philip Ben Greet Papers, New York Public Library Archives.

Yale Love = Love Family Papers, Manuscripts and Archives, Yale University Library.

Newspapers

BE = *Brooklyn Eagle*

BET = *Boston Evening Transcript*

BGl. = *Boston Globe*

CTr. = *Chicago Tribune*

PI = *Philadelphia Inquirer*

NYDM = *New York Dramatic Mirror*

NYH = *New York Herald*

NYMT = *(New York) Morning Telegraph*

NYS = *(New York) Sun*

NYT = *New York Times*

NYTr. = *New-York Tribune*

SFC = *San Francisco Call*

WH = *Washington Herald*

WTr. = *Washington Tribune*

Contemporary Theatrical Reference Works

JC(1902) = Julius Cahn, *Julius Cahn's Official Theatrical Guide*, VII (New York: Empire Theatre, 1902).

JC(1904) = Julius Cahn, *Julius Cahn's Official Theatrical Guide*, IX (New York: Empire Theatre, 1904).

JC(1905) = Julius Cahn, *Julius Cahn's Official Theatrical Guide*, X (New York: Empire Theatre, 1905).

JC(1909) = Julius Cahn, *Julius Cahn's Official Theatrical Guide*, XIV (New York: Empire Theatre, 1909).

C-L(1913) = Julius Cahn and R. Victor Leighton, *The Cahn-Leighton Official Theatrical Guide*, XVII (New York: New Amsterdam Theatre, 1913).

Acknowledgements

This study grew out of an invitation to deliver a lecture at the annual meeting of the Illinois High School English Teachers' Association. I would like to thank David Raybin, late of Eastern Illinois University, for introducing me to that lively crew and for suggesting I find a topic 'with an Illinois connection'. Little did we know. A few years later, I presented a more developed version of that talk at the University of Delaware. In the discussion that followed, several of my hosts — Jay L. Halio, Matthew J. Kinservik, Lois Potter — hypothesized on how Greet's work might connect to some of the better-known American Shakespearean achievements of the 1910s, '20s, and '30s. I remain grateful for their hospitality, interest, and ideas.

Making new friends while exploring archives is one of the pleasures of research. Kate Hutchens of the Special Collections Library at the University of Michigan may have been as keen as I was when she started carrying out the impressive Greet artefacts Isaac Newton Demmon preserved early in the last century. One of the world's leading authorities on circuit Chautauqua, Kathryn Hodson, Manager of the Special Collections Department of the University of Iowa Libraries, extended a gracious welcome and ensured that the days I spent working with the formidable Redpath Chautauqua Collection would be just as fruitful. Michael Frost of Yale University Library's Manuscripts and Archives was friendly and helpful. The staffs of the Folger Shakespeare Library, the New York Public Library's Manuscript and Archive Division, and the Victoria and Albert Museum's Theatre and Performance Archives were no less attentive and obliging. My thanks to them and the librarian-archivists who provided remote assistance with as much courtesy and skill as if I had been able to visit their institutions: Janice Braun of Mills College; Louisa Hoffman of Oberlin College; Amy McDonald of Duke University; Elspeth Healey and Letha Johnson of the University of Kansas; Tim Hodgdon of the University of North Carolina at Chapel Hill; Pam Beaty and Neil J. Guilbeau of Mississippi State University; Curt Hanson of the University of North Dakota; and Prudence Doherty, Nadia Smith, and Sharon Thayer of the University of Vermont.

A series of undergraduate research assistants helped retrieve the hundreds of newspaper articles and compile the 3,500+-date performance calendar upon which this study is founded. I am grateful to Hanna Brady, Jordan Canzonetta, Kasi Karr, Will Kucinksi, Molly MacLagan, Emily Rawlinson, Hagan Whiteleather, and Jillian Winter for their diligence, questions, and suggestions. I would also like to thank my colleagues in the Department of English, Kent State University, for their support, particularly the sabbatical leave they granted me during the 2012–13 academic year.

Kathryn Hume, Laura L. Knoppers, and Robert D. Hume taught me my craft; any shortcomings in the way I practice it are my own. To Paul D. Cannan, Kate Contakos, Paul M. Cobb, Colette M. Dugas, Estelle A. Dugas, Aoife Mooney, Mark Pilkinton, and Mary Volland, who provided advice and support during the long process of researching and writing this book, my thanks. Thanks, too, to Bob Peyak, Jim Voneida, and the great people at the Wheel and Wrench for keeping me on the road.

I am the beneficiary of the extraordinary generosity of Rosemarie K. Bank and Richard H. Palmer, who not only read my sprawling first draft, but also offered invaluable suggestions for improving it. Thank you both for your kindness, encouragement, and sage counsel. I am grateful to Donald G. Dugas and Harold H. Robinson, who read and commented on a more polished version to ensure it would be accessible to non-specialists. To Michael Dobson, who endorsed it at a critical juncture, my deep thanks. That Franklin J. Hildy accepted the editorship of this volume has been my good fortune; I am grateful to Frank for his support, attentiveness, corrections, and many fine contextual recommendations. To designer Leigh Forbes, indexer

Cynthia Savage, and image restoration specialist Paul Hasson of Tomorrow's Treasures, thank you for making such a handsome book.

I remain in a happy state of amazement that this project should have attracted the interest of Simon Callow. I am obliged to that renowned theatrical polymath for taking time out of his hectic schedule to help restore Ben Greet to the history of Shakespearean performance.

My final and most fulsome thanks go to Marion O'Connor, to whom I owe a debt of gratitude that is beyond repayment, but not, I hope, beyond acknowledgment. As the world's foremost authority on William Poel, she spotted my errors and directed me to resources I had missed. As chair of the Society for Theatre Research's Publications Subcommittee, she championed this study, urged her colleagues to ratify it, and oversaw its publication. I hope the world will think it a credit to her and the society.

FOREWORD

When I first went to work at the National Theatre as an actor, one of the senior members of the company, the great Michael Bryant, having detected a certain extravagance in my acting, nicknamed me Ben Greet. His implication was that I was a bit of ham, which was probably true, but very unfair on the subject of this illuminating new book. Greet was that unusual thing, an actor-manager who played secondary roles, only occasionally leading his companies, and then only in comedies. In fact, as Don-John Dugas's admirably lucid book makes clear, he was a remarkable, innovative, and somewhat radical figure whose contribution to the theatre of his time (and by extension the theatre of our time) was immense. Insofar as he is known at all — and Bryant's joke at my expense was lost on most of my fellow actors, who had never heard of him — he is remembered as one of Lilian Baylis's directors of production at the Old Vic during the immensely difficult First World War period.

What I think none of us suspected is what the present book makes abundantly clear: that Greet was something of an experimentalist. Though not in the front rank either as an actor or a director, he blazed trails in all directions, first as a pioneer and leading practitioner of what was then known as Elizabethan Manner productions, with their emphasis on clarity of text and fluidity of scenes, then as a discoverer and trainer of actors (he founded an Academy of Acting a good eight years before the creation of RADA), and finally as a promoter of what we would now call outreach — encouraging young audiences, both schoolchildren and university students, to experience Shakespeare live. Having toured productions for years before he came to the Vic, playing in every possible space, however unsuitable, he had become remarkably adaptable in his approach to staging, with results that were almost accidentally radical. During his time at the Vic, this same flexibility enabled him to counter the dearth of male actors by casting women in male roles, an experiment with which we are only now catching up. He brought his legendary production of *Everyman* to the Old Vic, staged *Hamlet* in its entirety, and dramatized Mendelssohn's oratorio *Elijah* — another innovation which has only recently become commonplace. Underpinning all of this was his deeply committed Christian Socialism, which he shared with Lilian Baylis (their singing from the same hymn-sheet, so to speak, did not prevent them from having epic altercations, in the course of which not once, but twice, Greet forcefully tweaked Baylis's nose).

Greet's career spanned a remarkable 56 years; in 1929 he was knighted for his services to the Old Vic and his devotion to Shakespeare. It was a rich, full career, over the course of which he contributed immensely to the life of the theatre, the gratification of audiences, and to proper appreciation of Shakespeare. He was a strong-minded and colourful character, and not without personal bravery: during the First World War, he would go on stage in costume and make-up to warn the audience of the imminence of Zeppelin raids, giving them the opportunity to leave the theatre if they so desired. Few did, but one night he went onstage dressed as a character who met a rather grisly end in the play, and large numbers of the audience fainted. This is a life which deserves to be much more fully chronicled, but Mr Dugas has done us an immense favour by recording in great detail and with immense sympathy an aspect of that life which even those of us who are fascinated by theatre history will scarcely have known of — Greet's American years. These were no mere diversion from his British career: they were in many ways the making of him. But more importantly, they were the making of modern Shakespeare in America. Dugas arrestingly tells us that Greet's *New York Times* obituary noted that he had done 'more to popularize Shakespeare than any one who ever lived'. That was in 1936, since when it is doubtful whether anyone has appeared to challenge that position. Mr Dugas justifies the claim in the enthralling pages that follow, and we should all be grateful to him for pulling a great man unfairly relegated to the shadows back into the limelight where he properly belongs.

Simon Callow, Islington, 2016

INTRODUCTION

Early in the afternoon of 14 May 1903, a few thousand members of New York society set out in their carriages and automobiles. Their destination: Columbia University. Their purpose: attend a benefit performance of William Shakespeare's *As You Like It*. But this promised to be no ordinary presentation. The first open-air production ever staged in Manhattan (or so all the newspapers claimed), it was a novelty witnessed by few Americans. And the company mounting it was none other than the English one led by Ben Greet, whose much-discussed production of the medieval Morality play, *Everyman*, had been the surprise critical and commercial hit of the 1902–03 theatrical season. One of the major events on the social calendar that spring, the fundraiser was organized and attended by some of the most distinguished women in the country.

The *New-York Tribune* provided the most comprehensive coverage:

New-York society and New-York lovers of the drama to the number of 3,500 sat in the sun and witnessed a production novel to this city [...] 'As You Like It', played on the lawn with shrubs and flowers for a foreground, and the trees and interlaced boughs for a background [...]. The players [...] were all from Ben Greet's 'Everyman' company [...]. They were well trained in their parts, and the result of the performance was much more than a pleasant novelty; like 'Everyman', it was a real glimpse into an earlier time.

The performance was given in aid of the kindergartens of the University Settlement, under the patronage of many of the best known women of the city so that the audience was exceptionally brilliant, and, sitting on camp stools in the open field facing the wooded mound where the play was given, made a bright picture [...]. Outside the canvas fence which bounded the amphitheater, scores of automobiles, carriages and coaches were gathered [...] and neighboring roofs and windows were filled with faces. Mr. Greet probably never played to a larger audience.

The reporter did not exaggerate the importance of the affair's patroness listed later in the article, the names of several of whom still retain their Gilded Age lustre. Under the leadership of the wife of international financier James Speyer, the event was organized and sponsored by Mrs Astor, Mrs Carnegie, Mrs Drexel, Mrs Gould, Mrs Harriman, Mrs Huntington, Mrs Juilliard, two of the Mrs Rockefeller, two of the Mrs Vanderbilt, and Mrs Whitney. Among the less famous persons it attracted were a pair of Shakespeareana collectors from Brooklyn, a couple by the name of Henry Clay and Emily Jordan Folger, though they were hardly prominent enough to interest anyone from the papers. That the event raised $10,000 (£2,000) — some $260,000 (£183,000) in today's money — indicates how much affluent Americans enjoyed Shakespeare, a good cause, novelty, and an opportunity for display, if not necessarily in that order.[1]

Seven months after first setting foot in North America, Ben Greet had arrived. The way Shakespeare would be presented on the continent would never be the same.

$*$ $*$ $*$

This book chronicles the North American career of the man whose epitaph in the *New York Times*, 'Did more to popularize Shakespeare than any one who ever lived', was as simple as it was meaningful.[2] The English actor-manager Sir Philip Barling Greet (1857–1936) had an extraordinary impact on American culture. He brought Shakespeare's plays to millions who would not otherwise have seen them. At the same time, he established practices and expectations that endure to this day. Americans who attend performances of Shakespearean plays presented out of doors or at festivals participate in traditions Greet inaugurated. Americans who attend performances of Shakespearean plays mounted at universities, colleges, and high schools do likewise. Americans who think the best way to present a Shakespearean play is on a bare stage using a full text delivered swiftly and unexaggeratedly by actors wearing Elizabethan dress do so at least partly because of him. In short, Ben Greet fundamentally changed how and where Americans 'do' Shakespeare.

For eighteen years between 1902 and 1932, Greet and his companies performed, indoors and out, for audiences that ranged from traditional to unlikely. They played for middle- and upper-class audiences in commercial theatres in the country's largest cities, for middle-class audiences in theatres in smaller ones, and for socialites on the grounds of private estates, country clubs, and resorts. They introduced professional Shakespeare to college campuses; appearing at more than 265 institutions on more than 780 dates, they performed more Shakespeare for more undergraduates and professors than any company in history. They introduced professional Shakespeare to schoolchildren in halls, auditoriums, and theatres. More surprising, they introduced it to two huge audiences whose religious beliefs had previously compelled them to eschew dramatic performance: educationally minded Lyceumites in the halls and auditoriums of cities and towns, and similarly inclined Chautauquans on the grounds of religious summer camps and in huge tents raised outside rural communities. Sitting presidents Theodore Roosevelt, William Howard Taft, and Woodrow Wilson patronized Greet's work. Mrs Roosevelt was such an admirer that she invited the Ben Greet Players to be the first professional company ever to appear at the White House. Standard Oil executive and Shakespeareana collector *par excellence*, Henry Folger, and his wife, Emily, were also interested in Greet, attending performances by his company, initiating a correspondence that continued for decades, and entertaining him at their home. During Greet's final weeks in the United States in 1932, Emily Folger invited him to formally represent the English stage at the signal Shakespearean event held in the country that year: the dedication of the library she and her husband founded in Washington, DC.

Greet was — and is — an important figure in the history of Shakespeare in America. Like many in that story, he was an energetic entrepreneur. He never grew rich, but his talent for artistic and managerial innovation as well as his tireless quest for new audiences enabled him to effect cultural change on an unparalleled scale

Greet was an innovator whose work had a democratizing effect on American culture. He created several new productions, a business model that enabled him to continue to stage them, and a simple, robust Shakespearean production method that endures to this day. But his greatest contribution was to bring Shakespeare to a vast and disparate audience. Ironically, the overwhelming success of his Elizabethan Manner production method may be the reason so few people have commented on it or heard of Greet. Starting in the 1910s, so many people began adopting it that Greet's introduction of it, and his protracted, costly, and at times bitter fight to establish it, receded into the cultural background. Another method, Spectacular Realism, had once dominated, and the way we now assume is 'natural', 'obvious', and 'normal' did not exist. Greet's method was, in fact, an invention, and things today might be different had he not successfully developed and spread it. And yet one of the most influential Shakespearean interpreters of the modern era is missing from every story of Shakespeare in America.

Accounting for how we have almost forgotten Greet is more difficult than explaining why he is worth remembering. The entry on him in *The Dictionary of National Biography* (1949 supplement) judged his importance to have been less than that of contemporary Sir Frank Benson and roughly comparable to that of contemporary William Poel, a hierarchy replicated in Phyllis Hartnoll's *The Oxford Companion to the Theatre* (1951) as well as in American reference works such as F. F. Halliday's *A Shakespeare Companion: 1550–1950* (1952) and Oscar James Campbell and Edward G. Quinn's *The Reader's Encyclopedia of Shakespeare* (1966).

That the only biography of Greet should emphasize his work in England is logical given that less than a third of his long career was spent in North America, but what *Ben Greet and the Old Vic* (1964) signals about its subject is more problematic. Benson's and Poel's biographies were written by men of some theatrical standing and published by respected presses known for their strong theatrical lists. Greet's was written by the less-well-known Winifred F. E. C. Isaac. More interested in programme transcriptions than in analysis, unedited, often failing to specify (let alone cite) its sources, lacking an index, and self-published, it is as frustrating to use as it is scarce. That Greet did not receive a proper biography implied he did not deserve one.

As wayward as it is, Isaac's book hints at an American career so exceptional that it inspired two doctoral dissertations. The haphazard deployment of a handful of newspapers not as well-chosen as they might have been, narrow use of the least significant of the four major American Greet archives, and topical organization (Greet as director, Greet as producer, Greet as actor) seriously limit the usefulness of Dale Erwin Miller's 'Ben Greet in America: An Historical and Critical Study of Ben Greet's Theatrical Activity in America' (1972). Considerably more worthwhile is Lew Sparks Akin's 'Ben Greet and His Theatre Companies in America: 1902–1932' (1974). Akin selected his handful of newspapers judiciously and worked them systematically. He, too, knew of the existence of only a single archive, but he sourced one of the richest and proficiently used the part of it he accessed. Although Akin overlooked several major accomplishments and failed to recognize the significance of others, he pieced together the first adequate overview of Greet's American career, and the revelations made possible by his chronological organization persuaded me of the wisdom of following his example. Neither of these studies nor any parts thereof being published, they did little to stimulate interest in the actor-manager.[3]

Ben Iden Payne's autobiography, *A Life in a Wooden O* (1977), cast Greet in a disreputable light. Payne recounted that Poel refused to allow photographs to be taken of his 1908 production of *Measure for Measure* because he feared that Greet, then touring on the other side of the Atlantic, would acquire and use them to 'steal' the production the way he had done *Everyman* in 1902.[4] By so doing, Payne called Greet's ethics and originality (not to mention Poel's mental stability) into question. Perhaps more surprising is the fact that this is his sole reference to Greet. Payne's chapter-long description of the process by which he began developing his Modified Elizabethan Staging method beginning in the 1910s implies that he introduced Elizabethan performance to North America. I do no doubt Payne came up with his own method based on the principles Poel taught him with a few refinements taken from Harley Granville Barker. I am less certain no one in the United States could have attested that Greet had successfully introduced Elizabethan Manner to Broadway in 1904, that it had provoked a long and heated debate there, that a major Broadway company used it in 1910, that Greet had lectured on and demonstrated it at the Carnegie Technical Institute immediately prior to Payne's first residence there in 1914, and that the consensus by the time of the Shakespeare Tercentenary of 1916 was that it was the method ultimately destined to prevail in North America. Clearly, there is ample evidence to suggest that Payne's account is not the only story to be told.

J. L. Styan's influential *The Shakespeare Revolution: Criticism and Performance in the Twentieth Century* (1977) was ideally positioned to identify Greet as one of the practitioners who radically altered the way Shakespeare's works were presented, especially because Styan possessed two facts needed to do so: that Greet was influenced by and collaborated with Poel, and that prominent American dramatic critic William Winter condemned Greet's Shakespearean offerings on Broadway. But Styan chose not to consider what these signified, perhaps because he assumed the revolution was staged entirely in Great Britain.

More than passively neglected, however, Greet was deliberately excluded. Charles H. Shattuck's *Shakespeare on the American Stage* (1976–87), at the urging and with the assistance of the Folger Shakespeare Library, set out to chronicle the history of Shakespearean performance in the United States during its first two centuries. Unfortunately for us, Shattuck died before he could complete the projected third and final volume. Unfortunately for Greet, Shattuck's undertaking was so massive that he limited his coverage to the most famous stars performing in the biggest cities. Volume two, which covers the period 1870–1910, mentions the actor-manager but once, and then only in reference to *Everyman*. Leaving Greet out of this seminal study essentially erased him from the history of Shakespearean performance in the United States.

The authoritative silences of Styan and Shattuck effectively doomed Greet to omission from subsequent studies of Shakespearean performance, Shakespeare on the American stage, and Shakespeare in American culture. Douglas Lanier's *Shakespeare and Modern Popular Culture* (2002), Robert Shaughnessy's *The Shakespeare Effect: A History of Twentieth-Century Performance* (2002), Frances Teague's *Shakespeare and the American Popular Stage* (2006), Virginia Mason Vaughan and Alden T. Vaughan's *Shakespeare in American Life* (2007), Joe Falocco's *Reimagining Shakespeare's Playhouse: Early Modern Staging Conventions in the Twentieth Century* (2010), Coppélia Kahn, Heather S. Nathans, and Mimi Godfrey's *Shakespearean Educations: Power, Citizenship, and Performance* (2011), and Vaughan and Vaughan's *Shakespeare in America* (2012) are the most prominent recent studies that do not incorporate Greet, and they would be richer for having done so rather than reinscribing the Greet-less narrative. So eminent a theatre historian as Don B. Wilmeth, in following Shattuck's lead in the 'Shakespeare on the American stage' entry in Wilmeth's *The Cambridge Guide to the American Theatre* (2007), dutifully recapitulates Shattuck's stars — Richard Mansfield, Robert B. Mantell, the Julia Marlowe-E. H. Sothern combination — before jumping to Granville Barker and

John Barrymore, neither of whom exerted anything like the influence Greet did. *Shakespeare for Everyman* makes the case that the current, unstated consensus that Greet did not exist or does not matter must be abandoned and the history of Shakespearean performance in the early decades of the twentieth century rewritten to acknowledge the accomplishments of the person 'who did more to popularize Shakespeare than any one who ever lived'.

Greet's work in the United States has not, of course, escaped scholarly attention altogether. In his analysis of Chautauqua's origins, growth, management, and operations, *The Romance of Small-Town Chautauquas* (2002), James R. Schultz acknowledges Greet's eminence among that institution's presenters. The entry on him Jill Line contributed to the *The Oxford Companion to American Theatre* (2004) references the quasi-religious vocation that compelled him to bring Shakespeare to new audiences as well as the open-air work so integral to his popularizing mission. In *Ritual Imports: Performing Medieval Drama in America* (2004), Claire Sponsler outlines the story of *Everyman*'s arrival in North America and conjectures as to why the actor-manager liked performing at universities and colleges. In her *The Most American Thing in America: Circuit Chautauqua as Performance* (2005), Charlotte M. Canning is more attentive to the unique cultural position Greet occupied, noting that the combination of his professional expertise, moral and scholarly reputation, long-standing work as a theatrical reformer, and devotion to and mastery of Shakespeare is what enabled him to introduce dramatic performance to that conservative institution. Only Michael Dobson, in his *Shakespeare and Amateur Performance: A Cultural History* (2011), recognizes the astonishing impact Greet had. Identifying the 1884 amateur production that inspired Greet to form the professional company with which he pioneered open-air performance at educational institutions, in London's Regent's Park, at the White House, and a host of other sites on both sides of the Atlantic, Dobson rightly contends that the actor-manager's presentations inspired hundreds of amateur ones and brought Shakespeare to the audience that has supported the open-air presentation of his plays ever since.[5]

The author of two articles about Greet, Richard H. Palmer is the foremost authority on the actor-manager. His first essay identifies the factors — the emerging interest in simplified presentation inspired by what came to be known as the New Stagecraft, the related growth in open-air production, the reaction to the limited offerings of commercial theatre, the widening scope of higher education — that enabled Greet to successfully develop an important new market for Shakespeare: institutions of higher learning. Customers there were eager to buy his wares, and Greet opened it to others, most notably his first and most successful American imitators, Ivah M. and Charles D. Coburn. Palmer's second article persuasively argues that Greet 'did more than anyone else to expose Americans to minimalist staging of Shakespeare'. Near its end, Palmer notes that, as the number of professional Shakespearean productions began to fall as the theatre business began violently to contract in the 1910s, the number of university and college productions began to rise. Thanks to Greet and the Coburns, he concludes, institutions of higher learning and the annual festivals a few of them began sponsoring became important centres of Shakespearean performance.[6]

* * *

As the first comprehensive study of its subject, *Shakespeare for Everyman* is primarily concerned with reconstructing Greet's North American career and context. Because my scholarly practice is shaped by the method developed by Robert D. Hume, Archaeo-Historicism, I present my findings in terms the actor-manager worked and thought in: repertory, personnel, seasons, tours, venues, bookings, promotions, expenses, and receipts.[7] But having considered that career and context, I also advance four arguments I hope will encourage scholarship of a more analytical nature. First, Ben Greet fundamentally changed the way Shakespeare's plays were performed and received in the United States. Although Spectacular Realism dominated commercial theatre until 1917, Greet's

Elizabethan Manner introduced a viable alternative to it over the course of several Broadway seasons beginning in 1904. By so doing, he brought Shakespeare into the twentieth century some eight years before the person usually credited with that accomplishment, Granville Barker, did in London. But changing the look and content of period plays provoked the ire and condemnation of several influential commentators, most famously the conservative 'dean' of America's dramatic critics, the *New-York Tribune*'s William Winter. The debate that ensued placed the question 'What is the best way to perform Shakespeare?' squarely in the public forum. Although dwindling houses, fuelled by the rising popularity of cinema, drove Greet away from commercial theatres in 1910, his continuing efforts led to a cultural shift whose eventual outcome was the universal acceptance of the production practices he pioneered.

Second, Ben Greet changed America's understanding of Shakespeare's theatre through his championing of the Open-Air Theatre Movement, a significant development in the history of dramatic performance. Greet was the founder of the Anglophone world's first professional company dedicated to outdoor performance, the first to develop and successfully introduce a line of commercially appealing outdoor Shakespearean products to the English and North American markets, and the first to perform in Manhattan, at Harvard, at the University of California's magnificent Greek Theatre, on hundreds of campuses, and at official venues like the White House. Greet did more than anyone to spark nation-wide interest in the movement. By so doing, he brought professional Shakespearean performance to higher education, inextricably linked 'open-air performance' to 'Shakespeare' in the imaginations of millions, laid the cultural foundation upon which every outdoor Shakespearean festival rests, and placed Shakespeare in literally thousands of American landscapes.

Third, Greet was one of the pioneering figures of the Educational Theatre Movement. Drama and Theatre instruction in American higher education were barely in their infancy during the first two decades of the twentieth century, when all but a handful of degree-granting institutions remained firmly prejudiced against them. When scholars today recall the people who introduced those disciplines to the varsity, they think of academics like George Pierce Baker, Thomas H. Dickinson, Thomas Wood Stevens, Gertrude Johnson, and Frederick Henry Koch. But as far as people at the time were concerned, the internationally renowned practitioner-educator Ben Greet and what the *New York Times* later dubbed his 'travelling Shakespeare university' was the most prominent champion of that cause. In 1905, the president of the University of California very publicly offered to create for Greet what would have been the world's first university professorship in the Dramatic Arts — an unprecedented invitation reported as far away as New York and London. As the same newspaper later noted, Greet's decision to decline it had a tremendous impact on American culture; he was able to exert the influence he did *because* he was not tied a single campus.[8] His appearances at hundreds of institutions from coast to coast introduced and established a standard method for producing Shakespeare there; more than anyone, Greet was responsible for the creation of what we now think of as North American Academic Shakespeare. The students and professors who saw his productions were of the generation that created departments of Drama and Theatre all over the country starting in 1914, and more of them saw productions of Greet's companies than any other theatre artist. That Americans gradually came to believe those subjects were worthy of a place in higher education was due, at least in part, to Greet demonstrating their educational value to the people who founded the first programs. Although he spent considerably less time with schoolchildren than he did with undergraduates, his successful efforts to recruit school boards and philanthropies in New York, Chicago, Boston, and other major cities to sponsor educationally oriented seasons for poor schoolchildren was a ground-breaking effort to bring performed Shakespeare into the curriculum and to develop — and influence — a vast new audience.

My final argument is that Ben Greet brought dramatic perform-ance to legions of Americans whose religious beliefs had previously compelled them to eschew professional theatre. Issues of religion and morality once determined how significant numbers of Americans regarded and consumed plays, and several major Protestant sects condemned theatre *in toto* at this time. The rever-ence for printed Shakespeare, however, and the cultural aspirations shared by many of the members of these churches inclined them to embrace the person who could bring them performances of the Elizabethan's works free from the moral taint they believed attached to theatres and professional actors. The tremendous success of Greet's modified *Everyman*, in which God was usually not imperson-ated, Greet's international reputation as a Shakespearean purist, and his renown as a church-stage activist encouraged Lyceumites and Chautauquans in their millions to turn out to see his Shakespearean productions — a fact that disproves the part of Lawrence W. Levine's influential Highbrow/Lowbrow theory that claims popular audiences turned away from Shakespeare after 1890. Perhaps surprisingly, Greet's reputation for virtue is what enabled him to introduce professional Shakespeare to the campuses of hundreds of universities, colleges, and normal schools, where administrators and faculty permitted only persons of upstanding character to interact with undergraduates. Greet's Victorian morality, from whence his advocacy of 'plays worth while' — Shakespeare, *Everyman*, a handful of classic English comedies — stemmed, was vital to his success in Progressive Era America.

We are able to restore to the historic record the important changes Greet effected thanks to the letters the actor-manager wrote to his principal American correspondent, Lucy Love; the letters the future Dame Sybil Thorndike wrote to her family; the recollections of her brother Russell; the diary actor Stanford Holme kept; the memoirs published by Greet associates J. Bannister Howard, H. F. Maltby, and Harry P. Harrison; and the considerable amount of business correspondence that survives. Uniquely, we possess a wealth of information regarding the time his company spent on 'the road', a record under-represented in the history of the early twentieth-century American theatre. 'The road' was where the train-based touring companies that once dominated America worked. Year in and year out, these companies supplied Shakespeare and other offerings to more people than did the stars who served audiences in the metropolises. In 1910, the road went into a decline from which it never recovered, one driven by problems internal to the theatre business aggravated by the ascendancy of cinema. The history of Greet's company during these years gives us a richly detailed, insider's account of the road's final years and an opportunity to see how swiftly these forces transformed the entertainment landscape.

As I have established, there is little secondary material to use to write Greet into the historical record, a history that could not be written at all had primary evidence not survived. In this case, that evidence takes two forms: the materials noted above and contemporary periodicals. That I have been able to reconstruct such a detailed picture of Greet's activities is the result of the advances in digitization and optical character recognition made during the last two decades. These resources include free databases (the Library of Congress's *Chronicling America: Historic American Newspapers*, Tom Tryniski's *Old Fulton New York Post Cards*) and subscription services (*The British Newspaper Archive*, *GenealogyBank.com*, *NewspaperArchive*, *Newspapers.com*) that give us access to literally hundreds of newspapers. They explain in a moment why Miller, Akin, and Shattuck, who lacked them, used only a handful of papers published in the largest cities — the ones most readily accessible on microfilm. Although our knowledge of what Greet did in rural America is still scrappy compared to what we know about his urban activities, the primary evidence has enabled me to compile a more-than-3,500-date performance calendar that I hope to make available as an on-line resource. The level of detail our current tools make possible is striking.

Though *Shakespeare for Everyman* aims to provide a history of Greet's company, of its performances, and of contemporaneous dramatic criticism, it is also tells the story of Greet's commercial brand that increasingly became cultural shorthand for 'minimalistically-staged Shakespeare'. One reason Greet's collaborator on *Everyman*, William Poel, has received much more scholarly attention is that his ideas are comparatively easy to access thanks to the essays and books he wrote. Another is that he was an original theorist and uncompromising member of the avant-garde; the praise of supporters and the condemnation of detractors did not change what Poel did, and if the commercial failure of one of his experiments forced him to wait months to mount the next one, so be it (and hard luck to his supporters and amateur actors).

Ben Greet, on the other hand, was a veteran actor-manager as well as a devoted teacher whose educational values were an extension of his spiritual beliefs. Constantly touring, he expressed most of his ideas through performance, not writing. His own experiments, which tended more to the pragmatic than the theoretical, and what he learned from Poel and others convinced him he knew what the 'proper' way to stage Shakespeare was, and his desire to deliver it to any audience that would have him in many ways resembled a religious vocation. Knowing that the good work would come to a halt if he went out of business, Greet could temporarily turn his back on 'proper' to embrace 'popular', as he did in 1908 and 1909 by producing hybrid drama-music productions of *A Midsummer Night's Dream* and *The Tempest*, the profits from which helped to support the traditional Shakespearean company he operated at the same time. Although such compromises of avant-garde principles earned Greet critical scorn, and though his occasional obstinacy, arrogance, and one notable instance of sharp business practice made enemies, Ben Greet was also a superb teacher of acting, generous, adventurous, adaptable, indefatigable, capable of compromise, and possessed of a singular vision of Shakespeare. To these strengths he added the zeal to carry his vision to the distant corners of North America, earning a rightful place in theatre history as the greatest Shakespearean popularizer who ever lived.

INTRODUCTION

NOTES

1   'Shakespeare on Lawn, Was a Brilliant Sight', *NYTr.*, 15 May 1903, p.4. The presence of the Folgers from Elizabeth Forte Alman, 'Shakespeare's Stage in America: The Early History of the Folger Elizabethan Theatre' (unpublished doctoral dissertation, University of Maryland, 2013), p.104.

2   'Ben Greet Dies, 78; Famous as Actor', *NYT*, 18 May 1936, p.17.

3   Dale Erwin Miller, 'Ben Greet in America: An Historical and Critical Study of Ben Greet's Theatrical Activity in America' (unpublished doctoral dissertation, Northwestern University, 1972); Lew Akin Sparks, 'Ben Greet and His Theatre Companies in America: 1902–1932' (unpublished doctoral dissertation, University of Georgia, 1974).

4   Ben Iden Payne, *A Life in a Wooden O* (New Haven: Yale University Press, 1977), p.91.

5   Dobson's treatment of Greet in his earlier 'Shakespeare Exposed: Outdoor Performance and Ideology, 1880–1940', in *Shakespeare, Memory and Performance*, ed. by Peter Holland (Cambridge: Cambridge University Press, 2006), pp.256–77, is largely identical.

6   Richard H. Palmer, 'The Professional Actor's Early Search for a College Audience: Sir Philip Ben Greet and Charles Coburn', *Educational Theatre Journal*, 21.1 (March 1969), 51–59; Richard H. Palmer, 'America Goes Bare: Ben Greet and the Elizabethan Revival', *Theatre Symposium: A Publication of the Southeastern Theatre Conference*, 12 (2004), 8–19.

7   Robert D. Hume, *Reconstructing Contexts: The Aims and Principles of Archaeo-Historicism* (Oxford: Oxford University Press, 1999).

8   'Ben Greet', *NYT*, 19 May 1936, p.22

CHAPTER ONE
A Late-Victorian Actor-Manager, 1857–1902

Formative Years

The son of Sarah Vallance Barling Greet and Captain William Greet, RN, Philip Barling Greet was born in 1857 aboard *HMS Crocodile*, then anchored off the Tower of London. He received an education at the Royal Naval School at New Cross befitting a future officer, but chose not to follow the sea. After a period teaching at the Rev. J. G. Gresson's private school in Worthing, he embarked on a stage career. He made his professional debut in 1879 as a member of J. W. Gordon's stock company in Southampton. He joined Sarah Thorne's stock company in Margate soon thereafter. He remained with Thorne, a noted teacher who attracted aspirants from respectable families, for three years.[1]

His training as a performer barely complete, Greet made his debut as a Shakespearean actor-manager. He assembled an ad hoc company comprising younger London professionals, the most distinguished member of which was leading man Frank Rodney. In February 1883, it played a two-week engagement at the Theatre Royal and Opera House, Southampton, that included *Romeo and Juliet*, *Much Ado about Nothing*, *As You Like It*, Edward Bulwer-Lytton's *The Lady of Lyons*, and Richard Brinsley Sheridan's *The School for Scandal*. The *Hampshire Advertiser* reported that Greet made good on his promises to present 'as careful and complete representations as possible' of some Shakespearean plays as he unveiled an 'improvement on the old method of producing' them. Conforming somewhat to that old method, his *Romeo and Juliet* employed simple pictorial scenery and impressive calcium-light effects of his own devising. The improvement came in how and how much of the tragedy he presented:

> Each member of the company was perfect in the text, and the whole piece went off smoothly, and even rapidly. There were no tiresome 'waits' to try the patience of the audience, who had, indeed, but the merest breathing time between the various acts, or leisure to consider the merit of the various artistes engaged. In the short time allotted them, however, for that purpose it was evident that they made up their minds as to the talent that was displayed.

Other newspapers confirmed the artistic and commercial success of the engagement.[2] Creating strong ensembles to swiftly and continuously perform full (or markedly full-er) texts to present a more authentic kind of Shakespeare would occupy Greet for most of his long career.

He made his London acting debut later that year, playing Caius Lucius in *Cymbeline* with Ellen Wallis. Successful engagements with Minnie Palmer (*My Sweetheart*, in which his Dudley 'Dude' Harcourt achieved considerable fame) and Lawrence Barrett (*Yorick's Love, Richelieu*) established him in the capital.

Greet became a follower of one of the leading proponents of Christian Socialism, the Rev. J. Stewart Headlam, around this time. A Church of England clergyman, Headlam was a tireless social and educational reformer who counted theatre among his causes. In 1882, he founded the Church and Stage Guild, the goals of which were to harness the power of drama to educate the masses, to persuade society that acting, dancing, and singing were godly callings, and to bring an end to the Church of England's isolation and condemnation of the stage that had caused so many to turn against it. As Richard Foulkes discovered, Greet was an active member of the guild by the summer of 1885, when he brokered a meeting between Headlam and the new Bishop of London. That conference was a failure, but, as Wendy Trewin concludes, Greet would prove 'the staunchest of [Headlam's] allies' — a decades-spanning association marked by several, more successful collaborations.[3]

Actor-Manager and Teacher

Greet's skill as a comic actor earned him steady employment in the capital, including engagements with American expatriate Mary Anderson (with whom he formed an enduring friendship), Herbert Beerbohm Tree, and Walter Bentley. But it was an amateur production in the provinces that changed the course of Greet's life and, ultimately, the way millions produce and consume Shakespeare. Lady Archibald Campbell had the remarkable idea of mounting *As You Like It* on the grounds of Coombe House, Surrey, and she hired noted professional costume- and set-designer Edward Godwin to direct it. In July 1884, Campbell and her volunteer company of professionals and amateurs gave several open-air performances in aid of a local charity that drew distinguished audiences of aristocrats, socialites, and artists. The production being so unusual and its patrons being so prominent, it attracted enough attention for the *Graphic* to publish this engraving of it. As Michael Dobson concludes, 'Whether or not Greet saw [it], he certainly heard about it and recognized its commercial potential'.[4]

Greet set about transforming Godwin's method into a commercial product. He began mastering the fundamentals of outdoor performance by stage managing Seymour Dicker's open-air production of *A Midsummer Night's Dream* (that included musical excerpts from Mendelssohn) at Stanstead Lodge, Kent, in July 1885. He formed his first outdoor company immediately thereafter. Like the Southampton ensemble, it was an ad hoc group comprising younger London professionals. It gave its inaugural performance, *As You Like It*, on the grounds of Hollytrees in Colchester in August 1885 — a year before the career overviews state Greet established his famous Woodland Players. I have confirmed only a handful of performances from the

2. Anonymous. AS YOU LIKE IT.
Dir. Edward Godwin, Coombe House, Surrey, July 1884.

summer of 1886, but it was definitely a going concern by 1887; Greet later attributed the upsurge in business that year to the national fad for throwing garden parties to honour the queen's jubilee. Soon, the company was profitably touring *As You Like It*, *The Comedy of Errors*, *Love's Labour's Lost*, *Dream*, *The Tempest*, and *Twelfth Night* through England's parks, botanical gardens, zoological gardens, country estates, castles, palaces, and historic sites. Greet's commercial manager from 1895 to 1910, J. Bannister Howard, later stated that the 1887 ensemble included Frank Rodney, future *Punch* cartoonist Bernard Partridge, and the future Dame May Whitty. Worth bearing in mind is that Greet completely or partially cut the non-woodland scenes from *As You Like It*, *Dream*, and *Tempest*, and that a popular feature of his night-time *Dream* was the special calcium-light effects he devised. A few musical works inspired by those of Shakespeare being popular in Victorian concert halls, he often added musical selections from Mendelssohn and Sullivan to his open-air *Dream* and *Tempest*, respectively.[5]

New Ventures

The period 1896 to 1901 was one of great activity and experimentation for Greet. In 1895, playwright-actor-manager Wilson Barrett wrote *The Sign of the Cross*. A melodrama dealing with a sacred subject, it depicts the conversion of a Roman prefect through his love for a Christian woman in the time of Nero. Barrett first exhibited it in the United States. When he brought it to London in 1896, he presented it at the Lyric Theatre, the new lessee-manager of which was William Greet. The impressive run there of 435 consecutive performances helped make *The Sign* (as it soon came to be known) the most profitable play in the capital that year. As the younger Greet told the *Era*, its success was founded on something no one had ever seen: the ringing clerical endorsements it received enabled it to attract 'more choirs, Sunday schools, and kindred bodies than any piece ever put on the stage'.[16]

He secured the provincial touring rights from Barrett, and in March 1896 the Ben Greet Comedy Company began satisfying the considerable demand the play had generated outside the capital, with the actor-manager playing Nero in support of leads Frank Westerton (Marcus Superbus) and Irene Rooke (Mercia). Church support continued to grow. Not only did the Bishop of Norwich grant a dispensation to anyone in his diocese who wished to attend one of the performances the company gave there during Lent, but he also publicly endorsed the play and everyone associated with it by hosting the company at a garden party. By 1898, Greet's involvement with the production had become exclusively managerial: recruiting, training, fielding, and supervising the four companies that continued to profitably tour *The Sign* until audiences tired of it at decade's end.[17]

The venues and audiences Greet's companies encountered taught him important new lessons. One of the actors he hired, H. F. Maltby, later recalled that, most of the rural Welsh and Scottish towns his ensemble played in 1899 lacking theatres, the company deployed its fit-up in the proscenium-less, often stage-less halls and corn exchanges its small technical team would adapt as needed.[18]

Maltby attributed the play's phenomenal drawing power to its mix of sex (Marcus drags Mercia to a drunken orgy at which he almost rapes her) and Christianity:

> It piqued the desires on one end and, at the same time, gave the comfortable feeling of moral elevation. It was for that reason that people who never went to theatres, who disapproved of theatres, who even preached against theatres, all went to see *The Sign of the Cross*.[19]

That audiences in the provinces would be more religious than those in London was not surprising. That rural Protestants with strong anti-theatrical prejudices turned out in droves was.

Maltby identified another reason religious audiences were drawn to Greet's work: he actively courted them. He was widely known as a religious man, and one of the ways he maintained that reputation while touring was 'to read the lesson in Church the Sunday *before* he opened in each town, artful old dog!' His actors did not approve of this practice, not because they regarded it as insincere, but because it necessitated mortifyingly early train calls.[20]

Managing *The Sign* companies made Greet the Anglophone world's most experienced producer of toured religious drama. The show had not been his, but the fact that he had played a part in inspiring theatregoers and non-theatregoers alike must have been gratifying to the devoted Church and Stage Guild supporter. He had used the drama to teach moral principles to the masses, demonstrate that acting could be a godly calling, and induce tens of thousands, including members of the clergy and conservative Protestants actively opposed to theatre, to overcome their anti-theatrical prejudice, at least temporarily. That doing so was profitable (Howard later stated that the tours netted Greet's business some £40,000) did nothing to detract from the work's virtue.[21]

With money in his purse, Greet cast around for another mass in need of education, this time in his first love: Shakespeare. In the spring of 1897, he took London's Olympic Theatre for the purpose of mounting a four-production festival: his own *Hamlet* (with a young Gordon Craig playing the Dane), *Macbeth*, and *The Merchant of Venice* along with the *Antony and Cleopatra* of long-time associate Louis Calvert. Significantly, one of its stated purposes was preparing schoolchildren for the university entrance exams. By so doing, he was expanding upon an idea of William Poel, who had pioneered the practice on a much smaller scale in 1895. Greet's 'popular prices' (i.e. half-price) tickets scheme attracted classes from more than a hundred urban and suburban schools.[22] Possibly because he was flush, Greet mounted uncharacteristically lavish productions patterned on those of the recently knighted Sir Henry Irving, whose Spectacular Realism shows at the Lyceum Theatre epitomized the era's dominant production method. Greet had some money, thanks to *The Sign*, but not enough to afford the sets, costumes, and super-numeraries necessary for a Lyceum-style production. Moreover, even attempting one required cutting lines and transposing scenes, something Greet had always avoided or minimized. In his negative review of *Merchant*, William Archer scolded Greet for allowing fashion to turn his head:

It is curious to note how Lyceum methods are penetrating — not to say viti-ating — our treatment of Shakespeare on every hand. One might have imagined that Mr. Greet, being, by the very nature of his enterprise, dispensed from the obligation of scenic display, would revel in his freedom and seize the opportunity to let Shakespeare tell his own story after his own fashion. But not a bit of it! We must have all the drawbacks of a spectacular Lyceum setting without its beauties.

A few paragraphs later, Archer told Greet to acclaim the value of his tried-and-true method:

Mr. Greet would do very much better for art, and no worse, I am sure, for himself, if he frankly accepted the situation and said to the public: 'I cannot give you Lyceum archæology and luxury, but I can give what is not to be had at the Lyceum — Shakespeare's scenes, not more than necessarily abridged, and in the order in which he wrote them'.[23]

Greet's foray into spectacle was unsuccessful, but *The Times* reported that his Shakespeare-for-schoolchildren scheme answered very well. Schools had been taking students to productions at local theatres for years, but the idea of a theatre in a major metropolitan centre mounting productions for the express purpose of attracting students from scores of them was new. Thanks to Greet's improvement upon Poel's original idea, the large-scale educational matinee had been born.[24] Like undergraduates and religious people in the provinces, schoolchildren were another large, non-traditional audience worth remembering.

Having seen the kinds of profits a box-office sensation like *The Sign* was capable of generating and having begun to master the business of operating multiple touring companies, Greet now focused on supplying contemporary hits to the provinces. For the next three seasons, he fielded an ever-increasing number of ensembles to bring touring productions of West End successes like *The Belle of New York*, *East Lynne*, *The Great Ruby*, *Grip of Iron*, *Hearts are Trumps*, *A Night Out*, *A Royal Family*, *The Second in Command*, *The Silver King*, and *White Heather* to the hinterland. According to Howard, Greet had fourteen companies on the road by decade's end.[25] That he also continued to personally lead the Ben Greet Comedy Company and the Woodland Players gives evidence of his considerable energy.

Greet's reputation as a teacher and his immediate and considerable need for performers prompted him to found the Ben Greet Academy for Acting, which had opened its doors in Bedford Street by 1897 under the day-to-day management of instructor Frederick Topham. Howard recalled that it quickly became 'very large and popular' because it was unsurpassed for 'practical training for the Stage'. Its placement record spoke for itself: Greet promised to employ Maltby's sister, for one, if she completed the year-long course, and kept his word.[26]

But the West End hits touring business collapsed at the end of 1900. Maltby reckoned that, had the actor-manager

> stuck to his old comedies and fit-up tours he would have lived and died a wealthy man, but he never could keep money. Directly he made it over one thing he was never happy until he lost it all over something else.

Implicit in this remark is the fact that the West End productions included effects like an avalanche, a balloon launch, an undersea duel — even a real coach with six horses. Howard remarked that mounting even simplified versions of them meant coordinating and managing scenery, large properties, and machinery. Contemporary sources declining to identify exactly why the enterprise failed, Lew Akin Sparks persuasively theorized that the more complex logistical considerations, higher costs, and unpredictable expenses these effects introduced to Greet's operational model, coupled with inadequate oversight of personnel and payroll, may have been the cause. In short, the actor-manager violated the dictum that had served him well for a decade — travel light — and then failed to adapt his business accordingly. Maltby stated that Greet had 'cancelled all his tours, keeping only his old comedy company, in which he was a great favourite' by the Christmas of 1900.[27] Undeterred, the actor-manager formed a second company as soon as doing so became feasible. These two ensembles continued touring the above-listed works (the provincial rights to which he still controlled), *Sherlock Holmes*, and even a musical, *The Casino Girl* (which launched the career of Greet's famous protégée, Gabrielle Ray), into 1902.

As busy as managing these companies kept him, Greet always found time for his religious activities and Headlam. In 1898, he contributed an essay, 'The Stage and the Church', to the Rev. Nathaniel Keymer's popular *Workers Together with God* collection. I summarize its main points here because it is the most detailed statement I have found about the ideas that informed Greet's church-stage activism. He opens by declaring that the Church of England was still failing 'to touch or impress the actor'. Headlam had awakened it from its indifference to the profession, but there was still a great deal of work to be done. Half the clergy were antagonistic towards theatrical performance. Although many found their ways into theatres when they visited London, clergymen kept away from them in their home towns for fear of attracting the disapprobation of parishioners. These men needed the courage to lead and not be led. Like people in every other business, actors did what they did for commercial gain, but nine-tenths of them were honest in their work. The kingdom's few remaining Puritans continued to characterize the theatre as a 'den of wickedness', 'the gate of hell', etc., but most people agreed that few entertainments had 'the slightest tendency to impropriety'. People would always desire recreation. More than other members of society, clergy had a duty to ensure that those recreations were wholesome and beneficial. Indeed, the clergy should lead the public to 'support the best work of the theatre — that which is more elevating to the mind and the senses, for theatrical representation has its classification, as music, pictures, and books have'. Church and stage must become more sympathetic toward one another, acknowledge and forgive the failings that had divided them, and join forces. 'Our art is a beautiful one', he wrote, 'the workers are enthusiasts, the lessons they teach are the same as those taught by the Church; they can and do help each other — co-workers, I believe, to help men to live their lives happily'.[28]

Putting a few of these principles into practice, Greet teamed up with Headlam in 1899 to create an annual Shakespearean competition for poor schoolchildren. As an influential member of the London School Board, the cleric recruited more than a dozen schools, each of which fielded a troupe to present the scene Greet selected. The actor-manager travelled to the schools, heard the performances, identified the best ensembles and actors, and presented his findings to Headlam, who handed out the prizes and reported the results to the board. The idea was not uncontroversial. Another minister on the board, the Rev. W. Hamilton of the Baptist Tabernacle, publicly condemned it and the harm he believed it might inflict on schoolchildren: instilling in them a love of amusement, overwhelming them with a 'prodigality of pleasure', and even degrading them morally. Convinced its cultural, creative, and elocutionary benefits outweighed the potential spiritual pitfalls, Greet and Headlam repeated it in each of the next three years, expanding it a little each time. In 1902, Headlam also arranged for Greet's company to deliver a series of 'popular prices' evening performances of Shakespearean comedies to the poor adult students of the evening continuation schools.[29]

Greet increased both his knowledge of religious drama and the scope of his church-stage activities by attending the Oberammergau *Passionspiel* in 1900. Striking up a friendship with Anton Lang, the actor who played Christ, Greet would make a point of returning to Bavaria in 1910 when Lang reprised the role. He would also be among those who hosted Lang when the German visited Great Britain in 1902 and 1931.[30]

Another dramatic experiment Greet conducted at this time was open-air Shakespeare in London's Regent's Park, then leased to the Royal Botanical Society. The Woodland Players began appearing there during the summer of 1899, often in aid of charities. Its inaugural presentation, *As You Like It* on 21 June, was well received:

> The efforts of the Royal Botanic Society to popularise their beautiful gardens in Regent's Park has been crowned with the production of a short series of pastoral plays [...].
>
> The interest of the afternoon [...] centred on the production of the pastoral play. A very fine natural stage was formed in the trees on a slightly raised eminence on the east side of the conservatory. On the lower level about a thousand seats had been arranged in amphitheatre form, and so great was the demand for these that long before the commencement of the play every one of them was occupied [...]. The whole thing was, indeed, one of the most delightful treats to which either the student of Shakespeare, the ordinary playgoer, or the general seeker after amusement could possibly have been called.

The Times congratulated Greet for that night's presentation of
A Midsummer Night's Dream:

> As the performance did not begin till 9 o'clock, audience and actors alike
> were entirely dependent on artificial light. The former found their way to
> places by the dim glimmer of Chinese lanterns and fairy lamps hung from
> the trees, the latter manœuvred in a brilliant circle of limelight. The
> acting, on the whole, was distinctly good. Mr. Greet himself was
> admirable as Bottom, Miss Dorothea Baird and Miss Edith Matthison
> looked charming as Helena and Hermia, and Miss Maggie Bowman made
> a most picturesque and delightful Puck. The music was a judicious blend
> of Mendelssohn and Wagner, and the whole performance was most
> cordially received.[31]

As Isaac records, Greet's novel combination of method and place
delighted Londoners, who began turning out for performances and
thinking of the park as an open-air venue.[32]

Poel and EVERYMAN

In 1901, Greet entered into one of the most important collaborations
of his career. Though short-lived, it brought him to the production
that catapulted him to prominence in North America. More problematic, it ended in a falling out that embittered his partner for years.

The actor, director, and manager William Poel was the greatest
scholar, reconstructionist, and champion of Elizabethan staging and
performance of the late nineteenth and early twentieth centuries. The
productions of early modern plays he mounted, most famously for
the all-volunteer, mostly amateur Elizabethan Stage Society between
1895 and 1905, did more to rediscover the ways Shakespeare's plays
were originally staged and performed than any efforts hitherto. Poel's
experiments and the conclusions he and others drew from them laid
the foundation of what we now call Original Practice.

The two men had several interactions prior to 1901. Marion
O'Connor discovered that Greet claimed to have met Poel before

1879, that Poel directed Greet in *Lady Jane Grey* in 1885, and that, like Greet, Poel began a long association with Headlam in the 1880s. Poel's biographer, Robert Speaight, states that Greet attended a performance of Poel's 1895 *Twelfth Night*, after which he hired one of Poel's amateurs, Lillah McCarthy. And Greet patterned his Shakespeare for schoolchildren scheme on Poel's. That Greet knew and had worked with Poel, was interested in and admired his work, and found employment for at least one member of the ESS is certain. McCarthy may not have minded turning professional, and not just because doing so paid. Poel had singular ideas about how Shakespeare's lines should be spoken, but he was considerably less skilful than Greet as a teacher of acting. He also lacked the contacts that helped so many of Greet's protégés rise in the profession after they completed their training.[33]

Greet and Poel collaborated on three projects during the 1901–02 season. Alike in many ways, they also complemented one another. Both revered Shakespeare, considered his plays to be primarily an aural art, believed his lines should be delivered quickly and completely (good taste permitting), and were committed to mounting fast-paced productions. Crucially, both men were adept at using limited or no scenery. To paraphrase Richard H. Palmer, practical considerations kept Greet's stages bare, while philosophical ones did likewise for Poel's.[34] Greet had been managing professional touring companies for nearly fifteen years, during which time he had personally led more than 2,000 performances of Shakespeare's plays, including at Stratford-upon-Avon — field experience that utterly dwarfed Poel's. As a result, he brought a perspective that was pragmatic, applied, and audience-focused; he could compromise if doing so enhanced a production's effectiveness, which he defined more in terms of artistic and commercial success than of authenticity. He could offer a competent ensemble of actors capable of delivering performances to a professional touring standard, yet unformed enough to be receptive to the unique delivery method Poel espoused — a bugbear of Poel's that made him dislike working with veterans.[35] Equally important, Greet could offer professional leadership and access to capital. Managerial ineptitude need not accompany philo-sophical opposition to commercial theatre, but it did in Poel's case. As O'Connor observes, the reason the ESS's offerings trickled to a halt by the end of 1900 was that they consistently lost money, and of course Poel's string of commercial failures is what brought about the effective dissolution of the ESS in 1905.[36] For his part, Poel brought his scholarly theories and aesthetic principles, his impressive and uncompromising artistic vision, his unique method, his unrivalled collection of museum-quality reproduction costumes and properties, his antiquarian and cultural connections, and his growing renown as the producer of the most authentically staged and dressed (if not performed) Elizabethan productions in the world.

The pair mounted their first collaboration, *Henry V*, on 19 October in New Theatre, Oxford. Greet's company, supplemented by some of Poel's amateurs, presented what was advertised as an ESS production. Poel rehearsed them and staged the play 'in the Elizabethan manner'. This meant he presented it on a bare stage: no scenery was used, just simple curtains and a simulated inner-below. The action was performed swiftly and continuously, a ten-minute interval being the only concession to modern sensibilities. Almost all the text was spoken: one reviewer reported that the roles of Captains Jamy and Macmorris were cut and that some of Shakespeare's coarser expressions were 'softened', but that other-wise the play was performed practically in its entirety in 135 minutes. Not surprising given that it had not been staged in anything like original conditions for more than 250 years, the result 'was at once crisp, vivid, and interesting' to some audience members, though dull to those who wanted what they were used to: the spectacle of the heroic king leading an army of supernumeraries in an impressively choreographed Battle of Agincourt. Returning Greet alumnus Robert Loraine took the title-role, and the actor-manager's talented, increasingly skilful leading lady, Edith Wynne Matthison, played Chorus. Greet probably provided the financing as well as handled bookings and promotions. The company performed the play several times over the next few months, including at the Shakespeare Memorial Theatre in Stratford-upon-Avon, Peterborough School, Rugby School, and Cambridge University. It being on the university examinations that year, audiences comprised largely schoolchildren. That an instructor from Harvard University's Department of English by the name of George Pierce Baker liked what he saw at the performance he attended at the University of London would soon prove beneficial.[37] Greet produced it in more spectacular fashion at the festival he mounted at the Theatre Metropole, Camberwell, the following April, with Loraine, now riding the customary white charger, reprising the title-role.[38]

By far the most important Greet-Poel collaboration was *Everyman*. Poel's original plan had been to present it at Westminster Abbey, but he shelved the idea after permission there and Canterbury Cathedral was refused. He returned to it in 1901, when, between July and October, he and members of the ESS gave five, semi-private performances at the Charterhouse, London; University College, Oxford; and the Royal Pavilion, Brighton. In November, they gave two more at the Ladies' College, Cheltenham, that have previously gone unnoticed.[39]

Poel's *Everyman* was important. In the short term, it brought him to some prominence and the work of the ESS to the largest audience it had yet reached. In the long term, it sparked scholarly and even popular interest in medieval drama. The secret of its success was that it was almost as artistically and emotionally compelling as it was masterfully researched, designed, and executed.[40] Significantly, the *Morning Post* remarked 'The programme had indeed many of the elements of a popular success. To use a phrase that one must immediately explain, there is money in it'.[41] Famously deaf to the opinions of others, Poel let it lie.

Greet's desire to take it up again is what made it Poel's most influential and profitable experiment. The pair formed a partnership or otherwise contracted together, the particulars of which are unknown. In addition to supplying his professional company, Greet probably put up the money, hired the venues, and handled promotions. Matthison stated that ultimate directorial control rested with him. Significantly, she played Everyman in keeping with Poel's decision to cast a woman, May Douglas Reynolds, in the role in 1901. Another important element Greet retained was the lack of curtain; these would remain open for the duration of the performance, even when the play was often presented in venues that had them. Poel provided the production, his costumes, and perhaps part of his fit-up.[42] He also coached and rehearsed the members of Greet's company, most of whom Greet had trained.

The new version received its premiere in March 1902 at London's St George's Hall, a 900-seat venue well known to both men.[43] Like *Henry V*, it was advertised as an ESS production, this time 'by arrangement with Ben Greet'. Greet, who made a practice of scheduling engagements to coincide with dates and seasons he believed resonated with audiences, booked a week-long series of Lenten matinees — a tradition that would endure for decades. *Everyman* being relatively short, Poel had originally paired it with the Chester Cycle's *The Sacrifice of Isaac* to make for a more substantial offering. That Greet added a considerable amount of music, ritual, and business may have been the result of his determination that the production needed to satisfy the conventional run-time expectation for a mainpiece.

But the most important change was the decision, almost certainly Greet's, to partially conceal God. Owing to conflicting interpretations of Biblical prohibitions against speaking God's name, looking upon God's face, and worshiping graven images, Christians had been debating for more than a millennium whether representing the Godhead was blasphemy. English law effectively prohibited the depiction of religious subjects on the commercial stage, and a government official, the Lord Chamberlain's Examiner of Plays, was charged with enforcing it. As John R. Elliott notes, Poel's non-commercial production was not subject to it, but the Greet-Poel commercial production was. Elliott also finds that

Greet later stated that he and Poel duly submitted the play, that the examiner's office replied that, although it was so old it 'could hardly be licensed', they should 'omit the presentation of Deity [...] as much as possible, and upon any occasion to treat the subject with reverence and discrimination'. In the original outdoor production, Poel placed Adonai (as Poel and Greet usually called God in the programmes) on high. At St George's Hall in 1902, Adonai was but imperfectly visible, when, after the speech of the Messenger with which the play begins, the curtain rose 'to show, in a deep shadow, the form of God, or "Adonai", standing motionless with his arms uplifted from the elbows, like the Saints on old stained-glass windows and tapestries'.[44]

The Times praised the revival; nothing could match an actual medieval monastery for creating a medieval illusion, but the incongruity of the hall was counterbalanced by the greater dignity and reverence supplied by the professional actors. Its writer praised the company for so ably reproducing the thoughts and language of another age without falling into burlesque. The only criticism the reporter voiced was that the new production was more melodramatic, not to mention more Catholic, than Poel's original. At Charterhouse,

> Everyman's exit to receive the Sacrament [was] marked by nothing more than the allusions of the players. Now the voice of the priest chanting the office in Latin and the Sanctus bell are heard, and incense rises over the curtains which form the background of the stage. Criticism is disarmed somewhat by the fact that these curtains conceal all else from the audience, but the sounds are wanting in solemnity, and the effect is painful.

The *Evening Standard*'s praise was unqualified: the production was the most interesting thing the ESS had ever mounted, and the performer who played Everyman (Greet and Poel continued Poel's practice of omitting the names of the actors from the programmes) was excellent. As these and other reviews indicate, the revival featured the best of both worlds: the magnificent vision, costumes, and possibly fit-up of the 1901 production presented by a much more talented and experienced ensemble in a new version tailored to appeal to modern tastes and sensibilities.[45]

The run was successful enough to encourage Greet to secure the hall for another week-long engagement in May, half of which was sponsored by Headlam's Sesame House for Home-Life Training. The ownership formula 'under the direction of Mr. Ben Greet and the Elizabethan Stage Society' now appeared, and the public responded even more enthusiastically. The *St James's Gazette*'s critic stated that the production kept the large audience spellbound for the entirety of its intermission-less, 105-minute run-time. After providing a plot-summary, the writer declared 'It is impossible in this crude outline […] to give any conception of its impressiveness; and still less of the superb art and dignity with which it is presented' before noting that the actress who played the title-role 'with consummate art and power' gave 'in every way a masterly perform-ance'.[46] Greet's management, changes, and actors had launched Poel's production into the commercial mainstream.

Convinced they had a hit on their hands, Greet transferred the Morality to the more central, 1,150-seat Imperial Theatre, Westminster, where it roused even greater interest in a city teeming with visitors for a coronation that had been delayed on account of the king's illness. People had time on their hands, and the impending ceremony seems to have made them interested in rites ancient, English, and religious. The crowds that packed the Imperial during the show's month-long run of matinees (a few evening perform-ances were added the final week) made *Everyman*, in the words of the *Atheneaum*, the '"sensation" of the season'.[47] Like *The Sign*, it had provided an opportunity to advance cherished religious and social goals, and to do so with considerable commercial success.

The last Poel-Greet collaboration of 1901–02 took place at the close of the *Everyman* run. On 11 and 12 July, a company comprising the best comic actors of the ESS and the Ben Greet Comedy Company presented a Bowdlerized version of Ben Jonson's *The Alchemist* at the

Imperial in what was advertised as an ESS production. That the programme identifies Poel and Greet as co-directors of the ESS suggests Greet had acquired a substantial stake in the society. Poel rehearsed the actors and directed a production that was based on the one he had mounted in 1899. *The Times* regretted that the text had been so eviscerated because many of the performances had been excellent. A few weeks later, the company presented it to the summer extension students at Cambridge University.[48]

But the *Everyman* story was only beginning. In July, it caught the eye of the greatest American theatrical impresario of the era, Charles Frohman, who decided to produce it in North America. Greet was the natural person to approach; he was a known commodity in the world of English commercial theatre, his brother (like Frohman) was the lessee of a major London theatre, his name featured in virtually every *Everyman* ad in 1902 (Poel's appeared rarely), and he and Frohman had transacted business on at least two previous occasions.[49] Accepting the producer's invitation gave the actor-manager an opportunity to bring the Morality (and perhaps some of his other productions) to a fresh, proverbially affluent audience whose patronage might restore his business to its former profitability.

The impresario and the actor-manager came to terms: Frohman would sponsor *Everyman* in a season-long tour of North America that Greet would personally lead. (Greet handed over control of his UK operations to Howard while he was abroad.) Significantly, and as O'Connor discovered, Poel was not party to the deal Greet and Frohman struck. Moreover, Greet chose not to sign a document Poel had drawn up that would have protected the North American rights Poel asserted. Through his solicitor, Poel eventually recovered £500 ($2,500) and £1,000 ($5,000) in North American rights and royalties, respectively.[50]

That Greet sponsored the *Everyman* tour Poel led in the fall of 1902 proves he did not simply abandon Poel and the ESS. In early October, the *St James's Gazette* described the paths the two men would travel:

Mr. Greet and his company sail for America to-morrow […]. Mr. Poel, of the Elizabethan Stage Society, who is mainly responsible for the rehearsing and the stage setting of the play, retains his interest in the production. The tour opens in New York […] where the company will remain for three weeks […]. The title rôle will be taken […] by Miss Edith Wynne Matheson [*sic*] […]. Mr. Greet is also about to give audiences in the country the opportunity of seeing the piece, a company, in which Miss Reynolds will play the leading part, starting at Rugby next week for a tour round the provinces.[51]

The power of Poel's original vision had much to do with making that autumn's tour the most remunerative of his career, but Greet had made the production considerably more accessible and attractive to mainstream theatregoers. He instructed Howard to produce and publicize Poel's tour, and his name on its promotional materials and in the newspapers helped attract the provincial and religious audiences he had been cultivating since 1896. Greet's seeming sharp practice angered Poel, but what appears to have embittered him was the fact that Greet received most of the accolades *Everyman* was about to win on the other side of the Atlantic.

NOTES

[1]   Unless otherwise indicated, details of Greet's early career from Richard Foulkes, 'Greet, Sir Philip Barling Ben (1857–1936)', in *ODNB*, 2004, online edition, <http://www.oxforddnb.com/view/article/33548> [accessed 31 May 2016]; Winifred F. E. C. Isaac, *Ben Greet and the Old Vic: A Biography of Sir Philip Ben Greet* (London: for the Author, [1964]), pp.7–85; S. R. Littlewood, 'Greet, Sir Phillip Barling Ben', *DNB, 1931–1940*, 1949, online edition <www.oxforddnb.com/view/olddnb/33548> [accessed 31 May 2016]; 'Sir Philip Ben Greet', *The Times*, 18 May 1936, p.19; Ben Greet, 'In the Days of My Youth', *Mainly about People*, 14 June 1902, pp.612–13. For Thorne's reputation as a teacher, see Richard Foulkes, *Church and Stage in Victorian England* (Cambridge: Cambridge University Press, 1997), pp.157–58.

[2]   'Theatre Royal', *Hampshire Advertiser*, 10 February 1883, p.8; 'Theatrical and Musical Intelligence', *(London) Morning Post*, 19 February 1883, p.2; 'Southampton', *Era*, 24 February 1883, p.10.

[3]   Foulkes, pp.170–74; Wendy Trewin, *The Royal General Theatrical Fund, A History: 1838–1988* (London: Society for Theatre Research, 1988), p.133, qtd. in Foulkes, p.174; John Richard Orens, *Stewart Headlam's Radical Anglicanism: The Mass, the Masses, and the Music Hall* (Urbana and Chicago: University of Illinois Press, 2003), p.153.

[4]   'Shakespeare "Under the Greenwood Tree"', *Era*, 26 July 1884, p.8; Princess Lazarovich-Hrebelianovich, *Palaces and Pleasures* (New York: Century, 1915), pp.59–92; John Stokes, *Resistible Theatres: Enterprise and Experiment in the Late Nineteenth Century* (London: Paul Elek Books, 1972), pp.47–50; Michael Dobson, *Shakespeare and Amateur Performance: A Cultural History* (Cambridge: Cambridge University Press, 2011), p.165.

[5]   'Arrangements for This Day', *(London) Morning Post*, 18 July 1885, p.5; 'Promenade Concert and Open Air Play at Colchester', *Essex Standard*, 15 August 1885, p.5; 'Literary and Other Notes', *Bristol Mercury*, 24 August 1885, p.6; 'Dramatic Gossip', *Illustrated London News*, 5 September 1885, p.4; 'A Pastoral Performance', *Era*, 31 July 1886, p.12; 'Theatrical Gossip', *Era*, 7 August 1886, p.7; Sir Philip Ben Greet, 'Reminiscences of a Mummer, Part II', *(Singapore) Straights Times*, 14 November 1929, p.12; J. Bannister Howard, *Fifty Years a Showman* (London: Hutchinson, 1938), p.101; Roger Fiske, 'Shakespeare in the Concert Hall', in *Shakespeare in Music*, ed. by Phyllis Hartnoll (London: Macmillan, 1964), 177–241 (pp.179–81 and 227–28).

[6]   'Dramatic Gossip', *Athenæum,* 23 June 1888, p.805. For reports of a few of the company's appearances at perennial host Worcester College, Oxford, see 'University Intelligence', *The Times,* 23 June 1892, p.7; 'University Intelligence', *The Times*, 21 June 1893, p.10; 'University Intelligence', *The Times*, 25 June 1896, p.10; 'University Intelligence', *The Times*, 1 July 1897, p.6. Downing, Jesus, and St John's hosted it at Cambridge.

[7]   For a description of the effect open-air touring in England had on the health of one of Greet's most accomplished performers, see Mrs Patrick Campbell, *My Life and Some Letters* (New York: Dodd, Mead and Co., 1922), pp.69–70. For a discussion of Greet's criteria for site selection, see Florence May Warner, 'Sir Philip Ben Greet Produces', *Quarterly Journal of Speech*, 18.1 (February 1932), 102–08 (pp.103–04).

[8]   Kenneth Macgowan, *Footlights across America: Towards a National Theater* (New York: Harcourt, Brace and Co., 1929), p.75.

[9]   Department of English and the Woman's League of the University of Michigan and the Ben Greet Players, Sharing Contract, 29 April 1905, Isaac Newton Demmon Papers, University of Michigan Library (Special Collections Library).

[10]   Isaac, pp.43–46.

[11]   Russell Thorndike, *Sybil Thorndike* (London: Thornton Butterworth, 1929. rev. ed. London: Theatre Book Club, 1950), p.110.

[12]   C. B. Purdom, *Harley Granville Barker: Man of the Theatre, Dramatist and Scholar* (Cambridge, MA: Harvard University Press, 1956), p.5; Isaac, p.52; Ben Greet Comedy Company, Play Programme, Theatre Royal, Eastbourne, 15–21 August 1898. Author.

[13]   M. C. Day and J. C. Trewin, *The Shakespeare Memorial Theatre* (London: J. M. Dent, 1932), p.137.

[14]   T. C. Kemp and J. C. Trewin, *The Stratford Festival* (Birmingham: Cornish

Brothers, 1953), pp.36–37; J. C. Trewin, *Benson and the Bensonians* (London: Barre and Rockcliff, 1960), pp.84 and 86; Isaac, p.55.

[15] 'Stage Whispers', *Man of the World*, 25 March 1896, p.5; Edward Morton, 'At the Theatre', *West-End*, May 1897, 15–17 (p.17); 'Amusements', *London Evening News*, 23 April 1898, p.4. In the early nineteenth century, the phrase 'Shakespeare festival' connoted a Shakespeare-related pageant held in Stratford-upon-Avon to celebrate author's birthday. But the play performances given to inaugurate the Shakespeare Memorial Theatre when it opened in that town in 1879 quietly altered its meaning to connote a series of presentations of the Elizabethan's plays in Stratford-upon-Avon to celebrate the author's birthday. For details, see Day and Trewin, pp.19–20 and 38–48.

[16] Isaac, p.46; 'The Theatres in 1896', *The Times*, 4 January 1897, p.5; 'A Chat with Mr. Ben Greet', *Era*, 16 May 1896, p.10.

[17] Isaac, p.46; 'Stage Whispers', *Westminster Budget*, 3 April 1896, p.16. Number of companies from Howard, p.107.

[18] H. F. Maltby, *Ring up the Curtain* (London: Hutchinson, 1950), p.46.

[19] Maltby, 43–48 (p.43).

[20] Maltby, p.65. Although Maltby's reference is to 1901, that Greet had been doing this since at least 1897 is confirmed by 'Music, Art, the Drama', *Bristol Times and Mirror*, 31 August 1897, p.3.

[21] Howard, p.108.

[22] Advertisement, *(London) Evening Standard*, 24 June 1895, p.1; William Poel, *An Account of the Elizabethan Stage Society* (London: for the Society, 1898), p.10; 'Music, Art, the Drama', *Bristol Times and Mirror*, 18 May 1897, p.3.

[23] William Archer, 'Shakespeare at the Olympic', *The Theatrical World of 1897* (London: Walter Scott, 1898), 151–157 (pp.151–52 and 153–54). By attending only to part of Archer's review, Carey M. Mazer, *Shakespeare Refashioned: Elizabethan Plays on the Edwardian Stage* (Ann Arbor, MI: UMI Research Press, 1981), p.71, erroneously concludes that Greet preferred to mount scenic productions and that he did so whenever possible.

[24] 'Olympic Theatre', *The Times*, 28 May 1897, p.3; 'A Chat with Ben Greet', *Era*, 2 December 1899, p.15.

[25] Howard, p.19.

[26] Howard, pp.89–90; Maltby, p.37. Although Isaac, p.234, dates (without citation) the academy's opening to 1896, Maltby's account of his sister completing the course there in 1898 makes 1897 the earliest opening date I have been able to confirm. That the May 1896 *Era* interview cited above makes no reference to the academy supports the 1897 hypothesis; Greet would almost certainly have touted his academy if it had opened or was about to.

[27] Howard, p.91; Lew Sparks Akin, 'Ben Greet and His Theatre Companies in America: 1902–1932' (unpublished doctoral dissertation, University of Georgia, 1974), pp.36–37; Maltby, p.65.

[28] Ben Greet, 'The Stage and the Church', in *Workers Together with God: A Series of Papers on Some of the Church's Works by Some of the Church's Workers*, ed. by Nathaniel Keymer. 3rd ed. (Oxford and London: A. R. Mowbry, 1898), pp.323–26.

[29] 'Stage Duel', *(London) Evening News*, 15 July 1899, p.2; 'London School Board', *The Times*, 23 March 1900, p.12; 'London School Board', *The Times*, 20 July 1900, p.13; 'London School Board', *The Times*, 17 May 1901, p.13; 'London School Board', *The Times*, 19 March 1902, p.9; 'Shakespearian Recitals for Evening Students', *The Times*, 1 March 1902, p.12.

[30] 'The Oberammergau Passion Play', *Ipswich Journal*, 2 June 1900, p.8; 'Stage in Other Lands', *Duluth (Minnesota) Evening Herald*, 11 October 1902, p.4; "Anton Lang in a New Role," *Nottingham Evening Post*, 20 October 1902, p.2; 'Belasco — Ben Greet Lecture', *Washington Times*, 22 January 1911, evening ed., p.6; Anton Lang, 'Christus of Oberammergau', *Living Age*, 22 August 1922, pp.550–51; 'Et Cætera', *Tablet*, 6 June 1931, p.21.

[31] 'Pastoral Plays in Regent's Park', *(London) Evening Standard*, 22 June 1899, p.5; 'Open Air Plays', *The Times*, June 28, 1899, p.10. For representative reviews of performances in subsequent summer seasons at the park, see 'Royal Botanic Society', *The Times*, 12 June 1900, p.14; 'Pastoral Plays in Regent's Park', *The Times*, 26 June 1901, p.7; 'Pastoral Plays in Regent's-Park', *The Times*, 28 May 1902, p.9.

[32] Isaac, pp.216–20. Regrettably, Isaac, David Conville, *The Park: The Story of the Open Air Theatre, Regent's Park* (London: Oberon, 2007), pp.14–16, and Dobson, p.181, fail to identify 1899 as the year Greet first performed in Regent's Park.

[33] Marion O'Connor, *William Poel and the Elizabethan Stage Society* (Cambridge and Alexandria, VA: Chadwyck-Healey, 1987), p.71; Marion O'Connor, 'William Poel', in *Poel, Granville Barker, Guthrie, Wanamaker: Great Shakespeareans 15,* ed. by Cary M. Mazer (London: Bloomsbury, 2013), p.41; Robert Speaight, *William Poel and the Elizabethan Revival* (Cambridge, MA: Harvard University Press, 1954), pp.104 and 68. For a vivid description of Poel trying to teach his 'tones' to some actors, see Ben Iden Payne, *A Life in a Wooden O: Memoirs of the Theatre* (New Haven: Yale University Press, 1977), pp.88–89.

[34] Palmer, 'America', pp.10–11.

[35] Speaight, p.41; Payne, p.86; O'Connor, 'William Poel', p.7.

[36] O'Connor, 'William Poel', p.34; Speaight, p.180. For Poel's views on commercial theatre, see Simon Shepherd and Peter Womack, *English Drama: A Cultural History* (Oxford: Basil Blackwell, 1996), p.106, ctd in Robert Shaughnessy, *The Shakespeare Effect: A History of Twentieth-Century Performance* (New York: Palgrave, 2002), p.35.

[37] '"Henry V." under Shakespearian Conditions', *St James's Gazette*, 22 November 1901, p.15; 'The Elizabethan Stage Society', *Manchester Morning Courier and Lancashire General Advertiser*, 22 November 1901, p.4; Kemp and Trewin, pp.59–60; Speaight, p.282; Isaac, pp.62–63; A. C. Sprague, *Shakespeare's Histories* (London: Society for Theatre Research, 1964), pp.96–97; 'Flotsam and Jetsam', *Hastings and St Leonards Observer*, 9 November 1901, p.6; Wisner Payne Kinne, *George Pierce Baker and the American Theatre* (Cambridge, MA: Harvard University Press, 1954), p.63.

[38] 'Henry V at Theatre Metropole, Camberwell', *Era*, 26 April 1902, qtd in Lanayre D. Liggere, *The Life of Robert Loraine: The Stage, the Sky, and George Bernard Shaw* (Newark, DE: University of Delaware Press, 2013), pp.52–53.

[39] 'Representations of the Old Morality Play', *Cheltenham Looker-On*, 2 November 1901, p.1056.

[40] For accounts of the first revival of *Everyman* and its impact, see Speaight, pp.161–68; Robert Potter, *The English Morality Play: Origins, History and Influences of a Dramatic Tradition* (London: Routledge and Kegan Paul, 1975), pp.222–25; O'Connor, *William Poel*, pp.70–76; John Elliott, Jr, *Playing God: Medieval Mysteries on the Modern Stage* (Toronto: University of Toronto Press, 1989), pp.42–44.

[41] *(London) Morning Post*, 15 July 1901, n. p., qtd in Potter, p.222.

[42] Henry Tyrrell, 'Edith Wynne Matthison — A Study', *Theatre*, June 1903, pp.139–40; '"Everyman" at the Imperial', *Illustrated London News,* 21 June 1902, p.898. Greet's American fit-up was different from Poel's original fit-up.

[43] Seating capacity from <http://www.victorianlondon.org/dickens/dickensque.htm> [accessed 31 May 2016].

[44] Elliott, p.43; Philip Ben Greet, 'England's Censorship', *NYT*, 2 February 1931, p.13; 'Everyman', *(London) Echo*, 22 March 1902, p.1.

[45] 'The Elizabethan Stage Society', *The Times,* 19 March 1902, p.14; 'St. George's Hall', *(London) Evening Standard*, 18 March 1902, p.3. For another detailed review, see J. T. Grein, *Dramatic Criticism, Vol. IV, 1902–1903* (London: Eveleigh Nash, 1904), pp.59–61.

[46] 'Every Man', *(London) Echo,* 22 May 1902, p.2; 'The Morality Play', *St James's Gazette*, 27 May 1902, p.6.

[47] Seating capacity from <http://cinematreasures.org/theaters/39335> [accessed 31 May 2016]; Isaac, pp.75–76; *Athenæum*, 20 July 1902, p.103, qtd in Potter, p.222.

[48] 'La Veine', *Saturday Review of Politics, Literature, Science and Art*, 19 July 1902, p.77; 'Imperial Theatre', *The Times,* 12 July 1902, p.12; Elizabethan Stage Society, *The Alchemist* Play Programme, Imperial Theatre, Westminster, 11 and 12 July 1902, <http://ccdl.libraries.claremont.edu/cdm/ref/collection/phl/id/1094> [accessed 31 May 2016].

[49] 'Town Hall, Edmonton', *Middlesex Gazette*, 20 November 1897, p.4.; W. Lestcoq to BG, 22 September 1900, NYPL. For a discussion of Frohman's importance in the United States, see Charles H. Shattuck, *Shakespeare on the American Stage*, 2 vols. (Washington: Folger Books, 1976–87), II (1987), pp.29–30.

[50] Poel and Others Regarding *Everyman*, 1902–1907 and undated, William Poel Papers, Victoria and Albert Museum Theatre Archive; Speaight, pp.165–166; O'Connor, *William Poel*, p.75.

[51] 'The Drama', *St James's Gazette*, 3 October 1902, p.6.

CHAPTER TWO
A Debut Like No Other, 1902–03

Religious Anti-Theatrical Prejudice in America

One reason *Everyman* appealed to Charles Frohman was that it was a religiously themed costume drama, a genre even more popular in the United States than it was in Great Britain. But religiosity could be a double-edged sword; a religiously themed play had the capacity to attract a huge audience, but it also had the potential to be ruthlessly dispatched if it offended moral sensibilities. The dramas the impresario knew had been adapted from recent, bestselling novels, which meant they already conformed to current tastes. But even altered to bring it more into line with contemporary preferences, the Morality remained a relic of another age. And the run in Westminster had generated one incendiary notice that had already been widely circulated in the United States by the time the company arrived. *Everyman* might have flopped had Frohman and Greet not worked to make it attractive to the new audience they hoped to capture.

Looking back on the fad for religiously themed costume dramas as it was beginning to wane in 1906, the *New York Times* noted the staggering popularity of works such as *The Sign of the Cross* (1895), *Ben Hur* (1899), and *Quo Vadis* (1900) before linking them to the Morality:

> Though the main aim of the theatrical manager in staging a 'religious' drama must be recognized as his desire to reach the non-theatregoing public, it is nevertheless true that a Biblical subject offers exceptional

45

opportunities for spectacular display [...]. Perhaps the most astonishing result of the 'religious' drama is the development of the so-called 'modern morality play'. This most recent return to an antiquated conception is primarily due to Ben Greet's revival of 'Everyman'.[1]

That the hits listed would inspire multiple film adaptations that would draw massive audiences for half a century illustrates not only how powerfully their stories and spectacles appealed to Americans, but also how strong and slow to change American religious attitudes were.

Everyman was neither Biblical nor spectacular, but its religious subject and rich production gave it some of the appeal of those other works. As this promotional 'character group' (the play contains no such scene) photograph illustrates, the fit-up included several levels behind which stood painted canvas flats depicting the cloister of Salamanca Cathedral. William Poel had the costumes copied from works by fifteenth- and sixteenth-century masters, and had coached Greet's actors to deliver some lines slowly and deliberately, and to chant others. Greet had added business, an organ playing ecclesiastical music, and burning incense. The programme requested that audience members refrain from applauding so as to strengthen the illusion that they were observing a religious rite rather than a play.

4. Byron. EVERYMAN.
Dir. Ben Greet, Mendelssohn Hall, New York, NY, October 1902.

Whether *Everyman* was tasteful and respectful enough for audiences in the United States remained to be seen. A few American critics regarded it as problematic, even sacrilegious, for the same reason the Lord Chamberlain's Examiner of Plays cautioned Greet and Poel: God appears in it as a speaking character. As Winifred F. E. C. Isaac and Stephen G. Kuehler note, the most negative and sensational account of the Greet-Poel production was written by Alan Dale, the pen-name of British-born Alfred J. Cohen, the dramatic critic for William Randolph Hearst's *New York American*, whose reviews were so notorious that managers and producers sometimes barred him.[2] Like Frohman, Dale saw *Everyman* at the Imperial, and his review, 'London Tolerates a Most Shocking Sacrilege', first ran on 30 July 1902; soon, Hearst-syndicate papers as far away as San Francisco were reprinting it. As its title indicates, it features all the scandal-mongering content and inflammatory editorializing style pioneered by the media tycoon's yellow journalists. After dismissing as 'ludicrous' and 'grotesque' the morality of Londoners, Dale admitted the play had outraged even his calloused sensibilities:

> if I don't wear a hard shell, it is not due to any lack of experience. But I confess right here that when I went to […] see […] 'Everyman', I gasped at what appeared to me to be the most shockingly audacious bit of sacrilege I have ever witnessed.
>
> We talk glibly for and against the Passion Play, and argue plausibly as to the advisability of presenting the Nazarene on the stage, but in America honest judgment is not smothered by one puny censor, and the right thing generally happens. Thanks to American outspoken-ness, and thanks — thousands of thanks — to an unmuzzled press — we get at the sentiment of the community, and that sentiment establishes itself.
>
> As I have often said, I hold that a presentation of religious plays for money-gain is an obnoxious idea, and that managerial venality when it touches this question should be ruthlessly balked and nipped.

The knowledge that he was paying to watch a professional actor play God on a commercial stage filled Dale with ersatz guilt: 'It seemed to me that I was assisting at a sacrilege, that I was aiding and abetting one of the most brazen "morality" efforts that I could have imagined'. Although he actually praised the production, its acting, and religious message, one must get beyond the sensationalized title and opening section to realize he believed a single change would make *Everyman* 'one of the most beautiful and touching events of the season': cut 'the unnecessary and audacious scene in Heaven' that opened the play.[3]

Dale's mention of the Passion Play spelled trouble because it raised the spectre of one of the most notorious episodes in nine-teenth-century American theatrical history: Salmi Morse's attempts to produce a lavish, Anglophone adaptation of the Oberammergau *Passionsspiel* in San Francisco (1879) and New York (1883), both of which aroused such vehement opposition from Protestant groups that the police shut them down.[4] When operatic impresario Oscar Hammerstein I contemplated mounting something similar in Manhattan in 1902, the objections of religious groups, coinciding with the Catholic Archbishop of Quebec's decision to shut down the Francophone adaptation of the *Passionsspiel* that had just opened in Montreal, persuaded him to find another project.[5]

Everyman is not a Passion Play, but the presence of a speaking God in it gave it the same offensive potential in religiously conser-vative America. In her study of religious anti-theatrical prejudice in the United States in the nineteenth-century, Claudia Durst Johnson argues that the churches and religious publics that condemned theatres and performers did so because they regarded these as inverting the functions of churches and ministers, respec-tively, as well as the Victorian moral values they espoused.[6] In the May 1902 issue of the country's leading theatrical monthly, *Theatre*, the Rev. Percy Stickney Grant, Rector of Manhattan's Episcopal Church of the Ascension, described this prejudice as it normally manifested itself, both in regards to plays in general and to the

Passion Play in particular. Grant stated that several mainstream Protestant sects condemned

> the theatre *in toto*. Baptists, Methodists, Congregationalists, and many other denominations, regard going to the theatre as unbecoming in a church member. Drinking, gambling, and theatre-going, according to the moral code in which many of us were reared, constitute a trinity of wrongdoing.

Even Christians from denominations not opposed in principle to theatre (Catholics, Episcopalians, and the more liberal Protestant sects) disapproved of sacred characters being played by professional actors, a group not known for its uniformly strong morality. Christians disapproved of theatres because they had multifarious uses:

> Religious people feel that playhouses have a very versatile description. The same edifice holds 'Ben Hur', 'Sappho', and the Rogers Brothers. They do not wish to see a stage with comic, sensational, spectacular or vulgar associations trodden on by the feet of Christ.

Finally, Christians objected to Jewish producers exploiting Christian piety for commercial gain:

> The leading theatrical managers of America, I do not doubt, are estimable men, but many of them are of a race and of a faith that does not presuppose deep attachment to Christ's religion. For these gentlemen, in despite of their own inherited and ancient faith, to present to the public a dramatic representation of Christ's Passion as a financial speculation would seem actual profanation.[7]

Frohman and Greet had some work to do.

As likely as Dale's mention of the Passion Play was to raise concerns, his critique was useful because it warned Frohman and Greet that their production might be unsuited to American tastes. The pair set about making it as appealing as they could. As a leading member of the powerful Theatrical Trust (detractors called it 'the Syndicate'), Frohman had at his disposal the most advanced promotional capabilities available anywhere.[8] His reputation for sponsoring only the finest, most important projects meant that the phrase 'Charles Frohman Presents' (in discreet type) in newspaper advertisements and on programmes promised the highest quality drama available on either side of the Atlantic. He had other means to boost *Everyman*'s chances. So as not to taint it with the opprobrium attached to theatres, he booked it into concert halls whenever possible. (That these more respectable venues were also good for the bottom line was a happy coincidence; concert halls lacking the functionality — curtains, machinery, advanced lighting — the simple production did not require anyway, they also cost less to hire.) Crucially, Frohman invited local clergymen as his guests every time the show opened in a new city. This proved an inspired idea because most of the churchmen who saw *Everyman* strongly supported it, and many promoted it from their pulpits, which simultaneously boosted attendance and made it more difficult for parishioners to credit cries of sacrilege. Last, he personally endorsed it. The day before it received its continental premiere, the *New York Times* published a long interview with the normally interview-averse impresario about his decision to produce it. He stressed the production's experimental nature and educational importance. After expressing doubts about its commercial viability (forestalling objections that he, a Jewish producer, was exploiting Christian piety for profit), he explained why he had decided to produce it nevertheless:

> I do not know for certain that the American theatregoing public will take kindly to the morality play and make it a sensation here as it was in London. It is a quaint and beautiful production, and it made such an impression when I saw it […] that I at once engaged the entire company […]. The morality play may not be of interest to the public, but it interested me, and from an educational point of view it is something to be desired […].

Frohman was sure to clarify that 'educational' meant more than a lesson in the history of English drama: 'I sincerely believe that those who may not like it from the modern play standpoint may still welcome and tolerate it for its highly constructive character and the undeniable potentiality for the good which it possesses'.[9] For his part, Greet retained the format of the English programmes, using 'Adonai' for 'God' and omitting the names of the performers to decrease theatregoers' awareness that they were paying to watch professional actors personate religious characters. More significant, he repositioned God once more. Mendelssohn Hall had two grated galleries on either side of the stage near the ceiling, and Greet placed God behind a curtain in the left-hand one. As one reviewer described the show's opening, 'the lights flash up in a latticed gallery [...] and God is seen, attended by two angels'.[10] Frohman and Greet had done much to make *Everyman* attractive to religiously conservative Americans.

Everyone Everywhere Loves Everyman

The theatrical season lasted forty weeks and ran from October to May. *Everyman* received its North American premiere in the 1,100-seat Mendelssohn Hall on 13 October 1902.[11] Promotional materials advertised the ownership formula 'Charles Frohman Presents *Everyman* as Presented by the Elizabethan Stage Society of London, under the Personal Direction of Mr. Ben Greet' throughout the season. As in London, the run in Mendelssohn Hall comprised primarily matinees. Dramatic critic Robert Grau later recounted that the opening-day receipts totalled a paltry $46 and that someone invited Greet 'to pack up his "props" and return to his native land', after the third performance, which invitation he 'politely and firmly declined'.[12]

The play attracted widely varied notices. The most prominent condemnation came from the *New-York Tribune*, which dubbed it 'A Dismal Experiment' possessing little dramatic value or ethical force. The only thing its critic did not condemn was Edith Wynne Matthison, who was fine in demeanor, dignified in pose and in movement, self-poised, deliberate [...] and continuously felicitous with expressive action [...]. She was viewed with respectful interest and sympathy by a melancholy audience of about four hundred persons, who felt somewhat sorry for her, exceedingly so for themselves.

The *New York World* pronounced it 'a sacrilege to enlightened intelligence and religious sense'. Having returned to America, Dale published another incendiary notice in the *New York American*, this one entitled 'Jehovah Seen in the Old Morality Play "Everyman" — Much That Church People Will Not Countenance'. In it, he acknowledged that, although 'the sacrilegious atmosphere' of the London production had been decreased, the still-visible deity, the fact that a professional actor was being paid to play God, the involvement of Frohman (who was not only Jewish, but was also producing Arthur Pinero's controversial *Iris*), and the impresario's importation of the show 'as a money-making scheme' still rendered the Morality deeply offensive.[13]

Other publications took more moderate positions. After acknowledging that a few people were likely to find the play sacrilegious, the New York *Sun* praised the production and noted that the audience registered no condemnation during the performance. *Life*'s James Stetson Metcalf objected to Christian teachings being 'set forth under Jewish managers simply as a money-making venture', but his overall assessment was positive:

It is naturally startling to see an impersonation of the Christian Deity, but it is brief and only incidental. The whole thing is done with such sobriety and earnestness that it is really less shocking than the familiar and flippant way [...] some clergymen refer to things sacred [...]. [*Life*] would suggest that if the management should give a special performance for New York's elderly millionaires, we might soon hear of some good acts of charity.

One of the country's leading theatrical weeklies, the *New York Dramatic Mirror* (*Dramatic Mirror* hereafter), preferred not to take a position: 'The question of whether or not a religious play of this character should be presented as a commercial enterprise is […] decidedly debatable. Churchmen and conservative laymen are at variance […] and the controversy will doubtless be without end'.[14]

A few positive notices appeared. The *New York Times*'s critic (possibly John Corbin) called it 'an impressive mediaeval parable' that 'touches the deepest chords of religious feeling' before pronouncing the personation of Matthison (depicted here in one of the drama's most powerful moments) 'a very real triumph'. But the critic disapproved of the decision to abandon the frank, vigorous spirit of the original play to make the production more appealing to restrained contemporary tastes, the overall effect of which was to make it tedious at points. The *Brooklyn Eagle* likened it to 'a draft of a fresh, cool spring to people who been wandering through the metropolitan desert athirst' before lauding Matthison's performance. A second review in the *New York Times*, this one carrying Corbin's by-line,

5. Byron. EVERYMAN.
Dir. Ben Greet, Mendelssohn Hall, New York, NY, October 1902.

criticized *Everyman* almost as much as it praised it. Corbin asserted that changing 'God' to 'Adonai' was as ridiculous as the 'shuffling self-consciousness' that prompted Frohman to recruit local ministers to 'chaperon the début', which surpassed 'the possibility of satire'. He dismissed as canting old women the critics who attacked the play before ironically noting that those who typically favoured new drama were the ones praising the old play, while those who typically championed faith and traditional morality opposed it. He praised the production's magnificent design and execution, but believed it betrayed the play's essentially medieval (fast, earthy, Catholic) spirit by pandering to 'the terrible spirit of puritanical piety'.[15]

Everyman began drawing larger audiences in early November, at which point *Theatre* and *Harper's Weekly* dubbed it one of most interesting and artistic productions on Broadway. Swelling attendance induced Frohman to extend the run, which he was able to do by transferring it into the 500-seat Madison Square Theatre, where it presented another string of matinees. A fortnight later, he transferred it to the enormous (3,815 seats) New York Theatre for a week-long run of two performances per day.[16] Business was robust by the time the show left the metropolis.

Greet made the final, most radical alteration to the production at some point between its departure from Mendelssohn Hall and its opening in Boston. Finally taking Dale's suggestion, he completely removed God from sight, transforming the character into a booming, disembodied voice that spoke from behind the scenes. (Greet restored God to the stage for performances at select educational institutions.) Kuehler implies Greet made this change after the production left Manhattan; he may be correct, but we should recall that the gallery Greet placed God in was an architectural feature unique to Mendelssohn Hall.[17] That fact, coupled with our ignorance of how the production was staged at the other New York venues, should leave us open to the possibility that Greet changed the show the first time Frohman transferred it. The gallery enabled Greet to stage a compromise between a represented and an unrepresented

God. Forced to choose, he catered to his audience. An offstage God at the other Manhattan theatres might at least partially explain why attendance swelled at the end of the run.

Whenever the change came, it made the show; *Everyman* toured to nearly universal acclaim thereafter. It caused a sensation at its next stop: a week-long engagement at Boston's 550-seat Steinert Hall in late November. An enthusiastic endorsement in the *Harvard Crimson* from English instructor George Pierce Baker helped boost student attendance. More influential in terms of overall turnout were the good opinions of the clergymen Frohman invited as his guests; many accepted and then praised *Everyman* in their sermons. Word of mouth and the good notices in the local papers supplemented the academic and religious endorsements that began rolling in. Suddenly, all of Boston wanted to see it. The *Dramatic Mirror* reported a box-office under siege:

> They wanted to stand on the stairs and hear the play even if they could not see it. Four times as many were turned away as could possibly get inside the hall. With such a week as that it will not be surprising to see Everyman have its route changed so as to bring it back to Boston again in the near future. Harvard professors made their students pass examinations on it, and Wellesley girls came to the matinees, and the Catholic priests who saw it — and dozens of them did — all advised their parishioners to go.

Greet told his principal American correspondent, Lucy Love, that the company made more money during its first three days in Boston than during its first week in Manhattan. A fortnight later, the *Boston Globe* reported that the run 'closed with hundreds disappointed when they found out they would be unable to secure seats'.[18] Frohman and Greet had a hit on their hands.

Because Lucy Cleveland Prindle Love (1855–1936) was Greet's closest American friend and is the reason we know so much about his years in the United States, a few details about her here are necessary. After teaching for a period, in 1878 the New York native married Dr Edward G. Love, the Hamilton- and Columbia-educated chemist who served as the City of New York's first Gas Examiner as well as the Gas Analyst for both the city's Board of Health and New York State. The couple's only child, Helen Douglas Love, was born the following year.[19] Lucy Love was active socially, and her support of cultural causes in the metropolis brought her into contact with prominent artists, educators, thinkers, and philanthropists, the correspondence of whom she saved and now compose the bulk of the Love Family Papers preserved at Yale University. But because the family solicitor counselled daughter Helen against making public Greet's more candid remarks about the famous people he encountered, Helen kept, but chose to not bequeath to that collection, most of the letters Greet wrote to her mother. Decades later, these were acquired by the University of Michigan.

Lucy Love's relationship with Greet was founded upon their mutual love of opera. I have been unable to determine how they met, but Greet was writing to her within a month of his arrival in the United States. The pair frequently attended musical events together when he was in Manhattan, and she introduced him to a number of prominent New Yorkers, including Walter Damrosch, Hamilton Wright Mabie, and Charles Sprague Smith. She also rendered more practical assistance — following up on orders placed with costumers, getting scripts copied, hiring musicians, finding suitable lodgings for the female members of the company — when Greet was on the road.

The actor-manager wrote to her regularly from 1902 until he returned to England in 1914, and then sporadically until his death in 1936. The more than two hundred letters, notes, and cards from him she saved are an invaluable resource for anyone interested in Greet's thoughts, plans, and activities. His usual practice while touring being to write to her on Sundays, he often listed his contact information (city and theatre) for each date of the upcoming week so she could reply. Thus, his letters are also an invaluable resource for reconstructing his company's performance calendar.

Early December 1902 found it playing short stands in the smaller New England cities to large, attentive crowds comprising not only each municipality's religious and civic dignitaries, but also its common labourers.[20] Significantly, Greet made his first appearance on the campus of an American institution of higher learning, Vassar College, at this time.

Perhaps inspired by Greet's success, Hart Conway decided to direct the students of the Chicago Musical College in his own production of *Everyman*. Conway's solution to the God problem was simple and effective: he blacked out the theatre for the entirety of the character's opening speech. The *Chicago Tribune's* W. L. Hubbard warmly commended 'the skill, taste, and dignified manner' of the presentation.[21] Equally impressed, the *Dramatic Mirror's* critic singled out Conway and his leading player, Rudolph Magnus, for praise.[22]

From Boston came an endorsement of Greet's production that helped ensure its fame and success for years to come in parts yet unknown to the Englishman. The Rev. Edward Everett Hale devoted a considerable part of his long life to the ministry, most famously as the pastor of Boston's South Congregational Church. His national reputation was equally impressive. A tireless activist for Abolition, educational reform, and the rights of immigrants, he was also the celebrated author of more than sixty books as well as hundreds of stories, essays, and poems. Frohman and Greet must have been thrilled when they learned that the influential clergyman had extolled the play's virtues in the pages of the *Christian Register*, America's leading Unitarian weekly. Hale's essay opens by commenting:

> The performance of a miracle play by an English company in our different cities suggests a great deal to those interested in religious education [...]. I doubt if any person who attends [...] does not come away with the serious question whether the play cannot teach us all what is good for us, and whether it cannot show us how we can teach those who are in our charge. The attendants at these performances are better men and better women for attending.

After outlining *Everyman*'s plot and moral, Hale observed that

> Between the year 1400 [*sic*] and the year 1903 this [message] has been said
> substantially by books and from the pulpit ten million times by ten million
> teachers. These miracle-play people succeeded in representing it in an
> hour and a half to the people who saw their play, so that they saw it, and
> never forgot it. It was a case of 'seeing, they shall see', as the Saviour said
> of his parables […].
>
> Whether young people in their passion for 'dramatics' — a very natural
> and worthy passion — cannot be set on some play which shall carry with
> it lessons as vividly portrayed as these, that is the question which suggests
> itself even to the most rationalistic of Protestants.[23]

Hale's testimonial, an excerpt from which Greet would reprint on
promotional materials and programmes for years, brought
Everyman to the attention of liberal Christians throughout the
United States. For the first time, people in rural America who had
nothing to do with theatres, plays, or East Coast cities not only
heard about the play, but were also urged to see it by a distinguished divine nationally renowned for his impeccable moral and
literary judgment.

The company's next engagement was a week in Philadelphia's
1,800-seat Horticultural Hall. The *Philadelphia Inquirer* enthusiastically praised the Morality, noting that, although there had been
'much discussion as to the good taste of introducing the Deity in
performance', the production contained nothing that would offend
'any religious scruples'. The *Philadelphia Evening Bulletin* likewise
assured readers that it contained nothing that would 'jar the most
devout minds'. Halfway through the run, another prominent
American man of letters endorsed the play. The University of
Pennsylvania's H. H. Furness was internationally renowned as the
world's foremost editor of Shakespeare's works. In a letter to the
Philadelphia Public Ledger that was widely reprinted, Furness exhorted

every student of dramatic literature, every lover of the drama, every reader
of the history of manners and customs, every student of theological history,
every Protestant clergyman, with his congregation, every Roman Catholic
priest, with his congregation, to see the old morality of 'Everyman'.

Such was the power of Furness's name that Greet would also have
his endorsement reprinted on promotional materials and
programmes for years. Unfortunately, warm notices and a scholar's
praise failed to draw audiences. Although the *Philadelphia Inquirer*
stated that *Everyman*'s success had been pronounced, a disappointed Greet told Love that Horticultural Hall was 'all hall, no
people. We're a dead Failure here I'm sorry to say [...]'.[24]

The plays he selected and the ways he staged them inspired
legions of imitators, both professional and amateur. One of the
latter, a clergyman in Manhattan, came to public attention while
the company was playing a week-long engagement in Baltimore's
1,710-seat Academy of Music. *Outlook* reported that the Rev.
Walter E. Bentley was cleaning up the basement of New York's
Episcopal Church of the Holy Sepulcher (a name he was about to
change to the Church of the Transfiguration) so that it could host
the performances of his newly formed St George's Dramatic
Society, the purpose of which was to attract the predominantly
working-class teens of the neighbourhood to the church by
having them mount plays that conveyed inspirational messages.
Everyman would be the society's first production.[25] That Bentley
saw Greet's *Everyman* is certain. Although I cannot prove he also
read Hale's endorsement, the purpose of the dramatic society he
formed was an excellent answer to the question Hale posed. One
of the reasons *Everyman* was important is that it inspired religious
feeling and renewed interest in using drama in religious education
and outreach.

Far more important to Greet's American story is the other, more
famous, body Bentley established. In 1899, the English-born cleric
founded the Actors' Church Alliance, which he modelled directly

on the Rev. J. Stewart Headlam's Church and Stage Guild. Bentley served as its general secretary, while the Rt Rev. Henry C. Potter, the Bishop of the Episcopal Diocese of New York, served as its president. Bentley recruited Greet and several members of the *Everyman* company into the organization within a month of their arrival in Manhattan. By 1904, the alliance had grown to 400 chapters nationwide.[26] The Actors' Church Alliance gave Greet access to an impressive network of people who shared similar ideas about drama and religion.

Rerouting the tour the way the *Dramatic Mirror* predicted, Frohman brought *Everyman* back to Boston a few days before Christmas — this time to the Park Theatre (1,580 seats), where the play cemented its reputation as a hit. The *Boston Globe* dubbed it 'the event of a lifetime' and reported clergymen, students, professors, and women's clubs thronging every performance. As Kuehler discovered, the Roman Catholic Archdiocese of Boston tacitly endorsed *Everyman* by allowing performances of it to be advertised in the diocesan paper. The archdiocese also joined forces with other churches and 'the university settlements among the slums' to buy a performance in Boston's largest theatre, the 2,600-seat Grand Opera House, on 20 January, all the tickets to which were distributed, gratis, to the city's poor.[27]

A streetcar accident briefly incapacitated Greet and left him with a permanent souvenir of the city in the form of a long gash above his left eye. A row of stitches and packed houses were all the physic he needed. As he told Love,

> I'm alright [*sic*] with a bit of a scar on my head, over which my silver locks will soon fall […]. Boston really appreciated us + this last week we've had some splendid audiences + the Universities & Colleges are captured, I think, for as long as I like to give them good things.[28]

In three months, *Everyman* had enabled the Englishman to attract not only an enthusiastic and growing religious following, but also an academic one. Having performed at Vassar (3 December) and Bryn

Mawr (12 December), Greet added another American institution of higher learning to the list on 19 January, when Brown University sponsored two performances.

Moving on to the Midwest, the company opened a three-week engagement in Chicago in late January. As he had in the other major cities, Frohman booked it into a concert hall, this time the 850-seat Steinway Hall. Chicagoans embraced *Everyman* even more enthusiastically than Bostonians had — so much so that Frohman laid on extra performances to satisfy unexpectedly high demand.[29]

Hubbard's glowing notice in the *Chicago Tribune* gives evidence to how successful Frohman and Greet had been at making the show appeal to religiously conservative Americans:

> The absence of all theatrical device […] the serious nature of the play itself […] and above all the pronouncedly reverent manner in which the entire production has been prepared and given — all these make the performance unique and distinctly apart from all that is usually associated with the theater. The auditor has the feeling of participating in something not far removed from a religious ceremony, and yet the appeal made to the esthetic [*sic*] sense is so strong that he cannot but realize that it is an art work he is contemplating, and an art work of exceptional beauty and power it is.

Like virtually every other critic, Hubbard lavished praise on Matthison, whom he described as 'an actress of exceptional abilities'.[30]

Hubbard became the first American dramatic critic to interview Greet when he did so near the end of the run. As Kuehler observes, a noteworthy feature of Greet's debut in the American press was his fulsome acknowledgment of Poel as the scholarly and artistic force behind *Everyman*:

> Nine-tenths at least of the credit should go to my friend and confrère, William Poel, the founder of the Elizabethan Stage society of England. He is the greatest authority on the medieval, Tudor, and restoration drama, from the setting point of view, of any one in our country.

Asked what his own plans were after he had finished touring the Morality, Greet stated that he hoped to bring 'the best specimens' of Elizabethan drama to the United States.[31]

The *Tribune* published another piece about *Everyman* the same day. Its writer explained how the Morality had compelled many Chicagoans to face spiritual issues they normally never acknowledged, let alone contemplated:

> The audiences at 'Everyman' […] have been proof that religious emotion is not quite dead. Perhaps the 'all earthly things are vanity' moral […] had an overpowering effect […] on people accustomed to exploit earthly things to the limit, but even if this is the explanation, there is still cause for astonishment in the reverence, awe, and almost terror with which Chicago people have been watching 'Everyman' stripped of all material things and brought face to face with the fundamental facts of life and death.[32]

Everyman's power to inspire genuine religious thought and feeling was as undeniable as it was considerable.

The company headed into Canada, first for an indifferent week in Toronto's 1,800-seat Princess Theatre, then for a slightly more lucrative one in Montreal's 1,972-seat Academy of Music. As Kuehler finds, the Morality drew positive notices in both cities.[33]

Turning south in March, the company returned to Philadelphia, where its run at the Garrick Theatre (1,884 seats) was significantly more successful than its initial appearance in the city. Indeed, one New York paper reported that the first Saturday matinee there took in more than $2,200. This surge in popularity (and profitability) may have been at least partially the result of another endorsement the production picked up, this one from Catholic Archbishop Patrick John Ryan of Philadelphia: 'I have heard many sermons and preached many, but never anything as powerful as this' — another testimonial Greet used in his promotional materials.[34]

The next week was all trains and short engagements. A large and enthusiastic audience welcomed the company to Princeton

University, whose students enjoyed Matthison's performance almost too much; they refused to leave Alexander Hall after the play ended, so eager were they to see her emerge from the grave. Leaving New Jersey, the company fulfilled engagements in Brooklyn, Providence, New Haven, and Hartford before returning to Manhattan, where it concluded the season with a seven-week run at the 1,110-seat Garden Theatre.[35]

New Yorkers enthusiastically welcomed the production back to their city. One reporter compared the *Everyman* phenomenon to the one that had attended the stage adaptation of *The Strange Case of Dr Jekyll and Mr Hyde* starring Richard Mansfield a generation earlier, when 'people went night after night, unable to withstand the sensational fascination'. Writing in the *Independent*, a gratified Elizabeth Luther Cary noted that New Yorkers had finally awakened 'to the fact that they had among them something worthy of their most distinguished consideration'. In its review of the 1902–03 theatrical season, *Forum* described *Everyman* as the 'one really striking poetic feature, the sole grand emotion, rising like a cloud-capped promontory above the level mediocrity of the dramatic year'. Shortly after the production opened at the Garden came the announcement that Frohman would sponsor two companies that fall to satisfy the strong demand the production had created; *Everyman* would undertake a transcontinental tour.[36]

Greet attracted the attention of two Brooklynites who would go on to achieve considerable cultural prominence. As Elizabeth Forte Alman discovered, Emily Jordan Folger and Henry Clay Folger attended two presentations of the Morality that spring. The greatest collectors of Shakespeareana who ever lived would prove reliable supporters of the Englishman's offerings in the years to come.[37]

Corbin chronicled the *Everyman* tour for the *New York Times* as the season drew to a close. As the Manhattan critics had quibbled the previous autumn about whether the production was an actual sacrilege or merely an archaeological bore, audiences grew, slowly but steadily, to the point that it was turning a profit by the time it left the city. Theatregoers everywhere else enthusiastically embraced it:

> There was no talk of archaeology, boredom, and sacrilege. The churches united with lovers of art in acclaiming it. In Boston and Philadelphia there were evenings on which it was necessary to turn people away from the door. Curiously enough, the city that appreciated it most warmly was Chicago [...]. Already the effect of the tour [...] is evident in the fact that in Boston three of the Chester Mystery plays have lately been revived by the Actors Church Alliance [...]. Next year Mr. Greet is to send two 'Everyman' companies on the road, and plans to revive other morality and mystery plays.[38]

Corbin relished the prospect of other smart, powerful productions of old plays coming to the American stage. Frohman and Greet wasted no time obliging him.

Shakespeare's American Pastoral

As the Manhattan papers were touting the Morality's final performances, Frohman and Greet were readying the actor-manager's American Shakespearean debut. Characteristically, Greet had wanted to organize something for 23 April, but Frohman insisted on biding their time.[39] The wait was worth it; the event the impresario put together was not only more ambitious than anything Greet had ever attempted, but it also launched the actor-manager's American Shakespearean enterprise in magnificent fashion. The *New York Times* announced the details: on 14 May, the *Everyman* company would present *As You Like It* on Columbia University's South Field to benefit the University Settlement Kindergarten. Matthison would play Rosalind opposite the Orlando of Greet's former leading man, Robert Loraine (who happened to be in Manhattan). Greet would play Jaques as well as direct. After listing a few of Greet's accomplishments — his over 1,000 open-air Shakespearean performances in England, his many appearances at Oxford and Cambridge, his development of Regent's Park as an open-air venue — the writer listed the event's three-score organizer-patronesses, several of whom I named in my Introduction. Their participation and attendance guaranteed the performance would attract considerable publicity.[40]

Greet invited Corbin to attend a rehearsal, and what the critic saw thrilled him:

> It is not our custom to plead the cause of long runs for Shakespearean performances, but in the case of Mr. Ben Greet's open-air production of 'As You Like It', it does seem as if such a plea were justified. The beauty of the out of doors, the sylvan charm of the play, the grace and virtuosity of Miss Wynne Matthison, and the intelligence of Mr. Greet's management, are so many conclusive reasons why we should have, instead of one, two, and even three or four representations.[41]

Greet had made a believer of Corbin.

To appreciate what made the Columbia performance revolutionary, we must first understand the way Shakespeare's works were staged at this time. Charles H. Shattuck explains that stars and spectacular display were the priorities of late-nineteenth and early twentieth-century Shakespearean producers and audiences.[42] As famous and respected as a play might be, everyone understood it was a vehicle for, and subservient to, its star. Leading actor-managers on both sides of the Atlantic — Edwin Booth, Henry Irving, Richard Mansfield, Herbert Beerbohm Tree — were famous for their deliberate, highly stylized deliveries of the playwright's most famous speeches. If those speeches and/or their contexts were not sufficiently dramatic, they could be rewritten and/or transposed to make them so.

If stars pleased the ear, Spectacular Realism pleased the eye. The religious content of *Ben Hur* and *Quo Vadis* had contributed to their success, but their unparalleled use of Spectacular Realism is what made them hits. For Shakespeare, spectacle was normally touted in terms of 'historical accuracy', but that phrase did not mean what it does to us: staging and performing Shakespeare's plays the way we think they were staged and performed in the late sixteenth and early seventeenth centuries. Rather, it meant producing them to look as though they were taking place in the historical periods in which their stories originated. Thus, the task of the *Hamlet* designer was to create archaeologically authentic reconstructions of places in and around tenth-century Elsinore Castle, while the job of *The Merchant of Venice* designer was to accurately represent what parts of that city looked like in the fourteenth century. Designers consulted with architectural historians and supervised teams of stage carpenters and painters that built elaborate sets depicting these spaces, which were increasingly expected to include three-dimensional elements to achieve greater realism. Large and complex sets required between five and fifteen minutes for the stagehands to change, and a production might have many of them — Booth's 1869 *Othello*, for example, had fifteen sets, including one that depicted a 45-foot-tall turreted building with bastions and towers.[43] Long changes produced long 'waits', which in turn made bridging orchestras a necessary component of Spectacular Realism. In addition to entertaining audiences during waits, orchestras also performed, overture-like, before a play began, during its intervals (plural), and then, recessional-like, after it ended. The need to minimize the number of time-consuming changes led to the routine transposition of scenes.

Spectacular Realism also affected the size of companies. Eager to dazzle, producers liked to depict scenes set in public spaces so they could fill their stages with corps of lavishly costumed supernumeraries. Booth advertised his 'full and efficient company' to assure audiences that his supers were as numerous as they were adept at mounting crowd scenes.

So strong was the desire for spectacle that producers sometimes added new scenes — even new acts — when they spotted opportunities for pageantry Shakespeare had missed. Contemporary dramatic critic Norman Hapgood applauded the changes to *Henry V* 'so magnificently produced by Richard Mansfield at the Garden Theatre in the fall of 1900 that an immediate popular success was scored by this, one of the least dramatic of Shakespeare's plays'. Cutting several early scenes and pulling the Battle of Agincourt back into Act Three enabled Mansfield to insert a new, dialogue-free Act Four. His 'Historical Episode — The Return of King Henry V to London after the Battle of Agincourt' depicted

> a London street, where the populace hailed the arriving troops, marching in battalions […] passing rapidly forward through an arch in the rear and off through the crowd to the side. Now and again a soldier was joined by his wife or by a waiting maiden, and amidst the excitement of it all the harder side of war was suggested by one woman's fate; she rushed among the soldiers to ask one question, and then was carried senseless from the ranks. A dance of girls with flowers was one feature of the pageant, which ended with the entrance on the stage of King Henry on his battle horse.

Another new, dialogue-free scene, 'The Ceremony of the Espousal of King Henry V to the Princess Katherine of Valois' in Troyes Cathedral, served as the grand finale. Hapgood heartily approved these additions because 'they were well executed in themselves, not inharmonious with the drama, and the means whereby thousands were led to spend an evening in the company of gorgeous language and noble sentiments'.[44] Mansfield gave theatregoers a joyful ending perfectly seasoned with pathos, patriotism, and pomp. Shakespeare's original vision (that at one time included other sentiments expressed at play's end by Pistol and the long-since-banished Chorus) was unimportant so long as the production delighted audiences.

The success of Mansfield's *Henry V* demonstrates that New Yorkers were happy to turn out for a Shakespeare play provided it was spectacularly staged. Indeed, another critic argued that one of the main reasons some of the Elizabethan's plays retained their commercial viability was because they made such fine vehicles for Spectacular Realism:

The mass of people go to the theatre to be entertained; and the fact that they find Shakespeare entertaining is a triumph of stage management. Critics talk a great deal of dramatic unity; but the truth is that if you want to keep a miscellaneous audience interested for three hours or even two, variety is the more important requisite. And the intelligent actor-manager finds that no dramatist gives such scope for varied interest as the great Elizabethan (to whom no author's fees need be paid). Apart from the variation of tragedy with comedy, Shakespeare's plays are all in the highest degree spectacular and full of lively action; they lend themselves naturally to the most elaborate staging.[45]

The writer went on to observe that, although Shakespeare's poetry was unsurpassed, his plots, humour, and sentiment could be uneven. The addition of colour, pageantry, detail, variety, and music had the power to correct the playwright's deficiencies.

Many of these priorities are illustrated in this pair of photographs of a production of *Hamlet* featuring one of America's rising Shakespearean stars, E. H. Sothern, in the title-role. Directed by Charles Frohman's brother, Daniel, it, too, received its premiere at the Garden in 1900. As Hapgood notes, it and Mansfield's *Henry V* were the two most popular and critically acclaimed Shakespeare productions

6. Anonymous. Hamlet.
Dir. Daniel Frohman, Garden Theatre, New York, NY, September 1900.

mounted in the United States during the period 1897–1900.[46] The set depicts the throne room of tenth-century Elsinore. That canopied dais may have been relatively easy to manoeuvre, but the bigger scenic unit — the twin staircases and balcony creating a simulated inner-below — probably required time to get on and off stage. The performers wear costumes based on tenth-century Danish, Norman, and Saxon dress. A flaming brand raised in his right hand, Hamlet detains and taunts his uncle ('What, frighted with false fire?'). Nearly overwhelmed by guilt, Claudius melodramatically attempts to pull away whilst calling a halt to *The Mousetrap* ('Give me some light. Away!'). Taken aback, the sixty-three other performers on the stage — more than forty-five of whom are supernumeraries — perform shock and surprise. The production's designer ensured that Ophelia's burial, shown here, was represented with equal richness. What these photos do not depict is the Garden's proscenium arch, which framed the action for the audience as well as distanced them from the actors. Within it hung its curtain, which signalled when the action began and ended as well as concealed the stage during the changes and intermissions. Also absent is the Garden's orchestra.

The overwhelming majority of theatregoers at this time regarded spectacle as completing Shakespeare. Few appear to have been

7. Anonymous. HAMLET.
Dir. Daniel Frohman, Garden Theatre, New York, NY, September 1900.

bothered by the fact that it also significantly decreased the number of Shakespeare's lines they heard. Producers who mounted shows that did not conform to the 150–210-minute run-time expectation did so at their peril. Uncut, some of Shakespeare plays already fell within that window. But Spectacular Realism producers had the additional responsibility of ensuring that their stars were front and centre, their sets and supers got on and off stage, and their audiences got their intermissions (plural). Something had to be cut to make the show come in on time, and that something was Shakespeare's text. Propriety required the excision of a few lines, but the playwright did not employ so much vulgarity that trimming it restored much time. Producers chose to cut the 'least important' lines (ones not spoken by the stars and others), but the routine elimination of hundreds of them — frequently whole scenes — made Spectacular Realism productions significantly different from the Shakespeare texts we know today. Professional productions of complete Shakespeare plays were unknown in America prior to Greet, a point worth bearing in mind. More than any theatrical professional of his age, the actor-manager Ben Greet would be the one to change what 'normal' Shakespeare looked like.

That change began on 14 May 1903. As noted in my Introduction, *As You Like It* on South Field was an extraordinary event. All the papers declared that it was the first outdoor production of a play — amateur or professional, non-Shakespearean or Shakespearean — ever mounted in Manhattan. Few, if any, audience members had ever attended a play performed out of doors and were excited to experience such a novelty. And the occasion also gave fans of the *Everyman* company (especially of Matthison) an opportunity to see the performers in a new play. One of the major social events in the metropolis that spring, the benefit was organized and attended by some of the most prominent women in America. The extensive newspaper coverage of who went and what they wore indicates that the costumes worn by Matthison, Loraine, Greet, and the other actors were not the only garments in which people were interested.

Professionals had presented Shakespeare's plays out of doors in America prior to 1903. The first known performance, a production of *As You Like It*, was staged on 8 August 1887 by an ad hoc company on the grounds of the Masconomo House Hotel in Manchester-by-the Sea, Massachusetts, a resort owned and operated by Agnes Booth-Schoeffel, a retired actress and the widow of Junius Brutus Booth, Jr. The event was successful enough that Booth-Schoeffel arranged for a lavish, night-time production of *A Midsummer Night's Dream* (accompanied by a forty-piece orchestra playing selections from Mendelssohn's Opus 61) to be staged there on 30 July 1888.[47] A casual search of the *New York Times* yields reports of another half-dozen professional or semi-professional presentations of *As You Like It* at diverse vacation-spots between 1891 and 1899.[48] More significant, an ad hoc professional company staged the comedy in a sylvan dell in Jackson Park in August 1893 as part of the official programme of the Chicago World's Fair.[49] Greet's production was considerably more substantial and polished than these, and Frohman had given it the power to be something more than a novelty by arranging for it to be presented in America's cultural capital on the grounds of a distinguished institution of higher learning before some of the most influential people in the country.

So intent were the Manhattan reporters on the event's uniqueness and distinguished patronesses that they failed to remark upon the unusual performance space the company used: a platform. If Columbia supplied what Trinity College (now Duke University) and the University of Michigan did later, it provided suitable grounds on which it erected a wooden scaffold 32–36' wide, 24' deep, and 3.5–4.5' high with two sets of steps at the back about 3' from the corners, all of which was dressed with a wagon-load of fresh-cuts boughs and grass. Sponsors were also required to provide a sufficient number of chairs, a hall or theatre in case of rain, and ushers and ticket sellers. As at South Field, canvas screens were raised to prevent the curious from watching (as well as listening) for free. For night-time performances, sponsors also supplied Japanese lanterns or electric footlights.[50] Greet did not use platforms in England, insofar as I have been able to determine, hence his use of a scaffold may have been a nod to the medieval, to the abundance of low-cost lumber in North America, or to a new production requirement even the least theatrical sponsor might supply.

As the *New-York Tribune* piece quoted in the Introduction noted, an estimated 3,500 members of New York society attended. Its claim that Greet had never played to a larger audience nor raised so much money in a single performance also seems to have been accurate.[51]

Socially, philanthropically, and critically, the production was a success. The *New York Herald* pronounced it excellent and as having surpassed the considerable expectations of the many *Everyman* fans in attendance, its critic praising the performances of Matthison (pictured here), Loraine, Greet, and B. A. Field (Touchstone) before commending the uncommonly strong ensemble Greet had created.[52] The *New York Times*'s critic (possibly Corbin) praised everything save the omission of the first act. Greet's design and direction was a revelation; although specific elements of the comedy had been sur- passed on the stage, 'the harmony and force of the play as a whole […] never shone forth in such undimmed and persuasive beauty'. Similarly, although other actresses had captured specific facets of the heroine more perfectly, none had rendered a completer Rosalind than Matthison.[53] *Theatre* rapturously declared

8. Byron. *Edith Wynne Matthison as Rosalind in* AS YOU LIKE IT. Dir. Ben Greet, Columbia University, New York, NY, May 1903.

that the date would be 'marked for long and lovely memory' in the minds of the 'spellbound audience of New York's finest four thousand' fortunate enough to have witnessed a performance 'the gods and muses smiled upon'. The ensemble had been strong, but the 'chiefest and constant enchantment' of the afternoon had been Matthison, whose Rosalind was probably unequalled in the history of the New York stage.[54] The flattering interview with her the magazine ran a few pages later signalled she was on her way to becoming a star.[55]

Other notices were more subdued. The *Morning Telegraph* judged the presentation 'interesting and credible'. Matthison spoke her lines 'with distinction and intelligence', Loraine was 'manly, straightforward and convincing', and the ensemble was unusually competent, but Greet the actor failed to live up to expectations. *Life*'s Metcalf declared Matthison's performance 'a most remarkable one and entitles her to rank with the best *Rosalinds* of our generation', but found the others disappointing. More problematic, the unorthodox staging method prevented him from accepting the illusion: '"As You Like It" out of doors [...] is interesting as a dramatic novelty, but the drama itself is really more effective acted within the walls of a theatre and by artificial light'.[56]

Greet's production proved extremely successful as a fundraiser (the philanthropy quickly laid on four more performances for June), but most people dismissed it as a novelty. No one seems to have realized that it had begun to change the way Americans staged Shakespeare.[57]

Shakespeare Plays the Varsity

Because he was not a star, Greet was used to working year round. Recruiting and rehearsing a new company in time to open *Everyman* in San Francisco in early September made returning to England impracticable, but readying a road company would not take up all his time. Where else might the current ensemble perform before its members sailed home?

As the *New-York Tribune* reported, the actor-manager had hit upon an excellent answer to that question by mid-May:

Ben Greet [...] has entered into a series of lucrative contracts with various universities and colleges of the East to present old plays in the open at the various college grounds [...]. [He] has a comfortable guarantee from every university and college where he is to appear, and as he carries no scenery, pays rent to no theatre and percentage to no booking agency, his profits promise to be snug.[58]

Greet's open-air Shakespeare productions had been annual traditions at Oxford and Cambridge for more than a dozen years. Now he would bring them to the campuses of several American and Canadian institutions, including Brown, Harvard, McGill, Princeton, Wellesley, and Yale. Significantly, Greet also played the University of Toronto. Performing there during every commencement week from 1903 to 1906, he seems to have tried to establish there the tradition he had inaugurated at Oxford and Cambridge. By so doing, he also created what we probably should regard as the continent's first annual Shakespeare festival, although the actor-manager did not call it that because it did not take place in late April.

Bringing professional productions of Shakespeare's plays to college campuses, another important Greet innovation, was an idea whose time had come thanks to the playwright's status in American culture in general and in higher education in particular. In his analysis of the American audience, Lawrence W. Levine theorizes a process by which Shakespeare was transformed in the mid-nineteenth century from a popular playwright into a rarefied genius. Initially, literate people of every stripe read and revered Shakespeare, whose plays were also popular entertainments for literate and illiterate alike, whether in major cities or in small towns. A shift from an oral culture to a literary culture occurred after the Civil War with the increasing heterogeneity of society resulting from the immigration of millions of non-Anglophone people, and culture became more hierarchical and compartmentalized. Shakespeare's status changed as high and low grew more distinct as the century drew to a close: he came to be regarded less as a universally admired playwright whose

Shakespeare's words, spoken in greater number and more swiftly and continuously than audience members had ever experienced. Greet cut lines and scenes, but nothing like what Spectacular Realism productions routinely excised. (Fortunately, the ignorance of Greet's highbrow auditors shielded them from the corrupting lines he retained.) The company performed the scenes it performed almost *in toto* and in the playwright's original sequence. The production featured period music and high-quality reproduction Elizabethan costumes. This was rapid-fire, remarkably complete Shakespeare stripped of all the 'improvements' that had been layered onto it over the centuries. It was new, exciting, and unquestionably the closest thing to Shakespeare's original practice ever presented on the continent.

Just as Figures 6 and 7 (of *Hamlet*) illustrate the old normal, Figure 9 — of the final moments of this performance of *As You Like It* Greet's company gave at Mills College in 1904 — illustrates what in time would become, thanks to the actor-manager, the new normal. The seventeen actors on the platform (positively teeming by the standards of a Greet production) are there because Shakespeare put most of them there, not because a producer decided to increase

9. Anonymous. As You Like It.
Dir. Ben Greet, Mills College, Oakland, CA, 22 October 1904.

the play's 'variety'. The production restored hearing as the principal sense through which audience members received Shakespeare. By eliminating the proscenium to frame the action, the curtain to start and stop it, and scenery to locate it, Greet compelled his audience to actively participate in the creative process. By forcing people to engage their imaginations, the actor-manager enabled them to encounter for the first time in their lives the playwright whom stars and spectacle had upstaged for so long.

As important as the higher education market was to become, Greet entered it only briefly during his first two springs in America. Several explanations suggest themselves for why he did not develop it more completely. The profits to be had from mounting fundraisers were so large that accepting invitations from philanthropies was far more remunerative (not to mention simple) than organizing academic bookings. The universities and colleges the actor-manager visited those springs were not only the ones he is likely to have heard of, but they are also proximate enough to one another that they formed tidy tours presenting little in the way of cost or logistical complexity. Last, Greet may have been slow to comprehend the scope of higher education on the continent. His appearances at English universities had been limited largely to end-of-the-year festivities weeks. The sheer number of North American institutions and summer sessions meant that, in theory, one could book end-of-year appearances in May and June, and then tour from summer school to summer school. With proper planning, one might even be able to book an open-air season comprising nothing but university, college, and normal school appearances.

An echo of that first *Everyman* season deserves mention. In August, the recently formed (1901) Chautauqua Dramatic Club of the ecumenical Protestant Chautauqua Assembly on Lake Chautauqua, New York, gave two performances of the Morality directed by and starring Rudolph Magnus. According to promotional materials Magnus later produced, some 7,000 people attended each.[65] Demand among some conservative Protestant groups for literarily and morally excellent drama decorously presented was considerable.

NOTES

1   'Religious Subjects as Matter for Dramatic Treatment', *NYT*, 16 December 1906, p.2.

2   Isaac, pp.76–77; Stephen G. Kuehler, 'Concealing God: The *Everyman* Revival, 1901–1903' (unpublished master's thesis, Tufts University, 2009), p.13, n. 27.

3   Alan Dale, 'London Tolerates a Most Shocking Sacrilege', *New York American*, 30 July 1902, p.8.

4   For a history of Morse's production, see Alan Neilsen, *The Great Victorian Stage Sacrilege: Preachers, Politics and The Passion, 1879–1884* (Jefferson, NC: McFarland, 1991).

5   'No Production of Passion Play', *NYTr.*, 9 April 1902, p.9.

6   Claudia Durst Johnson, *Church and Stage: The Theatre as Target of Religious Condemnation in Nineteenth Century America* (Jefferson, NC: McFarland, 2007).

7   Percy Stickney Grant, 'The Passion Play on the American Stage', *Theatre*, May 1902, pp.10–11.

8   For an overview of the Theatrical Trust, see Shattuck, *Shakespeare*, II (1987), pp.24–30.

9   'Frohman's Ambition to Reflect Old World Drama', *NYT*, 12 October 1902, p.15.

10   Kate Carew, 'Morality Play Surely Quaint', *(New York) Evening World*, 14 October 1902, night edition, p.7; Bliss Carmen, 'Bliss Carmen Writes on "Everyman"', *CT*, 25 October 1902, p.20; 'A Dismal Experiment. "Everyman"', *NYTr.*, 14 October 1902, p.9; 'Like a Draft of Water from a Fresh Cool Spring', *BE*, 14 October 1902, p.5.

11   Seating capacity from <http://www.nycago.org/Organs/NYC/html/MendelssohnHall.html> [accessed 31 May 2016].

12   Robert Grau, *Forty Years Observation of Music and the Drama* (New York: Broadway, 1909), pp.300–01.

13   'A Dismal Experiment. "Everyman"', *NYTr.*, 14 October 1902, p.9; 'Barefoot Actors in the Audience', *New York World*, 14 October 1902, p.5; Alan Dale, 'Jehovah Seen in the Old Morality Play, "Everyman" — Much That Church People Will Not Countenance', *New York American*, 14 October 1902, p.10.

14   'Everyman', *NYDM*, 25 October 1902, p.19; 'An Old Drama in New Use: "Everyman" Brought Forward from Long Ago', *NYS*, 14 October 1902, p.7; James Stetson Metcalf, 'A Curious but Interesting Performance', *Life*, 30 October 1902, p.1044.

15   'A Morality of Death', *NYT*, 14 October 1902, p.5; 'Like a Draft of Water from a Fresh Cool Spring', *BE*, 14 October 1902, p.5; John Corbin, 'Topics of the Drama', *NYT*, 19 October 1902, p.14.

[16] 'Plays and Players', *Theatre*, November 1902, p.4; 'Some Shows of the Week', *Harper's Weekly*, 1 November 1902, p.1614; 'Theatrical Incidents and News Notes', *NYTr.*, 2 November 1902, p.3. Madison Square Theatre seating capacity from <http://www.wayneturney.20m.com/madisonsquaretheatre.htm> [accessed 19 December 2011]. New York Theatre seating capacity from *JC(1902)*, p.35.

[17] Kuehler, p.26.

[18] Seating capacity from <http://commons.wikimedia.org/wiki/File:1904_SteinertHall_BoylstonSt_Boston.png> [accessed 5 January 2012]; George Pierce Baker, 'Performance of Morality Play', *Harvard Crimson*, 20 November 1902, <http://www.thecrimson.com/article/1902/11/20/performance-of-morality-play-pito-the/> [accessed 31 May 2016]; 'Foyer and Greenroom Gossip', *BGl.*, 25 November 1902, p.2; 'Telegraphic News: Boston', *NYDM*, 6 December 1902, p.14; BG to Lucy Love, 25 November 1902 and 20 December 1902, Michigan Love; 'Plays and Players', *BGl.*, 7 December 1902, p.33.

[19] Ellwood Hendrick, 'Obituary: Edward G. Love, An Appreciation', *Journal of Industrial and Engineering Chemistry*, 11.10 (1919), 992; Guide to the Love Family Papers (MS 12). Manuscripts and Archives, Yale University Library, <http://drs.library.yale.edu/HLTransformer/HLTransServlet?stylename=yul.ead2002.xhtml.xsl&pid=mssa:ms.0012&clear-stylesheet-cache=yes.> [accessed 31 May 2016].

[20] 'Springfield, Mass.', *NYDM*, 20 December 1902, p.34.

[21] W. L. Hubbard, 'News of the Theatres', *CTr.*, 5 December 1902, p.7.

[22] 'Hart Conway's Pupils in Everyman', *NYDM*, 20 December 1902, p.41.

[23] Edward E. Hale, 'Everyman', *Christian Register*, 4 December 1902, p.1434.

[24] 'Three Plays New to This City', *PI*, 9 December 1902, p.4; 'At the Theatres', *Philadelphia Evening Bulletin*, 9 December 1902, p.9; H. H. Furness, 'An Earnest Plea for "Everyman"', *Philadelphia Public Ledger*, 11 December 1902, p.8; 'Quartet of New Plays Next Week', *PI*, 11 December 1902, p.6; BG to Lucy Love, 20 December 1902, Michigan Love. Seating capacity of Horticultural Hall from Henry C. Miner, *Henry C. Miner's American Dramatic Directory for the Season of 1887–'88* (New York: People's Theatre, 1887), p.225.

[25] 'The Theatre as an Adjunct of the Church', *Outlook*, 20 December 1902, pp.921–22. Seating capacity from *JC(1904)*, p.96.

[26] 'Actors' Church Alliance News', *NYDM*, 1 November 1902, p.17; 'National Reform Societies', *Social Progress: A Year Book and Encyclopedia of Economic, Industrial, Social and Religious Statistics*, 1 (March 1904), 212; Walter E. Bentley, 'The Coming Relation of Church and Stage', *Theatre*, 5 February 1905, pp.48–49.

[27] 'Drama and Music', *BGl.*, 23 December 1902, p.11; 'Foyer and Greenroom Gossip', *BGl.*, 28 December 1902, p.33; 'Foyer and Greenroom Gossip', *BGl.*, 4 January 1903, p.33; Kuehler, pp.34–35; 'Boston', *NYDM*, 24 January 1903, p.12. Seating capacities from *JC(1904)*, pp.71 and 75.

[28] BG to Lucy Love, 26 January 1903, Michigan Love.

[29] 'The Drama and Music', *CTr.*, 8 February 1903, p.39. Seating capacity from <http://chicagomagic.blogspot.com/2009/02/chicagos-lost-magic-theater.html> [accessed 31 May 2016].

[30]   W. L. Hubbard, 'Everyman, Inspired, Calls Knowledge and Good Deeds to His Aid', *CTr.*, 28 January 1903, p.5.

[31]   W. L. Hubbard, 'The Drama and Music', *CTr.*, 15 February 1903, p.47; Kuehler, p.37, n. 101.

[32]   'Religious Education', *CTr.*, 15 February 1903, p.18.

[33]   Kuehler, pp.37–38. Seating capacities from *JC(1904)*, pp.222 and 219.

[34]   'Not Easy to Pick a Winner', *NYMT*, 20 January 1904, p.5; Blanche Partington, 'With the Players and Music Folk', *SFC*, 26 July 1903, p.46; Ben Greet Players, *Everyman* Play Programme, Oberlin College, Oberlin, OH, 4 February 1907, Oberlin College Archives. Seating capacity from *JC(1904)*, p.87.

[35]   'To Play Shakespeare', *NYT*, 3 April 1903, p.9. Seating capacity from *JC(1904)*, p.23.

[36]   'Current Dramatic Notes', *NYT*, 10 April 1903, p.9; Elizabeth Luther Carey, 'The Summoning of Everyman: A Moral Play', *Independent*, 16 April 1903, p.906; 'The Recent Dramatic Season', *Forum*, July 1903, p.89; 'To Play Shakespeare', *NYT*, 3 April 1903, p.9.

[37]   Alman, pp.103–15.

[38]   John Corbin, 'Topics of the Drama', *NYT*, 19 April 1903, p.25.

[39]   BG to Lucy Love, 22 March 1903, Michigan Love; 'To Play Shakespeare', *NYT*, 3 April 1903, p.9.

[40]   '"As You Like It" Out-o'-Doors', *NYT*, 9 April 1903, p.9.

[41]   John Corbin, 'Topics of the Drama', *NYT*, 10 May 1903, p.25.

[42]   This paragraph and three that follow are based on Shattuck, *Shakespeare*, II (1987), p.139; and Charles H. Shattuck, 'Shakespeare Free?' *Journal of Aesthetic Education*, 17.4 (Winter 1983), 107–23.

[43]   *Othello* details from Shattuck, *Shakespeare*, I (1976), p.140.

[44]   Norman Hapgood, *The Stage in America, 1897–1900* (New York: Macmillan, 1901), pp.175–76.

[45]   'The Spectacular Element in Drama', *Eclectic Magazine of Foreign Literature*, December 1901, 748–60 (p.748).

[46]   Hapgood, p.174.

[47]   H. J. W. D. 'In the Forest of Arden', *NYT*, 9 August 1887, p.5; 'Played on Nature's Stage', *NYT*, 31 July 1888, p.5.

[48]   Hoboken, NJ (June 1891); Pittsburgh, PA (July 1891); Pocantico Hills, NY (July 1892); Orange, NJ (May 1893); Pleasure Bay, NJ (August 1893); Hoboken, NJ (August 1895); Asbury Park, NJ (August 1896); and Larchmont, NY (August 1899).

[49]   'Drama at the Fair', *CTr.*, 27 August 1893, World's Fair supplement, p.28.

[50]   Ben Greet Players and Trinity College, Sharing Contract, 8 February 1910, Duke University Archives; Ben Greet Players and the University of Michigan, Memorandum of Agreement, 1 May 1914, Isaac Newton Demmon Papers, University of Michigan Library (Special Collections Library).

[51]   'Shakespeare on Lawn, Was a Brilliant Sight', *NYTr.*, 15 May 1903, p.4.

52 "'As You Like It" Al Fresco Is a Picturesque Success', *NYH*, 15 May 1903, p.5.

53 'As One Likes It', *NYT*, 15 May 1903, p.9.

54 'Plays and Players', *Theatre*, June 1903, p.132.

55 'Edith Wynne Matthison — A Study', *Theatre*, June 1903, p.139.

56 "'As You Like It" Given Al Fresco', *NYMT*, 15 May 1902, p.12; James Metcalf, n. t., *Life*, 28 May 1903, p.493.

57 On the birth of the Open-Air Theatre Movement, see Sheldon Cheney, *The Open-Air Theatre* (New York: Mitchell Kennerly, 1918), especially pp.5 and 128.

58 'Notes of the Stage', *NYTr.*, 11 May 1903, p.3.

59 Lawrence W. Levine, *Highbrow/Lowbrow: The Emergence of Cultural Hierarchy in America* (Cambridge, MA: Harvard University Press, 1988), pp.13–81.

60 Andrew Murphy, *Shakespeare in Print: A History and Chronology of Shakespeare Publishing* (Cambridge: Cambridge University Press, 2003), p.160. Nan Johnson, 'Shakespeare in American Rhetorical Education, 1870–1920'; Elizabeth Renker, 'Shakespeare in the College Curriculum, 1870–1920'; Dayton Haskin, 'The Works of Wm Shakespeare as They Have Been Sundry Times Professed in Harvard College', in *Shakespearean Educations: Power, Citizenship, and Performance*, ed. by Coppélia Kahn, Heather S. Nathans, and Mimi Godfrey (Newark, DE: University of Delaware Press, 2011), pp.112–30, 131–56, and 175–200, respectively.

61 Palmer, 'The Professional', pp.52–54.

62 Clifford Eugene Hamar, 'College and University Theatre Instruction in the Early Twentieth Century', in *History of Speech Education in America: Background Studies*, ed. by Karl Wallace (New York: Appleton-Century-Crofts, 1954), pp.572–94.

63 John L. Clark, 'Educational Dramatics in Nineteenth-Century Colleges', in Wallace, pp.521–51; Domis E. Pluggé, *History of Greek Play Production in American Colleges and Universities from 1881 to 1936* (New York: Columbia University Teachers College, 1938), p.5.

64 'The Woodland Players at Harvard', *BET*, 1 June 1903, p.29. The reporter did not exaggerate when he observed that the audience included some experts on Shakespeare. Of the five members of the English faculty who organized and attended the performances, three of them — George Pierce Baker, George Lyman Kittredge, and William Allan Neilson – had already achieved some distinction.

65 'Chautauqua Program', *Fredonia (New York) Censor*, 5 August 1903, p.1; 'Chautauqua Program', *Fredonia (New York) Censor*, 12 August 1903, p.5; Rudolph Magnus Company, *Everyman* Promotional Pamphlet, <http://digital.lib.uiowa.edu/cdm/compoundobject/collection/tc/id/64308/rec/7> [accessed 31 May 2016].

CHAPTER THREE
Season of Plenty, 1903–04

Greet, the Greek, and the Autumn EVERYMAN Tours

Charles Frohman backed two *Everyman* companies in the autumn of 1903. Greet led the newly recruited and rehearsed Western unit, which was built around veteran couple Constance and John Sayer Crawley. Charles Rann Kennedy, who was Greet's North American business manager as well as Matthison's husband, led the Eastern unit, which included most of the 1902–03 cast.

In July 1903, Greet made the long train journey to San Francisco, where he wasted no time making connections. As he told Lucy Love: 'We have a special chance [...] of getting a magnificent audience in the new Amphitheatre [...] at Berkeley. It holds 8000 people + Wm Hearst guaranteed us a huge audience or its equivalent'. The dramatic critic for the *San Francisco Call*, Blanche Partington, introduced the Englishman to her readers in a long, flattering interview in which he outlined many of the ideas that informed his work. He stated that *Everyman*'s success was the product of its authenticity, beauty, and combined literary and moral excellence. He noted that the spring open-air mini-tour had proved that some Americans were receptive to something other than Spectacular Realism. He praised the country's few remaining stock companies as well as its institutions of higher learning, which were significantly more receptive to performed drama than were their counterparts in England. But he regretted that

America's deeply entrenched star system impeded the development of the drama, limited actors, and injured dramatic art by 'imposing the idea of a personality as the central interest of a play'.[1] He expressed his desire to help improve the situation.

Partington's reference to Greet's magnificent head of prematurely snow-white hair, rosy cheeks, and enormous eyes 'of a blue too precious to be wasted upon a mere man' prompt me to offer a description of the actor-manager's person and character for readers unlikely to have access to Isaac's biography, which devotes considerable attention to these matters.[2] Describing his facial features in 1904, the *New York Herald* wrote: 'While his blue eyes are those of a student and a dreamer, there is a humorous twinkle to them. His smooth shaven face shows a sensitive mouth, with good natured lines, where a smile is always hiding'.[3] Sturdily built, Greet forever had to watch his weight. When not in costume, his uniform invariably comprised a dark blue suit and black, Navy-pattern shoes. His constant activity, impressive physical health and energy, and unbounded passion for the theatre were famous in a business that prized those attributes. His voice was high-pitched and his diction was superb. All classes of people on both sides of the Atlantic found him courteous and charming. Colleagues called him 'BG'. Family members and close friends called him 'Phil'. Everyone else knew him as 'Ben'.

The values of his age and upbringing manifested themselves in a variety of ways. He was unreservedly, patriotically English. A devout member of the Church of England, he also held strong Christian Socialist beliefs, and the decades he worshipped at St Alban the Martyr, Holborn, attest to his Anglo-Catholic leanings. He loved children, and most of his outreach activities after 1897 were focused on bringing Shakespearean and other 'plays worth while' to poor ones. He was very particular about diction, and his ideas regarding pronunciation were as narrow as they were fixed. The Royal Navy captain's son educated from boyhood to military leadership was forever watchful of the comportment and conduct of those he led. The letters of his most famous protégé, Sybil Thorndike, make reference to his attentiveness to and commentary upon the turnout of his actors, including his repeated admonition of Thorndike's own tendency to gain weight.[4] His expectations for cleanliness were exacting; Isaac personally witnessed him on more than one occasion command actors in the midst of actual performances to wash their hands. His moral standards were equally stringent; he would not permit engaged couples in his company to travel alone in railway carriages, and he objected to actors and actresses conversing between adjoining dressing rooms if he deemed too flimsy the partition separating them. He was genial and fond of playing practical jokes, but his intolerance of slackness could make him 'very severe' at rehearsals. He knew every line, cue, and stage direction of every play he produced, and he felt duty-bound to correct actors who came unprepared to or failed to adequately acquit themselves at rehearsals or performances. He was slow to anger, but had a temper 'that had to be watched' once roused. He never married.

Greet was a third-rate actor, but his second-rate managerial skills and first-rate abilities as a teacher of acting enabled him to make a living as a theatrical professional for fifty-six years. Because he lacked the private means that allowed Frank Benson to run his Shakespearean company comparatively independent of mundane concerns like profit and loss, he had to care about the funding needed and his fiduciary responsibility to operate his company's business. So when Isaac states 'Money never troubled Ben Greet', she means he was motivated by something other than a desire to build personal wealth: the 'mission' for Shakespeare that he regarded, from at least 1897 onwards, as his life's work. Writing in 1938, the commercial manager of Greet's UK operations from 1895 to 1910, J. Bannister Howard, stated:

> Greet's whole life was bound up in Shakespeare, for which he had a genuine passion. All else was done to supply the means of satisfying that passion. He was ready to sacrifice everything for the sake of Shakespeare, and no doubt his enthusiasm often cost him dearly.[5]

In 1960, Dame Sybil Thorndike, who by that time had worked with many of the era's most celebrated Shakespearean interpreters, used these terms to describe her erstwhile mentor's reverence for the Elizabethan: 'I think he lived for Shakespeare — he was the nearest approach to Almighty God that BG knew'.

Greet was a fair and honest businessman for almost all his long career. Writing fifty years after working for him, stage and cinema veteran H. F Maltby recalled the actor-manager interviewing him for a place in one of *The Sign of the Cross* companies:

> I have a *very* great affection for the memory of BG. He was the first grown-up in authority I had met who treated me like a human being. He gave me my first taste of the stage, a pleasant taste that has always lingered with me. At the end of the interview he shook me by the hand, but he gave me no letter of contract, and I, in my innocence, never thought of asking for one. I had always regarded a spoken promise as something that couldn't be broken, and all my dealings with BG confirmed that belief. I have met others since who have undeceived me, but taken as a whole and with many years' experience in other trades and professions I am amazed at the spirit of honour and straight dealing I have encountered in the theatre managers of the old school.[6]

However, evidence exists that Greet failed to live up to that standard regarding *Everyman*. As we saw in Chapter One, he may have behaved unethically toward William Poel. That he continued to act in an acquisitive and duplicitous manner is attested by an undated letter written by Cecilia Radclyffe, one of the members of the 1902–03 North American *Everyman* company, that Marion O'Connor discovered. Reacting with alarm to Poel's statement that he had not been party to the deal Greet made with Frohman, Radclyffe urged him to bring his concerns before the famously honest impresario. A few pages later, her animosity toward Greet caused her to explode 'I can't express my feelings about this odious Pharisee who cloaks all his despicable doings with a <u>pretense</u> of religion'. The *(New York)*

Morning Telegraph's reference to him in 1904 as having a 'cynical smile and one ear turned toward the box-office' suggests he was more grasping than has been recognized.[7] And I read a kind of confession in a letter he penned to Love in 1907. Responding to her query about why he was not taking legal action against the companies that had sprung up to tour similar productions of the Morality, he wrote:

> Anyone can really play 'Everyman' it is only the 'business' that I have arranged with Mr. Poel. He originally gave it for the Elizabethan Stage Society in the old Charterhouse, then let it lie. I took it up + practically staged the play as you see it now. The scene is mine + all the stage business, added to which through my efforts a large debt on the ESS was entirely wiped out + a goodly sum besides put into Mr. Poel's pocket. Of course I need not have paid them [presumably Poel and his solicitor] a penny for as I say the play belongs to the world (like Shakespeare's), the women [i.e. the artistic decision to cast women in the roles of Everyman, Knowledge, and Good Deeds] only belongs to me (+ Poel). Other people have filched it like the Crawley people.[8]

Paying off Poel settled the matter legally, but Greet's chary phrasing and defensive tone suggests his conscience continued to trouble him.

Readers will judge for themselves how much of a shadow this transgression casts upon the portrait of kindliness and generosity Thorndike's letters and Isaac's account paint. It seems to have done little to alter the latter's conclusion that 'He was a man *greatly* beloved'. Greet may have wronged Poel, but not so gravely that it prevented the Rev. J. Stewart Headlam, who knew both men well, from very publicly backing Greet in 1915. The decades-spanning friendships Greet maintained with divines like Headlam and the Rev. Arthur Henry Stanton, socially and culturally active matrons such as Love and the notably religious Mary Anderson, and former protégées like Edith Wynne Matthison and the notably religious Sybil Thorndike give evidence of his decency. Matthison and Thorndike apprenticed under him as young women, and the latter worked for him throughout World War I. That both later asked him to train young members of their families indicates that decades of exposure to other managers on both sides of the Atlantic did nothing to diminish the high regard they had for their erstwhile mentor, not just as an excellent and painstaking teacher, but also as a trustworthy guide, nurturer, and protector of novices. Describing him some thirty years after working for him, another former protégée, Mrs Patrick Campbell, emphasized his importance and benevolence: 'Mr. Ben Greet was a great man to me […]. He was always smiling, cheerful, and courageous, whether it was a big audience or a small one, and won my love by his extraordinary kindness to my children'.[9] Isaac collected remembrances from a number of the actor-manager's former colleagues, all of whom agreed he inspired the devotion he did through something as simple as it was powerful: he was kind and ran a happy company. That I should even raise the topic of Greet's integrity might dismay (and possibly outrage) the notably religious Isaac, whose categorical admiration of him as a patriot, champion of improving drama, tireless educator, and deeply religious man was founded upon her twenty-years' acquaintance with him.

Under Greet's personal supervision, the Western *Everyman* unit opened its four-month tour with a performance at the University of California on 1 September. Partington's rave review described it as 'one of the most profoundly impressive, most interesting, valuable and human dramas' she had ever witnessed. She judged the representation of God to have been handled with 'profound dignity', although she later remarked that Greet had been 'wise to omit the personification' for the commercial performances in San Francisco's Lyric Hall. The *San Francisco Examiner*'s Ashton Stevens also thought highly of the Berkeley performance, but criticized 'the spectacle of the Deity', which he regarded as being at 'variance with the genuinely religious impress of the rest of the morality'. The *San Francisco Call* would echo these sentiments in a piece it published after the company presented the Morality at Stanford University later that month.[10]

Everyman retained its power to captivate theatregoers despite being presented by a less-talented and -experienced ensemble. People turned out in droves, and it received an additional publicity boost half-way through its run when Partington published another long, flattering interview, this time with Constance Crawley. As they had elsewhere, the performances stimulated religious interest: the Morality served as the subject of a sermon delivered at the Third Congregational Church as well as of a rabbinical lecture given at the Bush Street Synagogue.[11]

Greet's inaugural Shakespearean offering on the West Coast was no less impressive. The performance took place in the University of California's new Greek Theatre, a structure modelled on the amphitheatre at Epidarus, which had seating for 8,000 and standing-room for 2,000 more. Construction had been advanced enough for President Roosevelt to deliver the commencement address there that May, but the venue's formal dedication did not take place until September. Its opening was not only the most important event of the Educational Theatre Movement that year, but it also marked a major milestone in the Open-Air Theatre Movement.[12] That Greet was given a central role signalled his growing importance.

The ceremonies were spread over four days. On 24 September, the institution's president, Dr Benjamin Ide Wheeler, dedicated the amphitheatre in the presence of its donor, William Randolph Hearst, before a capacity audience. After the speeches came the first performance: an undergraduate production of Aristophanes's *The Birds* (in Greek), shown here, directed by a trio of faculty members from the Department of Greek.[13] On 25 September, Wheeler presided over speeches delivered to an audience of about 1,000. The topic of the keynote address by Archbishop George Montgomery, the Roman Catholic Coadjutor of San Francisco, was the importance of religious values in public education. Greet, who spoke next, proposed that dramatic instruction be added to the higher education curriculum and that the federal government should subsidize a theatre the way those of several European nations did. The following day, his company performed *Twelfth Night*. (One need look no further for proof that the

10. Anonymous. THE BIRDS.
Dir. Leon Richardson, James Allen, and Washington Prescott, Greek Theatre,
University of California, Berkeley, CA, 24 September 1903.

Educational Theatre, Greek Revival, Elizabethan Revival, and Open-Air. Theatre movements were not only contemporaneous, but also interconnected.) The ceremonies at Berkeley concluded on 3 October with an undergraduate production of Jean Racine's *Phèdre* (in French).[14]

Partington described Greet's *Twelfth Night* in glowing terms:

> How glittering well the old comedy stood the test of these conditions will be known only to the fortunate four or five thousand who saw it yesterday [...]. But the comedy was at one with the big verities that surrounded it. There wasn't a line of it that rang falsely. Its humor bubbled up as spontaneously as the bird songs that accompanied it, its poetry fell as tenderly as the light of the Turner sunset that blessed its close [...]. It was one more triumph for Shakespeare the immortal, one more proof that the play's the thing.[15]

If Partington's estimate is accurate, the performance drew one of the largest audiences yet gathered for a performance of a Shakespeare play. Whether it set an attendance record or not, it delighted thousands, linked 'Greet' and 'open-air Shakespeare' in their minds, and revealed some of the possibilities of the remarkable new theatre.

Its California engagement fulfilled, the company set off for Pennsylvania. In October, it opened in Pittsburgh's 1,950-seat Carnegie Music Hall, where it played for two successful weeks before moving on to a week-long engagement in Cleveland's Gray's Armory (2,600 seats). The final echo of its visit to California came after it opened in Detroit's 1,200-seat Harmonie Hall.[16] As they had in Manhattan and Boston, performances of the Morality in San Francisco inspired a local religious group to mount a production of its own: students from the Jesuit St Ignatius and Santa Clara colleges staged an impressive, all-male *Everyman* (in which God was not represented) before large audiences in St Ignatius College Hall.[17] One of the reasons Greet was so influential was that, more than the productions of any other actor-manager of his day, his inspired people to imitate what they witnessed. A student-actor from St Ignatius, Redmond Flood, would become one of the first Americans to join Greet's company.

The Western unit spent the remainder of the tour in the Midwest. It did such brisk business during its week in Cincinnati's magnificent, large (3,516 seats) Springer Auditorium that Frohman added another. The engagement generated tremendous profits as well as another religious endorsement, this one from the city's Roman Catholic Archbishop William Henry Elder, who attended the opening-night performance and later sent Greet a note about what he witnessed:

> *Everyman* holds a large and cultivated audience in deep attention to the end.
> It will give pleasure and benefit to all who see it. 'Everyman' who is foolish
> and frivolous will be taught the value of good solid sense, and 'Everyman'
> who has good solid sense will be strengthened to live a sensible life.

True to form, Greet reproduced Elder's words on programmes and promotional materials for years.[18]

The company made its first appearance on the campus of a Midwestern institution of higher learning at this time: the two, well-attended performances it gave at the University of Michigan were not only the first given by professional actors in Memorial Hall, but also inaugurated Greet's long association with the university.[19] A successful, three-week engagement at St Louis's 2,000-seat Odeon Theatre concluded the tour in December. Many of the city's most prominent religious leaders — the Bishop of the Episcopal Diocese of Missouri, Daniel S. Tuttle; the Rabbi of the United Hebrew Congregation, Henry J. Messing; the Rabbi of Temple Israel, Leon Harrison — accepted Frohman's invitations. The company's final performance in the city was a benefit for the *St Louis Post-Dispatch*'s Christmas fund for needy children.[20]

The Eastern unit opened its three-month tour in early October in Ottawa's 1,900-seat Russell Theatre.[21] It returned to the United States in late October following engagements in Quebec, Montreal, and Toronto. It spent November and early December working its way east through the small-but-prosperous cities of upstate New York and New England. *Everyman* continued to draw large audiences and garner religious endorsements, including one from the Bishop of the Episcopal Diocese of Central New York, Frederick D. Huntington, who expressed his hope that the elevation in theatrical tastes and standards it had produced would endure.[22]

Elizabethan Manner Takes the Stage

Greet disbanded the Western unit at year's end, folding the Crawleys, whom he had signed to extended contracts, into the Eastern one. The company opened a hugely successful, six-week run in Boston's Chickering Hall (800 seats) in late December.[23] Although the initial fortnight was devoted to *Everyman*, Greet was eager to introduce the elements that made his outdoor Shakespearean productions so compelling — full texts, rapid delivery, swift pace, strong ensemble, Elizabethan costumes — to American theatre-goers. 'Elizabethan Manner' was a phrase as evocative as it was

conditions' he promised usually looked like the Middle Temple.

Greet's first Elizabethan Manner production, *Twelfth Night*, received its premiere on Twelfth Night, 1904. The company no longer performing a religious play, the names of its members could appear in programmes. Matthison played Viola. Greet played Malvolio, one of his best roles. The performances of B. A. Field (Sir Toby Belch), John Sayer Crawley (Sir Andrew Aguecheek), and Millicent McLaughlin (Maria) were consistently praised. Although I have been unable to locate a photograph of the production as it looked at Chickering Hall, a series of fine ones exist showing how it looked in New York a month later. The first I have selected illustrates the Aguecheek-Viola duel that was one of the comic gems of the show. The other depicts the Viola-Sebastian reunion in the play's final moments, with not only almost the entire cast on stage, but also the Beefeaters, Bluecoat Boys, and musicians in their usual positions. Greet had made good choices. The atmosphere his method created caused a sensation, opened a major debate about how Shakespeare should be staged, and packed major East Coast houses until April.

After attending the sold-out premiere, the *Boston Globe*'s critic wrote:

> While there is room for doubt as to whether the audience was prepared to approve permanently the abolition of scenery in Shakespearean drama, it is undoubtedly true that [...] the lines of Shakespeare were probably listened to with more thorough appreciation last evening than they have been in any presentation of 'Twelfth Night' in Boston. In fact the general delivery of the lines of the text throughout the evening, was marked by an intelligence as delightful as it is rare in modern Shakespeare productions.

The critic judged Matthison's Viola the finest presented in the city since Adelaide Nielson's in the 1870s, and Greet's Malvolio the best contemporary Bostonians had seen. The only objection the writer could think to raise was that use of female performers in a revival otherwise so Elizabethan was anachronistic. The *Boston Evening Transcript*'s critic was even more enthusiastic:

11. Hall. TWELFTH NIGHT.
Dir. Ben Greet, Knickerbocker Theatre, New York, NY, February 1904.

12. Hall. TWELFTH NIGHT.
Dir. Ben Greet, Knickerbocker Theatre, New York, NY, February 1904.

> The so-called austerity of the Elizabethan stage has a refreshing and wholesome richness for a modern audience, so surfeited with the merely artificial in stage craft, and a charm that is altogether unique. All the traditional customs of the theatre of centuries ago Ben Greet has faithfully reproduced, so far as circumstances will permit […] with the result that the spectacular is fairly overwhelmed by the rare beauty of the ensemble.

Matthison's Viola could not be praised highly enough, and Greet's Malvolio was 'boldly original' and 'rarely […] equalled.' The other actors showed 'the results of painstaking effort and constant and intelligent drill, added to no small degree of native talent'. In short, 'To lovers of Shakespeare sanely acted and correctly read, the performances of the Ben Greet Company present rare delights'. Greet shared the good news with Love: 'Our Shakespeare plays are going to be a big success here. The box office is crowded all day'. Demand ran so high that he laid on extra performances, and one New York paper described Boston as '"Twelfth Night" crazy' before reporting impressive weekly profits of $6,000–$7,000.[32] Elizabethan Manner had not only arrived, it was also profitable.

Greet's next offering was a pastiche of several medieval plays entitled *The Star of Bethlehem*, which was the work of Charles Mills Gayley, an expert on early drama as well as the head of the University of California's Department of English. Seeing how receptive American audiences were to old religious plays tastefully produced, Greet had given some thought to how he might give them another. When he met Gayley in the summer of 1903, their conversations about early drama had produced an interesting solution: the professor would write a Nativity based on medieval sources for performance by Greet's company. The resulting work was founded on three plays from the Towneley Cycle — *The First Shepherds' Play*, *The Offering of the Magi*, and *The Second Shepherds' Play* — into which Gayley inserted passages from nearly a dozen others from three other cycles. He also added interlinking verses of his own to give the whole a greater sense of unity in order 'to reproduce the material, conditions and atmosphere of the miracles as far as may be appropriate to modern conditions'.[33] The play never came close to matching the success of *Everyman*, but the friendship Greet and Gayley struck up may have contributed to the interesting opportunity that would come Greet's way in 1905.

The Star of Bethlehem, which used the Clerkenwell fit-up, opened to a large audience in late January. The *Boston Evening Transcript*'s critic praised every aspect of production and performance, singling out for particular commendation the contributions of Greet, Gayley, and Matthison. The *Dramatic Mirror*'s correspondent dubbed it 'an even more interesting revival than Everyman', commended Gayley's harmonious blending of his various sources, and lauded Greet's 'impressive' production and direction. The *Boston Globe* judged it better than *Twelfth Night*, calling it 'an exceedingly entertaining and instructive exhibition, the most curious, as well as the most satisfactory offering the company has made, with the exception of the ever-popular "Everyman"'. Every aspect of the production — the acting, the pageantry, the music — was excellent. As for the members of the company, the critic described them as 'so conscientious and so fitted to their roles that practically nothing could reasonably be desired of them'. Interestingly, that paper's coverage reveals a problem that arose at the first performance that Gayley and Greet failed to anticipate: audience members were at first nonplussed by the medieval practice of combining the sacred with the profane. According to the writer, the audience

> showed its desire not to offend good taste by preserving during the earlier part of the performance an unnecessarily serious attitude, even to the extent of failing to appropriately respond to some of the situations which were legitimately and actually humorous, but as the play progressed, and it was gradually perceived that it had been the intention of the constructor of the play, as it was of the actors themselves, to create merriment, the audience entered heartily into the spirit of the story and doubtless enjoyed it all the more accordingly.

The critic was optimistic that 'one source or another' would teach future audiences how to respond, but the reason the play did not endure may have had something to do with the fact that its broad, slightly irreverent humour was something the sober Protestants who had made *Everyman* a hit simply could not allow themselves to enjoy.[34] The belief that Bostonians were educated, loved plays, and were receptive to theatrical experimentation was so proverbial that producers routinely used the city as the proving-ground for new shows before bringing them to New York. That this sophisticated, open-minded bunch did not know how to respond to the antics of Mak (Greet's role) and Gill must have given Greet pause. Despite the energy, time, and money that went into making it a well-designed, -performed, and -reviewed show, it did not enter the repertory. After briefly reviving it the following Christmas, the actor-manager quietly dropped it.

Perhaps the most intriguing performance of *Star* took place at Bryn Mawr that spring, when necessity forced a return to genuinely medieval conditions. When the company arrived on campus to give its open-air performance,

> it found no stage and no natural elevation to play on. A large truck, wide and flat, which had been used to transport the properties, was pressed into service as a stage, the wheels were covered with bushes, and the scenery erected on the wagon.

The company did an excellent job disguising the last-minute change. Indeed, the student who covered the performance for the yearbook assumed the wagon had been the intended venue all along:

> The wagon fitted in the fashion of the primitive English stage, the beauty of the words which red-robed Gabriel chanted in Miss Matheson's [*sic*] impressive, rich voice, the quaintly-costumed, humorous shepherds, the magnificent, barbaric Kings of the East, created an atmosphere so unusual, so different from commonplace, as to give us a sense of the charm of medieval times.[35]

An Anglophone cycle play not having been performed out of doors on a wagon in 300 years, Greet has some claim, however unintentionally, to being North America's first early drama reconstructionist.

The actor-manager unveiled his next Elizabethan Manner production, *The Merchant of Venice*, to Bostonians in early February. Matthison played Portia, and Greet Shylock opposite her. The *Boston Globe* thought the Christ's Hospital fit-up 'quite suggestive' of the Elizabethan period and praised the production's educational value. Its critic noted that Greet's nearly complete text introduced lines and scenes unknown to modern audiences and underscored Portia as the play's dominant character even more clearly than the famous Irving-Terry production of 1879. Matthison's performance

> had the buoyancy, grace, humor and tenderness needful in delineating the delightful creation of the bard. The clarity of her articulation, her clever by-play, her grace of movement and the intelligent delivery of her text made her embodiment of Portia very delightful. The 'mercy' speech was notably effective.

Greet's Shylock started off quiet, matter-of-fact, cynical, and very human, becoming increasingly vigorous, 'impressive and powerfully dramatic' as the action unfolded. Like the *Boston Globe*, the *Boston Evening Transcript* considered the production to be the least gratifying of Greet's offerings. The company took two and a half hours to perform the play almost in its entirety. The production did not recreate an Elizabethan stage, but it did recreate the Elizabethan atmosphere as closely as could be imagined. Matthison's Portia was 'beautiful to look upon and hear, and to this comment there need be nothing added'. Greet's conception of Shylock was 'prudent and wise', but his personation was uneven: 'At times absolutely enigmatic and inexpressive, at other moments it almost carries the spectator off his feet. Nevertheless, even when apparently at fault, it is unquestionably interesting and even intellectually dominating throughout'. As for the other members of the company, they acted with the same intelligence and unity that helped make their productions so successful.[36]

A darling of high society during his early years in America, Greet was pleased to make his company available for society functions. In late January it gave a private performance of Henrik Hertz's *King René's Daughter* for Boston's 'Four Hundred' at the residence of Mr and Mrs J. Montgomery Sears. Matthison's delicate and moving perform- ance as the blind princess, Iolanthe, was much admired. In mid- February, it presented Reade and Taylor's *Masks and Faces* at the 1,653- seat Colonial Theatre as a fundraiser for the Hampton Institute. The Victorian comedy was one of Greet's favourites, not only because the role of James Triplet was one of his best, but also because Matthison excelled as Peg Woffington. Audiences and critics alike adored it. The *Morning Telegraph*'s Boston correspondent wrote:

> Ben Greet was admirable as 'Triplet', and was fairly overwhelmed by the
> plaudits. It would not be stretching matters to say that his impersonation
> is one of the best ever given on any stage. Those who expected a splendid
> impersonation of Mistress Woffington by Miss Edith Wynne Matthison
> were not disappointed. Her vivacity carried her audience as if by storm,
> and her comedy work was especially good, while her pathos was both well
> done and effective.

The benefit sold out so quickly the Hampton Committee arranged for another the next day.[37]

The company's last stop in New England was the Groton School, where President Roosevelt's son was a student.[38] Theodore, Jr, would not be the last member of his family to attend a Greet performance.

The Talk of New York

A near-capacity house greeted the company when it opened in Manhattan's opulent Knickerbocker Theatre (1,283 seats) on 22 February. Unusual circumstances had created the opportunity to play such a prestigious Broadway venue: the previous tenant, a sumptuous production of *Twelfth Night* starring Viola Allen, had been forced to close when Allen developed an infection so serious that surgery was required to save her life. Back-to-back *Twelfth Night*s at the Knickerbocker had not been the plan, but the *Evening Post*'s theatre critic recognized the rare and instructive contrast they offered. The production starring Allen was

> entirely 'up to date.' For the eye there is almost everything; for the under-
> standing very little. Nothing could be much finer than the panorama, or more
> rich or tasteful than the costumes. To suit the convenience of the stage
> carpenter, the text was transposed, mutilated, and otherwise used most
> despitefully. Most of the actors uttered what was left of it as if they had no
> comprehension either of its rhyme or its reason. In Mr. Greet's revival a
> widely different method is employed. All spectacular distractions [...] all
> subterfuges ordinarily employed to conceal the poverty of the performance,
> are discarded, while the text is restored exactly as it was written originally —
> with the exception of some fifty lines — and offered as the one sufficient
> excuse and unsurpassable charm of the whole entertainment.[39]

Which *Twelfth Night* would New Yorkers prefer?

That more than a few favoured Greet's quickly became apparent. As crowds packed the Knickerbocker, newspapers and magazines debated the virtues and limitations of Elizabethan Manner, the value of Greet's production, and what the implications might be for the commercial theatre in general and the way people staged and received Shakespeare in particular. By so doing, they established 'Ben Greet' and 'Elizabethan Manner' as familiar phrases, linking the actor-manager with that particular style of production in the popular imagination.

Two papers strongly endorsed the production. The *New York Times*'s critic (possibly John Corbin) praised the strong ensemble. Matthison was supreme in sentiment, if less masterful in comedy. Greet's Malvolio was better than both Sir Henry Irving's and Herbert Beerbohm Tree's. The production's great virtues were its intelligence, near-complete text, absence of 'archeological tedium', and delivery of 'the play in something approaching the original manner in which it was written to be represented'. The reviewer challenged a few points of Greet's archaeology, but praised the production for capturing Shakespeare's 'authentic spirit'. The effect of performances and method was to hold the audience in 'rapt interest' and make it 'burst from time to time into hearty laughter or admiring applause, ending with call upon call for the company, that continued long after the theatre would have ordinarily been emptied'. The *Evening Post*'s critic was rapturous and verbose. Greet's production had national implications because it shattered several venerable, cherished, but ultimately unhealthy illusions: that a government-funded theatre was a prerequisite of improving the American theatre, that classical plays could not be profitable, and that productions required stars and spectacle to be successful. Like *Everyman*, it demonstrated that audiences appreciated strong ensembles. It had flaws, but

> it was so good as a whole, so infinitely superior to the great mass of recent theatrical achievement, that it would be in the highest degree ungenerous to dwell unduly upon the defects [...]. Certainly no Shakesperean [*sic*] performance worthy to be compared with it in general efficiency, or in sympathetic intelligent appreciation of the text, has been given in this city since Sir Henry Irving's earliest production of 'The Merchant of Venice'.

Greet had not recreated the Elizabethan stage; far more important, he had recreated the Elizabethan atmosphere:

> The one great object, triumphantly achieved [...] was to prove by demonstration that the play is the thing, that a work of literary genius is practically independent of accessories, that the imagination which it excites is amazingly able to supply the scenic details which are imperceptible to the actual vision, that if the actors play well their parts it is gilding refined gold and painting the lily to overwhelm them with panorama and smother them with costly draperies, and that it is nothing short of murderous sacrilege to mangle an inspired text and try to conceal the iniquity by dazzling the eyes of the crowd with the glitter of vulgar spectacle.

The critic praised the company's intelligence, comprehension, elocution, and cooperation. Matthison was the best Viola seen in the city since Adelaide Neilson played the role, and she might have been better than Neilson. Greet's Malvolio was not as good as Irving's, but it was still excellent, both in conception and execution.[40]

Other papers were less impressed. The New York *Sun* concluded that, although the production tended toward dullness and monotony, 'the music of the poet, which was distinctly audible', made one forget 'all the Elizabethan stage society flummery and the mock antiques of Poel and Greet'. Having virtually all of Shakespeare's text served up in a little more than two hours' time was impressive and no doubt good for one, but being force-fed it in 'one solid lump' (there was actually a five-minute intermission) was disagreeable. Short's feeble *Romeo and Juliet* had spoiled whatever novelty such a production possessed, and Greet had not attempted an Elizabethan theatrical reconstruction anyway. The play should have been bright and merry rather than drab. Matthison was good, but not great. Greet's Malvolio 'was adroit, but gross in its conception', and the actor-manager played to the galleries. But the critic acknowledged that much applause had come from there and everywhere else in the Knickerbocker, and concluded by endorsing the show. The *New York Herald*, which had found *Everyman* so objectionable, forsoothly mocked *Twelfth Night*'s Elizabethan pretensions. The use of female performers would have been 'abhorrent in the sighte even of the groundlings in the dayes of good Queen Bess', its critic quipped. Though the audience members frequently and heartily applauded Matthison, 'there were some that did say that her enactment was not sufficinglie joyous or blithesome for a young a spark, which she fayned herself to be'. (Translation: her interpretation of Viola was incorrect and she was too old to play the role.) Greet played Malvolio 'in laughable fashion, yet did he retain the laughter within meet and proper bounds. He bodied forth the gross and pompous vanitie of the man with many touches of true wit'.[41]

The reactions of the generalist magazines were similarly mixed. *Life* considered Greet's fit-up more misleading than educational.

Outlook pronounced his actors merely competent, but thought the production's success was important for demonstrating that 'it is possible to present the best things without such an enormous expenditure upon accessories' as the typical Broadway production and still turn a profit. The long, illustrated, enthusiastically positive appreciation Eleanor Franklin wrote for *Leslie's Weekly* was good publicity. Franklin believed the production's greatest virtue was that it enabled audience members to appreciate the full beauty of a poem long ago mangled by modern staging techniques, and considered very judicious Greet's tempering of authenticity with pragmatism; a production that failed to incorporate anachronistic elements like actresses, theatres with proscenium arches, and artificial lighting would never find an audience. She concluded by declaring that 'every student of Shakespeare or of English literature, history, manners, or men' should see Greet's *Twelfth Night*. 'It is not a true picture of the seventeenth century, to be sure, but is as nearly a reproduction of the manners of that period as "modern inconveniences" will allow'. And *Current Literature* praised the production's splendid and consistent completeness, Greet's unified vision and commitment to presenting the play in its original manner, and the strong ensemble of actors who actually knew how to speak blank verse.[42]

The two most influential specialist publications dismissed *Twelfth Night*. The *Dramatic Mirror*'s critic succinctly stated the pro-Spectacular-Realism position: 'Mr. Greet's company is to Viola Allen's in this play as flat beer is to wine'. Greet's production was pretentious and irritating: 'for five acts in one long act, with not over sixty seconds between each act to talk to one's neighbor and exchange views, or to give the bored the chance to [...] silently steal away, is too much for the active American mind'. Set and costumes alike were dark, cheap, and unimpressive, and the actors were amateurish. Matthison was neither pretty nor charming enough to play the Viola, and her characterization was too sombre. Greet 'slaughtered' his lines and played Malvolio as conceited rather than as vain. *Theatre* pronounced it a tiresome experiment and an unworthy successor to *Everyman*. The actors were good, but they faced an insurmountable obstacle: 'trying to convey to the audience the illusion that this bare room is in turn a seacoast, Olivia's house and garden, the Duke's palace and then the street'.[43] How could anyone be expected to know where a scene was set with only the playwright's words to guide them?

The actor-manager now having achieved sufficient renown, the newspapers introduced him to New Yorkers. The *New York Times* published an interview by Corbin in which he and Greet debated the architectural and scenic requirements necessary to authentically stage *Twelfth Night*. Corbin, who had studied at both Harvard and Oxford and was a published authority on Elizabethan drama, believed Shakespeare used significantly more elaborate properties (including set-pieces and scenery) than most experts believed. Like the over-whelming majority of scholars, then and now, Greet was convinced the playwright favoured the use of only such elements as were absolutely essential to the action, relying on words and his audience's imagination at all other times.

The *New York Herald*'s long interview featured photographs of the actor-manager and the production. Its critic praised Greet's 'remark-ably competent company' before stating what most of the city's serious theatregoers already knew: Greet's *Twelfth Night* was 'the talk of New York'. Whether the actor-manager would succeed 'in revolu-tionizing modern stage methods', as some were suggesting, remained to be seen. His production running between Allen's *Twelfth Night* and Johnston Forbes-Robertson's much-anticipated *Hamlet* at the Knickerbocker, Greet hoped audiences would judge it on its own merits, not compare it to those spectacular, star-centred shows. Citing the experiments of the Elizabethan Stage Society and *Everyman*, Greet extolled the value of simple, more authentic productions of good, old plays, which clearly had the power to educate, improve public taste, and delight. Disagreeing with Irving's assertion that public taste should dictate the method of representing Shakespeare's plays, Greet argued that those works had to be protected from the powerful forces — the star system, the actors who valued themselves above the plays they performed, the desire for spectacle and the textual havoc it wreaked — that had caused them to be misrepresented for so long. The *Morning Telegraph*'s interview focused on Greet's managerial ideas. The profits his English companies made touring 'rubbish' like *The Belle of New York* underwrote 'hobbies' like *Everyman* and Shakespeare. Greet hoped Matthison would remain with him after her contract expired in June, but previous experience encouraged him to think he might be able to find someone to take her place if she chose to move on. Thanking Frohman for bringing him to America, he closed by touting the Hamlet of fellow Headlam-follower Forbes-Robertson (another Frohman import), which he was certain would 'make Broadway sit up'.[44]

The *Evening Post* did not interview Greet, but its critic offered more thoughts on *Twelfth Night* in a follow-up piece. Its archaeology may have been inaccurate by Corbin's lights, but the production was significant: 'The simple truth is that there has been no Shakespearean performance in this city worthy of comparison for many long years'. The moral of bare-stage performance was not that scenery was bad, 'but that a good text, with good acting, is independent of it; that a masterpiece, capably interpreted, without scenery, is unspeakably more fascinating and potent than the same masterpiece, hacked and defaced, and smothered with vulgar decoration'. The writer commended the quality of the ensemble acting as well as the training and management that produced it:

> The admirable groupings, the sustained animation of the whole stage picture, the evidence everywhere of discipline and prompt and intelligent cooperation, the generally clear, rhythmical and sympathetic utterance of the text, the swift steady progress of the action, the avoidance of points of tableaux [...] all denote a stage management of that intellectual sort which has been mourned as obsolete.

Finally, the critic could not resist pointing out the absurdity of the *New York Herald*'s critique of Matthison. What intelligent interpreter would choose to play as 'joyous or blithesome' a character who survives a ship-wreck in which she supposes her twin brother has died, and then falls hopelessly in love with a man who not only fails to perceive that she is a woman, but who also commands her to woo another woman on his behalf? As for Matthison's maturity, Terry, Allen, and Ada Rehan had all achieved success in the role at the same age.[45]

While the New York press was debating Elizabethan Manner, Poel was in London reviving *Much Ado about Nothing*, which the Elizabethan Stage Society performed nine times between February and April, some for the London School Board. Significantly, the ESS's final offering was produced 'by arrangement with Mr. Ben Greet and at the special request of the Rev. Stewart D. Headlam, Chairman of the Evening Continuation Schools' — a detail that escaped Poel's biographer.[46] Either the deal Poel and Greet struck in 1901 included Greet financing another ESS production or the society's situation had become so precarious by 1904 that Poel and/or Headlam asked Greet to support its work once last time.

Back in Manhattan, business was so brisk that Frohman extended the Ben Greet Players in the city into April, which necessitated trans-ferring it into the 1,150-seat Daly's Theatre so that Forbes-Robertson's *Hamlet* could open as planned.[47] Ironically, one of the reasons that eagerly awaited production failed to live up to expectations was that Greet had just introduced New Yorkers to strong ensemble acting of a full text on a lightly dressed stage. Several papers noted that Forbes-Robertson based his text on the Cambridge and Variorum editions, implying that, like Greet, he was concerned with textual fidelity, if not completeness. The star cut lines and transposed and combined scenes, but only to ensure the performance came in under 210 minutes. Critics agreed that his alterations were intelligent, kept the action moving at a decent pace, and did not create an excessive number of waits. (The longest lasted 'only' ten minutes.) Forbes-Robertson's performance, if not inspired or inspiring, was intellectually interesting and a triumph of Naturalism. Unfortunately, almost all the other members of the company were woefully inadequate. The numerous sets were interesting and pretty, and their comparative simplicity allowed them to be shifted with comparative rapidity, which enabled the star to speak noticeably more lines than were usually delivered in Spectacular Realism productions. However, several critics noticed not only that touring had taken its toll on the sets, but also that they were less beautiful and evocative than the ones used in the last major *Hamlet* production mounted in the city: Daniel Frohman's (pictured in Chapter Two). The *Evening Post* suggested a remedy: Forbes-Robertson should combine with Greet on a full-text *Hamlet* using Greet's Middle Temple fit-up. With the former starring and the latter directing and supplying his ensemble and fit-up, such a venture would undoubtedly be novel, excellent, and profitable. The *Sun* seconded the motion, adding that 'the Greet company is superior at all points save one to the Robertson organization — that single superior exception being Mr. Robertson himself'. The scheme never materialized, but the *Dramatic Mirror* announced that Robertson would 'adopt the Ben Greet idea' when he presented the tragedy in April in Harvard's Sanders Theatre, now dressed in a new Elizabethan fit-up designed by George Pierce Baker and H. Langford Warren of the Department of Architecture.[48]

Greet unveiled his full-text, Elizabethan Manner *As You Like It* in March, the turnout for which was so strong that he held it over another week. The critics were as enthusiastic as theatregoers were, with Corbin remaining one of the actor-manager's most vocal admirers. As he wrote in the *New York Times*, Matthison's Rosalind might not have realized all of Shakespeare's wit and fancy, but her humour, rich warmth, and poetic imagination were unsurpassed. And the reviewer thought Greet's simple, exquisitely intelligent Jaques even better indoors. Outlets that had disapproved of *Twelfth Night* now praised *As You Like It*, including the *Dramatic Mirror*, which described it as 'simply but most attractively and artistically mounted'.[49]

As an actor, Greet was hardly extraordinary. As a manager, he had done nothing less than present a viable alternative to Spectacular Realism in a highly visible, critically and popularly successful Broadway season. Even if it had been produced by a non-star, the

Broadway debut of Elizabethan Manner Shakespeare is something Charles H. Shattuck ought to have noted, particularly because it caused such a flutter in the important New York newspapers he used. Thanks to Shattuck's silence, this major achievement has nearly been forgotten. The scholarly consensus since at least the time of J. L. Styan has been that *The Winter's Tale* and *Twelfth Night* Harley Granville Barker staged in London brought Shakespeare into the twentieth century.[50] Greet's productions did not employ a thrust like those did, but they featured all the other elements scholars credit Granville Barker for reassembling on a commercial stage for the first time since the seventeenth century: full text, fast pace, continuous action, rapid delivery of lightly inflected lines, and a strong ensemble. And, unlike Granville Barker's, Greet's costumes and settings were Elizabethan. Greet, not his erstwhile protégé Granville Barker, brought Shakespeare into the twentieth century, and he did so in Boston and New York in 1904, not in London in 1912.

Non-star though he was, Greet was quickly establishing himself as one of the leading Shakespearean interpreters in America, a reputation bolstered by yet another unusual endorsement. In March, a rumour reached the *New York Herald* that Andrew Carnegie was considering creating a trust to endow a theatre in the city for the specific purpose of supporting Greet's work. The paper sent a reporter to verify the story, but the philanthropist, constantly bombarded with solicitations, chose to clarify his position in a letter:

To the Editor of the Herald:—

Your reporter called to see me a few days ago to know if I were interested in the question of an endowed theatre, about which we hear so much these days.

I have attended the theatre twice in one week recently, and heard the British company play 'Twelfth Night' and 'As You Like It'. This breaks the record for me, I think, in recent years. I hope to go frequently, because here is something approaching the standard of the endowed theatre. One or two of the male members of the cast still rant a little and speak too fast, but with those exceptions I have not seen such acting except in France and now and then in London. It is the art which conceals art. Mr. Greet's Jaques is the best Jaques I have seen, and I have seen many. The stillness which pervaded the theatre last night as he spoke, sitting, 'All the world's a stage', was impressive to a degree — a sermon, indeed. It was exquisitely done.

The two leading ladies are unusually fine; Toby and Sir Andrew Aguecheek also. Here is an opportunity for those who call so loudly for an endowed drama to support a company which deserves support […].

If this be taken as an advertisement of a company, I feel it is as deserved as it is unsolicited. We should not need an endowed theatre if those who clamor for it would support acting of the highest standard when it is presented to them. Every lover of the highest and best should see this company.

Andrew Carnegie[51]

Carnegie's penultimate line may have disappointed Greet, who had to console himself with having the industrialist-philanthropist's last sentence and signature reproduced on the company's programmes and promotional materials.

The actor-manager unveiled his final production, Goldsmith's *She Stoops to Conquer*, in April. The play had been a staple of the Ben Greet Comedy Company for more than a decade, and English theatregoers loved both it and Greet's Tony Lumpkin. Sizeable Manhattan audiences turned out, but the reception was so dull that Greet probably regretted not extending *As You Like It*. The *Morning Telegraph* identified the problem: 'Capable actors […] have undertaken a work with which they have not the slightest sympathy'. The *Evening Post* judged Greet's revival to have been 'conceived in the right spirit' and the performances good and efficient, but the company's strength was Shakespeare, not eighteenth-century comedy. The *New York Times*, which usually gushed over Greet's work, was conspicuously dry. The production had educational value, if only because the play had not been respectably staged in the city for many years. Greet's contrived Lumpkin and Matthison's solid Kate Hardcastle were workmanlike, while the performance overall was 'an intellectual and diverting bit of ensemble acting'. A genial *New York Herald* declared that, for all its 'many defects last night's performance was a pleasure'. Matthison's Kate was 'delightful' and 'acted on the right spirit', but Greet's 'simulation of boyishness left much to be desired'. The same could be said of the production, but the critic ended by expressing his gratitude that the comedy had been revived at all. Similarly, although the *Dramatic Mirror* found the actual presentation 'mediocre, but enjoyable', it commended Greet for mounting 'this matchless and rarely seen play'.[52]

If the half-season in Boston and New York established Greet as an important force in American Shakespeare, the week he spent in Washington, DC's 1,350-seat Columbia Theatre was noteworthy for a different reason. That the company presented *Everyman* during its first visit to the city was not surprising. That the Missionary Society of the First Congregational Church co-sponsored the performances most certainly was. The *Washington Times*'s reporter declared the event one of the most significant unions 'of church and theatre in the history of Washington'. He reminded readers that the Protestant anti-theatrical tradition was as long as it was uncompromising. That such a prominent Protestant congregation would partially under- write — and, thus, publicly endorse — the performances with the intention of using the profits they generated to finance its activities was 'wonderfully pregnant with meaning'. Indeed, that at least a handful of discriminating thinkers had recognized that tasteful, intelligent, and uplifting drama could be a force for moral and cultural improvement was a sign that times were changing. The jour- nalist finished by praising the 'enlightened and courageous churchman' who had undertaken the 'mightily encouraging' venture:

> Its members must surely encounter the criticisms of a few who are either short-sighted or ill-informed. But those who appreciate the extreme wideness of the theatre's field, those who enjoy the wonderful richness of the best stage literature, and those who see in a clear light the great didactic influence of the performed drama, will be glad that an organization of this nature has given the best influences of the stage the help of its approval.

Greet was changing the way religious Americans thought about plays.[53]

Returning to Philadelphia, the company offered *Everyman* for a fortnight before presenting *Merchant* and *Twelfth Night* on Shakespeare's birthday. It staged the Morality in Buffalo's 2,200-seat Teck Theatre the following week before returning to Manhattan to close the regular season with a special engagement.[54]

Lucy Love had previously introduced Greet to Charles Sprague Smith, the founder of the People's Institute, a group dedicated to the cultural advancement of New York's working poor. The two men now organized an experimental collaboration: three Shakespearean performances for poor adults and schoolchildren in the 1,400-seat hall at Cooper Union. The financial arrangement they worked out combined elements of Greet's Concert Booking and 1897 'popular prices' models: the institute would sponsor the presentations, some of the money for which would come from the sale of drastically discounted tickets. These tickets would cost from between 15¢ and 50¢ — significantly less than the 50¢–$2.50 top-tier theatres like the Knickerbocker charged.[55] As this photograph illustrates, the performances were truly bare-stage affairs; the hall's tiny platform could support only the smallest of properties. That fact did nothing to dampen the excitement of the more than 4,000 people who turned out.

13. Byron. THE MERCHANT OF VENICE.
Dir. Ben Greet, Cooper Union Hall, New York, NY, 13 May 1904.

The *New-York Tribune* reprinted a letter one twelve-year-old eyewitness wrote to Smith after attending *Merchant* with her classmates and teacher that I reproduce because it gives evidence of how successfully Smith and Greet achieved their educational objective:

Dear Sir: Saturday morning I was so happy over the prospect of seeing 'The Merchant of Venice' that I thought of nothing else. While helping mamma I was continually saying 'In sooth I know not why I am so sad', until she said her ears buzzed. The whole morning I was dreaming of Portia, Antonio, Shylock, and Bassanio. We obtained good seats and saw very well.

In the morning Miss K. had shown me a picture of Miss Edithe Wynne Mathison [*sic*] as she appeared in 'Everyman'. There she was so beautiful, but when I saw her as my beloved Portia she was twice as lovely. When Antonio came out and said, 'In sooth, I know not why I am so sad', Miss K. gave me a knowing look. Even though I knew the pound of flesh was not to be forfeited I forgot it for the time being, and imagined that I saw it being confiscated, but that is because of the way in which Shylock sharpened that knife and then felt it to see if it was keen enough to serve his cruel purpose. In the Lamb's Tales I have at home there is a picture of Shylock sharpening his knife, and the likeness was very accurate. On the way home Miss K. asked me which I preferred, to read books or to go to plays. As I am very fond of reading, I did not know which I was more fond of. I said, 'Of course, if all plays were like the "Merchant of Venice", there would be no question about it'.

When I reached home my excitement knew no bounds. I did not know what to talk of first.

You do not know, Mr. Sprague Smith, how thankful I am to you for contriving such clever means to enable us girls to reap the profits of so beneficial and enjoyable a play. I have read many of Shakespeare's comedies and tragedies, but I have never seen any. I hope some more Shakespearian plays will soon fall my way.

Thanking you sincerely for the golden opportunity you presented to us, I remain, yours gratefully.

A. M.[56]

Greet would later recall his work with the institute with particular fondness because it had inaugurated an important social undertaking that led not only to the formation of that organization's Drama Department, but also to the introduction of discount, 'wage-earner' nights at the New Theatre in 1909.[57] His dedication to bringing Shakespeare to poor schoolchildren would eventually lead to a knighthood, not for services to the theatre, but to drama and education.

Greet made another important contact in New York that spring. As Elizabeth Forte Alman discovered, Emily Jordan Folger and Henry Clay Folger attended nearly a dozen performances by the company that season. One of them even braved the scrum at Cooper Union to hear *Twelfth Night*. (I suspect Emily, a former teacher at a preparatory school for girls.) Henry Folger wrote a letter to Greet expressing his admiration, suggesting organizational improvements for his next Manhattan season, and entreating him to mount his *Macbeth*, *The Taming of the Shrew*, and *The Tempest* at the earliest opportunity. By so doing, he established a longstanding, if sporadic, correspondence with Greet.[58]

The 1904 Open-Air Season

Now operating as the Woodland Players, the company kicked off a seven-week season in mid-May. Lucrative work at fundraisers accounted for a significant part of its schedule. Demand for tickets ran so high at its first engagement, two performances on the grounds of the U.S. Naval Observatory in Washington, DC to benefit Works of Mercy, that the charity laid on two more the following day.[59]

Greet unveiled his open-air productions of *A Midsummer Night's Dream* and the rarely staged *Much Ado*. Although the company would present the latter for years and reviews of it tended to be very positive, it never established itself as a top draw. In contrast, the former, one of the oldest and most-established plays in the actor-manager's outdoor repertory, quickly became an American staple. As noted in Chapter One, Greet eliminated the non-woodland scenes (all of 1.1 and much of 5.1). Depending on the circumstances, he also cut some of the lines spoken by the human lovers. And he would deeply cut the lines of Titania and Oberon on the occasions when local children, whom Greet would patiently rehearse, played the fairies. If enough of them participated, Greet would teach them a fairy dance to perform. Also as indicated, the most resource-intensive version was the night-time one featuring Greet's special calcium-light effects and a small musical ensemble playing selections from Felix Mendelssohn's Opus 61.

The company presented its most extravagant version of the production — children, lighting effects, music, the works — twice on the grounds of the Gardiner estate in Brookline, Massachusetts, to benefit Boston's Home for Crippled Children and St Augustine's Home for Convalescents. Unfortunately, the American premiere was a critical disappointment. The reviewer for the *Boston Evening Transcript* was impressed by Greet's staging (particularly of the supernatural scenes) and his use of the surprisingly effective children. But his cuts to the dialogue of the human lovers 'were so drastic that one could scarcely follow the transitions of character with any conception of its rationality'. By excising relatively few lines from the subplot, Greet gave it more weight than Shakespeare intended. To aggravate the situation, the actors personating the mechanicals indulged in far too much slapstick — Greet, playing his beloved Bottom, being the chief offender. If the production failed to impress the critics, it succeeded admirably as a fundraiser: Greet told Love the two performances grossed $6,000.[60]

The company appeared at eight educational institutions that spring: Princeton, Bryn Mawr, Yale, Mt Holyoke, and the universities of Pennsylvania, Rochester, Toronto, and McGill. Its last stop was a pair of performances on 1 July at the New York estate of English art critic Charles Henry Caffin, who had met his wife, Caroline, years earlier when the two had been members of the Woodland Players.[61]

The 1903 and 1904 open-air tours proved not only that Americans wanted professional performances of Shakespeare's works presented in that manner, but also that a company could turn a tidy profit presenting them. Put in starker business terms, by demonstrating both the demand and the business model to fill it, Greet encouraged competitors to enter the market.

The first ones wasted no time taking the field. In July, a company advertising itself as 'the Woodland Players' began touring an outdoor *As You Like It* through upstate New York. Its operations ground to a halt after but four engagements when its manager, Philip A. Kilfoil, left Oswego after passing bad cheques. Confined to their hotel by the police, the actors had to wait while a policeman travelled to Manhattan, arrested Kilfoil for grand larceny, and brought him back to stand trial. The judge made him settle all the company's debts, after which Kilfoil announced he was disbanding it and quitting the theatre business. The police then released the actors, who returned to Manhattan. Although the experience is unlikely to have engendered fond memories, it failed to sour the company's leads, two young professionals by the name of Ivah M. Wills and Charles D. Coburn, on the idea of spending summers touring Shakespeare together in the open air. In August, another 'Woodland Players' company presented *As You Like It* on the grounds of the Hotel Pilgrim in Plymouth, Massachusetts. According to one account, some of its performers had been members of Greet's company.[62] The actor-manager had established a name and method worth appropriating.

NOTES

[1]   BG to Lucy Love, 28 July 1903, Michigan Love; Blanche Partington, 'With the Players and the Music Folk', *SFC*, 26 July 1903, p.46.

[2]   Unless indicated otherwise, the information in this paragraph and the two that follow it are taken from Isaac, pp.vi–xxi and 17–20.

[3]   'Ben Greet Believes that "The Play's the Thing"', *NYH*, 28 February 1904, section 3, p.7.

[4]   Thorndike, pp.127, 167, and 184.

[5]   Howard, p.100.

[6]   Maltby, pp.40–41.

[7]   O'Connor, *William Poel*, pp.75 and 128 n. 200; Cecilia Radclyffe to William Poel, *c.* 1902–03, Poel and Others Regarding *Everyman*, 1902–07 and Undated, William Poel Papers, Victoria and Albert Museum Theatre Archive; 'Malvolio Greet and the Sceneless Shakespeare', *NYMT*, 28 February 1904, p.6.

[8]   BG to Lucy Love, 24 June 1907, Michigan Love.

[9]   Mrs Patrick Campbell, *My Life and Some Letters* (New York, Dodd, Mead and Co., 1922), p.58.

[10]   Blanche Partington, 'Centuries Fall Back as Intent Audience at University Watches Playing of "Everyman", Popular in Columbus' Time', *SFC*, 2 September 1903, p.4; Blanche Partington, 'With the Players and the Music Folk', *SFC*, 13 September 1903, p.50; Ashton Stevens, '"Everyman", a Play Like a Church Service, Almost a Rite', *San Francisco Examiner*, 2 September 1903, p.5; 'Morality Play Wins Stanford', *SFC*, 22 September 1903, p.4.

[11]   Blanche Partington, 'With the Players and the Music Folk', *SFC*, 13 September 1903, p.50; 'Pastors Select Topics for their Discourses', *SFC*, 6 September 1903, p.34; 'Jewish Origin of Everyman', *SFC*, 4 September 1903, p.9.

[12]   State of California Board of Education, *Twenty-First Biennial Report of the Superintendent of Public Instruction for the School Years Ending June 30, 1903, and June 30, 1904* (Sacramento, CA: State of California Board of Education, 1904), p.35. On the significance of the Greek Theatre, see Cheney, pp.31–36.

[13]   'Students Will Don the Sock and Buskin to Present Aristophanes' Immortal Greek Comedy "The Birds"', *SFC*, 20 August 1903, p.11; *Biennial Report of the President on Behalf of the Regents to His Excellency the Governor of the State, 1902–1904* (Berkeley, CA: University of California Press, 1904), p.37. The mistaken belief that Greet directed this production seems to have originated with the erroneous claim that he did in Arthur Inkersley, 'Oedipus Tyrannus at the University of California', *Overland Monthly*, August 1910, 230–37 (p.231).

[14]   'Greek Theater is Received by Enthusiastic Students', *SFC*, 26 September 1903, p.10. Dan Venning, 'Shakespeare and Central Park: Shakespeare under

(and with) Stars', *Forum for Modern Language Studies*, 26.2 (March 2010), 152–65 (p.153), erroneously states that the performance of *Twelfth Night* at the Greek Theatre was the first open-air performance Greet gave in America.

15   Blanche Partington, '"Twelfth Night" on Greek Stage', *SFC*, 27 September 1903, p.37.

16   Seating capacities from <http://www.carnegiemuseums.org/interior.php?pageID=30> [accessed 31 May 2016]; C. H. Daniels, 'Third Convention of the Student Volunteer Movement', *The Missionary Herald*, April 1898, p.138; 'Detroit', *Bulletin of the American Institute of Bank Clerks*, 1 June 1904, p.50.

17   'St. Ignatius Graduates to Produce "Everyman"', *SFC*, 17 October 1903, p.7; 'Gentlemen's Sodality in Morality Play', *SFC*, 29 October 1903, p.13; 'Big Attendance at Last Rendition of "Everyman"', *SFC*, 30 October 1903, p.3.

18   'Show Gossip', *Cincinnati Enquirer*, 19 November 1903, p.6; Ben Greet Players, *Everyman* Play Programme, Oberlin College, Oberlin, OH, February 4, 1907, Oberlin College Archive. Seating capacity from <http://en.wikipedia.org/wiki/Music_Hall_%28Cincinnati%29> [accessed 31 May 2016].

19   'At the Sign of the Ass's Head', *(University of Michigan) Inlander*, December 1903, pp.132–34.

20   '"Everyman", Morality Play, Holds a Fine Audience', *St Louis Republic*, 1 December 1903, p.3; '"Everyman", the Old Morality Play, Will Aid the Big Christmas Fund', *St Louis Post-Dispatch*, 17 December 1903, p.22. Seating capacity from Alfred Henry Nolle, *The German Drama in English on the St Louis Stage* (Philadelphia: University of Pennsylvania Press, 1917), p.71.

21   Seating capacity from *JC(1904)*, p.818.

22   'Bishop Sees Play', *Syracuse Journal*, 21 November 1903, p.3.

23   Seating capacity from <http://en.wikipedia.org/wiki/File:1904_Chickering Hall_Boston.png> [accessed 31 May 2016].

24   Speaight, pp.90–93. Arthur J. Harris, 'William Poel's Elizabethan Stage: the First Experiment', *Theatre Notebook*, no. 17 (1963) 111–14; O'Connor, *William Poel*, pp.26–32.

25   'As Done in the Olden Time', *NYT*, 3 February 1895, p.12; 'Old English Play at Harvard: from Stage to Spectators, All is to Be in Elizabethan Style', *NYT*, 18 March 1895, p.9; George P. Baker, 'The Revival of Ben Jonson's Epicoene; or, The Silent Woman, March 20, 1895', *Harvard Graduates Magazine*, June 1895, pp.493–501; 'An Elizabethan Play at Yale', *Werner's Magazine,* March–August 1901, p.266. Baker's biographer, Wisner Payne Kinne, *George Pierce Baker and the American Theatre* (Cambridge, MA: Harvard University Press), pp.59–60, states that, because the faculty at Harvard was unaware of Poel's work, the archaeological experiments conducted there developed independent of it. Whether that ignorance extended to Sargent, whose idea it had been to stage *Epicoene* in an Elizabethan fit-up in the first place, and everyone else associated with the original production in Manhattan has yet to be determined.

[26] 'Shakespeare in the Ark: "Romeo and Juliet" Revived with Noah's Archeology', *NYT*, 25 January 1903, p.9. For a photograph of Short's production, see *Theatre*, March 1903, p.65.

[27] Stanford University English Club, *Elizabethan Humours and the Comedy of Ben Jonson* (San Francisco: Paul Elder and Co., 1905), p.1.

[28] Ben Greet, 'Shakespeare and the Modern Theatre', *Harper's Weekly*, 4 November 1905, p.1604.

[29] 'Notes of the Day', *Literature*, 23 June 1900, p.469.

[30] As indicated in '"The Comedy of Errors" at Gray's Inn Hall', *Lloyd's Weekly Newspaper*, 8 December 1895, p.11, Poel had been using Beefeaters and Bluecoat Boys since at least 1895. For proof that the *Everyman* production at the Imperial in 1902 included Beefeaters, see 'Everyman', *(London) Echo*, 12 June 1902, p.2.

[31] Quoted in 'Malvolio Greet and the Sceneless Shakespeare', *NYMT*, 28 February 1904, p.6.

[32] 'Rare Delight: "Twelfth Night" as in Olden Days', *BGl.*, 7 January 1904, p.8; 'Continued Local Attractions', *BET*, 12 January 1904, p.13; BG to Lucy Love, 11 January 1904, Michigan Love; 'Not Easy to Pick a Winner', *NYMT*, 30 January 1904, p.5.

[33] Charles Mills Gayley, *The Star of Bethlehem* (New York: Fox, Duffield and Company, 1904), p.xvii.

[34] 'Chickering Hall: "The Star of Bethlehem"', *BET*, 26 January 1904, p.10; 'Telegraphic News — Boston', *NYDM* 30 January 1904, p.14; '"Star of Bethlehem": Latest Offering by the Everyman Players', *BGl.*, 26 January 1904, p.7.

[35] 'Ben Greet's Troubles', *Wasp*, 2 July 1904, p.811; *Bryn Mawr College Yearbook, Class of 1905* (Bryn Mawr, PA: Bryn Mawr College Class of 1905, 1905), [p.97].

[36] 'Everyman Players: "The Merchant of Venice" in Elizabethan Form', *BGl.*, 2 February 1904, p.8; 'Chickering Hall: "The Merchant of Venice"', *BET*, 2 February 1904, p.10.

[37] '"King Rene's [*sic*] Daughter"', *BET*, 27 January 1904, p.15; 'Miss Matthison in Benefit Performance in Boston', *NYMT*, 11 February 1904, p.10; 'The Hampton Benefit at the Colonial', *BET*, 4 February 1904, p.11. Colonial Theatre seating capacity from *JC(1904)*, p.69.

[38] 'Ben Greet's Company Achieves Great Success', *NYMT*, 8 February 1904, p.5.

[39] 'Viola Allen's Condition', *NYDM*, 20 February 1904, p.8; 'Dramatic and Musical Notes', *(New York) Evening Post*, 20 February 1904, p.4. Seating capacity from *JC(1904)*, p.31.

[40] 'The Elizabethan "Twelfth Night"', *NYT*, 23 February 1904, p.5; 'Music and Drama', *(New York) Evening Post*, 23 February 1904, p.5.

[41] '"Twelfth Night" in One Act', *NYS*, 23 February 1904, p.7; '"Twelfth Night" as in Ye Olden Time', *NYH*, 23 February 1904, p.11.

42 'A Curious Idea in Education', *Life*, 10 March 1904, p.246; 'The Elizabethan "Twelfth Night"', *Outlook*, 12 March 1904, p.630; Eleanor Franklin, 'A Seventeenth-Century Play Interests a Twentieth-Century Audience', *Leslie's Weekly*, 24 March 1904, pp.278 and 284; 'The Drama', *Current Literature*, April 1904, pp.443–45.

43 'Knickerbocker — Twelfth Night', *NYDM*, 5 March 1904, p.16; '"Twelfth Night" as Shakespeare Saw it Played', *Theatre*, April 1904, p.99.

44 John Corbin, 'The Sceneless Ben Greet', *NYT*, 28 February 1904, p.4; 'Ben Greet Believes that "The Play's the Thing"', *NYH*, 28 February 1904, section 3, p.7; 'Malvolio Greet and the Sceneless Shakespeare', *NYMT*, 28 February 1904, p.6. Forbes-Robertson's connection with Headlam from Orens, p.38.

45 'Dramatic and Musical Notes', *(New York) Evening Post*, 27 February 1904, p.5.

46 Speaight, p.180; Isaac, p.51; quote from *Much Ado about Nothing*, ed. by F. H. Mares (Cambridge: Cambridge University Press, 2003), p.17. I am grateful to Marion O'Connor for calling to my attention Greet's involvement.

47 'Echoes from Stageland from Casual Listeners', *NYMT*, 27 February 1904, p.5. Seating capacity from *JC(1904)*, p.19.

48 'Playbills of the Current Week', *NYH*, 6 March 1904, section 3, p.13; 'The Great Modern Version of Hamlet', *NYT*, 8 March 1904, p.9; Gustav Kobbé, 'Forbes Robertson and Gertrude Elliott Produce Shakespeare's "Hamlet"', *NYMT*, 8 March 1904, p.10; 'Dramatic and Musical Notes', *(New York) Evening Post*, 5 March 1904, p.5; 'Wouldn't a Greet-Robertson "Hamlet" Be a Winner?' *NYS*, 9 March 1904, p.7; 'Boston', *NYDM*, 26 March 1904, p.14. That the 1905 preformances were presented in a new fit-up from Franklin J. Hildy, 'Why Elizabethan Spaces?' *Theatre Symposium: A Publication of the Southeastern Theatre Conference*, 12 (2004), 99–120 (pp.106–07).

49 John Corbin, 'The Heyday of Legitimate Drama', *NYT*, 27 March 1904, Sunday magazine p.6; 'Daley's — As You Like It', *NYDM*, 26 March 1904, p.17.

50 J. L. Styan, *The Shakespeare Revolutions: Criticism and Performance in the Twentieth Century* (Cambridge: Cambridge University Press, 1977), pp.232–33; Mazer, p.123. More recently, Joe Falocco, *Reimagining Shakespeare's Playhouse: Early Modern Staging Conventions in the Twentieth Century* (Cambridge: D. S. Brewer, 2010), pp.93–97, argues that this accomplishment should be credited equally to Granville Barker and Walter Nugent Monck.

51 'Andrew Carnegie Praises Actors', *NYH*, 16 March 1904, p.5.

52 '"She Stoops to Conquer" at Daly's Disappointing', *NYMT*, 29 March 1904, p.10; 'She Stoops to Conquer', *(New York) Evening Post*, 29 March 1904, p.7; 'She Stoops to Conquer', *NYT*, 30 March 1904, p.5; 'English Comedy Seen at Daly's', *NYH*, 29 March 1904, p.12; 'Daly's — She Stoops to Conquer', *NYDM*, 9 April 1904, p.16.

53 'Church and Stage', *WTr.*, 27 March 1904, Metropolitan section, p.4. Seating capacity from *JC(1904)*, p.103.

54 'Philadelphia', *NYDM*, 23 April 1904, p.23. Seating capacity from *JC(1904)*, p.109.

[55] 'Twenty-Five Cent Shakespeare for the People', *Theatre*, July 1904, pp.179–80; Knickerbocker pricing from *JC(1904)*, p.31. Greet usually required a minimum guarantee of $500 for a single performance for a philanthropic and/or educational cause. The letter he wrote to Love on 14 April 1904 indicates he accepted $800 for the two performances he gave of *The Merchant of Venice* as a personal favour to her. The letter he wrote to her on 14 January 1905 indicates that $350 per performance was the company's break-even number.

[56] 'People's Institute Plays', *NYTr.*, 22 May 1904, p.4.

[57] Ben Greet, 'For the Greatest Theatre in the World', *World's Work*, April 1911, 14222–29 (p.14228).

[58] Alman, pp.104–08.

[59] 'Washington', *NYDM*, 14 May 1904, p.12.

[60] 'Ben Greet's Players at Brookline', *BET*, 21 June 1904, p.11; BG to Lucy Love, 26 June 1904, Yale Love.

[61] On the Caffins meeting while working as actors in Greet's company, see <http://www.aaa.si.edu/collections/charles-henry-caffin-papers-8566/more> [accessed 31 May 2016].

[62] 'As You Like It', *Amsterdam (New York) Evening Recorder*, 14 July 1904, p.8; 'As You Like It', *Oswego (New York) Times*, 16 July 1904, p.5; 'As You Like It Called Off', *Rome (New York) Sentinel*, 27 July 1904, p.2; "People of Rome Waited in Vain," *Oswego (New York) Times*, 28 July 1904, p.4; "Current Happenings," *Massachusetts Ploughman and New England Journal of Agriculture*, 13 August 1904, p.3.

CHAPTER FOUR
The Business of Playing, 1904–06

The 1904–05 Season

Frohman's biographers list the Ben Greet Players among the acts the impresario sponsored during the 1904–05 season, but the disappearance of the phrase 'Charles Frohman Presents' (in discrete type) from the company's newspaper ads and promotional materials indicates the producer and the actor-manager parted ways at the close of the 1903–04 season. Greet's best actors also chose to move on: Matthison and Kennedy to Sir Henry Irving's organization, Millicent McLaughlin to the Julia Marlowe-E. H. Sothern combination, and B. A. Field to John Craig's stock company in Boston. That Craig literally doubled Field's salary is indicative of both the low wages Greet paid and how highly the market valued his most accomplished alumni.[1]

Moving the Crawleys into the leading positions was simple, but Greet needed to bring on an especially large cohort of actors to keep the company at full strength. He recruited another experienced husband-and-wife team, Leonard Shepherd and Helena Head, as second leads. He brought in journeyman Eric Blind to support them. He hired his own niece and nephew, twins Daisy and Maurice Robinson, both of whom had toured with him in England. To take some of Field's parts, he engaged an already obese aspirant named Sydney Greenstreet. Although Greenstreet's work achieved distinction only years after he worked with Greet, his celebrated cinema performances give evidence of the delivery-style Greet drilled into his actors: swift cadence; clear diction; careful punctuation and accent; and light, natural inflexion.

But that summer's most famous recruit, the artist who ultimately achieved the greatest renown and influence of all Greet's protégés, was Sybil Thorndike. She and her brother, Russell, had enrolled in the Ben Greet Academy of Acting in London after seeing an advertisement. Their religious parents (their father was a minister) were uneasy with the notion of their children taking up a profession generally regarded as both insecure and slightly unsavoury, but Greet's reputations as a superb teacher of acting and a religious man overcame their reluctance. The actor-manager offered Sybil a position in his American company after watching the siblings give their graduation performances in England that summer. She accepted his offer of $25 a week — $10 less than he paid the more experienced Daisy Robinson. Thorndike was twenty-one years old, and the three seasons she spent touring America with Greet laid the foundation of one of the most distinguished careers of the twentieth-century English stage.[2]

Thorndike would not emerge as a significant presence in the company for some time, and she would not fulfil her artistic potential for years, but she is important for telling this chapter of Greet's American story because of the letters she wrote home. The details they include, combined with the recollections of her brother Russell (who joined Sybil in America the following autumn), would eventually make up a quarter of the biography he wrote of his sister. These provide the richness and colour only an insider's view can — an enthusiastic account of two young artists learning their craft the way Mrs Patrick Campbell and Edith Wynne Matthison learned it: at the feet of Greet as members of his touring company.

The Ben Greet Players gave a few presentations during the six-week journey from Scotland to California to begin forging the ensemble. In September, Lucy Love joined them for a few days in the Berkshires. Avid music-lovers both, Love and Thorndike formed an enduring friendship. A mother whose own daughter was studying piano at a conservatory in Berlin, Love offered a sympathetic ear to Thorndike, who was still struggling with the guilt she felt over abandoning her own piano studies. Love assured the young woman that acting could be just as demanding as music, that she had a considerable talent for it, and that she would someday be 'in the front rank of actors' if she devoted herself as completely as she had to her music.[3]

This anecdote illustrates an aspect of company life never revealed in newspapers: the performers interacted with one another as though they were part of a large family business, not a hard-nosed professional concern. Greet comes across as an exacting, eagle-eyed disciplinarian as well as an inexhaustible, attentive, devoted, and occasionally impish and indulgent teacher. His players were older than one might imagine, most ranging in age from twenty-five to thirty-two.[4] As indicated, he made a practice of hiring siblings and married couples. Doing so not only made for happier, more stable and cohesive companies, but also used strong, established pairings to simplify arrangements in hotels, lodging-houses, and sleeper-cars. The handsome and insouciant Blind liked to tease and flirt with the innocent Thorndike, but he and the more experienced hands were generous with their help. Several of the older women carried well-stocked tea-baskets on campaign, the contents of which they dispensed (along with homey comfort and guidance) to Thorndike, who was literally 'fresh from the vicarage'.[5] Rivalries and pettiness may have existed, but scant trace of them can be found in Russell's book.

Sybil's letters also reveal that religion was a regular topic of conversation among company members. That a minister's daughter would mention it in letters home is hardly unusual. That Daisy Robinson, Agnes Elliott Scott (who voraciously consumed books about religion and philosophy), Frank Darch, Greet, and even Blind discussed it with her indicates a more widespread interest. Like Greet, Sybil and Russell were followers of the Rev. J. Stewart Headlam, and Sybil's rapid, not-so-short-term acceptance of

Christian Science in America illustrates that faith was a living, active part of her life.[6] The company performed religious plays, and religion was important to several of its members.

The last facet of company life the letters broadly speak to concerns the health of Greet's performers. The actor-manager required his artists to learn multiple roles in every play in the company's repertory, and Sybil's letters make clear why: illness and injury went hand-in-hand with touring. Unfamiliar food and water, extremities of temperature, insects (especially mosquitoes), a rigorous travel schedule, strange hotels and lodging houses — all on top of the physical demands associated with performing eight times a week in alien theatres and/or out-of-doors — took their toll, and the company had to be able to operate with several of its members *hors de combat*. Sybil's letters record several serious illnesses and injuries that season. In October, Blind developed an unspecified malady so severe he was forced to drop out of the tour for six weeks. Daisy Robinson's emergency appendectomy later that autumn and long convalescence kept her off the boards until spring. In March, Constance Crawley fell down a marble staircase in a hotel, knocking herself unconscious and injuring her back — the direct cause of Sybil being assigned her first professional engagement in a leading tragic role.[7] The life of an actor in a touring company, especially one that performed out of doors, was demanding.

In late September, the company stopped in Chicago for an appearance at the exclusive Onwentsia Club. Greet told Love 'we had 500 yesterday, 400 of them at $2.50'.[8] $2.50 being the price of the most expensive class of seat in the most expensive Broadway theatres, country-club appearances could be very profitable. An insatiable theatregoer, Greet was always taking his actors to plays. While in Chicago, he took Daisy and Sybil to *Romeo and Juliet* starring Julia Marlowe and E. H. Sothern. Sybil, who had never seen the play and was wont to declare that love bored her, wrote that Marlowe brought tears to her eyes: 'I've never heard anything more glorious than Julia Marlowe'.[9] Along with Richard Mansfield and Robert B.

Mantell, Marlowe and Sothern were two of the greatest Shakespearean actors who called America home in the first decade of the twentieth century. Already acclaimed in their own rights, the pair teamed up under Frohman's management for the 1904–05 season to tour *Hamlet, Romeo and Juliet*, and the rarely staged *Much Ado about Nothing* through America's largest cities — an undertaking so successful that they toured Shakespeare for the two seasons that followed. Possessing considerable skill and experience, an on-stage rapport that occasionally hinted the two might be doing more than playing (they would eventually marry), and Frohman's backing, the power-couple created far more interest in and awareness of Shakespeare's plays than Greet did.[10]

That said, the priorities and method he had introduced had started to influence the way in which their offerings were reviewed, if not presented. The stars' productions were old ones dusted off and made new by the addition of the other performer opposite its original lead. As we saw in Chapter Two, Sothern's *Hamlet* had received glowing notices in 1900, but something had changed by the time he revived it in 1904. Critic Charles E. Russell, who declared the actor's personation of the title-character superior to Irving's, Tree's, and even Forbes-Robertson's, nevertheless decried the mutilation of the text in the name of spectacle:

> In the play we are dealing with the profoundest problems that beset men, — irresolvable doubts, supernal mysteries, inevitable dooms. To such stupendous matters the *papier-mâché* and ballet, corps supernumaries of spectacle are merely grotesque. All there is in 'Hamlet' that any one really cares about is in the lines.[11]

The *Boston Evening Transcript* praised the *Romeo and Juliet* revival because it delivered more than stars and scenery. 'It is rarely if ever that lovers of Shakespeare hear blank verse spoken so fluently by one and all of a company of players,' its dramatic critic wrote. More important, the 'fine scenic display was given without distressing mutilation of the text'. The text had been cut to bring the show in at 195 minutes, but the excisions were judicious 'insomuch that the story of the tragedy runs along lucidly and without serious interruption. It is not always in an elaborate production that we get splendid scenic effect together with something more than the bare bones of the play'.[12] Completeness of text and quality of ensemble had joined the criteria by which some people were judging Shakespearean productions.

Greet's company travelled on to Berkeley, California, where it officially opened the season with another high-profile, open-air performance at the Greek Theatre. To commemorate the tercentenary of the publication of the Second Quarto *Hamlet*, Greet had decided to mount a production of the complete play featuring himself in the title-role. Because only one such production had been staged in living memory, Frank Benson's at Stratford-upon-Avon in 1899, Greet reckoned a sufficient number of Americans would be curious enough to justify the effort.[13] That he offered it almost exclusively at universities, and that his advertisements including expectation-lowering phrases such as 'The present performance should not be judged as an ordinary theatrical performance' and 'No new readings will be attempted, the whole endeavor being to give the play, with the scenes usually omitted, in a primitive manner as nearly as possible like that in which it as produced just 300 years ago' indicates he recognized that, whatever educational value the production possessed, its entertainment value was negligible.

The warnings were prudent. The actor-manager was a comedian, not a tragedian. Worse, he had committed to learn the entire part — something Booth, Irving, Forbes-Robertson, and Sothern never did. Although he had played the Dane in the cut-text production he mounted in Camberwell in 1897, he underestimated how difficult mastering the full role would be. Sybil recorded that he spent the journey from Glasgow to San Francisco swotting, and that he had not learned it all by the time they arrived in Berkeley. To salvage the performance, Greet created the role of 'Elizabethan prompter'; book in hand and dressed in common Elizabethan male attire, the especially clear-voiced Daisy Robinson would follow him round the playing area, feeding him lines when he faltered.[14]

As if cramming to learn the largest, best-known role Shakespeare ever wrote hours before one was to perform it in front of thousands of people was not sufficiently stimulating, Greet had to run through the blocking with not only his own actors, but also the members of the university's dramatic society taking walk-on parts and featured as Player King, Player Queen, and Lucianus. The actor-manager's decision to stop in Chicago, coupled with a weather delay en route to California, meant the company arrived barely a day before the performance at the Greek Theatre, for which Greet had only himself to blame.

Like the operas of Wagner sometimes were, Greet presented *Hamlet* in two parts separated by an hour-long intermission. The entire event lasted four-and-a-half-hours, and the start-time was selected so that the funeral rites at play's end would be illuminated by sunset over the Golden Gate. To make the production conform to the text in every detail, he had enlisted a military band from the Presidio to play the 'soldiers' music' that accompanied the dead prince's passage. As the four captains carried Hamlet's body into the sunset, a pair of cannon (also supplied by the installation's obliging commandant) placed on the hillside boomed out the stipulated 'peal of ordnance'.[15]

Advance bookings were strong and several thousand people took their seats in the Greek Theatre on an October day so perfect even locals remarked on its beauty. What they heard disappointed many who assumed they would be witnessing a performance of the complete *Hamlet* delivered to a uniformly professional standard.

The brief notices published in New York were polite. The *Dramatic Mirror* described it as 'successful' and reported 'an immense audience' of about 3,000 — an adequate turnout, though noticeably shy of the 4,000–5,000 who turned out for *Twelfth Night* there the previous year. The *New York Post*'s Henry Anderson Lafler regretted that the 'imperfect knowledge of the lines by many players, requiring the frequent interposition of the prompter' marred an otherwise good and instructive performance.[16]

The reviews in the local papers strongly disagreed with one another. The *San Francisco Call*'s Blanche Partington made no attempt to disguise her contempt. Sarcastically and at length, she ridiculed the amateurish nature of a performance memorable for the scores of dropped, paraphrased, and mangled lines; for clunky, illusion-dispelling devices used to prompt its unprepared leading man; and for its poor stage management — the only instance of such a charge being levelled at a Greet show I have found. Contrasting with that assessment was that of the *Oakland Examiner*'s Austin Lewis, who excoriated the hundreds of pretentious, mean-spirited undergraduates 'sick with the maladies of self conscious-ness and sham culture' who barely attended to the performance because they were so busy poring 'over their miserable texts' as if listening to one professor giving them his opinion of the interpreta-tions of three others. 'It was a refreshing delight to hear a little boy exclaim on the fall of the wicked King: "I am so glad"', the critic wrote. Lewis judged the production to have been so artistic as to have been beyond the imaginative capabilities of the multitudes that Spectacular Realism had numbed to restraint, subtlety, and human artistry. As he saw it, Greet's sole failing was not fielding the highly drilled professional company necessary to deliver a uniformly polished performance. The critic neither knew nor cared whether the players spoke every line; the presentation had been 'highly meri-torious', and the performers had 'set a standard for well balanced elocution and artistic reserve' as 'they produced great artistic effects without mechanical means'.[17]

That some audience members liked it and that Greet's hosts at the University of California, President Benjamin Ide Wheeler and Charles Mills Gayley, continued to enthusiastically support his work did not alter the fact that his Second Quarto *Hamlet* was a critical flop. The company performed it fewer than a dozen times, almost always sponsored by major educational institutions (Stanford University, Washington University, and the University of Michigan) before dropping it from the repertory in 1907.

A traditional, twenty-week, *Everyman-* and Shakespeare-intensive tour of California, Oregon, Washington, and British Columbia followed.[18] Formally launching it in the familiar surroundings of San Francisco's Lyric Hall, the company returned to the repertory that made the previous season so successful. After a fortnight performing the Morality and Elizabethan Manner Shakespeare (now including the actor-manager's *Much Ado*) to large and enthusiastic audiences, the company took to the road, alternating short stands in picturesque small towns with extended urban engagements.

Halfway across the country, an American *Everyman* company was launching its first tour. The Morality was popular and profitable; that a competitor would enter the market to service regions Greet was not visiting is hardly surprising. The company was led by none other than Chicago and Chautauqua Institute *Everyman* veteran Rudolph Magnus. Most of its bookings were in commercial theatres, but the young actor-manager had noted that performing at institutions of higher learning could be both profitable and good for establishing one's highbrow credentials. À la Greet, Magnus opened his season at the University of Notre Dame where, according to the *Dramatic Mirror*, his company delighted a large audience of undergraduates.[19]

Greet never took for granted the religious theatregoers whose support had been so critical to the success of *Everyman*. In November, the company presented *The Star of Bethlehem* for the first time in a commercial theatre on the West Coast: a special Sunday fundraiser in San Francisco's 1,500-seat Alhambra Theatre sponsored by the Catholic Truth Society. The next day, it opened a week-long run of the play in Lyric Hall during which the pupils and nuns of the local convent-schools were conspicuous. But playing to crowds of discount ticket-holders was no guarantee of profitability; Greet told Love he lost $1,000 that week.[20]

The company got a cool reception in Los Angeles despite solid notices in the city's papers. The 4,000-seat Hazard's Pavilion/Temple Auditorium probably felt very empty.[21] Portlanders did not care for Greet any more than Angelenos did. Attendance at the opulent, 1,442-seat Marquam Grand Theatre was disappointing despite *Everyman* stimulating local religious thought in the form of a sermon Dr Stephen S. Wise preached at Temple Beth Israel on the moral and educational value of theatre, the text of which appeared immediately below the Portland *Morning Oregonian*'s review of the Morality. Wise believed theatre exerted as powerful an educational influence as the schoolroom, the press, literature, government, or religion. He urged the members of his congregation to reward through attendance 'clean, decent plays' like *Everyman* and Shakespeare, and to punish through non-attendance 'the insulting purveyors of idiocy and filth' so as 'to make the most and best' of the institution that was theatre. By so doing, they would shape theatre into an even more educational and uplifting social force.[22] *Everyman* continued to inspire real religious thought.

Disaster struck a few days later. Writing home, Sybil reported: 'The business manager has bunked, with all the money. Poor Ben Greet is nearly frantic'. Writing to Love, the actor-manager estimated that the thief had taken between $3,000 and $4,000.[23] Appointing Maurice Robinson acting business manager, Greet sallied forth to secure the loans that would enable the company to continue operating.[24] A few days in decidedly English Vancouver over Christmas boosted morale, but the company's finances — and future — had become uncertain.[25]

The return engagement in Los Angeles in January did nothing to improve things; once more, Angelenos stayed away despite strong notices. One local critic voiced his frustration:

> It would be almost impossible for an audience to resist the fascination of such a play as 'Much Ado About Nothing' in the hands of actors of such abilities as the company which is playing here now to audiences which it is sad to confess about half fill the auditorium. It is a real play interpreted by artists, although it is apparent that only a few realize the fact.[26]

Greet offered blocks of significantly discounted tickets to schools and clubs in the hope of attracting a following, but to no avail. The situation was becoming increasingly grave.

The company limped east in February. Although it spent a week in Denver's 1,624-seat Broadway Theatre, most of its time was spent traveling and playing short engagements in the smaller cities of Nevada, Utah, Colorado, Kansas, Iowa, Illinois, and Wisconsin.[27] Exactly when Magnus's tour came to Greet's attention is unclear, but the *Dramatic Mirror* published a statement from the Englishman disavowing any connection with the American *Everyman* and declaring the superiority of his own.[28] Good or not, Magnus's production had already satisfied demand for the Morality in the Midwest — a fact Greet soon discovered. Writing to Love from rural Illinois in March, he declared

> One reason of our bad business in these parts is the fact that <u>those villains</u> have been doing 'Everyman' everywhere + giving such an awful show that the managers would not let us give it so we've had to put on 'Twelfth Night' which has been played to death all around here the last few years.[29]

Financial collapse loomed.

Suddenly and spectacularly, Greet's fortunes turned. Two businessmen he had met at the Onwentsia Club the previous autumn invited him to play an extended engagement in Chicago's 1,549-seat Studebaker Theatre, which they had just leased.[30] Their proposal inspired him to devise an ambitious plan to salvage the season. Shakespeare's birthday falling during the engagement, Greet decided to produce and advertise what he had already mounted a few times in England: a 'Shakespearean festival' — a phrase and concept still novel enough in the United States that it was likely to attract attention.[31] The company would present seven productions in three weeks, and Greet would sell subscriptions, normal tickets, and blocks of discounted tickets to encourage masses of schoolchildren and undergraduates to attend. To increase its appeal even further, he

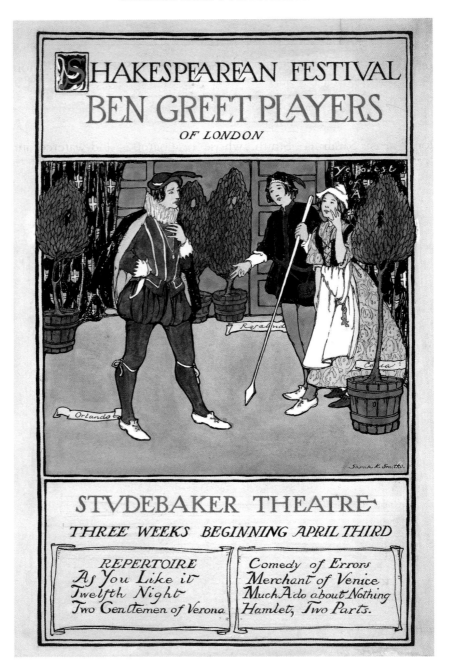

14. Sarah K. Smith. *Promotional poster for Shakespearean Festival, Ben Greet Players Studebaker Theatre, [Chicago, IL].* April 1905.

secured the services of Arnold Dolmetsch, the pioneering early music performer, historian, and instrument maker who had superintended the music for every Elizabethan Stage Society production before moving to Boston to work for Chickering & Sons.[32] Yet another enhancement came in the form of this handsome Arts-and-Crafts-style poster either Greet or the partners commissioned from local artist Sarah K. Smith, whose original pen-and-watercolour drawing Greet later presented to Emily and Henry Folger.[33]

Far more unusual — unique, in fact — was the proposal that arrived from the West Coast. In early April, the *San Francisco Call* reported that the president of the University of California, Dr Benjamin Ide Wheeler, was hoping Greet would accept a new professorship he wanted to create. Its duties would include mounting productions to supplement the courses in dramatic literature Greet would teach as a member of the Department of English and, in time, forming and heading a Department of Dramatics. The revolutionary nature of Wheeler's offer was not lost on the *New York Times*, which declared:

'Prof. Ben Greet, Department of Literature, University of California, Berkeley, California', will in all probability be the title and address of the Shakespearean actor- manager after this year [...]. This is probably the first time in history that an actor has been honored in this particular way. It is not an infrequent thing for prominent players to be called upon [...] to lecture upon drama [at ...] the leading institutions of learning [...]. But as far as is known the idea of including an actor in its Faculty has never before been seriously considered by any university.

Greet declined, but, as the same newspaper later observed, that decision had a tremendous impact on American culture because not being tied to a single campus is what enabled Greet to exert the influence he did. Although he had played barely a score of North American institutions by the time Wheeler made his offer, in time he and what the paper would dub his 'travelling Shakespeare university' would appear at more than 265 institutions on more than 780 dates.[34]

When scholars today recall the people who introduced Drama and Theatre instruction to American higher education, they think of academics such as George Pierce Baker (whose famous 'English 46' — the first course in the Dramatic Arts ever taught at an American institution of higher learning — had its inaugural run at Radcliffe during the 1903–04 academic year), Thomas H. Dickinson, Thomas Wood Stevens, Gertrude Johnson, and Frederick Henry Koch.[35] But as far as many Americans in 1905 were concerned, the most prominent champion of what would eventually be called the Education Theatre Movement was the internationally renowned practitioner-educator Ben Greet. His instructive mission and appearances at what in time became hundreds of institutions from coast to coast introduced and established a standard method for producing Shakespeare at American universities, colleges, and normal schools. More than anyone, Greet was responsible for creating North American Academic Shakespeare. And because he demonstrated the educational value of performed Shakespeare at so many institutions, he was also at the forefront of persuading Americans that Drama and Theatre were worthy of a place in higher education.

Back in the Midwest, popular response to Greet's Shakespearean festival idea was tremendous; the *Chicago Tribune* reported ticket sales strong enough to assure the financial success of the entire run. When Greet addressed the faculty and students of the University of Chicago's Department of English during the first week of the engagement, he remarked that, although most American audiences preferred theatricalism and trickery over substance and intelligence, there was cause for optimism: 'America is crazy over education [...]. It is a good craze, for it leads inevitably towards a greater interest in the true worth of the drama, and will result in the development of a truly artistic taste in higher development [i.e. education]'.[36] Gradually, people in higher education were developing a taste for Greet-style Shakespeare.

Chicagoans thronged the Studebaker to hear the company's performances despite almost entirely negative reviews in the *Tribune*. Greet was growing accustomed to the kinds of accusations levelled by supporters of Spectacular Realism, so statements from that paper's W. L. Hubbard and others that Elizabethan Manner taxed the imaginations and endurances of audience members were not especially surprising. New was the condemnation of the company as a whole, implicit in which was a criticism of the man who led it, trained many of its members, and designed its productions. Also new was the condemnation of full text on moral grounds. There were indecent words, ideas, and actions in these plays, and Greet should have cut them: 'Commonness and unpleasantness are not attractive, even if Shakespearean genius did put them on paper'. As far as the paper was concerned, the company's only virtues were its earnestness and educational zeal. *Twelfth Night* and *Everyman* were good, but every other production it reviewed it condemned. *The Merchant of Venice* displayed 'an almost total lack of all poetic or imaginative qualities', and Scott's Portia and Greet's Shylock were both found wanting. Several performers in *The Comedy of Errors* did not know all their lines, which state of affairs the commitment to full-text presentation rendered 'particularly evident and disturbing'. And of course the play contained the most vulgar passages. Although less controversial, *As You Like It* was a fiasco: 'A troupe of amateurs could not be more helpless and at sea in the delivery of the Shakespearean text than were the Greet players'.[37] The *Tribune* did not review Greet's *Hamlet*, *Much Ado*, or *The Two Gentlemen of Verona* — the only time Greet staged the comedy in the United States.

Strong advance sales helped insulate the company from the negative commercial effects of such harsh notices. Writing during the festival's second week, Greet told Love

> The audiences have crammed the theatre each time, + have been delighted + delightful, and the critics have simply <u>cursed</u> us. The Company is really <u>not</u> a good one, but they've been far better than the ordinary Cos of the day + the work + style is distinctly unique. But I think we shall take in some <u>$25000</u> […] or near it.

Demand for tickets to the only scheduled performance of the Second Quarto *Hamlet* was so heavy (500 people had to be turned away) that the actor-manager laid on another. (The absence of any reference to a prompter suggests he had finally mastered the title-role.) Although he revised downward the takings to $20,000 by run's end, the receipts were still strong. Chicagoans had rescued the tour and put the season solidly in the black. Greet was especially gratified to report to Love that thousands of area schoolchildren and undergraduates had attended the festival: 'I believe every school in the City came!'[38] His passionate belief in the educational value of Shakespeare's works was becoming fundamental to his vision of himself and his work.

The company was warmly received in the other Midwestern cities it visited. It became the first dramatic ensemble to play Minneapolis's new, cavernous (7,000 seats) Exposition Auditorium. The *Minneapolis Journal*'s W. B. Chamberlain reported the Morality 'kept the large audience rapt in attention' on opening night. Elizabethan Manner initially confused the same paper's Martha Scott Anderson, but the company's swift, spirited, and refined delivery completely won her over by the end of the performance. The company closed the regular season in the familiar surrounds of St Louis's 2,000-seat Odeon Theatre in May. Attendance was less robust than in 1903, but the papers commended Greet for giving Elizabethan drama 'a mighty impetus' in the city, particularly among the scores of high-school teachers who turned out. As he had at Berkeley and Stanford, the brave actor-manager invited local undergraduates — in this instance, members of Washington University's dramatic society — to join in the Second Quarto *Hamlet*.[39]

The 1905 Open-Air Season

Unusually, the company underwent two noteworthy personnel changes in the interval between the indoor and outdoor seasons. The sudden departure of Constance Crawley compelled Greet to replace her with an American journeyman named Adelaide

Alexander. More significant in the long term, the actor who would achieve the greatest renown of all of Greet's American protégés, Fritz Leiber, joined up with his brother, Allen.

For the first time in North America, Greet committed a company to an entire open-air season. It was a smart decision; the company did a roaring trade thanks to the growing demand for professional, outdoor Shakespeare that Greet had created, the highbrow celebrity the Berkeley offer had conferred on him, and the success of the Chicago festival.

Now aware that the continent was full of universities, colleges, and normal schools, and having established himself in the Midwest, Greet set about aggressively developing the higher education market in that region. Seats of higher learning accounted for more than a third of the company's bookings. The only familiar ones it visited were McGill, where the company presented its open-air *The Tempest* for the first time in North America, and Toronto, where the company gave six performances during commencement week.[40] The other institutions the company played were new to it and decidedly Midwestern, including Illinois, Milliken, Minnesota, Northwestern, Oberlin, and Purdue. Appearances by the Woodland Players would become annual traditions at several of them.

No North American university welcomed Greet on more occasions than the University of Michigan, which was the result of its Shakespeare professor, Isaac Newton Demmon, striking up a lasting friendship with the actor-manager.[41] That summer, the company gave six open-air performances on the Michigan campus. Gross receipts for the two it presented on 17 June totalled $1,371.00, of which the company's share was $959.30, or $259.30 more than the $350 per performance break-even figure Greet quoted to Love.[42] University work could be profitable. Another institution that hosted the company was the University of Cincinnati. Demand there was so strong that Greet doubled the length of the run, from four performances in two days to eight performances in four, *Billboard* reporting 'big business' at all of them.[43]

But the institution that gave the company the greatest support that season was the University of Chicago, which sponsored a week on the grounds of its School of Education's Scammon Gardens in July. Greet returning there for extended engagements in 1907, 1908, and 1909, to that institution goes the credit for hosting the United States's first annual Shakespearean festival. The university's students and the future teachers of the Midwest could not get enough of the actor-manager's open-air offerings.

While in the city, Greet noticed a private recreational development that had recently gone up in one of the northern suburbs. Its name was Ravinia Park, and it boasted a covered pavilion designed to host open-air concerts. He immediately booked twelve dates there.

The company gave a few private performances that summer, including one at the Burton estate on the shores of Minnesota's Lake Minnetonka that was the subject of a *Town and Country* article that featured this photograph of the actor-manager greeting attendees as they arrived. Another attention-getting appearance was the *As You Like It* presented in August at a farm near Sagamore Hill, the Roosevelt estate on Long Island. The entire First Family had originally been scheduled to attend, but the president was forced to bow out at the last minute. Still, the enthusiastic reception from Mrs Roosevelt, the president's children, and several members of the Roosevelt clan made for good publicity.[44]

One final detail from that summer bears mention. The leads of the ill-fated 'Woodland Players' tour of 1904, Ivah M. Wills and Charles D. Coburn, took the field once again. Wiser for having survived the collapse of Kilfoil's company, they formed their own open-air company, the Coburn Shakespearean Players, with which to tour their own production of *As You Like It* through the country clubs of New England and New York. With little outdoor experience and only one production to their name, they were hardly in a position to challenge Greet, but the considerable success his outdoor company enjoyed that summer encouraged them to set their sights on doing just that.

15. Sweet. *Ben Greet Observing the Audience.*
Burton Estate, Lake Minnetonka, MN, 1 July 1905.

The 1905–06 Season

In late October, the Ben Greet Players gave two performances in Poughkeepsie, New York, both of which were well-attended by the women of Vassar. One of the students wrote a poem for the college magazine about what she witnessed:

Ode on a Ben Greetian Urn
  (Apologies to Keats.)
Thou noted artist actor of our day,
Thou devotee of methods stale and worn,
Would-be Elizabethan, who dost press
On us the obsolete joys of a by-gone time,
A lack of foot-lights, and a dearth of paint,
An unchanged costume, and an uncurled wig,
A 'setting' sitting still from start to end,

145

No rising curtain, and no leading man,
No orchestra, no star to gaze upon,
No dear illusions, and no anything!
O portly shape! Fair actor Greet! with hoard
Of beef-eaters; and female page-boys lade
With sad old furniture. An organ cracked;
Some waiting ladies in ill-fitting gowns;
And men in rusty swords; yet Mr. Greet!
Though Edith Wynne hath left thy company,
Thou still dost draw, in midst of other shows,
Large crowds, *thyself* thy star, of whom we say,
'Benny is Greet, Greet Benny' — that is all
We know of him, and all we need to know.[45]

The image the poem evokes — a star-less, visibly shabby company whose manager's singular Shakespearean vision and method continued to enable it to draw audiences — was fitting prologue to the 1905–06 season.

Greet decried stars and the star-system, but if he wanted to remain in business he had to productively respond to the two star-related facts that confronted him: Shakespeare's plays were written for a company that had several, and Greet's company no longer had any. Equally problematic, his insistence on full texts and bare stages focused attention squarely on the actors and the words they spoke. Their skills needed to be good in order to hold audiences exclusively through their ability to deliver Shakespeare's lines. Greet knew the quality of his company's performances was inconsistent and sometimes poor. To make things worse, his most experienced players, Helena Head and Leonard Shepherd, had departed during the break. Of the twenty-eight members his company now contained, perhaps ten consistently achieved a professional standard. Until such time as he could bring them all to a higher standard, the actor-manager needed to find an audience willing to pay for — and accept — lower-quality acting.

Shakespeare for schools had proved as popular in Chicago in 1905 as it had in London in 1897, and Greet's collaboration with Charles Sprague Smith and the People's Institute in 1904 suggested the idea might have a future in New York. Exhibiting the creativity that enabled him to survive for decades as a professional actor-manager, Greet turned his company into a travelling school. As he taught his players their craft, they would teach tens of thousands of schoolchildren what fast-paced, full-text, spectacle-less Shakespeare sounded and looked like. This enterprise received its baptism by fire in America's most cutthroat theatrical market in the face of semi-competition from the country's greatest Shakespearean interpreters, and it would test not only Greet's business acumen, but also the power of his vision and method.

With the help of Canadian actor-submanager Frank McEntee, Greet secured the official cooperation of William H. Maxwell, the Superintendent of the New York Public Schools, and Henry N. Tifft, the President of the New York Board of Education. *Julius Caesar* and *Macbeth* being curricular requirements in the city that year, Greet agreed to mount the tragedies, the former possibly for the first time in his career.[46] He now had access to a substantial new audience: the school-children of greater New York. To get it into his theatre (the authorities had granted their approval, not allocated funds), he reconnected with Smith and the People's Institute. Together, they recruited a dozen philanthropic and social outreach organizations to sponsor a month-long Shakespearean festival. The schools, clubs, and societies of some of the city's poorest citizens snapped up the blocks of discounted tickets they offered, and the idea got some good press thanks to an article Greet penned for *Harper's Weekly* in which he expressed his eagerness to bring Shakespeare to poor children and adults.[47]

Careful management would be needed to ensure he stayed in business while he played teacher. When a philanthropy fully sponsored a performance (hiring the venue and paying the company's fee), the audience could comprise primarily discount ticket-holders. When one partially sponsored a performance (hiring the venue), the audience needed to comprise primarily full-priced ticket-holders. Greet needed to determine commercially feasible ratios of full-priced-to-discount-priced tickets, which he seems to have fixed at 4:1 and 1:4, respectively. More difficult, he needed to continue to attract a substantial number of full-priced customers despite having a company known to lack experience that appeared before audiences known to contain many more schoolchildren than normal. The slightly discounted festival subscriptions and full-priced tickets would be purchased by Greet's usual clientele: New York highbrows attracted to his method and new productions. Possessing both money and choice, these were the customers for whom Greet had to directly compete against the big-time Shakespearean operations, offering Elizabethan Manner while the others offered stars and Spectacular Realism.

Greet's first home in America, the 1,100-seat Mendelssohn Hall, would serve once again as the company's base of operations. His productions requiring no curtains, machinery, or advanced lighting, he could stage them in a concert hall, which cost less to lease than a theatre in an equally central location. The company would give six performances a week there rather than the normal eight so it could play two non-Broadway venues its sponsors had secured: the well-appointed, 1,300-seat hall in the Brooklyn Institute of Arts and Sciences, and the bare-bones, 700-seat auditorium in the Educational Alliance on the Lower East Side. The *New York Press*'s Edward E. Pidgeon described the latter neighbourhood, then commonly referred to as 'the Ghetto', as 'more densely and disgracefully populated than any other place in this world', before noting that young people there were abandoning the Yiddish theatre (including Shakespeare in Yiddish) of their immigrant parents for the popular Anglophone entertainment called 'Bowery melodrama'. The Educational Alliance, which sought to bring 'elevating' drama (i.e. productions of classical and morally uplifting plays normally mounted by amateurs) to the area's inhabitants, was delighted to announce that 'Shakespeare, in the person of his apostle, Ben Greet' would personally lead the latest mission to deliver the area's residents 'from the darkness of decadence'. Pre-performance lectures and discussions of the plays would be laid on to enhance their educational value. The critic also reported that

> Mr. Greet is very enthusiastic as to the possibilities […]. He realizes what a great and noble work it is to open up unexpected realms to mentally benighted thousands […] to whom the intellectual beauties of English drama never before have been disclosed […]. If entertainment alone is afforded by the drama, it has a slight mission. These performances not only will entertain and edify, but stimulate the intellect and the heart.[48]

As patronizing as Pidgeon was, he correctly identified the evangelical fervour that animated the actor-manager.

The festival comprised *Henry V*, *Macbeth*, *Julius Caesar*, *Much Ado*, *Merchant*, and *Twelfth Night* in the Elizabethan Manner. Greet would stage them in a fit-up that represented a public Elizabethan playhouse, either because his experiences in 1904 taught him that audiences wanted that or because Maxwell and Tifft made it a requirement. I have been unable to locate a picture of the one he used, but the newspapers described it including a sizeable set-piece that simulated two pairs of pillars representing the ones that supported the sloping roof of the tiring-house. Like Poel and his American imitators, Greet hung a traverse curtain between the downstage pair.[49] Once again, Dolmetsch and his ensemble provided period music.

Four weeks' steady work (soon extended to five) would give Greet the time he needed to book the rest of the season. More important, it would give the company a substantial period in one place in which to rehearse, perform, and generally improve the quality of its work. The impact Greet's energetic tuition had on his actors soon became apparent. Now writing for the New York *Sun*, John Corbin described them at the beginning of the festival as 'intelligent and well-schooled amateurs'. After hearing them a few weeks later, he revised his assessment of the ensemble's quality to nearer to that of a 'very able stock company'.[50] The challenges the company faced were certainly sufficient to stimulate its members to work hard. A big company and a roof over one's head were comforting, but presenting a repertory of seven plays, three of which were entirely new to them (and one of which may have been new to Greet), was not. Equally sobering was the knowledge that the company would be doing so when Manhattan was rife with top-tier Shakespearean offerings, a few of which duplicated its own. For, wittingly or not, Greet had scheduled it into the city at the same time the two biggest Shakespearean operations in America were kicking off their seasons there.

Produced by Frohman at the elegant Knickerbocker Theatre, the Marlowe-Sothern combination launched the second of its three Shakespearean seasons. From mid-October to late November, the stars presented Spectacular Realism productions of *Merchant*, *Romeo and Juliet*, *The Taming of the Shrew*, and *Twelfth Night*. In late October, one of the last of the old-school tragedians, Robert B. Mantell, opened his season at the Garden Theatre. There, he offered his famously lavish Spectacular Realism productions — his management team liked to advertise the fact that he toured with five, 60'-long baggage cars full of sets, costumes, and props — until mid-December in a repertory that included *Richard III*, *Othello*, *Hamlet*, *Macbeth*, and *King Lear*. At the same time and in the same place, three very different companies were about to test the old Broadway adage 'Shakespeare does not pay'.

Following several weeks of rehearsal, Greet tested the company with a few performances outside of the city. Apart from the ones in Poughkeepsie referenced above, probably the most notable was the *Henry V* in Princeton University's Alexander Hall pictured here. The company's official opener took place on 30 October, when it began one of the most culturally influential seasons in its history.

The festival got off to a rocky start. Reviews of *Merchant* stated that the company's standard had dropped appreciably since its last appearance in the city and that many of its unidentified performers could only be described as amateurs.[51] (Our knowledge of who played what this season is obscured by Greet's decision to print in the programmes a *dramatis personae* and a separate, alphabetical cast-list so that neither

16. Anonymous. HENRY V.
Dir. Ben Greet, Princeton University, Princeton, NJ, 2 November 1905.

praise nor blame could be individually apportioned.) The *Dramatic Mirror* thought highly of the trial scene and of Dolmetsch's music, commenting that Greet's simple staging was just as effective as the magnificent settings Marlowe and Sothern employed. However, its critic noted that Alexander's unconvincing Portia, Greet's uneven Shylock, and several of the supporting players' unfamiliarity with their lines made for a disappointing performance.[52]

Henry V drew mixed notices that agreed on two points: the acoustics in the newly renovated hall were dreadful and capacity audiences attended closely and applauded enthusiastically. The *Evening Post's* negative review described it as having 'been dulled by the lack of animation, intelligence, and vigor in the speed and action of some of the chief performers', none of whom possessed the skill or power of their predecessors. The *Morning Telegraph* likened the Elizabethan fit-up to a Punch and Judy booth, which would have been a preferable entertainment given that puppets knew and projected their lines. The reviewer found the Chorus, a character long-since banished from the stage, a ridiculous conceit and asked why not just have one character narrate the whole play? The *New-York Tribune's* negative review noted that, although Greet's method allowed the full text to be spoken, his players' disappointing elocution and the hall's bad acoustics rendered the play literally unintelligible at points. More encouraging, the *Dramatic Mirror* found the presentation 'interesting and instructive'; no strong individual performances were delivered, but, judged as a whole, the company was conscientious and able. The *Evening World* commended 'the universal excellence' of the performers and asserted that 'No Shakespeare play has been acted in more scholarly and generally acceptable fashion in years in New York'. The *Sun*'s Corbin pointed out what he believed were the archaeological inaccuracies of Greet's stage and traverse curtain, but he found much to praise about the performance, which, by presenting the playwright's original vision, maintained and promoted audience interest: '[it] kept my attention and sent me away in a glow of enjoyment — which is more than I can say for the rival and scenic production', meaning the Marlowe-Sothern *Merchant* he had negatively reviewed in the preceding paragraphs.[53]

Greet's strength as an actor being comedy, his *Much Ado* elicited considerably more praise. The *Evening World* lauded production and performances alike. The *New York Press* liked it even more, stating that it marked a return to the company's 1904 standard. The *Evening Telegram* considered it flawed in several respects, but praised the careful delivery of the lines and the textual reverence it exhibited. Its critic reported that Alexander's Beatrice and Greet's Benedick had delighted a large, appreciative, and unusually attentive audience, many of whose members followed along in the texts they carried. Others similarly praised the work of the leads and noted the enthusiastic reception the performance elicited.[54]

Greet's only direct clash with a star came the following week when he and Mantell simultaneously unveiled very different productions of *Macbeth*. (The appearance of the latter, costumed as the thane, on the cover of the November issue of *Theatre* spoke to the skill of those who managed and promoted him.) Critics praised the star's nervous and fearful interpretation as well as Marie Booth Russell's sweetly sly Lady Macbeth, but noted that the skills of their supporting players, many of whom did not know their lines or understand their meaning, was shockingly low.[55]

Several papers commented on the large audience that turned out for the first presentation of Greet's production, at which schoolchildren followed along in their texts and frequent and hearty applause was common, especially for the actress who played Lady Macbeth. The *Morning Telegraph* judged the show insufficiently Elizabethan. After restating his stage-depth and traverse-curtain objections, the *Sun*'s Corbin criticized the cauldron scene, which he regarded as being not only ineffectively staged, but also textually inaccurate because the actor-manager had failed to cut from it the interpolated lines by Thomas Middleton. Otherwise, the critic had been impressed, particularly by Greet's restoration of Shakespeare's 'Enter the Ghost of Banquo, and sits in Macbeth's place' — a stage direction abandoned generations earlier in favour of the protagonist shouting at the empty air. Corbin concluded by reiterating the value of the company's work:

> The signal fact [...] is that [they] present the text entire, with the scenes played in the order in which they were written to be played, and run off with desirable rapidity. Of the effect of this performance on the audience there is no question. Applause was frequent and spontaneous, and when the fighting climax approached many affrighted ladies got up and left — a tribute seldom paid to Shakespeare when the narrative is cut, distorted, and dragged out to make way for supposedly effective scenery.

The *Dramatic Mirror* conceded that Greet's mediocre company had held a large audience spellbound for several hours using little more than Shakespeare's words. What marvels might a similar production accomplish were 'really competent artists' to present it? Possibly borrowing some of Corbin's erudition, the writer criticized Greet for not cutting the Middleton passages before stating that, as interesting and educational as Elizabethan Manner was, the restoration of Banquo's ghost to the boards ultimately confirmed the superiority of modern practice.[56]

The dearth of coverage of Greet's *Julius Caesar* indicates the papers considered it unworthy of review. The *Dramatic Mirror* described an attentive audience pleased to hear a full-text version of a tragedy that was frequently produced, but always with spectacle and large sections of the text excised, before reminding readers of why Greet continued to draw audiences: 'Mr. Greet has not sufficient resources to command the most superior talent, yet the artistic, literary, and educational value of his work is as undeniable as it is obvious'.[57]

Outlook published the only detailed account of one of the Lower East Side performances I have found, a review also notable for being audience-focused in describing important matters rarely mentioned — specifically, the effect Greet's work had on a diverse, non-Protestant, lowbrow audience. Perhaps even more important, it records a rowdy, sustained, 'Elizabethan' interaction between an audience and a company of players — a phenomenon that had been theorized, but never witnessed. The magazine's critic, 'Spectator', had seen Matthison's Viola in 1904, and declared that, although her successor was inadequate to her in every way, *Twelfth Night* at the scruffy Educational Alliance had been 'an incomparably more dramatic occasion' than the one at the magnificent Knickerbocker:

> 'Doesn't it seem to you,' whispered one of the Spectator's companions
> [...] looking about into the faces, young and old, of the crowd that filled
> every inch of the hall, 'as if it were a Shakespearean audience as well as a
> Shakespearean play? I mean, Shakespeare wrote for the public, and the
> Elizabethan public wasn't always able to read and write, and lived under
> rude conditions. I have heard that Mr. Greet especially enjoys playing here,
> and that the company says it inspires them far more than the regulation
> Mendelssohn Hall uptown audience [...].' It certainly looked that way. Play
> and audience reacted to one another. There was a freedom, an enjoyment,
> up and down the aisles [...] that uptown theatres know nothing of.

Realizing that Viola, a role Shakespeare wrote for a comparatively inexperienced performer, was going to provide them with little of the entertainment they craved, the members of the audience shifted their attention to the comic subplot:

> In response, the actors did practically the same thing. Malvolio, Maria, Sir Toby, Andrew Aguecheek, and the Clown were applauded to the echo, and threw themselves with unction into the frolic. Was it so, the Spectator wondered, in the Globe Theatre, when a boy took the part of Viola […]? The sea-captain, too — was his impassioned fidelity to Sebastian one of the best climaxes of the performances at the Globe? It was so on the East Side, which gave Orsino's exquisite speeches only a languid attention in contrast. How even the children — and it was a family affair, that audience — laughed over Malvolio's reading of the letter, and Sir Toby's by-play! The mirth was uproarious whenever Andrew Augucheek made a point, and reached its climax in his duel with Viola […]. A more responsive audience in these scenes the Bard of Avon never saw.

Spectator had feared the hall would be crammed with school-children, their noses buried in textbooks. Instead, he saw only eager young faces

> manifestly unconscious of anything but the play, and ignorant of what was going to happen next in the story. 'Isn't it encouraging', said one of the party, as they came out among the crowd into the dinginess of East Broadway, 'to feel how really great things belong to everybody, and that Shakespeare cannot be cornered by the cultured? And did you ever see Shakespeare more sympathetically through the eyes of others, than to-night? I'm sure the Educational Alliance educated me this evening, for one'. Which was just what the Spectator felt, too.[58]

By gutting Shakespeare's subplots for the sake of star speeches and spectacle, producers had warped his plays and extinguished much of their fun. Similarly, the highbrow cultural position Greet occupied often obscured the fact that few things gratified him more than showing poorly educated audiences how much fun those works could

be when presented in something like their original form. At least one
audience repaid him by throwing itself into a performance so enthusiastically that it became the engaged audience Poel, Sargent, Baker, and
Short had had to dress and rehearse supernumeraries to simulate. Such
extraordinary experiences might explain why Greet was so passionate
about playing for schoolchildren and the poor; if the spheres aligned
just so, he just might feel the embrace of an Elizabethan audience.

Three Shakespearean tours simultaneously turning profits in
Manhattan had become unusual enough that the *New York World*
published a tongue-in-cheek field-guide to the distinct species of
Shakespeare devotees flocking to the various houses. Greet attracted
'fair aenemic damsels' who affected sandals, 'prim little women with
neatly parted hair' who wore thick glasses and carried playbooks, and
tortured poets with long hair and soiled linens.[59] One of the leading
Catholic magazines declared that the runs demonstrated nothing less
than the superiority of American virtue and taste over those of the
English, whose new-found and misplaced passion for the immoral
George Bernard Shaw had threatened to cross the Atlantic. That
Shaw would conquer the United States seemed all but certain at the
outset of the season, but Shakespeare's champions — Mantell, the
Marlowe-Sothern combination, and Greet — had united to hurl the
invader back into the sea: 'It is a great satisfaction that in New York
Shakespeare swatted [Shaw] good and hard, perhaps forever'.[60]

As some of the above-referenced notices indicate, the tours
touched off another round in the Spectacular Realism vs.
Elizabethan Manner debate. Rebuking those who questioned the
value of scenic display, the pro-spectacle *Billboard* demanded to
know how anyone could be so misguided as to advocate the aban-
donment of two centuries of progress in stagecraft:

> The eye must be pleased along with the intellect for perfect effect, and the
> gems of thought in the master playwright's work must be mounted with
> all the magnificence befitting them. New York has never before enjoyed
> such a feast of Shakespeare as the present. The Sothern-Marlowe combi-

nation [...] and Robert Mantell's company [...] are providing intellectual provender for those who have grown lean on dramatic food of a less substantial quality. Of an entirely different order is Ben Greet's revival [...]. True, it is Shakespeare as Shakespeare is supposed to have been played [...] when stage effects were an unknown quantity, and acting was in the embryo. But it attracts rather because of its eccentricities than through merit of the tried and true variety.

In a separate piece, the paper described the Ben Greet Players as able, but 'terribly handicapped' by its lack of 'accessories and up-to-date stage management'. Its leader may have drawn audiences, but his method would never attract imitators. The perennially pro-Elizabethan Manner *Evening Post* advocated nothing less than the violent overthrow of spectacular staging of Shakespearean plays, and proclaimed Greet's productions to be the ideal weapon with which to strike down the tyranny of theatrical excess and textual butchery:

The real importance of Mr. Greet's work lies in its demonstration that great plays are comparatively independent of the added attractions of scenery, even when they are represented by performers of ordinary ability. Incidentally, they demonstrate also the absurdity of reducing a play to a skeleton, or utterly destroying its natural proportions, coherence, and sequence for the sake of extravagant spectacular adornments, which, in nine cases out of ten, are ridiculously out of place [...]. It is absurd [...] to pretend to produce a play because it is universally admitted to be an immortal masterpiece, and then chop and hack it remorselessly in order to give the stage carpenter time to prepare an elaborate panorama. Of late the rule with Shakespearean revivals has been a minimum of text with the maximum of glitter produceable [*sic*] by the painters and costumers. Mr. Greet's work is a protest against, and is utterly destructive of, these barbaric and childish notions. He puts the creator of these works foremost, in the place where he belongs.[61]

Greet's ideas had taken root.

Shakespeare for schoolchildren had been a huge success, generating so much interest and demand that Smith asked Greet to extend the festival for another fortnight. Reluctant to throw the company's next engagement into too much disarray, Greet offered him a one-week extension followed by a week-long return to Brooklyn in January. Smith accepted . . . and then immediately invited Mantell to supply the desired sixth consecutive week. The star accepted, generously supplying blocks of discounted tickets for all eight performances. His profits probably dipped a little, but he could afford it, especially when doing so enhanced his personal reputation in New York — a state he had been forced to avoid for more than a decade because of a rigorously enforced arrest warrant that had once awaited him there, the result of an adultery-divorce-remarriage scandal that the New York authorities believed also involved bigamy because Mantell had failed to obtain a divorce in that state before marrying his next wife.[62] By helping the People's Institute, Mantell made an ally of the morally upright Smith, who seems to have been thrilled to have secured the services of a genuine (if once-notorious) star. Instilling a love for theatre was a commendable educational goal, and the tragedian's shows excelled at doing that. And most Americans still believed that their impressive costumes, sets, and special effects more than compensated for their non-Shakespearean scene-orders and dearth of Shakespearean lines.

Greet seems to have led a more sedate personal life. As Alman discovered, he accepted an invitation to dine at the home of the Folgers that December. Never one to let a promotional opportunity pass him by, he wrote to them a few weeks later asking whether they might be willing to 'stir up a few people' when his company returned to Brooklyn.[63]

Another event touching upon Greet happened as 1905 drew to a close: William Poel made his first visit to the United States. Poel's biographer states that he did so to promote Greet's *Everyman* tour, but the fact that Greet did not present the Morality once that season indicates otherwise. As the American newspapers and George

Pierce Baker's biographer make clear, Poel came to tour a lecture. With Baker's assistance, he presented 'The Shakespearean Play-House' at Brown, Columbia, Cornell, Harvard, Johns Hopkins, Mt Holyoke, Toronto, and Wellesley that November and December.[64]

Back in Boston for the first time in two years, the Ben Greet Players opened a month-long educational festival at the New England Conservatory's 1,000-seat Jordan Hall, Dolmetsch and his ensemble once again providing the music.[65] Subscription sales were strong and sales for individual performances were fair, but the run proved considerably less remunerative than Greet anticipated. Several factors worked against him. The Marlowe-Sothern tour offered stiff competition, not only because the stars were turning in fine performances, but also because their special effects were unusually impressive. Jordan Hall was a beautiful venue with perfect acoustics, but its out-of-the-way location depressed the walk-in trade. And owing to the extension of the Manhattan run and miscommunication with one of the Boston sponsors, Greet's festival had failed to secure the agreed-upon number of schools. Upon learning this, he immediately contacted the Boston School Committee, which responded so enthusiastically that it hurt his profits: it ordered twenty, 200-seat blocks of 25¢ tickets over and above the blocks the sponsors had already sold. Greet fulfilled the order almost certainly knowing that doing so would cause several performances to lose money. In mid-December, he confessed to Love that the financial situation had become so shaky that he might have to abandon the tour.[66]

Critical reaction to the company's first offering was negative, the usually supportive *Boston Evening Transcript* having little good to say about *Henry V*. The audience had been large, but the performance 'missed the spirit and atmosphere of the play'. Save for Alexander's commendable Katherine and Greet's excellent Pistol, the performances had been awful: the actors' 'faces were as blanks. Gesture was unknown to them, except as a rare afterthought. They shunned movement as though some fearsome peril lurked in it. They just stood [...] and recited verses they had learned not too accurately'.[67]

The paper was considerably more impressed by *Much Ado*. Its critic lauded the superb staging and commented that its simplicity proved how unnecessary spectacle was to successfully mount the rarely performed and underappreciated comedy. Greet's Benedick was excellent, Scott's Beatrice graceful and energetic, and the other parts 'more than respectably well done', revealing the 'unfailing intelligence and evidently pious and painstaking preparation' of Greet's actors.[68]

Like Corbin, the paper's dramatic critic reserved the highest praise for Greet's *Macbeth*. The writer thought the performances were solid and occasionally fine, but was most impressed by Greet's imagination, which in that production rivalled that of the world's most inspired directors. His use of off-stage sounds, his handling of the witches, and his deliberate slowing and speeding of the pace at key moments were excellent. The play was more powerful when Banquo's ghost was omitted, but the way Greet made him 'appear from the group of courtiers and then vanish through them' was 'uncannily illusive'. For the first time, Elizabethan Manner achieved the full power and immediacy of the modern professional theatre:

> In a word, Shakespeare was dramatically alive for Mr. Greet and kindling his imagination. He was no longer a 'snuffy' Shakespeare of folios and quartos [...]. He had ceased to be Shakespeare, educator of preparatory schools. He was Shakespeare, dramatist and poet of December, 1905, and in his fittest place, acted, really acted, on the stage.[69]

The tragedy's prominence in high school curricula, coupled with the accolades the production received from influential papers in New York and Boston, encouraged the actor-manager to put it into frequent rotation.[70] Although Dolmetsch stopped touring with the company at the end of the Boston engagement, Greet hired other musicians to continue playing his arrangements for the remainder of the season.

The week-long engagement in Brooklyn's Institute of Arts and Science in early January, during which the company gave ten, sold-out performances to schoolchildren, officially closed the New York educational festival and returned the company to a more solid financial footing. From there, it moved on to educational festivals in other major cities for the remainder of the season. Newspaper accounts and Greet's letters attest to the company doing good-to-excellent business before large and appreciative audiences.[71] The actor-manager gleefully reported receipts of $5,500 at the four performances it gave in Philadelphia's 3,100-seat Academy of Music, the audiences of which were made up primarily of schoolchildren for whom the Philadelphia Teachers' Association had procured blocks of discounted tickets.[72] Such profits would have pleased him any time, but generating them when the Marlowe-Sothern *and* Mantell tours were also in the city increased their symbolic value.[73] Playing Washington's Belasco Theatre (1,548 seats) for a week, the company had to lay on an extra matinee of *Macbeth* to accommodate the massive demand for student tickets that Greet helped drum up by delivering lectures on Elizabethan drama at area high schools.[74] The week in Montreal's 2,000-seat His Majesty's Theatre was disappointing.[75] Not so the engagement in Toronto's 4,000-seat Massey Hall, where a capacity crowd composed almost entirely of schoolchildren attended the extra matinee performance of *Merchant* Greet added. He reported profits of $8,000 in Toronto during a week-long run that the *Dramatic Mirror* confirmed was 'highly successful from a monetary standpoint'.[76] With sufficient planning and big enough venues, Shakespeare for schoolchildren could be money-maker.

The company launched a two-week educational festival in the familiar surroundings of Chicago's Studebaker Theatre in late February. Its last indoor appearance in the city had been a critical flop but a commercial success. The 1906 visit failed on both counts. Writing to Love at the end of the run, Greet confessed 'we have been dropped like a hot coal except by the schools. The Women's Clubs let us right alone: — the critics either scorned or ignored or violently abused'.[77] As sarcastic as W. L. Hubbard's review of Greet's *Macbeth* was, it was more positive than several of the ones he and his colleagues at the *Chicago Tribune* had penned the previous spring.

Hubbard dryly observed that Greet's decision to rehearse his company had produced good results: the actors not only knew their lines now, but they also moved like they understood their meanings. True, they still lacked subtlety, poetry, and imagination, but they spoke all the words, and they did so accurately, intelligibly, and distinctively. The critic conceded that watching the performance had almost been as good as reading the play, which remained the superior experience because it did not overwhelm one with copious amounts of 'gory, red gore', and other 'artistic touches' best left to the imagination.[78] The imposing presence of Mantell, who opened at the city's Grand Opera House while Greet's players were still in town, did not help matters. Chicago's theatregoers and critics wasted no time lavishing praise on the star and his work, particularly on his performance as King Lear, which was uncommonly fine that season. The Chicago Shakespeare Club threw a dinner to honour him, an event for which Greet was asked to deliver one of the after-dinner speeches, which he did.[79]

Leaving Chicago in mid-March, the company spent the remainder of the season playing venues in the Midwest, including St Louis's 2,000-seat Odeon Theatre, Cincinnati's Springer Auditorium (at 3,623 seats, the city's highest-capacity venue), and the 1,700-seat Caleb Mills Auditorium in Indianapolis's Shortridge High School.[80] It closed the season on May 1.

Strategically and systematically, Greet developed a major new audience for Shakespeare during the 1905–06 season: schoolchildren. His imagination, managerial creativity, and religious-educational beliefs had inspired the idea. His competence as a producer, his prominence as an early drama practitioner-educator, and his moral reputation enabled him to realize it. Although the evidentiary record is not complete enough to permit an exact tally of all the schoolchildren who heard the company that season, a projection based on seating capacities and confirmed performances in the primary and secondary cities in which it played yields an estimated attendance of 77,149. The lessons this season-long experiment taught Greet would help him reach nearly twice that number of schoolchildren every year between 1915 and 1921.

TABLE 1.
Estimated Attendance by Poor Schoolchildren and Adults, 1905–06 Season

Fully Sponsored Performances
(poor schoolchildren/adults = 80 per cent of house)

City	Venue	Seating Capacity	Performances	Total
Manhattan	Education Alliance	700	4	2,240
Brooklyn	Academy of Arts & Sciences	1,300	15	15,600
Philadelphia	Academy of Music	3,100	4	9,920
Washington	Belasco T	1,548	1	1,238
Toronto	Massey Hall	4,000	1	3,200
Indianapolis	Shortridge HS	1,700	5	6,800
Sub-total				38,998

Partially Sponsored Performances
(poor schoolchildren/adults = 20 per cent of house)

City	Venue	Seating Capacity	Performances	Total
Manhattan	Mendelssohn Hall	1,100	26	5,720
Boston	Jordan Hall	1,000	32	6,400
Washington	Belasco T	1,548	8	2,477
Montreal	His Majesty's T	2,000	8	3,200
Toronto	Massey Hall	4,000	8	6,400
Chicago	Studebaker T	1,549	16	4,957
St. Louis	Odeon T	2,000	8	3,200
Cincinnati	Springer Auditorium	3,623	8	5,797
Sub-total				38,151
TOTAL				77,149

The actor-manager's importance as a popularizer was growing, but critics were paying less attention to his work now that the novelty of Elizabethan Manner was wearing off. In an assessment of the most disparate Shakespearean offerings of the 1905–06 season, a writer for the monthly *World To-Day* wrote:

> The most strenuous effort in the way of real acting is that exhibited by Robert Mantell. His 'Lear,' Macbeth,' 'Othello' and 'Hamlet,' pitched in a fervent melodramatic key, are yet done with laudable sincerity.

> The Ben Greet Players have not met with a reception worthy of their intelligent attempts to subordinate the actor to the greatest of playwrights. But no thoughtful listener has come from their performances without a new sense of the dignity of Shakespeare simply staged and without appreciation of the self-sacrificing effort of Mr. Greet to make the theater a vehicle of something other than questionable sensations.[81]

Stars were what attracted audiences, not complete texts, strong ensembles, or authentic atmosphere.

The 1906 Open-Air Season

That Greet mounted a less-ambitious (nine-week) open-air tour that summer was the result of him having booked several high-profile appearances in England, including one at Carisbrooke Castle before the kings and queens of England and Spain.[82] After six months of Shakespeare for schools, he was ready to bring a smaller, more talented company (only the most accomplished members of the Ben Greet Players were invited to tour with the Woodland Players) back to wealthy American highbrows. Playing to smaller audiences of wealthier people was almost always more profitable than playing to large audiences of poorer ones. As he had at private and/or philanthropic performances in previous seasons, Greet regularly charged between $2.00 and $3.00 a ticket — the price of an excellent seat in a top-tier Broadway theatre.[83]

One prominent engagement the company fulfilled that season was a series of performances in Washington, DC's Woodley Park to benefit the Cathedral Close School. On 18 May, the double bill of *The Tempest* and *A Midsummer Night's Dream* attracted some 2,000 people, including Mrs Roosevelt and daughter Ethel, Justice and Mrs Oliver Wendell Holmes, and an impressive list of foreign diplomats and their families. Other benefits followed: a philanthropy in Baltimore sponsored a pair for a local orphanage, while one in Boston sponsored one for African-American women and abandoned children.[84]

Cattily (and correctly), the *Dramatic Mirror* predicted that news of the company's upcoming appearance before King Edward and Queen Alexandra would 'make all the anglomaniacs of Boston tumble over themselves' to attend the company's appearances in the city. Originally scheduled to take place on the grounds of the Lowell Estate in Chestnut Hill, the four performances had to be moved to Jordan Hall on account of the weather. Boston society turned out in force, but the hall's limited seating capacity forced the sponsors to turn away many would-be attendees. Those who managed to find seats to the first performance, *The Tempest*, entered into the semi-improvisational spirit of the event with good will. The last-minute transfer caused the company's properties to go astray, forcing the actors to scramble to improvise costumes, but no one seems to have cared.[85] The *Boston Evening Transcript* printed the first American description of Greet's *Tempest*, another work rarely staged at this time. The critic described Greet's intelligent cuts and ingeniously simple setting creating an excellent, direct, and forcible version that lasted a little over 120 minutes. The acting was 'decidedly uneven, some of it so excellent that it seemed out of place as it was joined to much that was bald and unconvincing', but the comic skill and physical characterization of Greet's Caliban was as excellent as it was original, even if it failed to adequately develop the character's bestial side. The performances of Greenstreet, George Vivian, Scott, and Sybil Thorndike were also commended.[86] The play quickly established itself as one of the company's standards.

Campus performances remained central to Greet's open-air touring formula. Notable institutional appearances that year included Tennessee, Sewanee, Virginia, Pennsylvania, Mt Holyoke, Yale, Princeton, Lehigh, Syracuse, Toronto, Michigan, the Western Michigan Normal School, Oberlin, the U.S. Military Academy, and New York University. The company's fourth appearance at the University of Toronto (another six performances during commencement week) prompted one professor there to express his hope that the visit, coupled with the soon-to-be-completed Convocation Hall's potential as a theatrical venue, would inspire students to form a drama club.

As this list indicates, the company made its inaugural visit to the South, where it was warmly received; one student at the University of Virginia described the company's appearance as 'without a doubt the most talked of, the best patronized and the most enjoyed function' of the year. The same leg of the tour included several memorable experiences that Russell Thorndike (who had joined the company the previous fall) later recounted. Seeing Sybil sweltering in her Abbess's costume before a presentation of *The Comedy of Errors* at an unnamed southern institution, a sympathetic co-ed offered the tee-totalling actress a delicious iced beverage to counter the oppressive heat. When the performer failed to answer her cue an hour later, first her colleagues and then the audience joined in the hunt. Eventually, a group of students found her, sleeping, and chaired her to the stage: 'I'm afraid she looked a very disreputable Abbess, when she said, "Oh, Mr. Greet, it was that awful mint julep". However, she certainly played the Abbess with rare gusto that day, and was most popular with the audience'. And in South Carolina a young man killed his stepfather in the street directly outside the company's hotel during a rehearsal. Russell recalled that Greet 'got very much annoyed' that the gunshot and subsequent ruckus forced him to end it early: 'I believe if the Last Trump were to sound while BG was rehearsing, he would finish the scene before passing to the Judgment'.[87] By July, the number of North American institutions of higher learning that had sponsored appearances had topped forty. Slowly but steadily, Greet was imprinting the pattern that would eventually become Academic Shakespeare.

Back in Manhattan, the Englishman was keen to organize the kind of event he had pioneered so successfully in London: a high-profile performance in a park. He laid out the particulars to Love, whom he asked for help obtaining the consent of the unresponsive Mayor McClellan:

> You remember I told you I tried to get the Mayor to let me give a Play [...] in Central Park? I still want to do it on July 2nd. I've written to William

Delafield our Tuxedo [Club] sponsor to see if he knows Mr. McClellan. Perhaps you know someone who would give it a fillip? Mr. Mabie probably could. I've looked out a lovely spot almost secluded in the Park + if the Park would fund the Seats I'd found [*sic*] the Play […]. I think that the press would take it up very warmly.[88]

Permission not forthcoming, more than four decades would pass before another director fond of performing Shakespeare on the Lower East Side, Joseph Papp, would give New Yorkers a taste for Shakespeare in the park.

Open-air Shakespearean performances continued after the Woodland Players sailed back to England. Now married, Ivah M. and Charles D. Coburn once again toured their sole offering, *As You Like It*, through the country clubs of New England and New York. Their promotional materials that summer touted both their debt and superiority to Greet:

It was Mr. Greet who first presented the outdoor play to the American public, the availability of certain of Shakespeare's plays for presentation in a forest landscape being satisfactorily tested by the superb company that Ben Greet first brought […]. [But the] commercial value of the aggregation at once became apparent to Ben Greet, the manager, and the actors were soon in the clutches of the theatrical syndicate which scattered a well balanced company into different companies and filled in with very inferior players. In toto the performance of the Coburn players last night almost equaled that of the early Woodland Players, and it easily excelled the recent Ben Greet productions.[89]

The facts were somewhat different than represented, but 'as good as the Woodland Players were before Greet sold out' made for a compelling pitch. The Coburns had thrown down the gauntlet; they would continue supplying the demand Greet had created after he and his players returned to England.

Notes

1 Dallas Anderson to Lucy Love, 28 September 1904, Yale Love.

2 For the story of Sybil Thorndike's recruitment, see Thorndike, pp.109–26. Salary information at p.142. For a good overview of her years with Greet, see Jonathan Croall, *Sybil Thorndike: A Star of Life* (London: Haus Books, 2008), pp.35–55.

3 Thorndike, pp.137–39.

4 The ages of all the members of the company at this time, recorded upon their arrival at Ellis Island, are available at <http://www.ellisisland.org/shipping/FormatTripPass.asp?sship=Numidian&BN=P00256-5&line-shipid=629&shipid=> [accessed 3 December 2012].

5 Thorndike, p.142.

6 Orens, p.38.

7 Thorndike, pp.158, 167, and 183–85; 'Constance Crawley Injured', *NYMT*, 17 March 1905, p.10.

8 BG to Lucy Love, 26 September 1904, Yale Love.

9 Thorndike, p.139.

10 Shattuck, *Shakespeare*, II (1987), pp.261–63.

11 Charles E. Russell, 'A Notable Dramatic Achievement: Miss Marlowe and Mr. Sothern in Shakespeare', *Critic*, December 1904, 525–31 (p.529).

12 'Hollis Street Theatre: Romeo and Juliet', *BET*, 29 November 1904, p.11.

13 Day and Trewin, p.83.

14 Thorndike, p.149.

15 Oscar Sidney Frank, 'San Francisco', *NYDM*, 1 October 1904, p.3; Henry Anderson Lafler, 'Literary News and Reviews', *(New York) Evening Post*, 29 October 1904, p.6; Frank McEntee, 'Notes of Plays and Actors', *NYS*, 14 April 1918, section 2, p.3.

16 'California', *NYDM*, 15 October 1904, p.4; Henry Anderson Lafler, 'Literary News and Reviews', *(New York) Evening Post*, 29 October 1904, p.6.

17 Blanche Partington, '"Hamlet" as Burbage Played It Centuries Ago', *SFC*, 2 October 1904, p.37; Austin Lewis, 'Hamlet by Ben Greet an Artistic Production', *Oakland Examiner*, 1 October 1904, p.1.

18 Oscar Sidney Frank, 'San Francisco', *NYDM*, 29 October 1904, p.3.

19 'Indiana', *NYDM*, 5 November 1904, p.5.

20 'Greet Players Appear', *SFC*, 26 November 1905, p.9. Oscar Sidney Frank, 'San Francisco', *NYDM*, 17 December 1904, p.3; BG to Lucy Love, 6 December 1904, Michigan Love. Seating capacity from <http://ohp.parks.ca.gov/pages/1072/files/RedwoodCity.pdf> [accessed 31 May 2016].

21 Blanche Partington, 'With the Players and the Music Folk', *SFC*, 20 November 1905, p.19; 'Los Angeles', *NYDM*, 19 November 1904, p.3. Seating

capacity of Hazard's Pavilion, which was renamed Temple Auditorium in late 1904, from <http://en.wikipedia.org/wiki/Hazard%27s_Pavilion#Clune.27s_Auditorium> [accessed 31 May 2016].

22 '"Everyman" an Impressive Drama', *(Portland) Morning Oregonian*, 10 December 1904, p.14; 'Story of the Nativity Re-Told', *(Portland) Morning Oregonian*, 31 December 1904, p.12; Seating capacity from *JC(1904)*, p.664; Stephen S. Wise, 'Theater as an Educational Factor', *(Portland) Morning Oregonian*, 10 December 1904, p.14.

23 BG to Lucy Love, 15 March 1905, Michigan Love.

24 BG to Lucy Love, 14 January 1905, Michigan Love.

25 Thorndike, pp.173 and 177–78.

26 '"Twelfth Night" Well Played', *Los Angeles Herald*, 19 January 1905, p.3; 'What the Theatres Are Offering', *Los Angeles Herald*, 22 January 1905, Sunday supplement, p.5; 'Artistic Work Not Appreciated', *Los Angeles Herald*, 25 January 1905, p.5.

27 Seating capacity from *JC(1904)*, p.191.

28 'Everyman', *NYDM*, 18 February 1905, p.25.

29 BG to Lucy Love, 15 March 1905, Michigan Love.

30 BG to Lucy Love, 15 March 1905, Michigan Love. Seating capacity from *JC(1904)*, p.158.

31 The first Shakespeare festival held in the United States known to the *New York Times* was the one Lawrence Barrett mounted in Cincinnati in 1883, but that phrase features minimally in that paper prior to 1905 in relation to dramatic activities in America. However, a poster in the possession of Franklin J. Hildy advertising the 'Grand Shakespearian Festival' mounted in Manhattan's Park Theatre in 1898 but not covered by that newspaper offers clear evidence not only that other festivals were held in the United States, but also that the phrase enjoyed some currency there prior to Greet. For details of Barrett's festival, see 'The Shakespeare Festival', *NYT*, 9 January 1883, p.5. I am grateful to Professor Hildy for calling these facts to my attention.

32 Speaight, pp.102–03.

33 Hamnet Catalog Record, Folger Shakespeare Library, <http://luna.folger.edu/luna/servlet/detail/FOLGERCM1~6~6~471716~133579:Shakespearean-festival,-Ben-Greet-P?sort=Call_Number%2CAuthor%2CCD_Title%2CImprint&qvq=q:Ben%2BGreet;sort:Call_Number%2CAutho r%2CCD_Title%2CImprint;lc:FOLGERCM1~6~6&mi=2&trs=13> [accessed 31 May 2016].

34 'Famous Actor as Professor', *SFC*, 4 April 1905, p.6; 'Actor Asked to Join University Faculty', *NYT*, 12 April 1905; 'Ben Greet', *NYT*, 19 May 1936, p.22.

35 Kinne, p.90–91.

36 'News of the Theatres', *CTr.*, 28 March 1905, p.8; 'Greet Finds Low Taste in American Audiences', *CTr.*, 5 April 1905, p.7.

37 W. L. Hubbard, 'Elizabethan Players', *CTr.*, 6 April 1905, p.8; 'The Comedy of Errors', *CTr.*, 11 April 1905, p.8; 'As You Like It', *CTr.*, 13 April 1905, p.8.

38 BG to Lucy Love, 10 April 1905, Michigan Love; H. L. Hubbard, 'Notes of

the Theaters', *CTr.*, 12 April 1905, p.8; 'Chicago', *NYDM*, 22 April 1905, p.14; BG to Lucy Love, 25 April 1905, Michigan Love.

39   W. B. Chamberlain, 'Auditorium — "Everyman"', *Minneapolis Journal*, 25 April 1905, p.4; Martha Scott Anderson, 'Auditorium — "Twelfth Night"', *Minneapolis Journal*, 27 April 1905, p.4; 'Minneapolis', *NYDM*, 6 May 1905, p.3; 'St. Louis', *NYDM*, 13 May 1905, p.14; 'St. Louis', *NYDM*, 20 May 1905, p.12; 'Many Clubwomen Attend Ben Greet's Performance', *St Louis Republic*, 4 May 1905, p.4. Seating capacity of Minneapolis's Exposition Auditorium from *JC(1904)*, p.177.

40   D. R. Keys, 'The Pastoral Plays', *The University of Toronto Monthly*, June–July 1905, pp.244–48.

41   For a discussion of Demmon's pioneering Shakespearean work in the classroom, see Renker, pp.145–47.

42   Ben Greet Company, Receipts, 17 June 1905, Isaac Newton Demmon Papers, University of Michigan Library (Special Collections Library).

43   'Cincinnati', *Billboard*, 1 July 1905, p.22; 'Cincinnati', *Billboard*, 8 July 1905, p.9.

44   '"As You Like It" Sylvan Style', *NYS*, 24 August 1905, p.15.

45   R. L. M., 'Ode on a Ben Greetian Urn', *Vassar Miscellany*, December 1905, p.177.

46   'Ben Greet Players', *BE*, 22 November 1905, p.7.

47   'East Side Shakespeare', *NYT*, 29 October 1905, p.9; Ben Greet, 'Shakespeare and the Modern Theatre', *Harper's Weekly*, 4 November 1905, p.1604.

48   Edward E. Pidgeon, 'Doings in Stageland', *New York Press*, 8 October 1905, p.4. See also 'The Usher', *NYDM*, 21 October 1905, p.15.

49   For newspaper descriptions, see 'Before the Footlights', *NYTr.*, 12 November 1905, p.2 and E. H. C., 'Jordan Hall: The Greet Players', *BET*, 13 December 1905, p.19.

50   John Corbin, 'Dramatic Censor M'Adoo', *NYS*, 5 November 1905, p.6; John Corbin, 'Belasco and His Three Aces', *NYS*, 19 November 1905, p.6.

51   'Shakespeare Without Actors', *BE*, 25 October 1905, p.3; 'Was Shakespeare Driven to Drink?' *NYMT*, 2 November 1905, p.1.

52   'Mendelssohn Hall — The Greet Company', *NYDM*, 18 November 1905, p.3.

53   'Dramatic and Musical Notes', *(New York) Evening Post*, 4 November 1905, p.5; 'Was Shakespeare Driven to Drink?' *NYMT*, 2 November 1905, p.1; 'Henry V', *NYTr.*, 31 October 1905, p.7; 'Mendelssohn Hall — Henry V', *NYDM*, 11 November 1905, p.3; 'Ben Greet's Efforts Enjoyed', *(New York) Evening World*, 31 October 1905, p.13; John Corbin, 'Dramatic Censor M'Adoo', *NYS*, 5 November 1905, p.6.

54   'Elizabethan Shakespeare Attracts', *(New York) Evening World*, 7 November 1905, p.11; '"Much Ado" by Greet Co.', *New York Press*, 7 November 1905, p.8; 'The Ben Greet Players', *(New York) Evening Telegram*, 7 November 1905, p.7; 'Much Ado About Nothing', *(New York) Evening Post*, 7 November 1905, p.5; 'Shakespeare Sans Scenery', *NYS*, 7 November 1905, p.9; *NYDM*, 18 November 1905, p.3.

55   'Mantell Shines as Weak Macbeth', *NYMT*, 14 November 1905, p.16; 'Robert Mantell in Macbeth', *(New York) Evening Telegram*, 14 November 1905, n. p.; Advertisement, *NYMT*, 18 November 1905, p.5; 'Garden — Macbeth', *NYDM*, 25 November 1905, p.3.

[56] 'Ben Greet Gives "Macbeth"', *NYMT*, 14 November 1905, p.16; 'Ben Greet Players in Macbeth', *(New York) Evening Telegram*, 14 November 1905, n. p.; John Corbin, 'Belasco and His Three Aces', *NYS*, 19 November 1905, p.6; 'Mendelssohn Hall — The Greet Company', *NYDM*, 25 November 1905, p.3.

[57] 'Mendelssohn Hall — The Greet Company', *NYDM*, 2 December 1905, p.16.

[58] 'The Spectator', *Outlook*, 2 December 1905, pp.809–10.

[59] 'Bill Shakespeare Catches Town, But No Royalties', *New York World*, 8 November 1905, p.13.

[60] John Talbott Smith, 'Shaw and Shakespeare', *Donahoe's Magazine*, December 1905, 599–608 (pp.607–08).

[61] 'Three Shakespeare Co.'s in New York', *Billboard*, 11 November 1905, p.10; 'The Ben Greet Style', *Billboard*, 11 November 1905, p.10; 'Dramatic and Musical Notes', *(New York) Evening Post*, 11 November 1905, p.5.

[62] 'Shakespeare at Reduced Prices', *NYMT*, 11 December 1905, p.10; Shattuck, *Shakespeare*, II (1987), pp.227–28.

[63] BG to Henry Clay Folger, 30 November 1905 and 2 January 1906, Folger Papers, Box 21, Folger Shakespeare Library, cited in Alman, p.111.

[64] Speaight, p.183; Kinne, p.66; 'Columbia University', *(New York) Evening Post*, 11 November 1905, p.8; 'Mr. Poel's Lecture', *Wellesley College News*, 22 November 1905, p.5; 'Mr. Poel's Lecture', *English Graduate Record Columbia University*, November–December 1905, p.117; 'Shakespearean Lecture', *Cornell Sun*, 2 December 1905, p.1; 'University Saturday Lectures', *University of Toronto Monthly*, December 1905, p.80.

[65] Seating capacity from <http://www.ebooksread.com/authors-eng/federal-writers-project-of-the-works-progress-adm/massachusetts-a-guide-to-its-places-and-people-hci/page-21-massachusetts-a-guide-to-its-places-and-people-hci.shtml> [accessed 31 May 2016].

[66] BG to Lucy Love, 15 December 1905, Michigan Love.

[67] 'Jordan Hall: Henry V. a la Greet', *BET*, 6 December 1905, p.19.

[68] 'Jordan Hall: The Greet Players', *BET*, 13 December 1905, p.19.

[69] 'Jordan Hall: Macbeth', *BET*, 20 December 1905, p.17.

[70] 'In the Theatres', *Auburn (New York) Citizen*, 25 August 1906, p.10

[71] BG to Lucy Love, 14 January 1906 and 16 January 1906, Michigan Love; 'Philadelphia', *NYDM*, 20 January 1906, p.14; 'Washington', *NYDM*, 27 January 1906, p.13; 'Toronto', *NYDM*, 24 February 1906, p.4.

[72] Seating capacity from *JC(1904)*, p.88; the involvement of the Philadelphia Teachers' Association from 'In the Playhouses', *Auburn (New York) Citizen*, 25 August 1906, p.10.

[73] BG to Lucy Love, 14 January 1906, Michigan Love.

[74] 'Philadelphia', *NYDM*, 20 January 1906, p.14; Lillian Camp Whittlesey, 'Happenings in Washington', *Congregationalist and Christian World*, 3 February 1906, p.148; 'Washington', *NYDM*, 27 January 1906, p.13. Seating capacity of the Belasco Theatre, the new name of the former Lafayette Opera House, from *JC(1904)*, p.104.

[75] 'Montreal', *NYDM*, 10 February 1906, p.4. Seating capacity from *JC(1905)*, p.297.

[76] R. Dale, 'Toronto News Letter', *Manitoba Free Press*, 16 February 1906, p.10; BG to Lucy Love, 11 February 1906, Michigan Love; 'Toronto', *NYDM*, 24 February 1906, p.4. Seating capacity from <http://www.thecanadianencyclopedia.com/articles/massey-hall> [accessed 31 May 2016].

[77] BG to Lucy Love, 13 March 1906, Yale Love.

[78] W. L. Hubbard, 'News of the Theatres', *CTr.*, 28 February 1906, p.6.

[79] 'Chicago', *NYDM*, 10 March 1906, p.14.

[80] Seating capacities from *JC(1905)*, p.219 and 'Last Chance to Get Music Membership', *Indianapolis News*, 16 April 1932, p.3.

[81] 'The Drama', *The World To-Day*, April 1906, p.358.

[82] 'Boston', *NYDM*, 26 May 1906, p.12; 'Boston', *NYDM*, 2 June 1906, p.13; 'Summer Stage Notes', *NYTr.*, 12 August 1906, p.5; 'Purchased on the Sidewalk', *(New York) Evening Telegram*, 17 September 1906, p.8.

[83] BG to Lucy Love, 10 June 1906 and 23 June 1906, Michigan Love.

[84] 'Shakespeare on Greensward Stage', *Washington Times*, 19 May 1906, p.5; 'Dramatic and Musical Notes', *(New York) Evening Post*, 26 May 1906, p.5; 'Baltimore', *NYDM*, 26 May 1906, p.13; 'Boston', *NYDM*, 26 May 1906, p.13.

[85] 'Jordan Hall: Ben Greet Players', *BET*, 31 May 1906, p.13.

[86] 'Jordan Hall: The Ben Greet Players', *BET*, 29 May 1906, p.19.

[87] D. R. Keys, 'The Wood-Lawn Players', *University of Toronto Monthly*, 6 July 1906, pp.241–44; 'Everyman', *(University of Virginia) Madison Hall Notes*, 13 October 1906, p.1; Thorndike, pp.191–94.

[88] BG to Lucy Love, 10 June 1906, Michigan Love.

[89] 'Night Not Ideal', *Auburn (New York) Argus Democrat*, 4 July 1906, p.5.

CHAPTER FIVE

Shakespeare's Plays
as Shakespeare Wrote Them, 1906–08

The 1906–07 Season

Greet had reason to be optimistic about the 1906–07 season because he had attracted the interest of powerful Theatrical Trust members Marc Klaw and Abe Erlanger, invariably referred to as 'Klaw & Erlanger', who agreed to produce the company. The pair controlled the cartel's interests in the South, and their sponsorship ensured a full calendar in a region of the country that Greet had yet to tour during the regular season. That he now revived *Everyman* suggests their backing may have been conditional upon it being his principal offering.

The promise of higher profits encouraged Greet to recruit more skilful leading performers — a testament to his decision to try to capture this new audience by giving it the best experience he could afford, even if that meant using some of those higher profits to do so. Following Adelaide Alexander's departure for Richard Mansfield's operation, Greet hired able journeywoman Agnes Elliott Scott, to whom he gave the principal female roles. He assigned several important male ones to Milton Rosmer, a talented journeyman he also brought on during the break.

Following a series of previews in the Mid-Atlantic, the Ben Greet Players officially opened the season in early November with performances of *Everyman* and *The Merchant of Venice* at the University of Virginia sponsored by the campus chapter of the

Young Men's Christian Association. Significantly, these were presented as part of a Lyceum course.[1]

Lyceum was an old institution, but it still had some life in it. Josiah Holbrook had founded it in Massachusetts in the 1820s to educate agricultural and mechanical labourers during the winter months. It had achieved regional significance by the time James Redpath assumed the leadership of the Boston Lyceum Bureau (later renamed the Redpath Bureau) in 1868. The introduction of modern management and advertising techniques enabled Redpath and his successors to quickly transform it into America's foremost network of travelling mass cultural education. Bureaus like Redpath functioned as booking agencies, supplying high-quality talent (meaning culturally prominent persons with exemplary personal reputations presenting educational and/or uplifting content) to the local sponsors with whom it collaborated. These sponsors (typically local YMCA and YWCA chapters) secured venues and sold subscriptions to courses comprising six presentations (lectures, recitations, concerts, etc.) the bureaus supplied over the course of an eight-month season that mirrored the regular theatrical season. Good management and salaries enabled Lyceum to attract famous activists, politicians, theologians, and writers. Susan B. Anthony, Frederick Douglass, Ralph Waldo Emerson, William Lloyd Garrison, Edward Everett Hale, Theodore Roosevelt, Carl Sandburg, Elizabeth Cady Stanton, Henry David Thoreau, Mark Twain, Booker T. Washington — all worked as Lyceum presenters at some point. Although the institution was in decline by the first decade of the twentieth century, it remained a potent cultural force.[2]

Greet had expressed to Lucy Love his interest in Lyceum as early as 1904.[3] Although I have discovered little about the course he joined in 1906, that brief association indicates that anti-theatrical attitudes had continued to soften. Previously, the closest thing to performance the institution permitted was 'dramatic readings': Mrs William Calvin Chilton, David Betram Cropp, John O'Kane Rose, Mrs William Douglas Turner, and Frederick Warde were but a few of the elocutionists and dramatic interpreters whose offerings included Shakespearean recitations. But in 1905 a Lyceum bureau in the South authorized what may have been the first play performance in the institution's history when it booked Rudolph Magnus's *Everyman* into a South Carolina circuit.[4] A year and a half later, Lyceum endorsed performed Shakespeare when it added Greet to the course in Charlottesville.

The actor-manager's letters paint an uninviting picture of the smaller towns that composed much of the tour. Business was so bad that he quickly determined that he would limit future visits to the South to the open-air season and the 'very pretty + refined' colleges he had spotted. In December, he confessed to Love 'The last three weeks we have had some very very unpleasant experiences. Such awful places + I think I <u>must</u> shake off Messrs. Klaw + Erlanger'. He also reported the lowest one-day receipts he had ever taken in America, although he declined to name the town that achieved that distinction.[5]

Significantly more pleasant, critically successful, and profitable was the time the company spent in the region's cities. Large audiences turned out to Atlanta's 2,644-seat Grand Opera House; according to the *Atlanta Journal Constitution*'s Alan Rogers, *Everyman* left 'an impression on every hearer which must for all time set it absolutely and unquestionably apart from any other theatrical production given at the Grand [...] within the knowledge of the writer'.[6] The engagement in Knoxville's Staub Theatre (1,900 seats) was similarly gratifying.[7] The company wrapped up the tour with a week in Louisville's 1,900-seat Macauley's Theatre that attracted consistently big crowds.[8] As Fate would have it, Helena Modjeska had just vacated the same venue. Travelling by private Pullman car, the great Polish-born tragedienne was making her farewell tour, bringing her renowned interpretation of Lady Macbeth to America's cities for the last time.[9]

Greet parted ways with Klaw & Erlanger in January, at which point he launched a self-produced, Shakespeare-based tour of the Midwest and Northeast. A phrase that had occasionally appeared in the company's promotional materials, 'Shakespeare's Plays as Shakespeare Wrote Them', now became its official slogan, as this impressive, chromolithograph, Swan-Theatre-sketch-inspired poster he commissioned illustrates.

The company spent a week in Milwaukee's Davidson Theatre (1,600 seats), which had just been vacated by the Marlowe-Sothern tour. In 1906, Frohman had objected so strenuously to the stars' proposal to mount a third consecutive Shakespearean season that he asked to be excused from their contract. Obliging him, the couple placed themselves under the Shuberts (the brothers who would eventually break the Trust's theatre-management monopoly), who allowed them to present a repertory of their own choosing.[10] Frohman's decision illustrates that those who controlled the theatre business believed stars had something better to do with their time: make lots of money for themselves and their producers by performing the latest Broadway hits before huge audiences in major metropolitan centres. Marlowe and Sothern's star status and deep

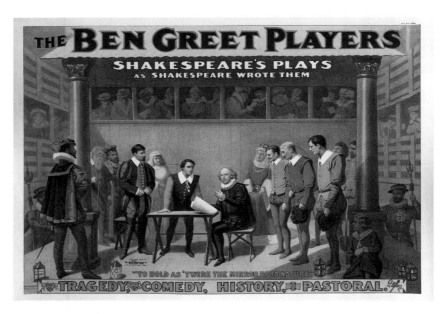

17. Anonymous. *Promotional Poster for The Ben Greet Players: Shakespeare's Plays as Shakespeare Wrote Them.* 1906.

pockets enabled them to give hundreds of Shakespearean perform-ances that season, but the following one would see them offering more modern repertories and touring separately from one another.

Other Shakespeare-inclined stars strictly limited the number of the playwright's works they included in their repertories. Mansfield could usually be relied on to mount at least one per season, but his large and varied repertory comprised mostly new and recent plays likely to turn a profit. The ever-popular visitor, Johnston Forbes-Robertson, was renowned for his Shakespearean roles, but soon he would find it next to impossible to play any character but the Stranger in the wildly successful stage adaptation of Jerome K. Jerome's modern Morality, *The Passing of the Third Floor Back.*

The only star for whom Shakespeare was a repertory mainstay was Robert B. Mantell. And apart from him, the only professional ensemble of national prominence offering a steady diet of Shakespeare, season in and season out, was the Ben Greet Players. It may have lacked stars, spectacle, first-rate management, and an advertising budget worthy of the name, but it was becoming ubiq-uitous. Mantell was excellent, but he was committed to Spectacular Realism, and thus to highly cut texts. Like other stars, he tended to play only the largest cities. Greet was slowly becoming an important Shakespearean popularizer, not because he was a great actor or because he drew audiences with the promise of dazzling scenes and effects, but because mounting complete, reasonably authentic productions of the playwright's works anywhere he could find an audience had become the sole purpose of his existence.

Returning to the East Coast in March, the company opened a five-week engagement at Manhattan's 1,110-seat Garden Theatre, where its repertory comprised mostly old Shakespearean produc-tions and *Everyman,* now with Rosmer in the title-role.[11] As in the fall of 1905, Shakespeare was well-represented in the metropolis. Marlowe and Sothern were nearing the end of their two-month engagement at the Lyric Theatre, where their popular *Hamlet, Merchant of Venice, Romeo and Juliet,* and *Twelfth Night* continued to draw. Theatregoers were also looking forward to the opening of Mantell's new, 'unadorned' (by the star's Spectacular Realism standards) production of *Julius Caesar* at Teller's Broadway Theatre.

Greet's choice of *Merchant* as his company's initial offering could hardly have been worse. New Yorkers were weary of old plays and productions, and Mansfield and Sothern had already exhibited strong Shylocks there that season. Greet's production was virtually identical to the one he presented in the metropolis in the fall of 1905 save for the alteration of his characterization of Shylock to make the role conform to the way scholars believed it had been played in Shakespeare's day: as an Elizabethan stereotype of a Jewish usurer. Greet had always worn the false nose and red wig and beard (clearly visible in this photograph), but now he played the character as a hideous, malicious, low-comedy figure. According to the *New York World*'s Louis De Foe, the new interpretation combined 'low transparent cunning, comic frenzies, and wild grimaces that in moments of mental tumult suggest the approach of an apoplectic fit'.[12] Although several critics conceded it was probably historically accurate, that fact did not stop them from hating it.

18. Anonymous. THE MERCHANT OF VENICE.
Dir. Ben Greet, Garden Theatre, New York, NY, March 1907.

A few commentators expressed dismay that Greet was still in business. *Town and Country* wondered how old productions, whose only value was educational, continued to attract theatregoers: 'One listens attentively; but one is likely to become drowsy, for some of Shakespeare's plays are tediously long for the average theatre goer'. The *New York Times* discreetly reminded readers that the reason Greet still drew audiences was because he remained the only purveyor of full-text, passably authentic Shakespeare in the United States, and that a few educators and highbrows had come to regard that as a good thing.[13]

Significantly, the reliably sympathetic John Corbin declared himself unable to continue supporting Greet. The critic still believed Shakespeare's plays should be acted as he wrote them and that this was impossible under modern conditions, but he could not disregard the fact that Greet's actors were little better than amateurs who reduced the playwright's lines to 'dull gray monotone'. More problematic was the contention of Corbin, who had published a prominent essay on Elizabethan staging conventions the previous year, that Greet's archaeology was inaccurate. The Middle Temple had indeed hosted a performance of a Shakespearean play, but erecting the Middle Temple fit-up so far downstage impeded the swift presentation Greet himself correctly advocated. The critic stated what had been true all along: Beefeaters and Bluecoat boys were inauthentic. He erroneously asserted that Shakespeare used more properties and scenery than Greet believed. More accurately and insightfully, he pointed out that the actor-manager was squandering a tremendous opportunity. The Garden had a huge stage, one of the few in existence comparable in size to that of the Globe. By failing to use all the space available to him, Greet was depriving New Yorkers of an opportunity to see Shakespeare's plays performed under more Globe-like conditions, square-footage-wise, than anyone then living had experienced. Such failings were of no consequence had only profit been at stake, but Greet had 'made himself sponsor of the cause of regenerating the art of producing Shakespeare. That is a cause of moment, and his pettifogging archeology and devitalizing management have given it what is sometimes called a black eye'.[14]

Corbin's denunciation encouraged others to pile on. One of the first to do so was *Life*, which accused the Englishman of fraud:

> Mr. Greet [...] inflicts on the public performances which have no real claim to the scholarliness they use as the excuse for their existence. Most atrociously read, acted not at all, wretchedly costumed and showing nothing but poverty in every resource, mental and material, they come very near getting patronage under false pretenses.

Its critic observed that Greet might have duped colleges and universities into believing his offerings had value, but New Yorkers knew better.[15]

But the coup de grace was delivered by none other than the 'dean' of American dramatic critics, the *New-York Tribune*'s William Winter, who declared that presenting Shakespeare's plays as he wrote them was a goal not to be desired because they were full of vulgarity, violence, and 'a considerable quantity of unnecessary language'. Several were unsuitable for public exhibition under any circumstances, as were a number of notorious episodes long since banished from the repertory for the sake of decency. (Winter had seen to it that nothing objectionable remained when he edited the plays for Edwin Booth decades earlier.) Having dispatched Shakespeare, the critic turned to Greet. The actor-manager's efforts had been received with considerable favour, particularly at universities, but he was nothing but a showman whose 'pose of scholarly superiority and educational purpose [...] savors somewhat of humbug'. His reputation in America had been founded on *Everyman*, but it was 'generally *understood*' that Edith Wynne Matthison had discovered and resuscitated the Morality. Greet was a veteran actor-manager who possessed 'a respectable endowment of commonplace talent', but he was also patronizing to the American theatre and press. Several of the productions he had mounted in New York had been pretentious and inadequate, but the latest crop was the worst yet. Winter's accusation that Greet was a huckster who traded in smut and savagery tarted up as 'education' caught the attention of *Literary Digest*, which reprinted several of the critic's statements in an article sensationally entitled 'Does Mr. Greet Overdo Fidelity to Shakespeare?'[16]

A few outlets offered guarded praise. The reliably supportive *Evening Post* reminded readers that Greet was the only manager in America mounting Shakespeare's plays in their entirety and reasonably authentically. The performances were far from perfect, but,

> considered as a whole, they are intelligent and illuminative, while the restoration of the text gives them a value which is quite incalculable. If he has no geniuses, he has no dolts in his company. His interpretations at no point fall below the plane of moderate excellence, and his players work together with a mutual understanding and cooperation which impart an uncommon vitality to their scenes.[17]

Nation drew inspiration from the fact that the under-resourced Greet had survived so long on the commercial stage because it confirmed the existence of American intellectuals who supported work that appealed to the mind. Of course Greet lacked distinguished actors; he was a master teacher whose company was internationally recognized as one of the finest schools of acting in existence. That wealthier managers snapped up his students as soon as they had learned their craft was inevitable. The current company lacked experience, but its performances were nevertheless 'smooth, interesting, and vivacious' because his actors 'supported one another loyally and with a mutual intelligence and sympathy'. Grotesque as it was, Greet's Shylock was competent and backed by traditional authority, but it would never win over admirers of Booth's, Irving's, and Possart's. Still, the actor-manager's production offered a more accurate version of the play than the more famous ones that cut it to shreds in the name of spectacle.[18]

The week after Corbin's review appeared, Mantell gave a reading at Harvard that included several scenes from *Othello*. (That the university invited a professional actor with a notorious past gives evidence of the institution's desire to overcome its own anti-theatrical prejudice.) Either the star or his agent, former wrestling and boxing promoter William A. Brady (who had represented 'Gentleman' Jim Corbett at the height of his career), instructed Mantell's personal manager, Frederick Donaghey, to address the students beforehand. Donaghey's widely reprinted attack on Greet and Elizabethan Manner (apparently, and imperfectly, cribbed from Corbin) made up for in animosity what it lacked in accuracy:

> Mr. Greet is making […] an archeological bluff. He sets his stage, he tells you, in reproduction of the stage of the Middle Temple, 'as Shakespeare did'. Now, as a matter of fact, Shakespeare's plays were not acted in the Middle Temple […]. It is true that Shakespeare has no scenery […] but he did the best he could […]. There were no beefeaters on the stage of the Globe Theater, and that stage was, in sheer acreage, larger by many square feet than the average stage of a modern theater. Wherever scenic illusion could be created with the materials of the day, it was created. This is not the case of my saying so and Mr. Greet's saying something else: but of fact. If you wish the proof of it, go to 'A Midsummer Night's Dream', turn to the last act, and read the tragedy of 'Pyramus and Thisbe'. Shakespeare therein made fun of the crude scenery of the Athenian mechanicals, in the smug belief that his own productions were very much Klaw & Erlanger.

Donaghey closed by asserting that the real difference between Greet's and Mantell's Shakespeares 'was the monetary difference between just enough scenery that may be carried for free […] and the cost of carrying scenery in five 60-foot baggage cars, at 15 cents per car per mile'.[19] By condemning Elizabethan Manner as a pretentious, archaeo-logically inaccurate justification for cheapness, Donaghey encouraged the men of Harvard to continue believing that Spectacular Realism was fully compatible with their highbrow educations and tastes.

Back at the Garden, the Ben Greet Players grimly soldiered on. Because they were old, the actor-manager's productions attracted few reviews. But the *New-York Tribune* could not resist the opportunity to denounce Greet's *Macbeth*, which it condemned as a 'desecration' that proved 'the superiority of the modern over the ancient method of presenting Shakespeare'. The situations and language aroused curiosity and concentrated attention, but the primitive staging dampened interest as the painfully common acting 'destroyed all possibility of illusion'. Scholars had known for some time that the text contained imperfections, but exactly how many 'were not known till now'. The critic (possibly Winter) concluded by describing the audience as 'small, patient, attentive, and resigned'.[20]

Attendance was indeed falling. The *Independent* declared that the waning interest in Greet's work proved that Matthison had been the real source of his success. Its writer observed that presenting Shakespeare's plays under original conditions might have some historical and educational value, but that it was also monotonous, wearying, and served only to 'emphasize the improvements made in stage management in the last two centuries — improvements that Shakespeare himself, if he lived now, would be the foremost to take advantage of'.[21]

Efforts at damage control made things worse. The New York *Sun* published a long, widely reprinted interview that might have done Greet some good had he not sulked or answered Winter. The actor-manager pointed out that his new *As You Like It*, which employed limited scenery, demonstrated that he was not opposed to modern staging. The company's costumes may have disappointed those addicted to spectacle, but they were evocative and historically accurate examples of Elizabethan dress. All his performers were professionals possessing several years' experience, but scathing notices and glib abuse had a dispiriting effect nonetheless: 'I don't think it's fair at all for people who are trying to do serious work to be treated in this flippant way'. Greet reminded readers that presidents of and internationally renowned Shakespearean authorities at august seats of learning had endorsed his work. He did not mind being called a showman so long as the term was not applied sarcastically; regardless of how artistic one's work was, professional theatre was a shop 'where you offer goods and the public comes to buy, if the critics don't run down your goods too much'. One critic, a learned dean no less, had erroneously stated that Matthison had been responsible for the revival of *Everyman*. Greet closed by posing a question that, unbeknownst to anyone at the time, would bear on Shakespeare's popularity in America: 'If the intellectual people don't want me, why not go to those people who are not usually considered intellectual?' For readers ignorant of the identity of the actor-manager's antagonist or the effects the bad press was having, one of the cartoons the *Sun* included, entitled 'Now is the Winter of Our Discontent', depicted a woeful Greet going over the daily receipts.[22]

The *New-York Tribune* published a letter from James Mavor, Greet's long-time host at the University of Toronto, who took issue with Winter's review, particularly with the critic's erroneous assertion that Matthison had discovered and resuscitated *Everyman*. Everyone knew Poel had been the first to do so. As for Winter's condemnations of Shakespeare and Greet, that the playwright and actor-manager had delivered a considerable amount of education and delight to persons not altogether uncritical could not be disputed.[23]

Winter responded to Mavor and Greet in the *Sun*. That such 'a cloud of woe' had 'darkened the land' as a result of his 'brief and not unkind article about Mr. Greet and his pretentious proceedings' was extraordinary. He had not stated that Matthison had discovered and resuscitated *Everyman*, but that it was 'generally *understood*' she had. Busy journalists did not have the luxury to choose their words 'with the deliberation easily possible to those persons who, apparently, have nothing better to do but to look for flaws and write letters to the press'. Sir Henry Irving and Frank Benson were more experienced Elizabethan revivalists than Poel, and they worked in public, not in a corner. (What Winter thought 'Elizabethan revival' meant we can only guess.) As for railing at Shakespeare, the critic

'gorgeous, magnificent, out-of-this world'[...]. [It] was generally felt that the Ben Greet players were in truth the greatest ever in the line of entertainment that Epworth had seen [...]. 'This method of Shakespeare was at once recognized by all who attended as the high form of art' the Epworth Quarterly for 1908 asserted. 'The presentations of the works of the great dramatist were perfect. Nothing was wanting. People were entirely satisfied. That this was so is proven by the fact that when it was learned there was a possibility of a return engagement within two weeks, enthusiastic requests came pouring in upon the management to secure the company again'. So it came about that a return engagement was arranged later in the summer and for succeeding summers through 1916.[45]

Greet's entry into Lyceum and Chautauqua were significant. Magnus had pioneered professional performance in Lyceum in 1905, but Greet introduced professional Shakespearean performance to it and Chautauqua during the 1906–07 season. That the Woodland Players appeared at the Presbyterian Winona Lake Assembly in 1908 and at all three — Epworth, Bay View, and Winona Lake — in 1909 illustrates how swiftly and warmly these important, educationally minded institutions embraced its work.

Concluding its engagements in the Midwest, the company travelled to Saratoga Springs, New York, for a popular and profitable half-week at Congress Springs Park. After appearing at a pair luxury hotels on Lake George, it ended the summer in late August with another successful, high-profile society performance, this time on the Maine coast. In collaboration with the Boston Symphony Orchestra, it presented the hybrid *Dream* at a fundraiser for the construction of Bar Harbor's Building of Arts, the *New York Herald* reporting several thousand dollars being raised from the large and fashionable audience in attendance.[46]

Greet's competitors had not been idle. The Coburn Shakespearean Players toured again, and again its promotional materials directly referenced Greet. According to the Coburns, demand for the Englishman's offerings was so high that 'only the larger colleges and universities' had any hope of receiving 'the occasional privilege' of a performance. Fortunately, their 'splendid company of American actors' was now offering four productions — *As You Like It*, *The Comedy of Errors*, *Much Ado*, and *Twelfth Night* — at country clubs and smaller educational institutions.[47]

As the *Doctor Faustus* performance at Princeton showed, not all those whom Greet inspired were professionals, nor were they all adults. The *New-York Tribune* reported that two children's companies presented *Merchant* and *As You Like It* 'in Ben Greet style' in New Rochelle that June.[48] As the *Washington Times* noted, 'The open air play seems to be growing in popularity since Ben Greet's outdoor productions and numerous college plays at commencement set the example'.[49] The Manhattan critics had savaged Greet, but he continued to dominate the Shakespearean wing of the still-burgeoning Open-Air Theatre Movement.

The 1907–08 Season

Three events occurred during the break that affected Greet. Perhaps the most important was Richard Mansfield's death on 30 August 1907. This not only deprived America of one of its greatest actors, but it also significantly decreased the number of nationally promi-nent Shakespeareans. Scores of touring and stock companies mounted productions of the playwright's works every season, but contemporaries increasingly regarded Mantell and Greet as the most dedicated Shakespearean interpreters in America.

In September, the People's Institute sponsored Mantell for a week of Shakespeare for poor schoolchildren and adults in Brooklyn. Greet had spearheaded the institute's first forays into professional performance and taught Charles Sprague Smith how to partner with local government and other philanthropies to bring Shakespeare to wider audiences, but Mantell had completely turned Smith's head.[50] Henceforth, the institute would sponsor the star's deeply cut, Spectacular Realism shows. Ironically, Greet's use of complete texts may have made Mantell more attractive to Smith;

Winter had branded Greet a trader in vulgarity and violence, and Smith was a vocal proponent of censorship. The last artistic descendant of Edwin Booth, Mantell was the greatest Shakespearean tragedian in America. His productions were a feast for all the senses and, thanks to the Winter-edited texts he used, they did not offend audiences by including any of the objectionable words or actions the Elizabethan had so inconsiderately placed in them. Greet held his tongue, but when *Theatre* prominently mentioned him in an article about the institute it published the following spring, he wrote a peevish letter to the editor declaring

> it was entirely through the efforts of my manager, Mr. Frank McEntee, and myself that the People's Institute was ever asked to mix up at all with the Board of Education of New York. The Institute showed its appreciation by signing a direct contract with Mr. Brady 'not to support the Ben Greet Players in New York'.

Contrary to *Theatre*'s implication, Greet and the People's Institute had parted ways.[51]

More gratifying, Greet received an indirect endorsement from one of the leading philosopher-practitioners of the American Arts and Crafts Movement. In a conscious rejection of Victorian extravagance, house- and furniture-designer Gustav Stickley advocated 'a return to a simple, vernacular aesthetic' that celebrated functionality, harmony, 'the natural beauty of pure materials, and the skill and acuity of the craftsman'.[52] One of the writers for his monthly *Craftsman* magazine, Selene Ayer Armstrong, saw in Greet's open-air work the embodiment of Stickley's aesthetic principles:

> Mr. Greet has achieved by perfectly simple means an art which, though stripped of every convention, is at once exquisite and satisfying. The test of this art, a test which must prove the undoing of any criticism that would measure it by conventional standards, is in the appeal it makes to the

spectator. The joy of the actors, the poetry of treatment and environment, never fails to communicate themselves to the audience [...]. The artistic success achieved by Mr. Greet and his players, entirely without the aid of artificial means, and by the sheer strength of the poetic and joyous spirit which marks their treatment of these pastoral plays, is the more significant in view of the dependency of both modern and classical productions upon spectacular effects. Their work is a movement in the direction of simplicity and naturalness in the art of the stage.[53]

Being a craftsman was all very well, but Greet would need to become a more effective manager if he was going to salvage the reputation of his indoor company.

Responding to the accusations of amateurism levelled the previous season, he devoted himself to delivering the highest-quality performances he could. He had not abandoned the ideas of 'Shakespeare's Plays as Shakespeare Wrote Them' and running a travelling school, but he now subordinated them to returning the company to artistic and critical respectability. To do so, Greet fielded a smaller company containing more experienced players whom he cast to greater advantage. To replace Sybil Thorndike, he hired Irene Rooke — a versatile performer with more than ten years' professional experience as well as some name-recognition thanks to her having played Mercia in the second, much more successful American tour of *The Sign of the Cross*.[54] Equally important was his decision to assign more leading roles to the increasingly compelling Rosmer and Scott. Although Fritz Leiber had left to join Julia Marlowe's company, journeymen Sydney Greenstreet and Redmond Flood continued to provide able support.

The actors had their work cut out for them because Greet had booked a full season: the company would present a repertory of ten plays in a six-month tour of Eastern Canada and the Northeast. Six of its Shakespearean productions were old; only Greet's Elizabethan Manner *Romeo and Juliet* was new. *She Stoops to Conquer* and *Masks and Faces* were technically old, but the company had performed them so rarely in North America that they were effectively new. Greet was also readying a newly written work.

The schedule was demanding, but he had planned it with care. From October to January, Greet sought new buyers for his old wares, drilling his actors and giving them time to thoroughly familiarize themselves with one another and the shows before they had to face more critical, urban audiences. To effect this strategy, the actor-manager booked short stands in the most familiar cities in Eastern Canada and the Northeast where he offered nothing but *Everyman* and Elizabethan Manner Shakespeare. The only major engagement the company played during this period was another well-attended week in Toronto's 4,000-seat Massey Theatre. The sole disappointment I have identified came during its half-week in Montreal's 2,000-seat His Majesty's Theatre, where business was only fair. Otherwise, papers reported good-to-excellent performances before consistently large audiences.[55] From the standpoint of quality, the actor-manager's decision to tour an ensemble of indisputably professional quality was proving sound.

In January, the company opened a week-long, all-Shakespeare engagement at Hartford's 1,817-seat Parson's Theatre that won considerable favour with 'good sized audiences'. In stark contrast to its last appearance in Philadelphia, the company's week in the city's new, 1,341-seat Adelphi Theatre, now with the limited-scenery *Masks and Faces* and *She Stoops* in the rotation, was a success.[56] The *Philadelphia Inquirer* did not review its presentation of the former, but called the latter 'another delightful production' that charmed the near-capacity house the company attracted in spite of severe winter weather.[57]

The most important critical trial came in Boston, where the company played three weeks in the New England Conservatory's 1,000-seat Jordan Hall in late January. Fully aware of the cries of amateurism raised the previous season, the *Boston Evening Transcript*'s critic admitted to feeling trepidation before the start of the limited scenery *As You Like It*. This was the play 'that the Ben Greet players in Shakespeare had first burst upon a charmed and delighted audience' in Cambridge in 1903 — a presentation that had astounded all that witnessed it. 'Would the fragrant memory of that other performance turn to dust as something dead and gone? Or could the spirit infused into the performance before make this one live?' The reporter spent two acts waiting for the answer, and, after a few false starts 'the spirit that made the other began to show'. Rooke was unusually effective, and Greet's Jaques was the same masterful character who had sat under 'a Harvard elm and claimed our applause for the artistry with which he gave the seven ages' speech. The audience soon

> forgot that the ugly curtains of Jordan Hall framed the picture. We never thought to remember it was a picture. The spell of Shakespeare and of finely active imaginations were about us. The care and toil of Mr. Greet had wrought the spell.

The critic expressed mortification that the rudeness and ignorance of the audience had spoiled the end of the performance; unaware that the play concluded with an epilogue and eager to pull on their galoshes, theatregoers partially drowned out Rooke's exquisite delivery of Shakespeare's almost-never-spoken closing lines.[58]

The same paper reported that *Everyman* failed to draw, not because the performances were lacking, but because the vogue for the Morality was over. Happily, *She Stoops* drew a near-full house and much praise, the *Boston Evening Transcript* stating that the company's fine ensemble work and Greet's careful stage management reminded everyone 'of the vitality of Goldsmith's sprightly comedy'. The stage business, the wealth of by-play, and the superb enunciation of Greet's players were an education in eighteenth-century comedy. The actor-manager was too old to play Tony Lumpkin, but he remained surprisingly effective. Rosmer made the best of the thankless task of playing Marlow, and Rooke's sprightly and attractive Kate Hardcastle kept the pace brisk and the improbabilities credible. Taken as a whole, 'the production demonstrated [...] that for wit, vigor, and keen characterization, we need only to go back to the old comedies, provided we use a little intelligence and pains in their presentation'.[59]

The paper was less impressed with *Merchant*. Significantly, its critic declared that, although experts continued to debate what Elizabethan Manner exactly comprised, Greet's 'method is, in general, the true one'. Equally doubtless, that method made the play's narrative and dramatic qualities stand out like never before. But the writer also noted that most people simply could not put themselves in the Elizabethan frame of mind, and that Greet's (meaning Shakespeare's) unfamiliar scene order and the 'helter-skelter entrances and exits' it exhibited diminished the comedy's appeal. The actor-manager's Shylock was similarly alienating. Irving and his legion of imitators had trained audiences to expect 'senile malice and crazy decrepitude', so theatregoers found difficulty crediting an interpretation that swung from ministerial to catty to hearty to buttonholing to vulgar, especially when Greet made his final exit as 'a baffled man' with no hint of the customary rage, humiliation, fear, hatred, or imminent collapse. If Greet's interpretation was problematic, the way he trained and deployed his actors was worthy of the highest commendation, especially in regards to Scott, Rosmer, and Greenstreet. The critic even took a moment to praise the collection of rich-but-understated Elizabethan costumes the Englishman had assembled ('a blessed relief from the pink satin horrors of the "legitimate" production') before concluding that, if the performance 'did not always create its illusions, it was at no point below a level of commendable achievement'.[60]

The *Boston Evening Transcript* described *Masks and Faces* as a quaint relic of the 1850s that had the potential to quickly be forgotten once an auditor was outside the theatre. But its critic thought the company had done a more-than-creditable job. Greet's Triplet was justifiably famous, and Scott's Woffington excellent.[61]

The company's new offering, *The Wonder Book Plays*, received its premiere in late January. The work was based on Nathaniel Hawthorne's popular *The Wonder Book for Girls and Boys*, in which the author offered moralized retellings of several Greek myths. In 1907, Rose Meller O'Neill, a young English playwright, dramatized three of them — *Pandora*, *Midas*, and *The Miraculous Pitcher* — as one-act plays suitable for both indoor and outdoor presentation. W. T. Hamiston supplied original music, and two of the tales featured dances Moore choreographed and performed. The initial performances were high-profile fundraisers for one of Greet's most loyal philanthropic sponsors, the Hampton Institute, which booked the 2,312-seat Castle Square Theatre for the event. The *Boston Evening Transcript* reported a 'long and influential' list of patronesses and a large audience comprising delighted children and adults. As Hawthorne breathed new warmth into the classic tales, O'Neill's sympathetic adaptation and the company's harmonious and cheerful performance made them live as never before. The reviewer described the presentation's effect:

> By picture, by word, by action, the players steadily gained with the end in view, the lesson which is as old as the world itself. The children in the theatre were silent, each growing mind absorbing what was passing, each being […] molded as the lesson would have it. These were wonder tales indeed, wonderful and beautiful.

The fundraisers were so profitable that the philanthropy immediately laid on four more performances.[62]

Halfway through the Boston run, another leading light of the American Arts and Crafts Movement offered his own appreciation of Greet. A printer and publisher of fine books, Elbert Hubbard was also the controversial philosopher, lecturer, and prolific author who founded the Roycroft Community of Arts and Crafts artisans in East Aurora, New York. On a date I have yet to identify, Greet's company gave an open-air presentation of *Twelfth Night* for the Roycrofters that inspired Hubbard to write this encomium:

> In giving a play out-of-doors, or without complex scenery, Ben Greet has made a discovery. The game is his, it is his idea, let those cheapen it or take it away from him who can. Merry villagers, fat moral bilge, obtuse persons drunk on what the world calls success, may say 'Oh, it is naught — it is naught!'[…].

The fact remains that Ben Greet has done something never done since William Shakespeare and necessity demanded it. He cuts the Gordian Knot of conventional stage-craft and just gives the play — we do the rest […].

Ben Greet allows the audience to supply the scenery; and so does he stir the imagination of even the orthodox unco gude, who stand outside the ropes, too conservative to pay for seats, that they forget to go, and stand breathless, silent or moved to bursts of bucolic mirth. Ben Greet allows us to construct palaces, such as no stage carpenter can boast.

Mind is the only material, and mind under proper treatment is plastic. He alone is great who can make men change their minds. These woodland players are psychologists. How they do it, they probably do not know; but that they do it I know. They capture young, old, innocent, intelligent, cynical, blase [sic], even the dull and tired, in the silken spider thread of their art and bind them hand and foot.[63]

It was among the most eloquent praises Greet ever received.

The company's next major engagement was in Washington, DC, where it attracted varied audiences and mixed notices during its week-long run in the 1,548-seat Belasco Theatre.[64] (That it conspicuously avoided Manhattan gives evidence not only of Greet's anxiety about the Broadway critics, but also his suspicion that his business might no longer be viable in the Metropolis.) The *Washington Herald*'s critic liked what he saw. *Masks* drew a smaller house 'than the merits of the comedy and the excellence of the acting deserved'. But the actor-manager seems to have taken to heart the main criticism levelled against *Merchant* because he played Shylock in more Irving-like fashion. The reporter described a large audience of schoolchildren, who found the play both educational and enjoyable.[65]

The *Washington Times* was more critical and thoughtful. 'The noticeable decline in enthusiasm' for Greet's offerings following his marked success in the city in 1906 proved that the novelty of Elizabethan Manner had worn off. A savvy manager, his introduction of scenery to select productions demonstrated that he understood he needed to introduce fresh ideas in order to stay in business. The most praiseworthy feature of the current engagement was his casting of good actors in even minor roles. The obsession with stars had given rise to 'execrable supporting companies as that with which Robert B. Mantell was surrounded last season', which damaged not only the tragedian's reputation, but also Shakespeare's. Even when he was struggling, no one could match Greet's ability to forge a strong ensemble. In terms of the company's specific offerings, *Merchant* had been of average competence thanks the actor-manager's decision to abandon playing Shylock as a low-comedy figure, however historically accurate such a characterization might be. There was 'much ranting and little really intelligent interpretation' in the company's *Macbeth*, whose only redeeming feature was Scott's 'illuminating and convincing' Lady Macbeth. *She Stoops* was noticeably better, but presenting the play in eighteenth-century fashion produced an overly broad comic effect unpleasant to auditors who valued 'smoothness and polish'. Dull, uninspiring, and crudely staged, *Wonder Book* was a source of 'considerable disappointment'. The 'mildly pleasing' tales may have dispensed 'wholesome morals administered in three homeopathic doses', but the work possessed none of *Peter Pan*'s impressive staging of human insight.[66]

Leaving the capitol, the company began a week-long engagement in Pittsburgh's 2,112-seat Duquesne Theatre. It was making expenses, but only barely. Greet told Love that 'Pittsburg [*sic*] liked us I think but only came out just enough to <u>scramble</u> through the week. If I could cut down my expenses <u>$500</u> per week I'd be alright. We never seem to get over the profit line'. While in the city, Greet delivered a lecture on pre-Shakespearean drama to the students and faculty of the Carnegie Schools of Technology, a vocational institution that would soon place itself at the forefront of dramatic instruction in American higher education.[67]

In March, the company travelled to the Midwest, where it played short stands mostly in familiar small cities and large towns until the close of the regular season. Although the *Dramatic Mirror* reported respectable houses, Greet painted a bleaker picture when he told Love that Mantell's recent tour of the region had poisoned the company's profitability and reputation there:

> we've had a very very bad week — + a great disappointment at three towns Wheeling a new place — Columbus + most of all Dayton which is always considered a <u>stronghold</u>. Business dropped off to a mere song. I really feel hideously vindictive because I believe Mantell's managers + their agents go into these towns, get hold of the Press + vilify us. The notices are so spiteful.[68]

As tempting as it might be to dismiss such a claim as exaggerated — even paranoid — we should recall that the star's business manager went out of his way to attack Greet at Harvard the previous winter and that papers reported his statements without checking their accuracy or getting a comment from Greet. Far more formidable than Mantell's business manager was his agent, Brady — the man Greet accused in print of having made the star's appearances for the People's Institute conditional upon that organization undertaking not to support the Englishman in Manhattan. That the star and his management team would aggressively seek to consolidate his position as America's foremost Shakespearean following Mansfield's death is only natural.

Greet's financial situation began to stabilize as the company worked its way east, but he was eager for the open-air season to begin. Not only was that shaping up handsomely, but it also promised significantly higher profits. In late April, he confided to Love that 'Things only just keeping us going but Pastoral affairs still going pretty promisingly. We go up and down so horribly — one night play to $600 or more the next down to 100 or 150'. With each passing season, the fact that open-air Shakespeare was where the money was became clearer and clearer.

The 1908 Open-Air Season

An astonishing, hugely profitable outdoor season made up for a commercially undistinguished (if more critically respectable) indoor one. At eighteen weeks, it was the longest Greet had yet to offer in North America. Demand for outdoor Shakespeare had never been higher, and Greet's position as the undisputed market-leader placed him in the best position to fill it.

The Woodland Players played a string of educational institutions in Virginia and Pennsylvania that May, including the University of Virginia, Washington and Lee, William and Mary, and Swarthmore. It played the University of Toronto once again that June, giving five performances during commencement week. Re-entering the United States in the Midwest, it played the campuses of perennial hosts Michigan and Oberlin. It also visited the Ohio State University, where it gave three performances during commencement week.

But the university engagement that summer that had the most enduring impact on American culture was the week it spent at Cleveland's Western Reserve University. The campus was hosting the annual convention of the National Education Association, and the NEA had arranged for Greet to perform for the hundreds of high school teachers and administrators in attendance.[69] Seeing these presentations changed the way many of the educators thought about and taught Shakespeare; that some tried to recreate with their students what they had witnessed is equally certain. Like the actor-manager's presentations at normal schools and schools of education, those at Western Reserve impacted not only on his immediate audiences, but also on the generations of students its members taught. Greet's performances made people want to mount their own Shakespearean productions, and to do so using his method.

The company enjoyed three excellent weeks in Chicago, which was bustling that July thanks to the presence of the Republican National Convention. As in previous years, the University of Chicago and the University of Chicago Settlement League sponsored a Shakespearean festival in the School of Education's Scammon

Gardens. The *Chicago Tribune* completely ignored the performances, inattention Greet attributed to the paper having already reduced the company's reputation to such a lowly state that nothing remained to knock down.[70] But who cared what the papers thought so long as people kept coming? And they did, and in crowds sufficient to warrant extending the festival by a week.

The company made a few short sallies out of Chicago, including to the daughter Chautauqua at Winona Lake. Like the Methodists at Epworth and Bay View, the Presbyterians at Winona found Greet's open-air Shakespeare sufficiently worthy to invite the company back the following summer. The cultural significance of the appearance was not lost on one English paper, which remarked

> Evidence of the extent to which in America the old Puritan attitude of hostility to the theatre has declined is afforded by the fact that the Ben Greet Company of Shakespearean players has recently fulfilled a week's engagement at Winona, under the auspices of the famous Bible School there.

Sensational for a different reason was a performance the company gave at the University of Wisconsin in late July, when a section of the temporary bleachers collapsed, severely injuring one of the 300 students thrown to the ground.[71]

Popularly and commercially, the high point of the Chicago season was the three performances of the drama-music hybrids the company gave at Ravinia Park in collaboration with Damrosch's New York Symphony Orchestra. Greet told Love that these grossed $8,600, which number would have been higher had season tickets been included in the calculation. The business case for making the hybrids his company's principal offering was becoming hard to ignore. The *Chicago Tribune* reported that a record-shattering 8,000 people went to Ravinia on one of the days, and that many remained through the evening to attend the sold-out, standing-room-only performance. Greet added four more performances in July, when he unveiled two more hybrids, *Romeo and Juliet* (with

Gounod's music) and *The Merry Wives of Windsor* (with Nicolai's), this time backed by the Theodore Thomas Orchestra under Frederick Stock. The *Dramatic Mirror* described the former as a 'complete success', but the fact that it featured minimally (and *Merry Wives* not at all) in the company's repertory afterwards indicates Greet believed otherwise.[72]

Returning to Manhattan for the first time in sixteen months, the company played a week-long engagement at Columbia University, where it presented the small-musical-ensemble *Dream* and *Tempest* featuring the dances of Moore, who now toured with the players. The low-point of the engagement came the night of 5 August when a storm, coupled with the university's failure to provide an adequate rain-venue, disappointed the very large audience that had assembled. The high-point was the matinee of *As You Like It* on 7 August, which garnered considerable attention thanks to Mrs Roosevelt and a gang of Roosevelt children and cousins steaming over from Oyster Bay specially for the event. A few days later, Greet was among the guests the President and First Lady hosted at Sagamore Hill. The Englishman was the last to leave, and Mrs Roosevelt personally escorted him to the train station in her car.[73] Greet's company appearing at Columbia again in the summer of 1909, and the Coburns there in 1910 and 1911, to that institution belongs the credit for hosting the United States's second annual Shakespearean festival.

A three-week tour of upscale resorts in New York and New England closed the season. The company was warmly received, especially in the Adirondacks. Greet told Love that the Sagamore Hotel's proprietor 'was so delighted with the plays that he handed the <u>entire receipts over</u>!' The Lake Placid Club christened its new, 600-seat, electrically lit outdoor theatre 'The Arden Forest Theatre' after the company inaugurated it with a performance of *As You Like It*. The presentation was so picturesque that Greet used this photograph from it to advertise the company for years.[74]

The Coburn Shakespearean Players presented *As You Like It*, *The Comedy of Errors*, and *Twelfth Night* that open-air season in a tour that

20. Bragdon. As You Like It.
Dir. Ben Greet, Lake Placid Club, Lake Placid, NY, 20 August 1907.

included country clubs not only in the Northeast, but also in Cleveland, Indianapolis, and Detroit. Significantly, the Coburns advertised their Terre Haute engagement as a 'Shakespeare festival'. That they charged appreciably less than Greet did ($1.50–2 per ticket rather than $2–3) for their country-club appearances indicates that competing on price was part of their expansion strategy. They resisted the temptation to reference Greet in their promotional materials that summer, but the *Dramatic Mirror* noted that some of their actors had formerly worked for him — a claim I have been unable to verify.[75] Contemporaries clearly had difficulty avoiding using the actor-manager's name when discussing his most famous creation; 'Ben Greet' had become cultural shorthand for the product 'open-air, bare-stage, full- (or full-ish)-text, Elizabethan-costumed Shakespeare'.

The actor-manager's influence was being felt elsewhere. In June, Harvard hosted Shakespearean performances by the star of the American *Peter Pan* tour, Maude Adams. *Twelfth Night* was the play, and the Sanders Theatre, once more dressed in the Baker-Warren fit-up, was the venue. As *Theatre*'s coverage indicates, attitudes about a host of issues touching Greet had changed appreciably since 1903. Adams's appearance (courtesy of Charles Frohman) was important to the university's authorities, who were reportedly keen to break away 'from the Puritanical prejudice against the actor'. Her reputation as a Shakespearean was not distinguished, but her success as

Peter Pan made her a natural to play a girl who disguises herself as a boy. Every detail of the fit-up

> had been approved by the scholars of the English department and, while it will probably never be decided upon authoritatively just how much or how little scenery was used in Shakespeare's time, there was at least an intelligent approximation in this case.

The text, reported to have been arranged by Adams herself, was cut, but 'no choice bit of poetry was omitted and every line necessary for the development of the plot had its due place'. Although the star's costumes were entirely the product of Spectacular Realism, the others approximated Elizabethan dress. The quality of the company supporting her was 'far above that usually accorded to a "star's" performance of Shakespeare'.[76]

What was different? Professional productions of Shakespearean plays had a place on the campuses of the country's most distinguished institutions of higher learning. Scholars continued to argue about what 'authentic' Elizabethan staging actually was, but everyone agreed it was the best way to present Shakespeare's plays, at least at the varsity. A complete text was superior to an incomplete one, and performing a cut and/or rearranged one required some explanation, or at least an acknowledgement. And people had grown sceptical of the notion that a star could carry an entire play single-handedly; a capable ensemble was necessary to bring out each work's full complexity and richness. Greet's ideas had achieved widespread cultural currency.

Adams's other offering at Harvard demonstrated that bare-stage presentation of Greek classics or Shakespeare was not the only open-air method. On the evening of 22 June, she, a company comprising professionals 'selected from the diverse forces of Charles Frohman', more than a thousand supernumeraries, and a full orchestra presented a colossally scaled version of Schiller's *The Maid of Orleans* in the football stadium to benefit the university's Germanic Museum. All the performers wore professional-quality, fifteenth-century costumes. Trees, foliage, and a massive set representing a castle and tower were carted on to the gridiron to transform it into a stage. The production featured a thirty-minute coronation scene, a massive battle, and giant spotlights that turned night into day as required. The diminutive Adams, playing Joan of Arc, impressed everyone with her ability to mount and ride a horse wearing full plate armour. 15,000 people, each of whom paid $2–3 per ticket, attended the sold-out performance. A massive, professionally produced version of a tragedy by one of the greatest German playwrights and performed by a 1,000+-person cast at Harvard before the largest audience ever assembled for an outdoor performance was a landmark in the Open-Air Theatre Movement.[77]

But live, spoken drama had nothing to do with the innovation that was about to shake the entertainment industry to its foundations. As Greet's players were enjoying their vacations that fall, *Theatre* published a long article, provocatively entitled 'Where They Perform Shakespeare for Five Cents', about a new business on Manhattan's lower East Side. The essay's author, Montrose J. Moses, opened light-heartedly, but conveyed with growing seriousness the enterprise's disruptive potential. The Tompkins Square Vaudeville Theatre had been converted into something called a 'Nickelodeon', and a German émigré named Oscar I. Lamberger, formerly Assistant Professor of Comparative Literature at Leipzig University, was showing moving pictures, or 'movies', there to 'an interesting mix of foreigners of all classes', children being especially well represented.[78] The variety of his offerings and the price of admission — ninety per cent less than the least expensive adult ticket to a Broadway show — kept his intensely loyal audience coming back for more. The absence of spoken dialogue and the negligible amount of text presented in the intertitles did not bother its members, many of whom could not read English anyway. Moses noted that, although they were not traditional theatregoers, traditional theatregoers would be wise to take them seriously:

In numbers measuring over two hundred thousand throughout New York City, the kinetoscopic *clientèle* is composed of people who cannot afford to go to the theatre, even though such an organization as the People's Institute strive to reduce for them the theatre prices along the way.

In terms of content, Lamberger screened 'inane comic pieces' to keep his business comfortably in the black, but his ultimate ambition was 'to present nothing but classical dramas for his little public'. To this end, he screened adaptations of Biblical episodes, *The Scarlet Letter*, and 'Rip Van Winkle', each of which he accompanied with a lecture. Several of the Shakespearean films produced by the Vitagraph Company that year, the first made in the United States, featured in Lamberger's repertory. All the major studios had their own stock companies, and they spared no expense to bring them to lakeshores, gardens, and wooded avenues in their 'anxiety and determination to obtain realism'. Moses chose to illustrate this point (and perhaps the threat he so clearly

21. ROMEO AND JULIET.
Dir. J. Stuart Blackton, Prod. Vitagraph, 1908.

perceived) with this still from the duel scene from *Romeo and Juliet*. Vitagraph being headquartered in Brooklyn, it filmed in appropriate locations nearby, one of which was the terrace of the mall in Central Park.[79] Significantly, the first professional Shakespearean production the park ever hosted was mounted, not by Joseph Papp (or even Ben Greet), but by J. Stuart Blackton, Vitagraph's director. Silently and subtly, cinema had begun to steal the scene.

NOTES

[1]   BG to Lucy Love, 9 December 1906 and 14 November 1906, Yale Love; 'Dramatic and Musical Notes', *New York Evening Post*, 27 October 1906 p.5; 'Everyman', *(University of Virginia) Madison Hall Notes*, 13 October 1906, p.1; 'Ben Greet', *(University of Virginia) Madison Hall Notes*, 3 November 1906, p.1.
[2]   Andrew C. Rieser, *The Chautauqua Moment: Protestants, Progressives, and the Culture of Modern Liberalism* (New York: Columbia University Press, 2003), p.101; French Strother, 'The Great American Forum', *The World's Work*, September 1912, pp.551–64; James R. Schultz, *The Romance of Small-Town Chautauqua* (Columbia: University of Missouri Press, 2002), pp.1–4.
[3]   BG to Lucy Love, 4 January 1904, Yale Love.
[4]   *Annual Catalogue of Furman University for the Year 1904–1905* (Greenville, SC: Furman University, 1905), p.36; *Wofford College Catalogue, 1904–1905* (Spartanburg, SC: Wofford College, 1904), p.39; 'Everyman before a Laurens Audience', *Laurens (South Carolina) Advertiser*, 22 March 1905, p.1.
[5]   BG to Lucy Love, 9 December 1906, Yale Love. For a description of one of those 'very very unpleasant experiences', see Thorndike, pp.195–96.
[6]   D. E. Moorefield, 'Atlanta, GA', *Billboard*, 29 December 1906, p.13; 'Atlanta', *New York Clipper*, 29 December 1906, p.1188; Alan Rogers, 'Ben Greet Players Present "Everyman"', *Atlanta Journal Constitution*, 16 December 1906, p.24. Seating capacity from *JC(1905)*, p.358.
[7]   'Knoxville', *New York Clipper*, 5 January 1907, p.1212.
[8]   'Kentucky', *New York Clipper*, 5 January 1907, p.1226. Seating capacity from *JC(1905)*, p.285.
[9]   'Kentucky', *New York Clipper*, 5 January 1907, p.1208.
[10]   Shattuck, *Shakespeare*, II (1987), pp.275–76.
[11]   Seating from *JC(1905)*, p.41. Rosmer details from 'Garden — Everyman', *NYDM*, 6 April 1907, n. p.
[12]   Quoted in 'The Week's Playshops', *WTr.*, 17 March 1907, p.2. See also 'Garden — The Merchant of Venice', *NYDM*, 16 March 1907, p.3.
[13]   'The Theatre', *Town and Country*, 9 March 1907, p.24; 'Ben Greet as Shylock', *NYT*, 5 March 1907, p.9.

[14] John Corbin, 'Shakespeare and the Plastic Stage', *Atlantic Monthly*, March 1906, pp.369–83; John Corbin, 'Drama by the Bootstrap', *NYS*, 10 March 1907, p.6.

[15] 'The Ben Greet Shakespearean Side-Show is Again in Town', *Life*, 14 March 1907, p.387.

[16] William Winter, 'Shakespearian Revivals', *NYTr.*, 5 March 1907, p.7; 'Does Mr Greet Overdo Fidelity to Shakespeare?' *Literary Digest*, 16 March 1907, p.432.

[17] 'Dramatic and Musical Notes', *New York Evening Post*, 9 March 1907, p.5.

[18] '"The Merchant of Venice" by The Ben Greet Players', *Nation*, 7 March 1907, p.229.

[19] M. McD., 'The Week's Playshops', *WTr.*, 17 March 1907, p.2.

[20] 'The "Ben" Greet "Macbeth"', *NYTr.*, 12 March 1907, p.7.

[21] 'The Drama', *Independent*, 21 March 1907, p.654.

[22] 'Ben Greet to His Critics', *NYS*, 24 March 1907, section 2, p.3.

[23] James Mavor, 'The Revival of "Everyman" and the Ben Greet Performances', *NYTr.*, 25 March 1907, p.7.

[24] William Winter, 'Grief of Greet — and Others', *NYTr.*, 28 March 1907, p.7.

[25] Emily Folger, 'Plays I Have Seen' theatrical diary, pp.5, 74, and 76, Folger Collection, Box 38. Folger Shakespeare Library.

[26] 'A Slight Difference of Opinion', *Life*, 4 April 1907, p.487.

[27] William Bullock, 'Player Folk', *New York Press*, 10 April 1907, p.6.

[28] William Winter, 'A Sair Greeting', *NYTr.*, 12 April 1907, p.7.

[29] George E. Macdonald, 'Unbidden Thoughts', *Liberty*, May 1907, 60–73 (pp.65–66).

[30] Thorndike, p.197.

[31] 'Editorial', *Nassau Literary Magazine*, May 1907, pp.66–67. For additional details, see *Theatre*, June 1907, p.148.

[32] 'The Call Boy's Chat', *PI*, 28 April 1907, p.10.

[33] '"Everyman" Well Received', *WH*, 30 April 1907, p.2; 'The Ben Greet Players', *WTr.*, 30 April 1907, p.5; '"Everyman" Morality Play Interests Big Audience', *WTr.*, 30 April 1907, p.6. Seating capacity from *Handbook of Continental Memorial Hall, Washington, DC* (Washington: Daughters of the American Revolution, 1915), p.13.

[34] *Marianne Moore Selected Letters*, ed. by Bonnie Costello (New York: Penguin, 1997), p.81.

[35] Seating capacity from <https://studentactivities.uchicago.edu/facilities/mandel.shtml> [accessed 18 April 2013].

[36] 'News of the Theatres', *CTr.*, 9 July 1907, p.8.

[37] Hannah E. Fabens, 'Lou Wall Moore's Interpretations of Ancient Dances', *Burr McIntosh Monthly*, April, 1908, n. p.

[38] 'Chicago', *NYDM*, 27 July 1907, p.3.

[39] 'Notes on the Stage', *WH*, 5 May 1907, section 3, p.4.

[40] <http://www.ciweb.org/our-history/> [accessed 31 April 2016].

[41] Cindy S. Aron, *Working at Play: A History of Vacations in the United States* (New York: Oxford University Press, 1999), pp.91–97 and 113–18.

[42] See Robert McGowen, 'Records of Redpath Chautauqua', from *Books at Iowa*

19 (November 1973) <http://www.lib.uiowa.edu/spec-coll/bai/redpath.htm> [accessed 31 May 2016].

43   For details about Bay View, Epworth, and Winona Lake, see Mary Jane Doerr, *Bay View: An American Idea* (Allegan Forest, MI: Priscilla, 2010), <http://ludingtonmichigan.net/index.php?page=epworth>, and <http://www.villageatwinona.com/village-history/>, respectively [accessed 31 May 2016].

44   Aron, pp.124–26.

45   'Famous Ben Greet Players to Open Epworth Program', *Ludington (Michigan) News*, 1 July 1915, p.1; Susan Averill, 'Beautiful Performances by Ben Greet Company at Epworth Are Recalled', *Ludington (Michigan) News*, 15 August 1947, p.6.

46   'Society at Benefit for Arts Building', *NYH*, 20 August 1907, p.10.

47   'Shakespeare Al Fresco', *Auburn (New York) Citizen*, 17 May 1907, p.6.

48   'New Rochelle a Stage and All the People Therein Merely Players — and Auditors', *NYTr.*, 9 June 1907, p.5.

49   'Kyrle Bellew's New Play', *WTr.*, 11 August 1907, Women's magazine, p.2.

50   BG to Lucy Love, 24 December 1906, Yale Love.

51   Francis Oppenheimer, 'New York's Censorship of Plays'. *Theatre*, May 1908, pp.134–36; 'Letters to the Editor', *Theatre*, August 1908, p.iv.

52   <http://www.fenimoreartmuseum.org/node/1055; http://www.apartment-therapy.com/gustav-stickley-the-american-a-127060> [accessed 29 April 2013].

53   Selene Ayer Armstrong, 'Under the Greenwood Tree with Ben Greet and His Merry Woodland Players: Their Happiness in the Simple Things in Life A Lesson in the Joy of Living', *Craftsman*, September 1907, pp.620–28.

54   'Fourteenth Street — The Sign of the Cross', *NYDM*, 2 October 1897, p.16.

55   'Toronto', *Billboard*, 9 November 1907, p.53 'Montreal', *NYDM*, 23 November 1907, p.10; 'Peterborough', *NYDM*, 16 November 1907, p.25; 'Geneva', *NYDM*, 30 November 1907, p.19; 'Kingston', *NYDM*, 30 November 1907, p.21; 'Springfield' and 'Worcester', *Billboard*, 14 December 1907, p.26. Seating capacities from *JC(1905)*, pp.297 and 662.

56   'Hartford', *NYDM*, 25 January 1908, p.17. Seating capacities from *JC(1905)*, p.343 and Julius Cahn and R. Victor Leighton, *The Cahn-Leighton Official Theatrical Guide*, XVI (New York: New Amsterdam Theatre), p.516, respectively.

57   'She Stoops to Conquer', *PI*, 24 January 1908, p.6.

58   'Jordan Hall: Ben Greet's Company', *BET*, 28 January 1908, p.13.

59   'Jordan Hall: Everyman', *BET*, 30 January 1908, p.14; 'Mr. Greet Revives She Stoops to Conquer', *BET*, 31 January 1908, p.14.

60   'Jordan Hall: The Merchant of Venice', *BET*, 5 February 1908, p.17.

61   '"Masks and Faces", Opera and Operetta', *BET*, 7 February 1908, p.12.

62   'Three Wonder Tales', *BET*, 31 January 1908, p.20. Seating capacity from *JC(1905)*, p.149.

63   [Elbert Hubbard, 'The Ben Greet Players',] *Philistine*, February 1908, 75–80 (pp.76–77). This essay was later reprinted in the author's posthumously published collected theatrical writings, Elbert Hubbard, *In the Spotlight: Personal Experiences of Elbert Hubbard on the American Stage* (East Aurora, NY: Roycrofters, 1917), pp.57–60.

[64] Seating capacity from *JC(1905)*, p.180 (under its former name, the Lafayette Square Opera House).

[65] 'Masks and Faces Given' *WH*, 20 February 1908, p.5.

[66] 'The Passing Fad for "No Scenery" Plays', *WTr.*, 23 February 1908, p.2.

[67] BG to Lucy Love, 2 March 1908, Michigan Love; 'M. M. C. S.', *The (Carnegie Technical Schools) Tartan*, 4 March 1908, p.5. Seating capacity from *Standard History of Pittsburg [sic] Pennsylvania*, ed. by Erasmus Wilson (Chicago: H. R. Cornell, 1898), p.886.

[68] 'Indianapolis', *NYDM*, 12 May 1908, p.12; BG to Lucy Love, 14 March 1908, Michigan Love.

[69] 'Shakespeare at the N. E. A.', *School and Home Education*, 27 (1908), 359.

[70] BG to Lucy Love, 29 July 1908, Michigan Love.

[71] 'Jottings', *Press*, 19 September 1908, p.13; 'Stand Breaks; 300 Fall; Ben Greet Averts Panic', *CTr.*, 28 July 1908, p.2.

[72] BG to Lucy Love, 29 July 1908, Michigan Love; 'All Records Go at Ravinia Park', *CTr.*, 26 July 1908, p.3; 'News from Chicago', *NYDM*, 8 August 1908, p.6. For a description of *The Tempest* performance, see 'News from Chicago', *NYDM*, 25 July 1908, p.6.

[73] 'Ben Greet's Players', *NYDM*, 15 August 1908, p.5; 'Real Tempest Drives "The Tempest" Indoors', *NYH*, 5 August 1908, p.12; 'Mrs. Roosevelt at Columbia', *NYS*, 9 August 1908, p.1; 'Many Guests Arrive', *WH*, 14 August 1908, p.3.

[74] BG to Lucy Love, 29 July 1908 and 16 August 1908, Michigan Love; *Lake Placid Club on Adirondacks Lakes* (Essex Co., NY: Lake Placid Club, 1908), pp.56–57; Montrose J. Moses, 'Pastoral Players', *Theatre*, December 1908, pp.320–21.

[75] For notices, see 'Twelfth Night', *Auburn (New York) Citizen*, 23 June 1908, p.5; 'Amusements', *Amsterdam (New York) Evening Recorder*, 29 June 1908, p.5; 'Amusements', *Rome (New York) Sentinel*, 29 June 1908, p.2; 'Shakespeare at the Country Club', *Terre Haute Saturday Spectator*, 18 July 1908, p.14; Advertisement, *Indianapolis Sun*, 28 July 1908, section 2, p.3. Quote from 'Detroit', *NYDM*, 15 August 1908, p.9.

[76] Mary Caroline Crawford, 'Maude Adams in "Twelfth Night"', *Theatre*, August 1908, pp.218–20.

[77] For production details, see 'Joan of Arc', *BET*, 23 June 1909, p.17; 'Maude Adams Again Scores in a Unique Performance', *Deseret (Utah) Evening News*, 23 June 1909, p.5.

[78] According to *The Business of the Theatre: An Economic History of the American Theatre, 1750–1932*, ed. by Alfred L. Bernheim (New York: Actors' Equity Association, 1932; repr. New York: Benjamin Blom, 1964), p.87, thirteen legitimate and vaudeville houses in New York City were showing films in 1908.

[79] Montrose J. Moses, 'Where They Perform Shakespeare for Five Cents', *Theatre*, October 1908, pp.264–65 and xi–xii. Biographical details about Lamberger from 'Poems by Longfellow Go on Ether at WOR', *Radio Digest Illustrated*, 13 January 1923, p.3.

CHAPTER SIX

The Giddy Round of Fortune's Wheel, 1908–12

The 1908–09 Season

As Greet began organizing the 1908–09 season, he had three important facts to confront: demand for his traditional indoor offerings
continued to fall, the drama-music hybrids had attracted huge audiences in Chicago, and the centenary of Mendelssohn's birth (just the
kind of anniversary he liked to use as a hook) was only a few months
away. In response, he launched the most ambitious venture he ever
undertook: a transcontinental tour of the hybrids that included
more than 85 performers. But the actor-manager could not abandon
his beloved Elizabethan Manner Shakespeare, which had become
fundamental to his vision of himself and his work, so he formed a
second company to continue delivering it. Novelties sold tickets, and
Greet was betting that the profits the hybrids generated would
underwrite his traditional business.

Before the season got under way, however, he had to fulfil a
commitment he had made to one of his most loyal and distinguished benefactors. Mrs Roosevelt's tenure as First Lady nearing its
end, she had invited the company to present *The Wonder Book Plays*
on the grounds of the White House on 16 October to benefit the
Washington Playgrounds Association.[1] She arranged another
performance there the following day, this time for an audience
comprising the thousands of schoolchildren she had invited to help
celebrate the president's birthday.

As the city's newspapers declared and this photograph indicates, an eminent and gracious hostess, a worthy charity, glorious weather, a concert by the United States Marine Band, and the novelty of a performance on the White House grounds by the foremost open-air company in the land combined to make the event one of the memorable happenings in the capital that autumn. *Billboard* reported that 'nearly all the official and residential society was present. The audience was one of the largest that ever witnessed a theatrical event in Washington'. The President, First Lady, and children Ethel and Quentin sat in the central box. Four cabinet members, several ambassadors, and their families sat nearby. With approximately 2,000 people attending the first performance and 3,000 the second (before which President Roosevelt gave a short address), the engagement was an artistic, social, popular, and philanthropic success. Thanks to Mrs Roosevelt, Greet had achieved the distinction of leading the first professional dramatic company ever to perform at (if not in) the White House.[2] The actor-manager still had the capacity to capture the national imagination.

22. Harris & Ewing. THE WONDER BOOK PLAYS.
Dir. Ben Greet, The White House, Washington, DC, 16 October 1908.

A new season always meant personnel changes: Agnes Elliot Scott went to work for Robert B. Mantell while Sydney Greenstreet joined Julia Marlowe. To replace Scott, Greet recruited Miss Keith Wakeman. A native of Oakland, Wakeman already had more than two decades' professional experience, during which she had supported the likes of Edwin Booth, Lawrence Barrett, E. S. Willard, Henry Ludlowe, and Otis Skinner.[3] Veterans John Sayer Crawley and Leonard Shepherd now returned to the company, and Greet took on a promising apprentice from San Diego, Grace Halsey Mills, who would establish herself as a vital member of the company in the years ahead.

The hybrids were the most personnel-intensive productions Greet ever mounted. The company would tour with a full orchestra; this was usually the fifty-member Russian Symphony Orchestra under Modest Altschuler, but others served upon occasion. For the first time, Greet would present *A Midsummer Night's Dream* accompanied

23. Bratzman. A MIDSUMMER NIGHT'S DREAM *with the Russian Symphony Orchestra.* Dir. Ben Greet. English's Theatre, Indianapolis, IN, 18 March 1909.

by the entirety of Mendelssohn's Opus 61. As she had in Chicago, Lou Wall Moore supplied a 'fairy ballet of children' to perform the dances she had choreographed for the comedy, she herself performing the ones she choreographed for *The Tempest*. Artists Troy and Margaret Kinney created small scenic set-pieces as well as translucent green draperies and painted canvas curtains depicting an abstract landscape.[4] The only promotional photograph of one the hybrids I have located, one depicting the *Dream* taken the following March, illustrates how the various elements came together.

The company spent November playing short stands in the Northeast, the *New York Times* reporting that the combination was 'enthusiastically received' in New Haven.[5] A few days later, the *Dramatic Mirror*'s Boston correspondent called the productions some of the most interesting Greet had ever presented, but noted that their success owed more to the music than to the acting — an assessment other papers would echo.[6]

In January, Greet divided the company in two. He led the Western unit, which included Crawley, Rooke, Rosmer, and the Vivians. Based in Manhattan, it would offer the hybrids, the company's new play, a few Shakespearean standards, and *Everyman* there and in select East Coast cities. In early March, it would launch its transcontinental tour with the RSO that would conclude at the end of June. Frank McEntee, who had faithfully served Greet both as an actor and in sub-managerial capacities since the spring of 1903, led the Eastern unit. Featuring Wakeman and Shepherd, it included those performers whose talents ran more to the tragic than to the musical and comic. Leaving Manhattan immediately, it presented Elizabethan Manner *Hamlet, Julius Caesar, The Merchant of Venice*, and *Macbeth* down the East Coast until the close of the regular season.

The Western unit's new production received its premiere in January. *The Little Town of Bethlehem* was written by Katrina Trask, the wife of Spencer Trask, the New York banker and chairman of the National Arts Club. Like *The Sign of Cross, Ben Hur*, and *Quo Vadis*, it is a moral tale of sin and redemption set in the Roman empire. W. T.

Hamiston, who had composed the music for *Wonder Book*, once again supplied original music. Edmond Parks created sets based on Tissot paintings, from which the costumes were also copied. Rooke took the leading role of Faustina. Although the production was significantly more lavish than most of Greet's offerings, it made only a slight impression. A capacity crowd turned out for the first performance: a fundraiser in Brooklyn's 2,000-seat Academy of Music for the benefit of long-time philanthropic sponsor the Hampton Institute.[7] The *New York Times*'s positive review described it as a 'tender and appealing play' that was 'dignified' and 'impressive' despite its simple language and uneven performances. The New York *Sun*'s negative review also noted the uneven acting, adding that, although the audience was large, it never grew enthusiastic. Its critic may have mistaken reverence for boredom, however. In its glowing notice, the *Brooklyn Eagle* reported the massive audience 'followed with an attention that was almost awe'. Both the *Sun* and the *Eagle* felt obliged to assure readers that St Joseph was the only sacred personage depicted, and then but briefly; old prejudices died, especially when the man who put God on the American stage was directing.[8] The company presented the melodrama only a handful of times that winter.

Far more important was its presentation of the hybrid *Dream* in collaboration with the New York Symphony under Walter Damrosch in Carnegie Hall on 1 February. Greet had wanted to play the venue for years; that he did before a full house as part of the official Mendelssohn Centenary Festival celebrations was probably gratifying. According to the *New-York Tribune*, the combination of Shakespeare and Mendelssohn enchanted a mirthful holiday audience comprising people of all ages. One of its members, Emily Folger, praised the music, regretted the absence of Sybil Thorndike, and criticized the horseplay Greet permitted his comedians (and himself), which she considered too rough.[9]

Recombining with the RSO, the Western unit departed Manhattan in March. It presented the hybrids across the Midwest and West on its way to the Pacific, its longest engagement being a week in Denver's 1,624-seat Broadway Theatre. Arriving in Los Angeles in April, it received the warmest welcome Greet ever got in that city. Large and enthusiastic crowds turned out for the performances it gave during a profitable week in the 2,776-seat Auditorium Theatre. The excitement generated by the White House appearance not yet having worn off, the *Los Angeles Herald*'s society columnist also covered the run.[10]

Heading north, the company played a week-long engagement in San Francisco's Garrick Theatre (1,750 seats).[11] Like other managers, Greet had not visited the city in years; spending the money needed to bring a company there in the aftermath of the earthquake and fire of 1906 was too risky an investment. The devastation had been staggering, and, temporarily at least, San Franciscans had better things to do than spend their money on plays. But the city had been rebuilt, and new theatres had sprung up to replace the many that had been destroyed. As it had in earlier visits to the area, the company performed in the University of California's Greek Theatre, where it presented the hybrids in May. The *San Francisco Call*'s Walter Anthony praised its work, but the interview with Greet he published makes clear the actor-manager rued the decision to make the long (and expensive) trip west:

> I have never in my life played to such small audiences as I have encountered [...] along my tour. They believe in 'Everyman' and like 'A Midsummer Night's Dream'. They dote on 'As You Like It' and say 'The Tempest' is great fantasy — but they do not go to see these plays. As some one of the wits has said of the classics, 'they are the books that everybody admires but nobody reads'.

San Franciscans had once thronged to his presentations, but now they stayed away even when he offered them classical drama backed by superb music: 'Perhaps its [*sic*] the moving pictures or the cheap vaudeville houses that are doing the damage, but legitimate theaters are suffering all over this country'. That the public preferred sensation over substance was the result of dramatic critics failing in their duty to shape taste by condemning immoral and frivolous entertainments. As a result, managers who provided enlightening, clean, and uplifting fare could not make enough money 'to pay the gas bill'.[12]

Greet carried his umbrage into the Pacific Northwest. When a paper in Portland interviewed him, he sarcastically warned readers about the 'excessive intellectuality' needed to appreciate his productions before explaining his approach to producing the Elizabethan's work:

> I believe in presenting Shakespeare from a human standpoint. His charac-
> ters speak naturally. They do not stride or rant. They were human. They saw
> life too, from a humorous standpoint, and I think there is as much satire
> and genuine humor in Shakespeare as in any modern dramatist.[13]

Such simplicity and sincerity might have served Greet better than the patronizing attitude he sometimes struck. The highlight of this leg of the tour was the week the company spent in Seattle's 2,436-seat Moore Theatre.[14]

Turning east, it presented the hybrids in Montana and North Dakota before crossing into Manitoba in June. Re-entering the United States, it worked its way to the week-long engagement in Dayton that closed the season. A complete lack of money for advertising (and everything else) may explain the dearth of newspaper coverage from this period. Incredibly, an embezzler — Greet named his advance man — had struck again. As in 1904, the thief made off with a considerable sum, although exactly how much remains unclear. Once again, the amount was too great for Greet to cover out of pocket; in addition to the transportation costs involved in moving his scores of performers from city to city, Greet had hired a freight-car to carry the combined ensemble's trunks and instruments. The payment failing to arrive, the railroad impounded the car. The tour literally ground to a halt.[15]

The 1909 Open-Air Season

Perhaps with the help of a loan, Greet paid the company's debts and got it back on the road. Parting ways with the RSO as planned, the Western unit travelled to Chicago, which served as its base of operations for the next two months. There, it gave a more ambitious, more musically intensive version of the 1908 summer schedule that also reflected Greet's latest assessment of the business environment. The open-air market was getting crowded, the effect of which had been to drive down both quality and price. Greet was still willing to play colleges, clubs, and charities, but his eye was now fixed on presenting the hybrids and appearing before audiences to which his competitors had no access. Apart from the universities of Chicago and Michigan, the only campus performances I have identified that summer took place at the half-dozen normal schools in Illinois and Michigan in easy striking-distance of Chicago.

The company settled into its usual Chicago-area haunts. It staged the hybrids more than a half-dozen times at Ravinia Park in collaboration with the New York Symphony and Theodore Thomas orchestras. The latter also supported it during the two-week festival it presented in the University of Chicago's School of Education's Scammon Gardens, where, in addition to offering the hybrids and musically enhanced versions of four other Shakespearean plays, it presented Hertz's *King René's Daughter* and W. S. Gilbert's *Creatures of Impulse*. The coverage in the *Chicago Tribune* and the *Dramatic Mirror* indicates that year's festival was especially well-received by Greet's core audience of undergraduate summer-school students.[16]

The company made its most extensive forays yet to Epworth, Bay View, and Winona Lake. Greet had completely overcome the anti-theatrical prejudice of the Methodist and Presbyterian education-vacationers, who now could not get enough. Knowing these people were of modest means, Greet did not charge anything like the prices he charged their counterparts in the Adirondacks. Still, the enthusiastic welcomes they afforded reminded him that, rich or poor, Americans loved his open-air Shakespearean offerings.

The company headed east in August. After presenting the hybrids at Pittsburgh's Schenley Hotel supported by the Pittsburgh Festival Orchestra, it revisited familiar resorts in the Adirondacks. Its final performance that season took place at the Sagamore Hotel on Lake George. Cold and rainy weather dampened turnout, but a happy Greet told Love that those who attended agreed that it had been

> a real artistic hit. Some people came miles for it + others who lived at the Hotel didn't but 300 people out of the 320 registered at the Sagamore bought $5 tickets — not bad. 9 men contributed $125 apiece for Boxes […]. I really think our artistic reputation has had a big up lift this year.[17]

Looking back on the open-air season as it drew to a close, he added

> We've had some wonderful audiences this tour, but I'm much afraid there's very little profit. We've had to have such cheap prices — over 2000 people at Winona Lake Assembly — all 25¢, but the cry that Shakespeare is dead or that he's not wanted by the people — the common-people is ridiculous. I feel keener than ever that I can get something going in NY. There's no doubt we have enormously enhanced our reputation this year.[18]

The actor-manager was ready to do it all over again.

The White House performances, the transcontinental tour of the hybrids, another successful season in Chicago, and the well-received (if barely profitable) Chautauqua and Adirondack engagements were not the only reasons to be optimistic. McEntee had done a fine job with the Eastern unit. With the coming of the open-air season in late April, he led it north. Working its way up the East Coast, it played more than a dozen institutions of higher learning, including the universities of Georgia and South Carolina, Converse College, North Carolina State Normal, Virginia A & M, Washington and Lee, William and Mary, St John's (Annapolis), and the University of Pennsylvania. After giving a handful of presentations of the hybrids in collaboration with the Victor Herbert Orchestra at Brooklyn's Pratt Institute in June, it turned to the lucrative (if more sporadic) business of performing for society audiences on the grounds of private estates in the Berkshires before disbanding in July. Recognizing an opportunity in Manhattan, in early August McEntee hastily assembled an ad hoc company comprising some of Greet's more accomplished performers, past and present — Eric Blind, Dudley Digges, Greenstreet, Wakeman — to play a week-long engagement on the grounds of Columbia University. They delighted the summer-school students and members of the public so thoroughly that McEntee booked a second successful week there. Writing from the road, Greet playfully scolded Love for not sending him press clippings about McEntee's 'extended Columbia engagement'; the lengthening of any run in Manhattan, however brief, was cause for celebration.[19] McEntee's first independent command had been a critical and commercial success. That two Ben Greet companies — one of which was known not to include the actor-manager — toured, simultaneously and profitably, for eight months indicates Greet's name had achieved the status of a brand. What Levi Strauss was to riveted denim work trousers, Ben Greet had become to open-air Shakespeare.

As for his outdoor rivals — a group that now included companies led by Constance Crawley and George Ober as well as by the Coburns — Greet noted that none of them was being extended anywhere. He also told Love that Mrs Damrosch had told him that the Coburns had been disappointing when she saw them in Gloucester. I have uncovered few details regarding Crawley's and Ober's activities, but the summer of 1909 was the Coburns' best season yet. They dropped the word 'Shakespearean' from the name of their company, perhaps to signal the inclusion of the works by other playwrights, notably Percy MacKaye, whose *The Canterbury Pilgrims* they presented at more than thirty colleges and universities between Georgia and Massachusetts.[20]

Unfortunately for Greet, published accounts of the Coburns' appearance on the Massachusetts shore convey an impression altogether different than Mrs Damrosch's. Pageants had been growing in popularity since the 1890s, but had been typically local affairs written and presented by amateur groups containing fewer than seventy-five participants. But the performance of the professionally written, semi-professionally mounted *The Gods of the Golden Bowl* in Cornish, New Hampshire, in 1905 attracted a considerable amount of national attention and, according to David Glassberg and Naima Prevots, inaugurated the American Pageant Movement.[21] On 4 August 1909, the Coburns presented a colossally scaled *Canterbury Pilgrims* in Stage Fort Park as the central dramatic entertainment of a Gloucester Day commemoration (under the overall direction of Eric Pape) celebrated on an unprecedented scale. Activities earlier in the day included the ringing of church bells, canon salutes from the six warships lying in the harbour, and a military and civic parade reviewed by the governor and mayor. The performance of the play that night began with a twenty-one gun salute from the men-o'-war followed by the igniting of a giant fire curtain. Supporting the Coburns were a 200-person adult choir, 600 children, and a 65-piece military band (playing music Walter Damrosch composed for the event), all of whom shared the 175' x 680' playing space. A joust was added to the last act, and dances by adults and children were liberally inserted. A fireworks display closed the festivities. The last-minute cancelation of the event's much-touted guest of honour, President William Howard Taft, was a disappointment, but by all accounts the rest of the First Family (which was in attendance) and the estimated 20,000–25,000 other audience-members enjoyed themselves. The Gloucester Day appearance was a transformative experience that catapulted the Coburns to national prominence. MacKaye may not have been Shakespeare, and the Coburns' performance may have been as unexceptional as Mrs Damrosch claimed, but being featured at such a well-attended spectacular represented unprecedented exposure. Their appearance at Harvard a few days later confirmed their highbrow *bona fides*.[22]

In September, *Current Literature* published a feature about America's growing love for pageants that declared that open-air performance had blossomed into a full-fledged, nation-wide theatrical movement. Although not pageant producers, Greet and the Coburns were its leaders, and their efforts had established university and colleges campuses as the venue of choice.[23] Greet had been America's foremost purveyor of open-air plays for seven years. Whether he could retain that position remained to be seen.

The 1909–10 Season

Responding to the departures of Rooke, Rosmer, and Shepherd, Greet hired back Blind and divvied up the leading male roles between him, Crawley, and McEntee. He assigned the leading female ones to Wakeman, who received support from Mills and the Vivian sisters.

Represented by New York's Pond Lyceum Agency for the first part of the season, the company offered the hybrids with the Russian Symphony Orchestra on a mediocre tour of the Northeast. Once again, critics judged the musicianship to be superior to the acting. Indeed, the *Dramatic Mirror* reported that the fine work of the orchestra 'was all that saved the performance; Mr. Greet's players were away [*sic*] below what he has given us heretofore'.[24] Although the combined unit made three well-publicized and -attended appearances at Carnegie Hall early in the new year, the collaboration between the Ben Greet Players and the RSO effectively concluded that December.

But the most important Shakespeare-related event in Manhattan that fall was the opening of the New Theatre. That enterprise's not-so-slow-motion failure gave evidence that Spectacular Realism's grip was weakening. The promise of seeing a new, dazzling, star-studded production mounted in a theatre that set new standards of luxury and technological capability still appealed, but so did hearing a good play ably performed.

The New Theatre was conceived and built to be nothing less than the epicentre of drama in the United States; what the Comédie-Française was to France, the New Theatre was supposed to be to

America. It was financed by a consortium of thirty eminent founders — men with names like Astor, Frick, Gould, Huntington, Morgan, Vanderbilt, and Whitney — each of whom contributed $100,000 so that it might exist independent of the commerciality that drove the rest of the theatre business. Fronting on Central Park West a mile north of Manhattan's theatre district, the magnificent, 1,700-seat, *beaux-arts* structure was declared one of the city's most beautiful buildings the instant it was completed. Its repertory was to be strictly regimented: classical plays two nights a week, modern American and European plays two nights a week, and light operas two nights a week. To prevent the most successful productions from being performed until theatre-goers wearied of them, only short runs were permitted. All the great playwrights were welcome, but Shakespeare was given pride of place. Indeed, the sonnet Richard Watson Gilder composed for and recited at the laying of the cornerstone opened by boldly declaring:

> Shakespeare's new home is this; here, on this stage,
> Here shall he reign as first in London town;
> Here shall the passion of that high renown,
> Embodied newly, know its ancient rage.

The plays and operas would be mounted by a stock company and production team comprising experienced and versatile professionals drawn from both sides of the Atlantic. It would be given virtually unlimited resources with which to achieve the highest possible level of artistic perfection. Making a profit, or even expenses, was not a priority. Discount, 'Wage-Earners' Nights' would be regularly offered to enable the city's poorest residents to attend performances. In short, the New Theatre was one of the most self-consciously highbrow ventures in American theatrical history.[25]

The management team (which included John Corbin) determined that a no-expenses-spared production of the rarely staged *Antony and Cleopatra* would make the perfect inaugural offering. With impressive credentials and deep pockets, it persuaded America's Shakespearean power couple, Julia Marlowe and E. H. Sothern, to bring to life one of the playwright's greatest power couples in what promised to be the most lavish production of the tragedy ever mounted. The performers found the idea so appealing that they agreed not only to play the lovers, but also to lead the New Theatre's stock company.

The choice of both play and leads was poor. The reason the tragedy was produced so infrequently was that it is one of the Shakespearean plays most antithetical to Spectacular Realism. With more than forty scenes, it powerfully resists the integration of sets of any kind, let alone the behemoths favoured by the period's producers. The company's designer and stage manager succeeded in cramming it into twelve scenes employing five large, historically accurate sets erected between a pair of gargantuan Egyptian columns. The result pleased the eye, but little else. Addresses by J. P. Morgan, Governor Hughes, Senator Root, and Johnston Forbes-Robertson before the by-invitation-only gala dress rehearsal were no proof against the fiasco that ensued. As Charles H. Shattuck recounts, the theatre's acoustics were bad, the heating-ventilation system loud, the scene-changes took significantly longer than rehearsed, electrical problems yielded stage lighting so low that many audience members could not see the actors' expressions (or even know who was speaking) at times, and the performers spoke their lines too quietly and slowly. These problems produced a nearly incomprehensible performance that lasted 265 minutes, by the end of which fully two-thirds of the audience had already walked out. Fixing the acoustical and technical problems, cutting two more scenes, and eliminating the Pompey's galley set produced a swifter pace and a less gruelling (220-minute) run-time, but the result still fell far short of expectations.[26]

As for the leads, Shattuck correctly notes that Marlowe specialized in playing virtuous, emotionally vulnerable women. She was seasoned, skilled, and intelligent, but she had yet to achieve the mature artistry needed to convincingly portray Cleopatra. Similarly, Sothern lacked Antony's majesty and virility, choosing instead to invest the character with a melancholy that had served him well as

Hamlet, but which ill-became the triumvir and lover of the Queen of the Nile. At best, the stars' performances were mediocre. Regretting their decision, they discontinued their association with the New Theatre after the thirteenth and final performance in mid-December, thereby depriving the management not only of its principal box-office draw, but also of its Viola and Malvolio for January's already widely publicized *Twelfth Night*.[27] Making things even more difficult for their erstwhile employers, the pair decided to spend the rest of the season performing Shakespeare together. They cleared out of Manhattan for a few weeks, but returned in February to revive their most beloved Shakespearean productions at the Academy of Music, to which admirers would flock in droves until April.

Marlowe and Sothern inconvenienced more than one management that winter: over the Christmas break they hired away Blind from Greet, who assigned his roles to newcomer Alexander Calvert.[28] More positive, between the New Theatre, the Marlowe-Sothern combination, and Greet, Shakespeare would be a robust presence in the metropolis once more.

In January, the Ben Greet Players opened a three-month run at the 1,100-seat Garden Theatre — the last extended engagement it ever played in Manhattan. Uncharacteristically, Greet leased the theatre until May. The Garden becoming less and less fashionable as the theatre district crept further north, it had become so unprofitable that its owner had recently closed it.[29] The terms the Englishman secured encouraged him to believe he could once again test the old Broadway adage 'Shakespeare doesn't pay'.

His first offering, *The Little Town of Bethlehem*, ran for two weeks. The play had failed to make an impression the previous winter, but the *Brooklyn Eagle*'s positive notice credited improvements to the production, good word of mouth, and endorsements from prominent religious leaders for the modestly successful revival. Perhaps in deference to Trask, who was reported to be inconsolable at the recent, sudden death of her husband, the *Dramatic Mirror*'s negative review was also unusually moral:

> Of the play as a drama and of the acting nothing much can be said […].
> If taken as an interesting way to teach the story of the nativity, the play
> fulfilled its purpose. The reverential handling of the production did more
> to inspire a religious feeling of love and gratitude than could a thousand
> sermons on the same subject.[30]

Greet quietly dropped it from the repertory.

He then kept the Garden dark for a fortnight to allow himself time to rehearse his actors through the ambitious season he had committed them to: five Shakespearean standards, two eighteenth-century comedies, one new Elizabethan play, two moral fantasies, and *Everyman*. As he had in 1905, he offered a limited number of modestly discounted season-ticket subscriptions to his traditional clientele as well as blocks of discounted tickets to schools and social organizations.[31] The actor-manager no longer enjoyed the sponsorship of the People's Institute, but he was able to sell a sufficient number of full-priced seats and blocks of discounted tickets to stay in the black. As in 1905, thousands of poor schoolchildren were exposed to classical drama through his efforts, although how many cannot be estimated.[32]

She Stoops to Conquer got the season off to a rollicking start and received strong notices in both the *New York Herald* and the New York *Sun*.[33] Although the *New-York Tribune*'s new critic (its old one, William Winter, had been fired in 1909) considered the production only acceptable, he went out of his way to thank Greet for saving New Yorkers from the ineptitude, mediocrity, and 'animalism' that had thus far characterized the season. After noting that many of the actor-manager's performers possessed only workmanlike skills, the critic declared they were guided by a fine sensibility:

> From the drivel of certain other houses one hastens to the Garden
> Theatre disposed again to proclaim the truism that great plays, old
> comedies and curious old plays, fairly well acted, are vastly to be preferred
> above the 'brilliant', pretentious, and ephemeral 'presentations' which

affect a meaningless 'modernism' and which insufferably bore when they do not intensely disgust spectators of ordinary decency and a reasonable outfit of intelligence.

Substantive and tasteful, Greet's productions delighted all who valued the abiding excellence:

> The Ben Greet Players speak well, and that is more than can be said of any other company in town, with two or three exceptions. A certain distinction of manner, a certain grace and lightness of style may be lacking, but what a comfort it is to understand the actors, to listen to players who realize that words have meaning, and who know what the author was about! It is an experience too seldom met with in continuing journey through Theatreland. Persons who must see 'stars' or consider themselves defrauded care little for Shakespeare, Goldsmith or Sheridan, or […] the pleasure to be derived from acting; their hope is for sensation and the fashion and the folly of the hour […]. Here is something with which fashion and faddism have no concern.[34]

The critic's comments reinforced Greet's fundamental belief that he should stick to what he knew because it was as timeless as it was sound.

The papers did not review his Elizabethan Manner *Macbeth*. That it was influential is hard to deny, if for no other reason than Andrew Carnegie paid for 250 public school teachers to attend the performance the company gave on 28 February.[35] The philanthropist wanted the city's teachers to do justice to the tragedy in their classrooms.

Patrons at the opening night of the company's next offering, *The Merchant of Venice* (now with Wakeman as Portia), enjoyed what they saw. The *New York Herald* reported that 'The play was given with sufficient spirit to please a large audience, and Mr. Greet's Shylock was greatly applauded. The trial scene was followed by enthusiastic recalls for the whole company'.[36] Greet was putting the humiliation of 1907 behind him.

Responses to Greet's first American production of *The Rivals* were mixed. The *New York Evening Telegram* noted the appreciative audience that heartily followed the opening night's performance and the fine work of Greet and newcomers Alice Gale and Douglas J. Wood. The *Dramatic Mirror*'s negative review compared it unfavourably to Joseph Jefferson's and declared that the actors had been unable to deliver a first-rate presentation because they 'took themselves too seriously'.[37]

True to form, Greet scheduled a special matinee of *Everyman* for every Friday of Lent. Newcomer Beatrice Irwin's performance of the title-role was not as strong as those of her supporting players, but demand for tickets was brisk enough that Greet laid on additional evening performances.[38] On 14 March, the company gave what was advertised as its 1,000th performance of the Morality.[39]

Greet's all-male, Elizabethan Manner *Doctor Faustus* drew strong notices. William Poel had staged it to critical acclaim in 1896, and his 1904 revival achieved enough popular success to justify one of the longest tours of his career.[40] Greet could have attended a performance of the former, and he definitely saw the one the Princeton Dramatic Society mounted in 1907. According to the *Sun*, the text was that of the 1604 quarto with two scenes omitted and one scene transposed from the 1616 quarto. The paper also reported that Greet used his Middle Temple fit-up, which, like the costumes his players wore, was tired and worn. The performance of Crawley in the title-role drew praise, as did the work of newcomers Robert Whitworth (Mephistopheles) and Louis Thomas (Wagner). The *Dramatic Mirror* judged much of the acting to have been mediocre, but concluded by declaring that a professional revival of such an important work 'compensated for incidental shortcomings and the production must be favorably charged to the credit of Mr. Greet's pioneering spirit'. Similarly, *Theatre* commented, 'It has been remarked that if, perhaps, the Ben Greet Players do not always give performances of splendid professional finish, they at least enable one to witness plays that by possibility could not be seen elsewhere'. And the *New York Herald* reported that a large opening-night audience 'watched the play with interest and whenever opportunity was offered applauded the players'. The company performed the tragedy but three times.[41]

The papers barely acknowledged Greet's Elizabethan Manner *Julius Caesar*. After remarking that Calvert's Brutus was the best performance given, the *Dramatic Mirror* observed:

> Since the play is put forth in the usual non-scenery Greet way and in its entirety, the audience was at a loss to know where they were at. It would help to a better understanding of locale if Mr. Greet would divide his productions into acts and state on the programme where each act is supposed to take place. The educational value of Mr. Greet's performances, for which he pretends to make his productions, is almost destroyed by the confusion of place.[42]

That Elizabethan Manner continued to bewilder at least one professional Broadway dramatic critic six seasons after Greet introduced it indicates what a radical innovation it was.

Something almost as revolutionary was afoot at the New Theatre. Critics had enjoyed the *Twelfth Night* staged there in January, but their praise was both muted and qualified; it would have been much better with Marlowe and Sothern. Deciding that the company needed star appeal if subsequent productions were to have any hope of drawing, the management recruited Edith Wynne Matthison. The first Shakespearean production she appeared in there, March's *The Winter's Tale*, was a revelation. One of the few shining moments in the New Theatre's brief existence, it was instantly hailed as the best offering of its inaugural season as well as the finest production of the Romance mounted in the city in more than a generation. Matthison's incomparable Hermione and Rose Coghlan's impressive Paulina were much praised. Significantly, the way the play was staged attracted just as much attention because the management decided to mount it with a nearly complete text, reproduction Elizabethan costumes, a set comprising a single painted Elizabethan-style backdrop, and simple props.[43] The best-resourced company in America was doing Elizabethan Manner.

Mounting a nearly bare-stage production in a brand new, staggeringly expensive theatre boasting state-of-the-art Spectacular Realism capabilities struck no one as incongruous. Only the *Evening Post* registered a note of irony:

> It is a good thing that the New Theatre has thought fit to profit by the example set by Ben Greet and William Poel and play Shakespeare in conditions somewhat resembling those he wrote for. Only after seeing a representation of this kind is it possible to comprehend the full effect of the mutilations of the text demanded by the exigencies of modern spectacles.[44]

The lesson was clear: text and performance were just as important as theatre, scenery, and effects — slavish devotion to which could lead to the chain of decisions that produced the *Antony and Cleopatra* debacle. By going to the other extreme with its *Winter's Tale*, the New Theatre's company became the second professional ensemble of the twentieth century to stage an important, widely publicized, critically and commercially successful, reasonably authentic Elizabethan production. Although most of the performers were unable to achieve the swift cadence; clear diction; careful punctuation and accent; and light, natural inflexion that Greet's did, Elizabethan Manner at the New was important for bolstering the method's legitimacy.

The New Theatre's modern productions fared better than its classical ones, but its management took only two seasons to realize that their audacious highbrow venture was one of the greatest follies in American theatrical history. In 1911, it disbanded the company, changed the building's name to the Century Theatre, and leased it out to other ensembles. Wherever Shakespeare's American home was to be, the New Theatre would not be it.

Downtown, Greet was presenting a week of *Wonder Book* matinees to attract schoolchildren enjoying their Easter holidays. To draw their parents, he offered *The Palace of Truth* at night. Both productions used scenery. The brief notice the papers took of the former indicates only that it was well performed and much applauded.[45] Critically and commercially successful, the latter commanded more attention. The *New York Herald*'s unqualifiedly positive review praised the performances of Greet, Mills, Violet Vivian, and Wood, and urged readers to hasten to see the production. Apparently they did just that; the *New-York Tribune* reported sizeable audiences. After stating that Greet deserved credit for reviving the play, the critic proceeded to lecture him on the lesson he should draw from his success:

> When Mr. Greet deserts his severe alleged Shakespearian stage and uses the modern devices of scenery and costume he is much more likely to convey something of the meaning of a play. Mr. Greet's companies are not of such extraordinary merit that they do not require all present devices for creating stage illusions. And when he attempts a comedy more or less modern in origin he finds a field more suited to his resources than most of the Shakespearian tragedies.

The *Dramatic Mirror*'s positive review contained its share of backhanded compliments. The production had succeeded because the company was interested in its work. The simple play was 'well within the scope of [Greet's] players, many of whom have not yet graduated from the amateur class, and it is given with scenery. The result is a production far superior to that of the usual Greet production'. After pronouncing most of the performances merely workmanlike, the critic admitted that those of Greet and the Vivian sisters had been good.[46]

In April, the *Dramatic Mirror* ran a feature declaring that the success of all the Shakespeare, Maeterlink, Hauptmann, and Ibsen in the metropolis indicated that 'effete' New Yorkers were finally abandoning the 'insipid' novelties that had distracted them for the last several seasons for substantive old plays penned by 'virile' dramatists. The staggering commercial and critical success of the Marlowe-Sothern combination at the Academy of Music, Greet's pioneering and moderately successful season at a theatre so out-of-the-way its owner had shuttered it the previous fall, and the impressive productions of the Matthison-led *Winter's Tale* and *Sister Beatrice* at the New Theatre boded well. Fashions came and went, but higher intellectual and artistic standards seemed to be reasserting themselves.[47]

Greet's hybrid *Tempest* attracted little notice. The *New York Evening Telegram*'s brief mention states that the opening performance was well-attended and that Crawley's Prospero, Violet Vivian's Miranda, and Greet's Caliban were effective. Emily Folger, who attended it, praised the music, the scenery, and Greet's performance before describing the production as 'an enchanted isle for sure'. More ominous, she also reported many empty seats and little applause.[48]

The company's final offering of the run, a full-text *Dream*, attracted even smaller houses. The *Dramatic Mirror*'s positive review declared that the only thing the low turnout proved was that New Yorkers disliked the comedy. Greet's production was as good as Nat Goodwin's and Annie Russell's had been, not in terms of scenery, 'but in the way of illusion, of getting over the poetic value and furnishing real amusement'. Greet's Bottom and Percival Vivian's Salome-inspired Flute were hilarious, but Calvert's Lysander was luminous: 'as good as any Lysander within memory, and quite the best player of Greet's company'.[49]

Greet had leased the Garden until May, but there was no point lingering if larger audiences could be found elsewhere. For what turned out to be the final time, his company left a commercial theatre in Manhattan. On 22 April, Julius Hopp's Wage Earners' Theatre League and Theatre Center for Schools sponsored Greet's company in Carnegie Hall, where it presented *As You Like It* and *Dream* for poor adults and schoolchildren.[50] The next day, Shakespeare's birthday, the Brooklyn Teachers Association sponsored a performance of the Elizabethan Manner *Julius Caesar* at the 2,000-seat Brooklyn Academy of Music before a near-capacity house comprising almost entirely schoolchildren. The *Brooklyn Eagle* reported that the actor who played Antony faced an unanticipated challenge during the funeral oration when 'a chorus of small boys impressively repeated with him, in slow accents, "That [*sic*] was a man"'. The Brooklyn *Standard Union* remarked that the 'unseemly conduct may serve in future to make Mr. Greet think twice before he entertains so many budding students of English again'. (Its writer did not know the actor-manager.) Emily Folger, who also attended, noted that the children ridiculed the romance, reveled in the violence, and applauded enthusiastically at the oration. She reserved her censure for the performance, which she condemned as 'pretty shabby'. In her estimation, its only real virtue was the full text Greet presented.[51]

The 1910 Summer Season

A positive mention in one of the country's most influential magazines appeared as the members of the Greet's company were clearing out of Manhattan. Writing in the *Saturday Evening Post,* America's first professor of Dramatic Literature, Brander Matthews of Columbia University, praised the managements that had made the previous three months so rich for lovers of old plays in New York: 'thanks to the New Theatre, to the Sothern-Marlowe company and to Mr. Ben Greet', playgoers had had the chance to see fifteen Shakespearean plays, *Doctor Faustus, Everyman*, and three eighteenth-century comedies. 'It is true that some of these performances were barely adequate, but yet again some of them were unusually interesting'. But Matthews's comment had no appreciable impact on turnout at the company's next engagement, a fortnight in Philadelphia's Adelphi Theatre (1,341 seats), which was low.[52]

A far more receptive audience awaited the company in Washington, where the *Washington Herald* noted that 'Having already established himself as a prime Washington favorite, Mr. Greet has no fear that his engagement will not be accompanied by profit to himself and his audiences'. Departing considerably from his normal practice, Greet had decided that his company would spend the next two months playing the city's 1,467-seat Belasco Theatre. Even more unusual, its large repertory contained a high proportion of modern plays, all of which used scenery. For the first time, one of Greet's ensembles would function as a summer stock company.

Its first offering, *She Stoops*, pleased, but did not delight. Its second, Greet's seldom-mounted (and Bowdlerized) *Merry Wives*, attracted decent notices and large audiences. The presence of President and Mrs Taft at the 21 May performance did nothing to decrease the play's popularity or the reputation of the actor-manager, whose Falstaff was only adequate. The Tafts would visit the Belasco several more times during the run.[53]

J. M. Barrie's *The Professor's Love Story* pleased Washingtonians after initially startling them. So used to and fond were they of E. S. Willard's personation of the title-character that that player had all but eclipsed the play in their minds. As it did for Shakespeare, Greet's company re-established the pre-eminence of the play. The result was as striking as it was revelatory: the comedy was superb, ranking after only *Peter Pan* among the playwright's works. The production attracted healthy and appreciative audiences.[54]

Response to his special student Shakespearean matinees (*Romeo and Juliet, Tempest, Merchant*) was so enthusiastic that Greet laid on others. Not daring to risk dispelling the magic of the experience with their applause, theatregoers at the first night-time performance of the tragedy remained silent until the curtain closed, at which point they exploded into a long ovation — an occurrence rare enough to be newsworthy once upon a time. Violet Vivian's Juliet was splendid, and Ruth Vivian's Nurse was a treat.[55]

The *Washington Herald* praised the company's ability to offer so many good productions at a time when one a week was becoming 'a feat which is sufficient to occupy the time and attention of a fairly capable stage manager and company of actors'. After applauding the acting skills of the Vivian sisters and the managerial and acting skills of Greet, the reporter commented on the large numbers of students benefitting from the company's Shakespearean matinees, 'which while not given on the sumptuous scenic scale [...] are [...] of immeasurable good in instilling into playgoers of all classes a love for the works of Shakespeare, who is the standard dramatist for all times'.[56]

Most uncharacteristically, Greet allowed himself a holiday. His company continued to perform, but it would soon pay a price for its leader's slackness. Its next offering, Barrie's *The Little Minister*, went off without a hitch. Ditto for T. W. Robertson's *David Garrick*. Not so the opening night of *School for Scandal*, which drew withering notices. Having just returned to the city, Greet discovered — possibly only after the curtain had gone up — that most of his players were insufficiently prepared. The result was an awful, truly amateurish performance in which only five actors both knew and creditably delivered their lines. That one paper praised Greet for singlehandedly saving the performance was cold comfort. A company that traded on reliable competence and strong ensemble playing could ill-afford such disastrous outings.[57]

It was not the only reversal Greet suffered that 16 June. For on that day the Coburns, in what was billed as their first appearance in Washington, performed *As You Like It* on the grounds of the White House. The first Shakespearean play ever presented there was followed the next day by *Twelfth Night*. Once again, the performances were given for the benefit of the Washington Playgrounds Association and were important social events, though not on the scale of Greet's 1908 appearances. The *Dramatic Mirror* reported that Mrs Taft invited the company because it had impressed her so much at the Gloucester Day celebrations the previous summer.[58] That the Coburns had achieved open-air prominence equal to Greet's could no longer be disputed.

The Shakespearean standards Greet mounted next attracted mixed houses and notices, although the papers judged *Tempest* the best production of the Belasco season. The critics also had good things to say about the educational value of the interesting and well-attended *Merchant*, though some expressed disappointment that Greet's Shylock lacked the repulsiveness of Sothern's.[59] Robertson's *Caste* followed. Papers praised the performances of Greet, Violet Vivian, Ruth Vivian, and Crawley, but noted that several supporting players did not know their lines.[60] Performances of a much more respectably presented *School for Scandal* carried the company into July.

Responding to the increasingly oppressive heat, Greet hit upon the notion of presenting the company's week-long run of *Palace of Truth* on the Belasco's roof, which had originally been built as a roof garden. The novelty of the idea and the cooling breezes to be found there caused a minor sensation. People turned out in droves, and by week's end the *Washington Herald* reported a smile permanently wreathing Greet's face for having caught the public's fancy so completely. Washingtonians responded so enthusiastically to the rooftop *Dream* that Greet shortened the holiday he had promised his actors in order to add more performances.[61]

The company's next destination was Cincinnati's Zoological Gardens, where it mounted a two-week, twenty-six-performance(!) Shakespearean festival. Significantly, that institution's management had built a permanent, wooden, semi-roofed, 1,000+-seat Woodland Theatre there for the express use of the company, Greet having previously selected the site and consulted on the design. The stage is known to have measured 21' x 41' — a respectably Elizabethan scaffold. The *Dramatic Mirror* regretted that a more dignified venue could not be found, but the actor-manager loved it. Writing to Love half-way through the run, he declared 'We're doing very well here — the "Woodland Theatre" is beautiful'. The *New York Clipper* confirmed his assessment, reporting that the company delighted the 'large and fashionable audiences of stay-at-homes' that turned out to hear it at the alluring new venue.[62] Angus L. Bowmer has rightly been commended for transforming the concrete foundation of a dismantled Chautauqua site in Ashland, Oregon, into an open-air theatre in order to produce an amateur, three-day, two-play Shakespearean festival in 1935. But we should not forget that the management of the Cincinnati Zoo built an open-air theatre so Greet's professionals could mount a fortnight-long, multi-play Shakespearean festival in 1910. The Woodland Players returning there during the summers of 1911, 1912, and 1913, to the Cincinnati Zoo goes the credit for hosting the United States's third annual, after the universities of Chicago and Columbia, (and first non-university) Shakespearean festival.

Cincinnatians were not the only ones anxious to hear Greet before summer's end. In the same letter to Love, he reported that Ravinia's manager had been so eager to reunite him with Damrosch that he had personally travelled to Cincinnati to obtain the Englishman's signature. In mid-August, the company offered a week of musically enhanced *As You Like It*, *Comedy of Errors*, and *Merry Wives* at Ravinia in collaboration with the New York Symphony Orchestra. Attendance was healthy, if not robust. A disappointing week in Interlaken, New Jersey, followed by a scattering of country-club appearances on Long Island closed the season.[63]

The same summer found the McEntee-led company of Woodland Players touring seven of Greet's Shakespearean standards through the South and Northeast. Once again, appearances at educational engagements — including the University of South Carolina, Converse College, Trinity College (now Duke University), the University of Virginia, Washington and Lee, William and Mary, Syracuse, the University of Pennsylvania, and several normal schools in Pennsylvania — were central to the tour. One of its highest-profile engagements took place on 16 May, when the ensemble presented *As You Like It* and *Dream* at the Governor's Mansion in Raleigh, North Carolina. The last performances I have confirmed took place in mid-August on the grounds of Pittsburgh's Schenley Hotel, where the company presented the hybrids in collaboration with the Pittsburgh Festival Orchestra. It had been another successful outing for McEntee and the Greet brand. By summer's end, the total number of universities, colleges, and normal schools that had sponsored performances by Greet's companies neared 100.

In late August, the New York *Sun* published a feature about the ever-increasing importance of the Open-Air Theatre Movement. The Victorian amateurs who had hit upon the novelty had been succeeded by skilled professionals who legitimized and popularized it. Their efforts eventually attracted the interest of stars like Maude Adams and Margaret Anglin, whose one-off, no-expenses-spared theatrical events at the University of California's Greek Theatre that summer

(*As You Like It* and *Antigone*, respectively) achieved new heights of scale and spectacle. But readers should not forget the less-prominent practitioners who presented solid, if less awe-inspiring, work:

> Of course there are as serious artistic and ambitious productions made by the Coburn and the Ben Greet company, although they lack such distinguished individual stars as Miss Adams and Miss Anglin. They offer, on the other hand, the advantages of smoothness and finish that comes from playing together through long periods.[64]

America had never consumed as much open-air drama as it had during the summer of 1910, the year in which pageant-scale productions with huge budgets featuring stars supported by massive casts presented to 10,000+-person audiences in performances that were never intended to recoup costs achieved cultural pre-eminence.

Greet's summer companies continued to command large and diverse audiences, but every year brought more rivals into the market, each hungry for a piece of the action. And their managers knew that the best place to find customers was in areas Greet had pioneered but was not servicing, either because he was working elsewhere or because his old patrons wanted something new. Although several open-air competitors — Constance Crawley's company, George Ober's company, John Nicholson's company — were now operating, the Coburns remained Greet's only serious rival. As we have seen, they aggressively entered the academic market in 1909. They consolidated their position there during the 1910 open-air season by appearing at the likes of Brown, Columbia, Harvard, Mt Holyoke, Princeton, and Smith — all of which had once hosted Greet. The Coburns may have dropped the word 'Shakespearean' from the name of their company in 1909, and their 1910 repertory may have included Euripides's *Electra* and MacKay's *The Canterbury Pilgrims*, but *Romeo and Juliet*, *Twelfth Night*, and *As You Like It* were their principal offerings that summer.[65] And of course Shakespeare is what they had presented at the White House.

Considerably more ambitious was the plan Charles D. Coburn devised to not only bring more performances to more institutions of higher learning, but also to increase his company's market-share. In an essay published in *Forensic Quarterly* that September (and as a pamphlet the following year), Coburn argued that Drama would be elevated to the cultural prominence of its sister art, Music, as soon as a critical mass of universities and colleges began regularly sponsoring professionally mounted performances of 'worthy' plays on their campuses. Once this happened, he claimed, institutions would begin adding Drama (by which he meant Theatre) to their curricula, which would eventually induce them to construct theatres. In time, he asserted, the uplifting, educative power Drama (by which he meant Theatre) had once had would be restored to the betterment of American culture. To effect this, Coburn called upon the country's educational institutions to form an academic society *cum* circuit he suggested be called the University Theatre Association. If at least fifty of them came together, designated the Coburn Players as their official company, and contracted to sponsor it in a tour of classical plays (repertory to be determined by himself subject to the approval of the UTA's officers) every winter, he would undertake this important cultural work in the most cost-effective manner possible. Although the idea proved to be impractical, it made manifest Coburn's intention to dominate the academic market.[66]

The 1910–11 Season

Greet's pioneering open-air tours and those of his outdoor rivals had inaugurated a nation-wide dramatic movement, but nothing was transforming the entertainment industry as drastically as cinema. Film had finally begun to affect theatre; theatrical professionals who failed to adapt to the new competitive environment were likely to find themselves out of work.

Like hundreds of touring companies, Greet's spent much of the regular season working what was known simply as 'the road', which economic theatre historian Alfred L. Bernheim defines as 'every place except New York City […] Boston, Philadelphia, Detroit, Chicago, St. Louis, Los Angeles and perhaps a half dozen other cities' where attractions could 'settle for a run of the play instead of merely passing through for a limited stay on a pre-arranged schedule'.[67] Although a vibrant force in late-nineteenth-century American culture, the road began to die in the second decade of the twentieth century.

Bernheim catalogues the external and internal forces that triggered its demise. Of the former, film was the most powerful; the irresistible combination of low admission price and breadth of appeal enabled it to seize control of the entertainment industry. The best adult seat in a cinema cost between 25¢ and 75¢, while the best seat in a theatre cost between $1.50 and $2.50. As well, the content of movies was more universally attractive and wholesome than that of plays. Other features enhanced its convenience and appeal in a nation of hard-working immigrants. Movies ran continuously, thereby eliminating the imperative of making a curtain. More important, a command of English was not necessary to enjoy them. Another mass-produced technological wonder, the automobile, was another instrument of change. Inexpensive and reliable, Henry Ford's 1908 Model T made traveling to the nearest city — where better shopping, restaurants, and entertainments awaited — an affordable and convenient alternative to the local theatre. It even prompted some people to abandon performed entertainments for automobile tourism, which soon established itself as a popular pastime. With breath-taking rapidity, these high-tech innovations became cultural forces that started taking substantial market-share from commercial theatre.

Bernheim also identifies the internal issues concerning quality and supply that further weakened the road. The protracted battle between the Theatrical Trust and the Shuberts for control of the theatre industry resulted in an oversupply of theatres. A town with a healthy Trust theatre might get a new Shubert theatre regardless of whether its population could support it. If its citizenry could not, the failure of both theatres might result. Exacerbating the over-supply problem was the dearth of good plays and players, which caused widespread dissatisfaction among theatregoers, especially when unscrupulous producers published shamelessly deceptive advertisements about the bad ones they were offering.

The days of the small-town theatre — and the companies that serviced them — were numbered. Bernheim describes how the road began to die as theatres in their hundreds started to close. And fewer theatres hosting fewer performances on fewer dates meant the road could no longer sustain the number of companies it once had. Unable to string together enough engagements to remain profitable, touring companies by the score started to fold. In 1910, the road went into a precipitous decline from which it never recovered. During the period 1905–09, the average number of companies touring the road was 298. During the period 1910–14, the average plummeted to 198 — a dizzying, thirty-four per cent drop in just five years. During the period 1915–19, that average had fallen to just 72, or fewer than a quarter of the companies that had operated a decade earlier.

Managers of touring companies quickly realized they needed to do whatever they could to stay off the road, which dealt yet another blow to America's already over-theatre-ed (yet under-served) towns. Going bust was a very real possibility for companies whose managers failed to secure enough extended engagements in major urban centres.

The assessment Greet made of the market in the late summer of 1910 convinced him that fielding an indoor touring company was too risky. Uncharacteristically (but perhaps wisely), he decided to sit out the season. Instead, he pursued a variety of lesser projects, few of which were Shakespeare-related. Taking a long-planned trip to Germany, he attended the Oberammergau *Passionspiel* to watch his friend, Anton Lang, reprise the role of Christ. Returning to North America, he toured an illustrated lecture about that year's *Passionspiel* on a Lyceum circuit that included Montreal, Manhattan, and Washington. In January, he directed Henri Bernstein's *The Redemption of Evelyn Vaudray* in Richmond, Virginia for Leibler Co.[68] In February, he formed an ad hoc company to present *Palace of Truth* and some other Gilbert comedies for a brief tour of New England and upstate New York.

In April, he published a long essay in the progressive *World's Work* in which he announced an ambitious scheme that brought together many of the ideas about management, repertory, actors, and audience he had championed over the years. The New Theatre clearly on his mind, he advocated for the construction of a Shakespeare Memorial Theatre in Manhattan. Like its counterpart being contemplated in London, it should be completed (or at least fully financed) by the tercentenary of the playwright's death in 1916. It should be located south of 15th Street so that it would be as close as possible to the greatest number of New Yorkers, the poorest of whom should be regularly provided with low-cost tickets. American money should endow it, and Americans should manage and direct it. It should house two companies that would include the ablest American performers available, neither of which should contain stars. The Shakespearean company should mount 'authoritative' productions (probably meaning that they should conform with Greet's ideas) of works by the playwright. The other company should present a miscellaneous repertory comprising good new plays that could not get a hearing elsewhere as well as one-hundred good-but-neglected older plays Greet would identify. Only short runs would be permitted in order to prevent the most successful productions from being presented until theatregoers wearied of them and enable the actors to master a wide array of roles and skills. The theatre should house a Shakespearean library as well as a school of acting, the latter of which the actor-manager would not be averse to operating. The stage, the profession, and the American people would be the ultimate beneficiaries of this important cultural undertaking. Wealthy benefactors might supply some of the projected $2–5 million that would be needed, but the ideal funding source would be a million high-minded Americans pledging $1 a year for five years.[69] Greet and others continued to champion the idea into 1912, but the scheme failed to attract sufficient support and was eventually dropped.[70]

The 1911 Open-Air Season

Greet fielded a single company of Woodland Players that included Mills, McEntee, Flood, the Vivians, and Dallas Anderson, who had been a member of the original North American *Everyman* cast. Its repertory included one new production, *The Winter's Tale*, along with seven Shakespearean standards. It opened the season on 22 April at Carnegie Hall, where, supported by the Volpe Symphony Orchestra, it presented two Shakespearean plays to celebrate the author's birthday. The matinee, *As You Like It*, featured prelude, entr'acte, and incidental music taken from Beethoven's Pastoral Symphony and a rustic clog-dance interpolated into the play. The hybrid *Dream* was the evening's offering. Hopp's Wage Earners' Theatre League and Theatre Center for Public Schools bought out the upper part of the house for the performances, both of which attracted large audiences. Advocates for Greet's New York Shakespeare Memorial Theatre plan promoted their cause during the intermissions.[71]

Greet's company was not the only one celebrating Shakespeare's birthday in Manhattan. On the same day, large audiences attended Daly's Theatre to see Mantell's *King Lear* and *Merchant of Venice*. The New York *Sun*'s critic found the former disappointing, even 'unnecessary'; Shakespeare's characters were unsympathetic or evil to the point of impossibility, but Rudolf Schildkraut's recent personation of the king rendered Mantell's even less convincing. The New Theatre's Elizabethan Manner *Winter's Tale* had confirmed beyond all doubt 'how much more swift and direct the dramatic progress of the story may be when it is not encumbered' with scenery, machines, and effects. Mantell's commitment to these remained unshakable, but the tragedy's often impressionistic localities did not lend themselves to scenic representation. The *New York Press* pronounced his Shylock unsubtle, weak, and too prone to provoking gales of laughter from the schoolchildren in the audience. In terms of spectacle, Mantell's now-dated productions failed to achieve the technological standard contemporary Broadway audiences demanded.[72]

As competitive as the open-air market had become, Greet secured an impressive number of bookings in a seventeen-week tour that encompassed the South, Midwest, and the Northeast. Longer engagements included a two-week, twenty-eight-performance(!) Shakespearean festival at the Cincinnati Zoo, a week at Indianapolis's Broad Ripple Park, and a week at Chicago's Ravinia Park. Institutional appearances included the universities of North Carolina, Virginia, Washington and Lee, Pennsylvania, Princeton, Lehigh, and Michigan. As it had the previous summer, the company performed at the governor's mansion in Raleigh, North Carolina. It also played a few country clubs. Significantly, the texts it presented on the boards of the Cincinnati Zoo's Woodland Theatre were cut; the *Cincinnati Enquirer* reported that every play in the festival had an intermissionless, 105-minute run-time.[73] Textual fidelity had become less important than delighting audiences (and staying in business).

The Coburns enjoyed another fine season. After playing East Coast universities and colleges that May and June, they settled down for a week-long engagement at the University of Chicago's School of Education's Scammon Gardens in July, breathing new life into the festival that had been allowed to lapse the previous summer. The festival they mounted later that month at another Greet-pioneered site, Columbia University, attracted large audiences and good press. Performances at Harvard and Dartmouth followed. In August, the Coburns presented three Shakespearean plays at the Thirty-Eighth Chautauqua Assembly at Lake Chautauqua, New York.[74] A feature published in the New York *Sun* described the Coburns and Greet as America's preeminent open-air producers.[75]

The last Greet-related event of the summer worthy of mention was the appearance of an educationally purposed ensemble in Manhattan that featured several alumni of the actor-manager's company, including Blind, Crawley, and Greenstreet. On 29 July, Hopp's Wage Earners' Theatre League and Theatre Center for Public Schools arranged for the players to present a bare-stage, full-text *Merchant* at P.S. 64 on the East Side. Swedish-born Warner Oland played Shylock. About 1,000 people attended, and senior representatives of the New York Board of Education delivered speeches about the educational and social value of drama.[76] Thanks to Greet, Hopp and others like him were eager that schoolchildren be exposed to professional productions of complete Shakespearean plays.

The 1911–12 Season

Once again determining not to field a company, Greet pursued other projects. In October and November, he directed Bernstein's *The Thief* and *The Whirlwind* at Manhattan's Daly's Theatre for Leibler Co. He also delivered a series of ten lectures on the plays of Shakespeare and their 'practical application to problems of the present day' at the West Side YMCA.[77]

Forced to find other employment, Frank McEntee and his wife, actress Millicent Evison, founded a company that used Greet's method, repertory, business model, and sometimes even name, the activities of which the *Dramatic Mirror* sporadically covered. Greet had had enough by February, when the paper reported that 'McEntee's Ben Greet Players' had appeared in Asheville, North Carolina; in a polite letter to the editor, he encouraged the journal to check its facts, noting that any company using his name that season did so without his permission.[78]

Greet spent part of that fall and winter editing some Shakespearean plays for Doubleday, Page & Company. In March, the publisher brought out the first volumes in its *The Ben Greet Shakespeare for Young Readers and Amateur Players* series, the stated purpose of which was to arouse 'a keener interest among young folks and amateurs in the presentation of Shakespeare's plays both in the home and on the stage'. The blurb on the backs of the dust-jackets touted the unique qualifications of their editor as well as the distinctive layout of the books:

If one were asked to select the ideal man of all the actors or experts in our generation to edit Shakespeare for the young of all ages, there could hardly be any choice but Mr. Ben Greet. Himself a most distinguished impersonator of 'Bully Bottom' and other Shakespearean rôles; a really wonderful stage manager and producer; an enthusiast on Shakespeare, on outdoor plays, on inexpensively staged home and amateur productions of good plays by young people — he has every qualification necessary to produce a classic. And that is what we firmly believe these books will become. Not only is there a continuous reading-text on the right-hand pages, but on the left-hand ones Mr. Greet has poured out his wealth of knowledge and novel ideas on how to stage the plays, the action and the 'business', the conception of different parts — the whole intricate and fascinating art of stage-craft applied to the greatest dramatist, as Mr. Greet has developed it in a lifetime of practical experience and study. There *couldn't* be better books for young people than these.

In the brief essay, 'A Few General Rules or Customs of Acting', that opens every volume, Greet lays out simple, practical advice on standing on a stage, breathing, projecting, and the importance of originality. He also explains his decision to cut the texts to a 120-minute run-time in order to make them conform to modern expectations and to simplify mounting them. (His target readership being students, a statement regarding his excision of all bawdy and suggestive passages was unnecessary.) The text and explanatory notes include suggestions for blocking, business, costume, music, and dance, as well as illustrative diagrams like this one from *Julius Caesar* — all keyed to the lines they face — that offer useful guidance to novices and more advanced practitioners alike. Thanks to Greet and Doubleday, mounting creditable amateur productions had just gotten much easier.

Sales were robust, and the editions attracted positive reviews in the *New York Times*, the *New-York Tribune*, and the *Dramatic Mirror*, which was uncharacteristically enthusiastic:

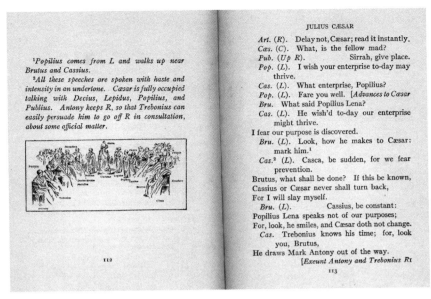

24. *The Ben Greet Shakespeare for Young Readers and Amateur Players: Julius Caesar*, ed. by Ben Greet [1912], Act 3, Scene 1, lines 8–26.

these books evidence most painstaking effort by Ben Greet, who has written ample prompt directions that face each page, not only describing action, but explaining motives and shedding light upon many points that might be doubtful […]. This rearrangement is exceedingly admirable, and has been accomplished with great care, reverence, and unremitting regard for detail.[79]

All told, the series comprised editions of six plays — *As You Like It, The Comedy of Errors, Julius Caesar, Merchant, Dream*, and *Tempest* — all of which had been issued by October. Greet had added editing to his list of Shakespearean accomplishments.

In February 1912, he signed a memorandum of agreement with the Redpath Bureau, pledging to field a company of Ben Greet Players that the bureau undertook to produce on the Lyceum circuits it operated during the regular 1912–13 season.[80] As we will see, this collaboration would have a profound impact on

Shakespeare's presence in American culture.

In March, English film studio Kinemacolor hired Greet to narrate its forty-five-minute colour adaptation of *Oedipus Rex* that ran for a fortnight in Manhattan's Kinemacolor Theater — the new name of Mendelssohn Hall, the venue at which *Everyman* had received its North American premiere. As the movie and orchestra played, Greet recited passages from Gilbert Murray's translation of Sophocles's tragedy and offered explanatory remarks that supplemented the intertitles. The *New York Times* and *Billboard* reported exceptionally large audiences. The *New York Times*, *New York Herald*, and *Evening Telegram* thought well of the experiment, the last pronouncing it 'remarkably satisfying from an artistic point of view'. The *New-York Tribune* was impressed by the images and the colour, but decried the textual violence that transformed 'stately Greek tragedy' into 'swift melodrama'. The *Dramatic Mirror* declared it pretentious, inferior to recent stage productions of the play, and marred by Greet's confusing tendency to continue speaking when new intertitles appeared on the screen. If Greet was slow to adapt to the new medium's timing, he immediately recognized its educational potential. On 11 March, 500 schoolchildren from the New York Institution for the Instruction of the Deaf and Dumb trooped in for a screening. The New York *Sun* described Greet speaking slowly and with even greater care for the students adept at lip reading. Its critic also noted that the fun of the field-trip Greet had organized heightened its educational impact:

> To-morrow everybody will have to write out the story of *Oedipus* in compositions, and nothing will be missed, for when Mr. Greet had [...] retired one girl pointed to her eyes, a boy thrust with an imaginary sword; there were real bits of acting all about.[81]

Few things gratified Greet more than bringing classical drama to life for children.

Rare was the April when Greet failed to formally celebrate

Shakespeare's birthday. That year, he and Henry Ludlowe assembled an ad hoc company that presented three Shakespearean plays in Philadelphia's 3,100-seat Academy of Music.[82]

Greet continued to explore other new opportunities. In late April and early May, he recorded fifteen speeches from more than a half-dozen Shakespearean plays for the Victor Talking Machine Company. Released that summer, the first of the records contained the actor's interpretations of 'Hamlet on Friendship' and 'Benedick's Idea of a Wife'.[83] Greet had added recording artist to his Shakespearean credits. Almost certainly of greater importance to him was his election at the national convention to the presidency of the New York (and founding) chapter of the Actors' Church Alliance, in which he had remained active since 1902. Greet was now one of the leading figures of the church-stage movement in the United States.[84]

The 1912 Open-Air Season

The company of Woodland Players he assembled that May contained a number of veterans, including George, Percival, and Ruth Vivian. The actor-manager also hired seasoned American professional Alma Kruger to take the leading female roles. A much younger American recruit made his first appearance at this time; William Keighley's managerial skills would soon prove a valuable asset. Greet had little interest in fighting the Coburns for one- and two-day stands at universities and colleges; his eyes were fixed on securing longer engagements. Travelling to Chicago, the company opened its most ambitious run of the season there in late May. More than the citizens of any other American city, Chicagoans loved Greet's hybrids, and the actor-manager was determined to give them the most magnificent versions yet mounted, and at 'popular prices'. He would stage them in the metropolis's foremost operatic venue: the 3,811-seat Chicago Auditorium. Its resident Chicago Grand Opera Orchestra and the Chicago Grand Opera Chorus under N. B. Emanuel would supply the music, and its Chicago Grand Opera Ballet would supply the dances. The result was truly spectacular. Although the run had originally been scheduled for two weeks, demand for tickets ran so high that it was extended to four.[85] Greet told Love that the initial fortnight had been gratifyingly remunerative, but that the locals had claimed the lion's share of the profits when the time came to negotiate the terms for the extra fortnight. Still, the exposure the company received in Chicago generated healthy Midwest bookings.[86] Another rewarding open-air tour loomed.

Greet offered an ambitious repertory comprising nine Shakespearean standards, *Palace of Truth*, *She Stoops*, and *Wonder Book*. Remaining in the Midwest, the company visited several educational institutions including Michigan State, Indiana State, and the universities of Indiana and Illinois. In early July, it opened its longest engagement of the summer: a three-week festival at the Cincinnati Zoo's 1,000+-seat Woodland Theatre.[87] Nearly a month of university and resort engagements, including appearances at old haunts — the University of Michigan, Bay View, Epworth — followed. After a half-week at the affluent Grand Hotel on Mackinac Island, Michigan, the company travelled to upstate New York, where it closed the season at the Lake Placid Club. The company's packed calendar, references in the papers to large and capacity audiences, and solid profits (Greet reported $1,000 per week) support the conclusion that the tour was lucrative, if not critically distinguished.[88]

As the Woodland Players worked a season notable for the number of indoor (or at least under-roof) performances, the Coburns offered more traditional open-air fare. They played educational institutions in the South, the Midwest, and the South Central region (a part of the country that had yet to host an extended tour by either company) before making their now-regular appearances at Columbia and Harvard. An advance notice for their appearance at Kenyon College included one of their most untruthful anti-Greet claims:

> In strong contrast to the Ben Greet players, the Coburn players base their
> claims for artistic ability on the fact that there are no individual stars — the
> company is exceptionally well-rounded and that the acting of no part, even

the smallest is suffered to be inferior.[89]

As they had the previous summer, the Coburns also performed at the Chautauqua Assembly on Lake Chautauqua, New York. More significant, they had toured during the regular 1911–12 theatrical season. Now possessing seven years' managerial experience, the Coburns determined that their expertise was sufficient to enable them to survive as a year-round concern.[90] At a time when companies were folding right and left, their decision — and success — was a bold statement.

Another couple, McEntee and Evison, fielded their own open-air Shakespearean company that summer. Although the *Dramatic Mirror* was careful to call it the Frank McEntee Pastoral Players, advertisements in local papers continued to reference 'Ben Greet' — a name that drew audiences in a way 'Frank McEntee' never would.[91] Greet would soon learn whether it appealed to another group, one that had always eschewed theatre.

NOTES

[1] Dobson, p.179, erroneously states that Greet's first performance at the White House took place on 14 November 1908. Considerably wider of the mark is the assertion by Charlotte M. Canning, *The Most American Thing in America: Circuit Chautauqua as Performance* (Iowa City: University of Iowa Press, 2005), p.211, that it took place in 1904.

[2] 'Ben Greet and His Players on White House Lawn', *Billboard*, 31 October 1908, p.46; 'Diplomatic', *WTr.*, 4 October 1908, Society, the Stage, and Personal Chat section, p.4; 'Mrs. Roosevelt Bids Children to Show', *WTr.*, 7 October 1908, p.6; 'Play Outdoors at the White House', *WTr.*, 13 October 1904, p.4; 'President Smiles on Greet Crowds', *WTr.*, 17 October 1908, p.1.; 'Society, in Force, Sees Ben Greet Plays', *WTr.*, 17 October 1908, p.4; 'About People and Social Incidents', *NYTr.*, 17 October 1908, p.6; 'Plays on White House Lawn', *NYT*, 17 October 1908, p.9.

[3] 'Bijou — The Merchant of Venice', *NYDM*, 29 February 1908, p.3; 'Miss Keith Wakeman', *NYS*, 18 October 1933, p.28.

[4] Details from 'Greet Players and Symphony', *Meriden (Connecticut) Morning Record*, 17 November 1908, p.5. The fact that the Kinneys were also Chicago-based artists and dance historians suggests Moore may have introduced them to Greet.

[5] 'Russian Music with Acting', *NYT*, 17 November 1908, p.9.

[6] 'Boston', *NYDM*, 28 November 1908, p.7.

7   Seating capacity from <http://www.lhat.org/historictheatres/theatre_inventory/NY.aspx> [accessed 5 June 2013].
8   'Appealing Play of the Nativity', *NYT*, 13 January 1909, p.9; 'Story of Christ in a Play', *NYS*, 13 January 1909, p.9; 'Katrina Trask's Play Deeply Reverential', *BE*, 13 January 1909, p.5.
9   'Shakespeare and Mendelssohn', *NYTr.*, 3 January 1909, p.9; Emily Folger, 'Plays I Have Seen' theatrical diary, p.51, Folger Collection, Box 38, Folger Shakespeare Library, Washington, DC.
10   'Greet Playeks [*sic*] in "Midsummer Night's Dream"', *Los Angeles Herald*, 20 April 1909, p.5; 'Greet Players in "The Tempest" Receive Much Applause', *Los Angeles Herald*, 22 April 1909, p.5; 'Society', *Los Angeles Herald*, 25 April 1909, p.2. Seating capacity from *C-L(1913)*, p.91.
11   Seating capacity from *Henry's Official Western Theatrical Guide, 1907–08*, ed. by W. R. Daily (San Francisco: n. p., 1907), p.51. The new Orpheum Theatre that was built in 1907 (the old one was destroyed by the earthquake) was renamed the Garrick early in 1909.
12   Walter Anthony, 'Ben Greet — Pessimist Mrs. Phipps — Optimist', *SFC*, 9 May 1909, p.27.
13   'Shakespeare by Track', *(Portland) Morning Oregonian*, 12 May 1909, p.4.
14   Seating   capacity   from   <http://www.historylink.org/index.cfm? DisplayPage=output.cfm&file_id=3852> [accessed 31 May 2016].
15   BG to Lucy Love, 30 June 1909, Michigan Love.
16   'In the Theaters', *CTr.*, 13 July 1909, p.10; 'In the Theaters', *CTr.*, 19 July 1909, p.8; 'Chicago's Summer Activities', *NYDM*, 7 August 1909, p.9.
17   BG to Lucy Love, 1 September 1909, Michigan Love.
18   BG to Lucy Love, 27 August 1909, Michigan Love.
19   'Gossip about Actors Managers & Events', *NYDM*, 24 July 1909, p.7; 'Columbia University — The Ben Greet Players', *NYDM*, 14 August 1909, p.5; BG to Lucy Love, 27 August 1909, Michigan Love.
20   'Open Air Play at Barnard', *NYS*, 23 May 1909, p.10.
21   David Glassberg, *American Historical Pageantry: the Uses of Tradition in the Early Twentieth Century* (Chapel Hill: University of North Carolina Press, 1990), p.75; Naima Prevots, *American Pageantry: A Movement for Art & Democracy* (Ann Arbor: UMI Research Press, 1990), p.5. For a contemporary discussion of pageants, see Percy MacKaye, 'American Pageants and Their Promise', *Scribner's Magazine*, July 1909, pp.28–35.
22   'Boston Making Preparations', *NYDM*, 14 August 1909, p.10; 'Great Day in Gloucester', *NYS*, 5 August 1909, p.7; '25,000 Witness Pageant', *BET*, 5 August 1909, p.12; 'Gloucester Day, 1909', *The Massachusetts Magazine*, 2 (1909), 184; 'Boston Making Preparations', *NYDM*, 14 August 1909, p.10.
23   'The Return of Drama to Nature', *Current Literature*, September 1909, pp.312–15. This article is heavily indebted to Percy MacKaye, 'American Pageants and Their Promise', *Scribner's Magazine*, July 1909, pp.28–35.
24   'The Pond Announcement', *Lyceumite and Talent*, September 1909, p.48; 'Trenton', *NYDM*, 11 December 1909, p.30.
25   Seating capacity from *C-L(1913)*, p.427. For details about the enterprise's origins, organization, management, and personnel, see *The New Theatre* (New

York: For the Theatre, 1909). Gilder's sonnet p.8.

[26] 'First Production in New Theatre Splendidly Staged', *New York Press*, 9 November 1909, p.1.

[27] 'New Theatre Opens', *BE*, 9 November 1909, p.11; Shattuck, *Shakespeare*, II (1987), pp. 279–82; New Theatre advertisement, *NYS*, 13 December 1909, p.5.

[28] 'Academy of Music — As You Like It', *NYDM*, 2 April 1910, p. 6.

[29] Asmodeus, 'A Change in Standards', *NYDM*, 2 April 1910, p.5. The Garden Theatre was located at 27th Street and Madison Avenue.

[30] 'Little Town of Bethlehem', *NYS*, 18 January 1910, p.9; 'Mrs. Trasks's Play of the Nativity Coming into its Own at Last', *BE*, 25 January 1910, p.3; 'Garden Theatre — The Little Town of Bethlehem', *NYDM*, 29 January 1910, p.7.

[31] Isaac, p.115, reprints an announcement in which Greet outlines the financial and repertory particulars of his eight-week season at the Garden.

[32] Asmodeus, 'A Change in Standards', *NYDM*, 2 April 1910, p.5; 'Drama at Home and Abroad', *New York Evening Post*, 9 April 1910, p.5; 'Notes of Interest to Theatregoers', *New York Evening Telegram*, 8 March 1910, p.6.

[33] 'Mr. Greet Reopens the Garden Theatre', *NYH*, 22 February 1910, p.11; 'Ben Greet Revivals', *NYS*, 22 February 1910, p.9.

[34] A. W., 'Garden Theatre', *NYTr.,* 24 February 1910, p.7.

[35] 'Theatrical Notes', *NYTr.,* 2 March 1910, p.7.

[36] 'Greet Players in "The Merchant"', *NYH*, 4 March 1910, p.13.

[37] 'Notes of Interest to Theatregoers', *New York Evening Telegram*, 8 March 1910, p.6; 'At Other Playhouses', *NYDM*, 19 March 1910, p.8.

[38] 'Garden Theatre', *NYTr.,* 5 March 1910, p.7.

[39] 'Plays and Operas', *NYH*, 13 March 1910, p.12; 'Ben Greet in "Everyman"', *NYTr.,* 24 February 1910, p.7.

[40] Speaight, pp.113–19.

[41] 'A First View of 'Faustus',' *NYS*, 19 March 1910, p.5; *NYDM*, 26 March 1910, p.7; *Theatre*, May 1910, pp.xxv–vi. 'Faustus Here after 300 Years', *NYH*, 19 March 1910, p.12.

[42] 'Ben Greet Produces Caesar', *NYDM*, 2 April 1910, p.8.

[43] 'Notable Revival of "The Winter's Tale"', *NYH*, 29 March 1910, p.13; 'A Review of The New Theatre's First Season', *NYTr.,* 10 April 1910, p.6. Several photographs of the production taken by the Byron Company can be found at the website of the Museum of the City of New York: <http://collections.mcny.org/C.aspx?VP3=SearchResult&VBID=24UAYWRP186HR&SMLS=1&RW=1680&RH=939> [accessed 31 May 2016]. The fourth photograph is a miscatalogued image from some other production.

[44] 'The Winter's Tale', *(New York) Evening Post*, 29 March 1910, p.9.

[45] 'The Ben Greet Players Present Three Hawthorne Wonder Book Tales', *Billboard*, 9 April 1910, p.6.

[46] '"The Palace of Truth" Revived, Still Charms', *NYH*, 29 March 1910, p.13; 'Garden Theatre', *NYTr.,* 31 March 1910, p.7; 'Garden — Palace of Truth', *NYDM*, 9 April 1910, p.6.

[47] Asmodeus, 'A Change in Standards', *NYDM*, 2 April 1910, p.5.

[48] 'Notes of Interest to Theatregoers', *New York Evening Telegram*, 5 April 1910,

p.6; Emily Folger, 'Plays I Have Seen' theatrical diary, p.81, Folger Papers, Box 38, Folger Shakespeare Library, Washington, DC.

[49]   'Garden — A Midsummer Night's Dream', *NYDM*, 23 April 1910, p.8.

[50]   'The Wage Earners' Theatre League', *NYDM*, 19 April 1910, p.6.

[51]   'Ben Greet as Caesar', *BE*, 24 April 1910, p.21; 'Ben Greet Players in Julius Caesar', *(Brooklyn) Standard Union*, 24 April 1910, p.7; Emily Folger, 'Plays I Have Seen' theatrical diary, p.85, Folger Papers, Box 38, Folger Shakespeare Library, Washington, DC.

[52]   Brander Matthews, 'The Drama Today', *Saturday Evening Post*, 23 April 1910, p.16; 'Philadelphia Stage Gossip', *NYDM*, 7 May 1910, p.16. Seating capacity from *C-L(1913)*, p.551.

[53]   'The Week's Programme', *WH*, 22 May 1910, part 2, p.6; 'Washington', *NYDM*, 28 May 1910, p.17; 'In the Social World', *WH*, 21 May 1910, p.1; 'Washington', *NYDM*, 4 June 1910, p.13. Seating capacity from *C-L(1913)*, p.123.

[54]   'The Week's Programme', *WH*, 29 May 1910, p.29; 'Washington', *NYDM*, 28 May 1910, p.17.

[55]   'Ben Greet Players Given an Ovation'. *WTr.,* 31 May 1910, p.9.

[56]   'The Week's Programme', *WH*, 5 June 1910, p.6.

[57]   'Leader Returns to Greet Company', *WTr.,* 17 June 1910, p.14; 'Belasco — "The School for Scandal"', *WH*, 17 June 1910, p.9; 'Washington', *NYDM*, 11 June 1910, p.13; 'Washington', *NYDM*, 18 June 1910, p.13.

[58]   'Washington', *NYDM*, 11 June 1910, p.13; 'Washington', *NYDM*, 18 June 1910, p.13. For details of these performances, see 'Visions Realized in Play Setting', *WTr.,* 17 June 1910, p.14; 'Give Outdoor Plays', *WH*, 18 June 1910, p.5; 'Shakespeare Performed in Miniature Arden', *WTr.,* 18 June 1910, p.5; 'Mrs. Taft at Plays on White House Lawn', *NYH*, 18 June 1910, p.10.

[59]   'The Belasco', *WH*, 21 June 1910, p.4; 'Ben Greet Players Surpass Former Efforts in "The Tempest"', *WTr.,* 21 June 1910, p.10; 'The Merchant of Venice', *WH*, 23 June 1910, p.5; 'Ben Greet Takes the Role of Shylock', *WTr.,* 23 June 1910, p.7.

[60]   'Washington', *NYDM*, 25 June 1910, p.15; 'In Aid of Clara Morris', *WH*, 27 June 1910, p.5; 'The Belasco — "Caste"', *WH*, 28 June 1910, p.4; '"Caste" at Belasco Amusing at Times', *WTr.,* 28 June 1910, p.4.

[61]   'Washington's First Open-Air Roof Theatre to Open To-Morrow', *WH*, 3 July 1910, p.6; 'The Week's Programme', *WH*, 10 July 1910, p.7; 'Belasco Roof — Return of Ben Greet', *WH*, 21 July 1910, p.5; 'Comedy Presented on Moonlit Stage', *WTr.,* 22 July 1910, p.7; '"As You Like It" Given by Ben Greet Players', *WH*, 22 July 1910, p.3.

[62]   'The Outdoor Stage', *Cincinnati Enquirer*, 8 July 1910, p.2; 'Cincinnati', *NYDM*, 30 July 1910, p.18; BG to Lucy Love, 6 August 1910, Michigan Love; 'Players at the Zoo', *New York Clipper*, 13 August 1910, p.660; 'An Out-of-Door Ice Skating Rink', *Ice and Refrigeration*, 1 November 1917, p.184; 'Cincinnati', *Music News*, 11 August 1922, p.3. Seating from 'Cincinnati', *NYDM*, 2 July 1913, p.15.

[63]   'Chicago News', *New York Clipper*, 27 August 1910, p.699; BG to Lucy Love, 28 August 1910, Michigan Love.

[64]   'Drama in the Open Air', *NYS*, 28 August 1910, p.5. For a description of

Adams's acclaimed, attendance record-setting *As You Like It* at Berkeley, see Walter Anthony, 'Maude Adams Pictures Shakespeare's Rosalind', *SFC*, 7 June 1910, p.5. For a description of the even more impressive *Antigone* starring Anglin mounted at the same venue the following month, see Walter Anthony, 'Miss Anglin Makes "Antigone" Live Again', *SFC*, 1 July 1910, p.3.

[65] 'Maryland' and 'Massachusetts', *NYDM*, 21 May 1910, p.23; 'Princeton University', *New York Evening Post*, 21 May 1910, p.8; 'Providence', *NYDM*, 18 June 1910, p.14; 'Notes of Interest to Theatregoers', *New York Evening Telegram*, 26 July 1910, p.6; 'Plays of the Week', *NYDM*, 6 August 1910, p.10; 'News from Boston', *NYDM*, 13 August 1910, p.15.

[66] George Townsend, 'Classic Plays in the Holiday Season', *Forensic Quarterly*, 1.4 (September 1910), 235–44; Charles Douville Coburn, *The University Theatre Association: A Practical Plan for the Presentation of Acted Drama as an Educational Factor in the Universities, Colleges and Higher Schools of America* (New York: Gotham Press, [1911]). On the unworkability of Coburn's proposal, see Thomas H. Dickinson, *The Insurgent Theatre* (New York: B. W. Huebsch, 1917), pp.191–93.

[67] Bernheim, p.75. This paragraph and the three that follow it summarize Bernheim's findings, pp.75–97.

[68] 'Ben Greet to Lecture Here', *(Montreal) Gazette*, 24 October 1910, p.3; 'Belasco — Ben Greet Lecture', *WTR.*, 22 January 1911, evening edition, p.6; '"Midsummer Night's Dream" by the Ben Greet Players', *New York Evening World*, 3 January 1911, night edition, p.13; 'Ben Greet Comes along Now in Rather a New Role', *Richmond Times-Dispatch*, 20 January 1911, p.3; 'Reflections', *NYDM*, 8 February 1911, p.16.

[69] Ben Greet, 'For the Greatest Theatre in the World', *World's Work*, April 1911, pp.14222–29.

[70] Ben Greet, 'A Shakespeare Theater', *BE*, 14 May 1911, p.2; 'Sir Philip Lights a Candle', *NYT*, 24 April 1932, p.2.

[71] 'Society', *NYH*, 9 April 1911, p.8; 'Greet Players Appear Twice', *New York Press*, 23 April 1911, p.5; 'Carnegie Hall — As You Like It', *NYDM*, 26 April 1911, p.7.

[72] '"Lear" and Other Dramas', *NYS*, 23 April 1911, p.12; 'Robert Mantell as Shylock', *New York Press*, 23 April 1911, p.5.

[73] 'Stageland Gossip', *Cincinnati Enquirer*, 17 July 1911, p.4.

[74] 'Amusements in Chicago', *NYDM*, 12 July 1911, p.13; 'Shakespeare Revivals', *Billboard*, 5 August 1911, p.8; 'Chautauqua Program', *Fredonia (New York) Censor*, 9 August 1911, p.2.

[75] 'Theatricals in Summer', *NYS*, 30 July 1911, p.5.

[76] 'School Drama Not a Big Success', *NYT*, 27 July 1911, p.11; 'Drama on School Platform', *NYT*, 30 July 1911, p.9; 'Drama for the East Side', *NYDM*, 2 August 1911, p.7.

[77] 'Ben Greet to Lecture', *NYH*, 25 September 1911, p.5; 'Gossip of the Town', *NYDM*, 4 October 1911, p.11; 'Daly's — The Thief', *NYDM*, 18 October 1911, p.10; 'News of the Theatres', *NYS*, 5 November 1911, p.6; 'Gossip of the Town', *NYDM*, 15 November 1911, p.10.

[78] 'Pennsylvania', *NYDM*, 8 November 1911, p.22; 'Pennsylvania', *NYDM*, 29 November 1911, p.20; 'Asheville', *NYDM*, 28 February 1912, p.21; 'Letter to the Editor', *NYDM*, 13 March 1912, p.11.

[79] 'Ben Greet's Shakespeare', *NYT*, 10 March 1912, book review section, p.125; 'Heroes of Letters and Life', *New York Tribune*, 7 December 1912, p.13; 'Book Review', *NYDM*, 8 May 1912, p.5.

[80] Redpath Lyceum Bureau and Ben Greet, Memorandum of Agreement, 1 February 1912, Iowa.

[81] '"Oedipus Rex" in Pictures', *NYH*, 5 March 1912, p.9; 'Oedipus Rex in Pictures', *NYT*, 5 March 1912, p.11; '"Oedipus Rex" in Kinemacolor', *NYTr.,* 5 March 1912, p.7; 'Greek Trilogy Condensed for Kinemacolor', *New York Evening Telegram*, 5 March 1912, p.8; 'Oedipus Rex at Kinemacolor', *Billboard*, 9 March 1912, p.6; 'Deaf Mutes See the Show', *NYS*, 12 March 1912, p.9; 'Oedipus Rex Disappointing', *NYDM*, 13 March 1912, p.26; 'New Kinemacolor Theatre', *NYDM*, 20 March 1912, p.25.

[82] Seating capacity from *C-L(1913)*, p.551.

[83] For a list of the recordings Greet made, see <http://victor.library.ucsb.edu/ index.php/talent/detail/8451/Greet_Ben_speaker> [accessed 31 May 2016]. Curious readers can listen to the ones named as well as to 'The Duke's Speech' from *As You Like It* and 'Strike upon the Bell' from *Macbeth* at the Library of Congress's National Jukebox: <http://www.loc.gov/jukebox/search/ results?q=Ben%20Greet> [accessed 31 May 2016].

[84] 'Philadelphia', *NYDM*, 1 May 1912, p.23; 'Reflections', *NYDM*, 8 May 1912, p.10; 'Actors' Church Alliance Meets', *NYDM*, 29 May 1912, p.13.

[85] Glenn Dillard Gunn, 'Ben Greet Players Join with Chicago Opera Singers', *CTr.,* 29 May 1912, p.6; 'Chicago', *NYDM*, 5 June 1912, p.19; 'Chicago', *NYDM*, 19 June 1912, p.19; 'Chicago', *NYDM*, 26 June 1912, p.7; 'Three Plays Close', *NYDM*, 26 June 1912, p.12.

[86] BG to Lucy Love, 1 July 1912, Michigan Love.

[87] 'Ben Greet Players Attract', *NYDM*, 24 July 1912, p.15.

[88] BG to Crawford Peffer, [n. d.] June 1912, Iowa; BG to Peffer, Cablegram 9 August 1912, Iowa; 'Road Notes', *NYDM*, 14 August 1912, p.11; 'Coldwater', *NYDM*, 21 August 1912, p.20.

[89] 'Coburn', *Mt Vernon (New York) Democratic Banner*, 28 May 1912, p.3.

[90] 'Reflections', *NYDM*, 3 July 1912, p.11; 'Dates Ahead', *NYDM*, 17 July 1912, p.23; 'Dates Ahead', *NYDM*, 24 July 1912, p.23; 'Dates Ahead', *NYDM*, 7 August 1912, p.23.

[91] 'Amusements at Parks', *NYDM*, 10 July 1912, p.15; 'Shakespeare Plays Today', *Bourbon (Kentucky) News*, 23 April 1912, p.5; 'Students' Conference', *Berea (Ohio) Citizen*, 2 May 1912, p.4.

CHAPTER SEVEN
The Buzzing Pleased Multitudes, 1912–21

The 1912–13 Season

Placing the company under Redpath's management enabled Greet to revive his regular-season business, but the ensemble's success in Lyceum was not assured. As Andrew C. Rieser finds, that institution had become more entertainment-oriented during the 1890s. And, as we have seen, it had permitted at least two professional companies to present *Everyman* and Shakespeare in a few minor circuits beginning in 1905. But the decision to feature professional performance as a head-lining, season-long attraction was something of a gamble. The bureaus were eager to please, not offend, their conservative, middle- and working-class, educationally oriented patrons, many of whom still held anti-theatrical prejudices. But one of the attributes that made Redpath so successful was the ability of its executives to perceive what their customers wanted. Approaching Greet had been the idea of the owner-manager of Redpath's New York territory, Crawford Peffer. He would learn soon enough whether his assessment that Lyceumites were ready to embrace performance — so long as it was of 'dramatic liter-ature' and the company presenting it was Greet's — had been correct.[1]

Redpath provided what Greet had lacked for years: strong manage-ment with national reach. The Englishman turned out a product that consistently delighted new consumers, but he was far less adept at promoting, booking, and distributing it. Redpath's coast-to-coast consortium of territories and modern managerial practices enabled it to schedule presenters for months on end and to assure reliable (if modest) profits for one and all. And an important efficiency of Peffer's idea was that normal operations would not have to be altered to accommodate the actor-manager's bare-bones productions, which mounted easily in the armouries, auditoriums, halls, schools, and theatres that had been hosting Lyceum presentations for decades.

Redpath contracted to make the bookings, promote the performances, pay the actors' salaries, and remunerate Greet $100 for every week the company toured. In return, Greet agreed to supply productions, costumes, fit-ups, and a company of professionals coached, prepared, directed, and disciplined by him so as to produce 'the best results artistically'. He also licensed until the end of the season the exclusive use of the name 'Ben Greet Players' to the bureau, which owned whatever profits and losses the tour generated.[2]

There were nine major Lyceum bureaus in 1912: Redpath, Mutual, Coit, Alkahest, Central, Eastern, White, Midland, and Davidson. During the 1911–12 season, these and more than forty minor bureaus serviced an estimated 12,000 cities and towns. As we have seen, a typical Lyceum course comprised six presentations delivered over an eight-month season: an inspirational lecture, an evening of magic, a humorous lecture, and three concerts. Estimated average attendance at a Lyceum presentation in 1912 was 500.[3]

More than a thousand municipalities had their courses booked by the Redpath Bureau, which in 1912 comprised eleven, independently owned territories: Boston; New York; Pittsburgh; Columbus, Ohio; Chicago; Cedar Rapids, Iowa; Kansas City; Columbus, Mississippi; Denver; Seattle; and Chatham, Ontario.[4] Each was a separate legal entity, but one of the reasons the consortium was successful was that its operational model was built on the efficient circulation of presenters between territories.

As soon as Redpath and Greet came to terms, Peffer announced to Lyceumites across the country that the Ben Greet Players would soon be touring the Redpath circuits. The fulsome feature he published in *Lyceum News* declared:

It is with no little satisfaction that we announce our success in arranging with Mr. Ben Greet for a company of [...] players, personally trained and coached by him, to give plays [...] for the lyceum courses. This is a great step in advance for the lyceum. Mr. Greet presents the best in dramatic literature with true histrionic art in a way that has not been excelled by any other producer. Mr. Greet is considered today one of the greatest living authorities on the English drama and is world famous for his remarkable productions of Shakespearian plays and old English comedies. He has been connected with the stage for thirty years and has taught many actors; perhaps more than any other man living today. For twenty years Mr. Greet has been prominent in England for performances in [...] London, Cambridge, Stratford-upon-Avon and other places in 'Shakespeare's England'. Mr. Greet became well-known in America several years ago through his presentation of the morality play 'Everyman' under the management of Charles Frohman [...]. This was later followed by the production of Shakespearian plays and classical comedies [...]. Some years ago the Ben Greet 'Woodland Players' gave their first open air play at Columbia University before an audience of over three thousand persons. This was followed by performances at Harvard, Yale, Princeton, Oberlin, Universities of Chicago, Pennsylvania, Virginia, Michigan, Minnesota, California, etc., and repeated ever since almost annually. Mr. Greet's company was the first to be invited to appear at the White House grounds [...]. The plays presented by him are given in pure fashion with the minimum stage effect. There is nothing to detract from the play. These are real educational productions of masterpieces of classical comedy and drama. There are no stars in the cast, but every actor is experienced and competent [...]. Absolutely correct diction and pronunciation is a distinguishing characteristic of Mr. Greet's players.[5]

Clearly, Peffer believed that Lyceumites would be drawn to Greet's authority, experience, teaching prowess, and highbrow accolades, as well as to the educational value of his offerings.

Greet rehearsed the company before it left New York. Grace Halsey Mills, Leonard Shepherd, and Percival Vivian were its leading performers, with Margaret Gallagher and Charles Hanna appearing in support. The actor-manager not touring, he appointed an executive staff to handle daily operations: Vivian (business manager), Shepherd (director), and William Keighley (stage manager).[6] An abridged version of *The Comedy of Errors* would be its principal offering with *She Stoops to Conquer* available on request. In 1958, the former owner-manager of the Chicago Redpath Lyceum Bureau, Harry P. Harrison, offered a colourful account of how the Shakespearean text came to be cut, which he remembered as having taken place in the spring of 1913:

> To make doubly sure [it] would not offend even the most moralistic audience, Peffer, Keighley, and everyone else with money invested in the venture went over the script line by line, deleting every tart Elizabethan phrase that might wound soft sensibilities.

Specifics provided by an old showman recalling events more than forty-five years after they transpired should always be used with caution, especially in this instance when we know that the company had been using cut texts since the summer of 1911.[7] Peffer may have reminded Greet that bawdy was impermissible, but the inexperienced and non-stake-holding Keighley is extremely unlikely to have collaborated with him and unnamed others on a line-by-line edit with the likes of Greet, Shepherd, and Vivian present — all of whom were vastly senior to Keighley and knew the play inside and out. Using the sanitized edition Greet prepared for Doubleday would also have been an option.

As bare-bones and trimmed as they were, the productions delighted Lyceumites. Newspapers reported that the 1,480-seat Griffin Opera House in Woodstock, Ontario, was filled to capacity when the company performed there in November, that 'An audience of culture packed the auditorium' of Buffalo's Central YMCA to hear it a few weeks later, and that the company's presentation in Brunswick, Maine, in December was an 'excellent performance, to [a] large and fashionable audience'. Although I have been unable to locate a photograph of one of Greet's audiences, *World's Work*

25. Anonymous. *A Typical Lyceum Audience*, 1912.

published this one in 1912 illustrating a characteristic Lyceum audience. Harrison wasted no time congratulating Greet: 'You have made good, and in making good, you are doing good. We are honored in having you in the Redpath family'.[8] The texts were less authentic and the venues smaller, but the company was back in business.

Peffer had been right: Lyceumites could not get enough dramatic literature presented by the Ben Greet Players. In February, the institution's official organ trumpeted that the experiment had been wildly successful, and that the results had 'been so gratifying that at a recent meeting of the managerial heads, the Players were retained for next year — an unusual proceeding for so large and expensive an attraction'. The writer concluded by moralizing:

> So the lyceum has a place for such educative attractions as the Ben Greet Players in the field of classic drama. And the people are responding with enthusiasm beyond the expectation over the rare work of this company. Their success has inspired other lyceum presentations of the classics, as the tendency is to supplant them on the stage by the film-shows, the frivolous and trashy appeals […] the amusing and spectacular and the long line of offerings that betray the dramatic degeneracy of the times.[9]

The institution that had disdained theatre for decades never became a bastion of classical drama, but, thanks to Peffer and Greet, it embraced professionally performed Shakespeare.

The company's success continued as it worked its way to the Pacific, the *Dramatic Mirror* confirming excellent performances delivered before large-to-capacity houses from Iowa to New Mexico.[10] The tour closed in May in California, where someone took this photograph of the presentation the company gave on the campus of the San José Normal School that would grace its promotional materials for years to come.

Originally scheduled to last twenty weeks, the first Lyceum tour ran twenty-nine. The impact it had on Shakespeare's popularity was significant. Many of the tens of thousands of Lyceumites who saw it had previously been leery of — even opposed to — theatre, and yet the productions delighted them so much that they clamoured for more. Under Redpath, the Ben Greet Players would survive the decline of the road.

26. Anonymous. THE COMEDY OF ERRORS.
Dir. Ben Greet, San José Normal School, San José, CA, 22 April 1913.

Greet spent the winter running the New York chapter of the Actors' Church Alliance, whose president he remained. By February he had added the vice presidency of the organization's National Council to his collection of offices, further increasing his influence as one of America's leading advocates for moral actors performing moral plays in moral theatres. For Lent, he directed a revival of *Everyman* for Leibler Co. — the principal attraction of which was Edith Wynne Matthison reprising her career-making role — that ran for three weeks in the Children's Theatre atop the Century Theatre (formerly the New Theatre). The papers fell in love with the Morality all over again, several declaring that the revival was better than the one that originally brought the two Britons to the United States. According to the *Dramatic Mirror*, it delivered 'an emotional experience rarely obtained these days in the theatre'. Significantly, Dorothy Mavor played Beauty when Greet brought it to Oberlin College in April. The daughter of James Mavor, Greet's long-time host at the University of Toronto, Dorothy had attended one of the performances of *A Midsummer Night's Dream* the Woodland Players presented on the Toronto campus in 1906, and what she witnessed inspired her to pursue a career on the stage. Greet mentored her for a time after she obtained her formal dramatic education in Canada and England — privately coaching her, introducing her to the Shuberts, and finding occasional employment for her between 1912 and 1914. As Paula Sperdakos discovered, the actor-manager's discipline, practicality, no-nonsense approach to directing, and passion for Shakespeare exerted a powerful influence on the young artist who, as Dora Mavor Moore, would go on to become the first lady of the Canadian theatre as well as one of the founders of the Stratford Ontario Shakespeare Festival.[11]

Also that March, Greet accepted a proposal from Harrison. Would the actor-manager be interested in fielding a company to tour the more entertainment-oriented, spring and summer circuits Redpath also operated?[12]

The worlds of Lyceum and Chautauqua had grown increasingly interconnected during the 1890s. Lyceum bureaus had booked presenters exclusively for Lyceum circuits until that decade, at which point some independent Chautauqua assemblies realized that Lyceum bureaus were better at booking desirable presenters than they were. Soon, independents were outsourcing to Lyceum bureaus the booking of Chautauqua presenters.

Thus it was that a Lyceum manager named Keith Vawter and his assistant, J. Roy Ellison, came to be booking presenters into small, independent Chautauqua assemblies in Iowa in the early years of the new century. Getting good presenters to appear at the independents was not easy. As Rieser explains, not only were many assemblies remote, but most of them also did not coordinate their sessions with one another, which complicated the efficient circulation of presenters between them. Recognizing a business opportunity when they saw it, Vawter and Ellison devoted themselves to figuring out how to bring efficient booking to the independents. The model they began experimenting with in 1904 would make them famous. The solution they devised was simple and effective: put together a quality three-to-seven day lecture-entertainment package and offer it at a reduced rate on the condition that every assembly take it. Refinements born from failure and conflict enabled them to perfect it by 1910. The presentations would be held in tents so that the operation would be independent of potentially problematic local venues and/or collaborators and that the bureau's veteran superintendents could control every facet of the proceedings. The assemblies had to accept the dates Vawter and Ellison selected. They were also responsible for advance ticket sales; the assemblies, not the bureau, had to absorb the losses if gate receipts were low. Most important, Vawter and Ellison devised 'tight booking', of which James R. Schultz provides the best definition:

On a seven-day circuit, chautauqua tents were raised simultaneously in seven nearby towns. The talent that performed in one town on Monday would move to the next town for Tuesday's performance. When the rotation was completed by the end of the week, the seven tents, each with its own crew, were moved to seven more towns in a different geographical area.[13]

One last feature requires explanation. Vawter and Ellison called this enterprise 'Chautauqua'. Their decision to appropriate an established, culturally resonant, but not legally protected name made good sense at the time, but it can be a source of confusion today. The only thing the travelling, tent-based phenomenon had in common with the lakeside assembly in upstate New York with which it coexisted for nearly three decades was in the delivery of 'improving' content in rural settings. To decrease misunderstanding, historians use the terms 'circuit Chautauqua' or 'tent Chautauqua' when discussing the former.

Circuit Chautauqua grew explosively between 1905 and 1915. In 1904, Vawter and Ellison booked nine assemblies. In 1913, the various Redpath territories collectively booked 600 . . . of the more than 1,200 that had come into existence. With hundreds of assemblies springing up every year, there was more than enough work to go around. Junior partners and up-and-coming managers struck out on their own, old territories expanded and/or divided, and new territories were created as the old Lyceum hands fanned out to organize and service the rapidly expanding circuits. These owner-managers chose names for their businesses that advertised their Lyceum origins while signalling the shift to the flourishing new market. Vawter called his Redpath Chautauqua. When Ellison and new partner Clarence White headed out to Oregon to form a territory that quickly encompassed Western Canada, the West Coast, and the Southwest, they called theirs the Ellison-White Lyceum and Chautauqua Association.[14]

The number of Americans who attended tent Chautauquas is difficult to determine, Charlotte M. Canning's conservatively estimated 9–20 [sic] million during its peak years being the most realistic range offered.[15] By figuring out the crucial business pieces — the attractive bundling of presenters, efficient logistics, favourable contracting — Vawter and Ellison created a wildly popular, extremely powerful engine for delivering cultural content.

Redpath and Greet came to terms. Under the energetic and hardworking Vivian, the Lyceum company would tour tent Chautauqua from late May to Labor Day, during which it would play 110 dates.[16] Redpath would pay the actors their Lyceum salaries and Greet a flat $500 for the use of his name, productions, and company. Having already booked and committed himself to lead the larger, more elaborate Woodland Players, the actor-manager would not accompany the Ben Greet Players — an absence mentioned in the disclaimer that appears in fine print toward the back of the brochure Redpath produced.[17] Greet also allowed the bureau to fill the remaining gaps in the Woodland Players' calendar by scheduling it to appear at a number of summer schools, independent assemblies, and larger tent Chautauquas it also booked.[18] Thanks to Peffer's idea and the success of Greet's company in Lyceum, the first play the powerful cultural engine that was circuit Chautauqua delivered to its massive, still-burgeoning audience was Greet's *Comedy of Errors* (the costumed cast of which this promotional postcard depicts) with a few performances of *She Stoops* for variety's sake.[19]

The Ben Greet Players and the Woodland Players both enjoyed robust open-air seasons. The former worked its way through the circuits of Georgia, Alabama, Tennessee, Kentucky, West Virginia, Indiana, Michigan, Ohio, and Pennsylvania. Taken the week it appeared in this very tent in Richmond, Kentucky, this photograph illustrates what a teeming Chautauqua presentation looked like. The players consistently drew audiences large enough to generate receipts significantly in excess of the guaranteed minimum Redpath required from the local assemblies — a fact Vivian kept squarely before Harrison.[20] But the packed calendar and sweltering heat took a toll on the actors. The letter one of them, George Seybolt, sent to Harrison in July seeking the back-wages Vivian refused to pay him (the cause of Seybolt quitting) describes an exhausted, demoralized company led by a capricious bully.[21] Nevertheless, considerably more people heard the company during the fifteen-week Chautauqua season than had during the twenty-nine-week Lyceum season. Newspapers reported it drawing not only the largest crowds of the various weeks, but also the biggest audiences many assemblies had

27. Anonymous. *Ben Greet Players—Redpath Chautauqua*. 1913.

28. Anonymous. *Auditorium Tent, Richmond [KY] Chautauqua*. 1913.

ever seen. In the world of tent Chautauqua, that meant throngs in excess of 1,700.[22] According to figures published that December, daily attendance across the Redpath circuits that summer averaged 1,500, with the Ben Greet Players and Bohumir Kryl Orchestra sharing the distinction of having drawn the largest single-day attendances recorded: 2,200.[23] That the company played to more than 160,000 rural audience members that summer is therefore likely.

Redpath publicly acknowledged the company's success in the Lyceum circuits by engaging it for the 1913–14 season. The bureau's reaction to its success in Chautauqua was even more enthusiastic: it engaged two companies to tour in 1914. Convinced that strong demand for Shakespeare existed in rural America, Peffer, Harrison, and their colleagues made sure that they and the Ben Greet Players would be the ones to satisfy it.

Led by Greet, the twenty-five-member Woodland Players launched its 1913 tour in April, newcomers Malcolm Dunn, George Somnes, and sisters Elizabeth and Isobel Merson joining veterans George Hare, George Vivian, and Ruth Vivian. For the next month it appeared in theatres, colleges, and high schools in and around greater New York. Its size enabled it to offer a large (ten-play) repertory. True to form, the actor-manager formally marked Shakespeare's birthday. He delivered one of the five addresses spoken at the commemoration ceremonies that opened at the Ethical Culture School that morning and closed at John Quincy Adams Ward's statue of Shakespeare in Central Park that afternoon. That evening, he and his company presented *Twelfth Night* using the now-ancient Middle Temple fit-up before an audience of 3,000 gathered in City College's Great Hall.[24]

In May, it played a scattering of engagements in the Northeast that included familiar haunts Lehigh and Bucknell. Heading into the Midwest, it stopped off at perennial hosts Michigan and Indiana before opening a two-week, twenty-four-performance(!) Shakespeare festival in the 1,000+-seat Woodland Theatre on the grounds of the Cincinnati Zoo in June. The engagement being inadequately publicized on account of a scheduling change, turnout at the zoo was initially low. Attendance soon picked up, however, Cincinnatians being 'right glad [...] for Shakespeare in hot weather to break the monotony of summer vaudeville'.[25]

Alarmed by the meagre profits generated by the early Redpath-booked appearances, Greet reproached the bureau for failing to negotiate better terms. After reminding it of some of the ones he had secured during the previous fourteen months, Greet urged Redpath to contract a minimum guarantee of $500 for a two-performance day plus a percentage of the gross receipts over that amount plus transportation costs. Redpath got him much of what he asked for: decent guarantees — between $300 and $500 (depending on the size of the assembly) plus fifty per cent of the gross receipts above that for one-day, two-performance engagements, and a flat guarantee of $800 for two-day, four-performance engagements — plus all transportation costs for the remaining Woodland Players dates it booked.[26]

Its run at the zoo concluding in early July, the company spent the rest of the month playing a variety of venues — educational institutions, independent Chautauqua assemblies, even a few permanent Chautauqua assemblies — in the Midwest. As busy as it kept and as solid as its performances seem to have been, profits remained dispiritingly low. Writing to Lucy Love in early August, Greet confessed

> We've had a strenuous tour + last week was the only one in which he had any profit! It seems to me I'd better give it up as it's really rather sinful to go on working so hard + getting nothing beyond salary, printing + railroad money. Our work has been really good + it vexes me.[27]

His outlook improved when the company's return engagement at the Cincinnati Zoo put it solidly in the black.[28] It brightened considerably on 19 August, when attendance at the performances of *As You Like It* and *Dream* the company gave in the huge, permanent (steel and concrete), 4,500-seat Chautauqua Auditorium in Lincoln, Illinois, topped 6,000.[29] Redpath having negotiated a $350 guarantee plus fifty per cent of the gross receipts above $400, the actor-manager's share of that day's takings exceeded $1,250.[30] That amount being the weekly operating budget (excluding transportation costs) of the Woodland Players, the enormous crowds in Lincoln represented a tidy windfall.[31] After stopping off at the familiar (if less crowded) grounds of Pittsburgh's Schenley Hotel, the company closed the tour with two well-attended performances at Hershey Park in Hershey, Pennsylvania, on Labor Day. Hardly the most gratifying season, but it brought enough acclaim and profit to induce Greet to do it again.

The 1913–14 Season

For years, Greet had personally involved himself with nearly every aspect of his company's operations, but his positive experience with Redpath encouraged him to outsource his bookings. As his performers took well-earned breaks that September, he contracted with the former tour-manager of the Coburn Players, L. M. Goodstadt — whose newly formed General Managing Bureau was focused on 'exploiting open-air companies in classical dramas' — to book the Woodland Players for the 1914 and 1915 open-air seasons.[32]

The departures of Shepherd and Gallagher necessitated adjustments to the Lyceum company. To replace Shepherd, Greet recruited veteran Leslie King to play Shylock opposite Mills's Portia. He brought in Dorothy Conrey, who would be singled out for particular praise that season, to replace Gallagher. Once more, Greet rehearsed the ensemble in Manhattan before it took to the circuits. *Comedy of Errors* and *Merchant of Venice* would be its offerings.

Under Percival Vivian, it set off in October on a twenty-one-week tour of the Midwest and Northeast. As it had the previous season, the company drew large audiences. Seizing the opportunity for cross-promotional sales, the company, Redpath, and Doubleday began selling in lobbies copies of Greet's Shakespeare editions, which they promoted with testimonials from David Belasco and Mrs Lucretia J. McAnney, the founder and head of the Department of Oratory at Dickinson College.[33] Less positive, the mercurial

Vivian precipitated an unpleasant incident that attracted some notoriety. Following the company's appearance at the North Missouri Normal School, the institution's president, John Kirk, issued a public accusation, published simultaneously in the *St Louis Globe-Democrat* and *Kansas City Star*, that the company had pulled down the large American flag normally displayed above the stage and then left it lying on the auditorium floor. Kirk added that the company's electrician had inexplicably lowered the lights an instant before the performance began, the actors had hauled down the flag in the darkness, and no one in the audience had noticed. He also claimed that the vandalism had been partially motivated by spite:

> Last year the Greets appeared in Kirksville and objected to the presence of the big flag over the stage. They were given the alternative of playing or not getting their money and they played. This year they said nothing about the flag, but pulled it down before they began the play.

Kirk declared that the company would never again be permitted to appear at the institution so long as he headed it. Vivian acknowledged lowering the flag, but stated he had done so to improve sightlines and that he had left it folded respectfully over a chair. The episode generated enough coverage that several New York papers picked it up. Kirk's implication, that the members of the company harboured anti-American sentiments, does not seem to have harmed business significantly, but the publicity the story generated was hardly the kind that Greet (not to mention Redpath) welcomed. The companies that toured the Chautauqua circuits the following summer conspicuously advertised their pro-American sentiments by displaying a pair of American flags, one on each side of the platform, at every performance to assure those familiar with the controversy that they were, in fact, pro-American. The Missouri unpleasantness notwithstanding, that year's Lyceum tour was successful enough to induce Redpath to renew the company for 1914–15, which fact the bureau announced in February.[34]

Greet was re-elected to the presidency of the New York chapter of Actors' Church Alliance in January. His acceptance speech referenced the 'sociological plays' (some called them 'sex plays') sweeping America — works like Eugène Brieux's *Damaged Goods (Les avariés)* that had generated so such controversy that fall that they provoked aggressive censorship efforts by some local police forces. Greet assured his constituents that theatre was not going to the dogs; the 'unpleasant plays' not being as profitable as was supposed, they would die out soon enough.[35] He was wrong, but this type of drama was not something he was likely to approve.

In November, the *New York Times* had reported that an architect had completed the plans for the proposed Edwin Booth Memorial Theatre in Manhattan, an initiative backed by a consortium of Wall Street investors. Conceptually and operationally, it would be organized along the lines of the New Theatre, with a stock company, a regimented repertory, and regular 'wage-earner nights' for the poor. The work of American artists would receive greater emphasis than at the other house, but the planners reckoned that opening the Booth with a Shakespearean festival would be appropriate given that the renowned actor achieved his greatest successes in Shakespearean roles. Another feature that would distinguish the Booth from the New would be its theatrical library 'devoted principally to collections for the information and delight of the Shakespearean scholar a well as for the serious student of the theatre'.[36] That so many of these elements, including the on-site Shakespearean library, feature in the Shakespeare Memorial Theatre proposal Greet championed in 1911 suggests he may have consulted to the planners of the Booth, an inference supported by the fact that the consortium offered him the artistic directorship of their proposed theatre in January.[37] As Alman discovered, Greet immediately sent two letters to Henry Folger asking him to invest in the scheme and/or promote it to his wealthy friends. Folger ignored the first and politely but firmly declined the second. Intriguingly, she wonders whether this episode may have inspired

Folger to insist that the plans for his library include space for a theatre.[38] The Booth Theatre idea was dropped a short time later.

In February, a hundred friends and colleagues threw a dinner for Greet at the Salmagundi Club, the *Dramatic Mirror* reporting that 'Mr. Greet's activity in behalf of popularizing Shakespeare in every hamlet in America was the keynote of the half-dozen brilliant speeches that were delivered by members of the club'.[39] That contemporaries recognized his importance as a popularizer in the winter of 1914 is significant because his most ambitious American season still lay ahead of him. Greet used his own speech to attack Brieux's play again. Responding to a recent review of Sir Johnston Forbes-Robertson's production of *Othello* in which one critic stated that Shakespeare was no longer anything but an 'illusion', he warmly replied

> the real illusion is the illusion of the so-called sociological play as it has been presented this year. Managers have found that they don't go and I believe that we shall see no more of them […] until such time as some master comes along to treat the subject in a masterly way.[40]

In March, Greet's position in the Actors' Church Alliance required him to weigh in on the controversial topic of Sunday-night performances, which conservative religious groups were seeking to outlaw in major cities (notably Chicago and St Louis) where the practice was long-established and widely accepted. The topic generating considerable interest, Greet made it the subject of the chapter's next meeting. Ministers and theatrical professionals packed the hall, and many strong convictions were passionately expressed. The alliance's founder (and Greet's friend), the Rev. Walter E. Bentley, read a statement prepared by its absent president, of which I have found only an abstract. The *Dramatic Mirror* reported that Greet stated that, if all the theatres were to be closed, then the all churches should be open. A vote by clergy, theatrical professionals, and the public might deliver a clear verdict, but a single, national solution was unlikely to work given how widely attitudes differed from region to region. Only vulgar audiences desired performances on Sunday nights. If these were encouraged, competitive pressures were likely to compel respectable managers to offer them, even if doing so meant losing money. Actors presenting successful vulgar plays to large houses might not mind selling their day of rest for the right price, but actors presenting worthwhile ones to small houses were likely to be ill-repaid for the loss of theirs.[41]

Greet had been forced to absent himself because, as he had the previous March, he had organized an ad hoc company to undertake a mini-tour that opened with a performance at perennial host Oberlin College. The following week, it made its only known appearance at the Carnegie Technical Institute in Pittsburgh. The performances of *As You Like It* and *Dream* it gave there were sponsored by the Department of Drama. That department — the first of its kind in North America — had just been created by the institution's president, Dr Arthur A. Hammerschlag, who had appointed Thomas Wood Stevens its head. Greet, his Elizabethan Manner method, and his professionals seem to have made an impression on Stevens, who immediately invited one-time William Poel collaborator Ben Iden Payne to mount the first of what turned out to be many Modified Elizabethan Staging student productions to commemorate Shakespeare's birthday.

Returning to Manhattan, Greet's company presented the comedies in high schools in poor neighbourhoods sponsored once more by Julius Hopp's Wage Earners' Theatre League and Theatre Center for Schools. Thanks to Hoop's equally zealous belief in the improving power of classical drama, the educational scheme Greet had introduced to New York in 1904 continued to enable the actor-manager and others to keep delivering engaging, meaningful productions to thousands of poor schoolchildren and adults.[42]

The 1914 Open-Air Season

The burgeoning Chautauqua phenomenon and first-class management now combined to enable Greet to deliver Shakespeare to an unprecedented number of Americans. As the list of assemblies grew, so did Redpath. In May, one newspaper projected that 2,200 Chautauqua assemblies would convene in North America that spring and summer, approximately 1,000 of which were under the bureau's management. Three months later, Chautauqua's official organ stated that 3,064 assemblies had actually convened, and that total attendance that season topped 1,000,000 — a first in the institution's history.[43] Redpath was hungry for content to fill all those engagements, and the unsurpassed drawing power of the Ben Greet Players the previous season and the still-exciting novelty of dramatic performance in tent Chautauqua combined to drive up demand for its offerings to an unprecedented level. That the company would present Shakespeare as America celebrated the 250th anniversary of the playwright's birth made it even more desirable. Redpath had previously contracted with Greet to supply two companies, but, as the calendars began to fill, the bureau increased its order to four. Moreover, Goodstadt had organized the finest, most efficient tour in the history of the Woodland Players. There would never be another summer like it.

While Greet scrambled to recruit and rehearse the companies, the less successful visit of another prominent English Shakespearean interpreter was drawing to a close. Actor-manager Frank Benson had been a mainstay of Stratford-upon-Avon and the English provinces for two decades. In 1912, he brought his Stratford-upon-Avon Players to North America for a two-season tour of some of its major cities. Significantly, he avoided Manhattan on the advice of Charles Frohman, who told him his company was not good enough for Broadway. Benson's productions delighted Canadians, but drew disparate reactions from Americans. The company was $5,000 in the red by the time its tour ended in May 1914.[44] That Greet owed his continuing North American success to the specialized businesses he developed, the non-traditional audiences he served, and Redpath's management could not have been more evident.

Redpath had plenty of work for the four Greet companies it fielded. Percival Vivian led the thirteen-member Number 1 Chautauqua company, which featured Dorothy Conrey, Hanna,

Erskine Sanford, and leading lady Mills. From late April to Labor Day, it presented *Twelfth Night* before 130 assemblies in the South and the Midwest — a record-shattering achievement the bureau repeatedly touted. Its remarkably efficient operations were temporarily disrupted when a platform collapsed during a performance in Tennessee, which caused Vivian to be hospitalized for more than a week. The knowledge that the company delighted Chautauquans even more than it had in 1913 may have provided some comfort; the acting remained solid, and audiences strongly preferred *Twelfth Night* to *Comedy*. Its performances in the towns of Augusta and Americus, Georgia, both drew audiences in excess of 2,750, while its presentations in Athens, Georgia; Columbia, South Carolina; Columbus, Georgia; and Montgomery, Alabama attracted the largest crowds of each city's respective Chautauqua weeks.[45] No Greet open-air company reached more people than the one Percival Vivian led that season.

George Vivian led the thirteen-member Number 2 Chautauqua company, which presented *Comedy*. The first performances I have confirmed took place in North Dakota in mid-June. Moving east and then south, the company systematically worked assemblies in Minnesota, Iowa, and Missouri for twelve weeks.

Eric Blind led the thirteen-member Number 3 Chautauqua company, which presented *The Taming of the Shrew* at assemblies in Ohio and upstate New York for eleven weeks. Rosalie De Veaux played Katherine opposite Blind's Petruccio. The fact that this company operated in Ohio suggests it was the one featured in the promotional film Redpath produced that summer.[46]

William Keighley led the thirteen-member Number 4 Chautauqua company, which presented *Twelfth Night* at assemblies in Pennsylvania and West Virginia for eleven weeks. As Sperdakos discovered, the company included Greet veterans St Clair Bayfield and Sydney Greenstreet as well as Dorothy Mavor, who may have played Viola.[47]

If Percival Vivian's Chautauqua tour was impressive in terms of the total number of people reached, the Greet-led Woodland Players tour was notable for bringing the actor-manager's most authentic Shakespearean offerings to a vast new academic audience. The twenty-five-member company opened its outdoor season in South Carolina. Somnes and the increasingly popular Elsie Herndon Kearns were its leading players. Harry Calver, Hare, and Ruth Vivian appeared in support. From April to August, it offered a repertory comprising *As You Like It*, *Dream*, *Tempest*, and *Twelfth Night*. The impressive string of engagements — I have confirmed more than 120 performances at more than 75 venues — Goodstadt booked took it through the South, South Central, Midwest, and Northeast in what was unquestionably the best-attended open-air season in the history of the Woodland Players.

At least forty-nine institutions of higher learning sponsored the company that spring and summer. Greet had become personally acquainted with scores of universities, colleges, and normal schools during his years in America. Thanks to his work with the Coburns and his own researches, Goodstadt knew of scores more. Many of these were located in the South Central United States, a region the Coburns had partially explored, but that a Greet company had never visited. So in addition to playing the large Midwestern universities where open-air appearances by the Woodland Players had become annual traditions, the company made its debuts at Mississippi State, Louisiana State, the Southwest Louisiana Institute, Oklahoma State, Kansas State, and the universities of Oklahoma and Arkansas. It became the first major open-air company to tour Texas, where institutions such as Texas A & M, the University of Texas, Texas Christian, and Baylor sponsored appearances. Two performances a day being common, and students and faculty tending to be well-heeled and appreciative, the packed, college-focused tour Goodstadt organized achieved a new standard of cultural influence (not to mention profitability) as it introduced Greet's productions to a massive new audience.

In July, the Woodland Players visited a number of old haunts in the Midwest, including the Lake Winona Assembly, the University of Wisconsin, and Northern Illinois State Normal. Establishing new institutional relationships being an important goal of the tour, it also played a number of Midwestern campuses previously unknown to it, including Drake, Iowa State Teachers College, Eastern Illinois State Normal, Ohio Normal, and Kent State Normal, where someone took this impressive photograph of its presentation of *Twelfth Night*. The company closed the month with a two-day visit to the exclusive Greenbrier Hotel resort in White Sulphur Springs, West Virginia, where many dignitaries were then in residence. According to the *New York Times*, President and Mrs Wilson, Vice President and Mrs Marshall, Chief Justice and Mrs White, two governors, and a senator were among those who heard the company there.[48] Wilson, who had hosted it many a time at Princeton, made the third sitting president for whom it performed. Pushing on to Philadelphia, the company played an engagement at its favourite open-air venue in the city, the University of Pennsylvania's Botanical Gardens, before heading to New York and the final outings of the season, which included appearances at New York University, a private estate, and a country club.

Greet's importance as a Shakespearean popularizer had already been recognized that winter. That the five companies touring his productions presented them to at least 600,000 more people that spring and summer is likely. The Englishman had many successful open-air seasons in North America, but that of 1914 represented the pinnacle of his popularizing work.

Greet's fame was greater than it had been in years. Thanks to Redpath and the dynamic Percival Vivian, his winter business was back on a solid footing. Thanks to Redpath, Goodstadt, and his four loyal franchisees, his open-air offerings had never reached more people. The actor-manager had been contemplating a trip to England since learning of the death of his brother, William, in April, but he planned to be back in New York by October to rehearse the Lyceum company.[49] Viewed from the perspective of late July, the 1914–15 season promised to be another extremely successful one provided nothing out of the ordinary happened.

29. Anonymous. TWELFTH NIGHT.
Dir. Ben Greet, Kent State Normal School, Kent, OH, 21 July 1914.

The 1914–15 Season

The outbreak of the First World War kept Greet in England. William Greet's widow immediately converted the couple's Thames-side residence into a hospital and convalescent home for Belgian refugees, and the newly returned Ben pitched in to help her run it.[50] A few weeks later (and at the suggestion of Estelle Stead), Lilian Baylis invited him to assume the artistic directorship of her theatre.[51] He jumped at the opportunity. That Baylis shared his educational values and missionary zeal, and that many of her patrons were poor probably added to his eagerness. In December, the *New York Clipper*'s London correspondent described the new arrangement:

> Ben Greet, who came over for a holiday […] is lending a hand with the 'popular' performances of Shakespeare at the Victoria Theatre, a big house in the slums, now run by people who believe in the drama as a humanizing influence. Mr. Greet told me the other day that the Shakespeare cult has never been so strong in America as now it is.

Greet's work in America having achieved an impressive momentum, he was eager to see if he could get something similar going at Baylis's theatre. His storied years at her Royal Victoria Theatre — now known as the Old Vic — had begun.[52]

But America was reluctant to let the actor-manager go. The Rev. Dr William Carter, president of the Church and School Social Service Bureau Motion Picture Company, invited him to direct a series of Biblical films to be shot on location in the Holy Land.[53] Greet had no interest in making movies, but staging plays in the United States continued to appeal to him. The letters he wrote to the New York papers assured readers that he would be back by February, mount another Lenten revival of *Everyman*, and personally lead another open-air tour of the Woodland Players.[54]

His mentor's mantel squarely on his shoulders, Percival Vivian readied the Ben Greet Players to present *As You Like It*, *Comedy*, and *Twelfth Night* during the 1914–15 Lyceum season. Viola Knott took over for Mills, who departed along with King during the break. Although Vivian rehearsed the company, Redpath continued to pay Greet the agreed-upon $100-per-touring-week Lyceum fee.[55] The Englishman's name, productions, costumes, and goodwill were valuable, and everybody acknowledged that extraordinary circumstances delayed his return. That year's tour comprised twenty weeks in the Northeast, Midwest, and West. One of the best-attended performances the company gave took place in January in the 3,000-seat Mormon Assembly Hall in Salt Lake City, Utah, where it presented *As You Like It* before a large audience made up mostly of schoolchildren.[56]

Although Greet had thrown himself headlong into his work with Baylis, he issued more statements that he would return to the United States in time to personally lead the Woodland Players. The many people who believed his arrival was imminent planned accordingly. The leader of the Ethical Society of St Louis, Percival Chubb, wrote to the actor-manager in February. The society was forming a committee to organize the American celebrations of the tercentenary of Shakespeare's death in 1916; would Greet like to join George Pierce Baker and Thomas Wood Stevens (confirmed) and Margaret Anglin and Horace Howard Furness, Jr (invited) on it? As a story about Chubb's efforts *Theatre* published in May suggests, Greet seems to have responded by sending details about the plans being developed in London.[57] (That Chubb placed Greet in such company reminds us of his prominence as a Shakespearean and pioneer of the Education Theatre Movement.) More immediate (and problematic), Goodstadt had been booking engagements of 'the Ben Greet Woodland Players with Ben Greet' for months. Having to explain to scores of local sponsors that the Englishman would not be appearing as contracted was likely to prove awkward — perhaps even costly.

The 1915 Open-Air Season

Greet's behaviour placed Goodstadt in a difficult position. That the business immediately field a company of Woodland Players was imperative, but there was no money for salaries or transport. No funds arriving from Greet, Redpath refusing to turn over to Goodstadt any of the monies it owed Greet, and the very real prospect of breach-of-contract suits being brought if something was not done quickly, Goodstadt and George Vivian, to whom Greet had assigned financial control of the Woodland Players, made a decision. In April, they reassembled most of the 1914 Woodland Players veterans, including Calver, Hare, Kearns, and Somnes, whom Greet had previously appointed company manager.[58] Vivian and Calver rehearsed them through Greet's productions. Last but not least, Goodstadt and Vivian personally put up the $1,200 needed to get the company on the road.[59] The tour was on.

Goodstadt had booked another remarkable tour for the Woodland Players. From April to July, it presented seven Shakespearean productions and *She Stoops* before audiences in the South, South Central, and Midwest. As in 1914, most of its appearances were at institutions of higher learning, at least forty-five of which sponsored it. Major university appearances that season included Florida, South Carolina,

285

Clemson, Louisiana State, the Southwest Louisiana Institute, Texas A & M, Texas, Oklahoma, Oklahoma A & M, Arkansas, Kansas State, Kansas, Wisconsin, Minnesota, Illinois State Normal, Indiana, Iowa State A & M, Drake, Ohio Normal, and Michigan. *The Tempest* seems not have been up to the old standard, but the company's other offerings delighted audiences, who were especially taken with Kearns and Somnes.[60] That I have been able to confirm nearly 100 performances on 80 dates indicates a robust and profitable season; although slightly less impressive than that of 1914, the tour still brought Greet's productions to a vast audience.

In May, Goodstadt launched a second company of Woodland Players, which he advertised as undertaking an extensive tour of the Northeast under Greet's personal supervision.[61] Its offerings included four Shakespearean standards and *She Stoops*, which it presented at universities, colleges, normal schools, prep schools, country clubs, and resorts from Virginia to Vermont until July. I have discovered few details about it other than that it had twenty-eight members, newcomers Inez Buck and Rupert Harvey were its leading players, and Greet did not lead it.[62]

Goodstadt and Vivian's decisive action saved the season. Regrettably, the heroes soon turned to villainy; after recouping their initial outlays, they began helping themselves to profits rightly belonging to Greet. Perceiving what was afoot, Percival Vivian wrote a letter to his erstwhile mentor in early July telling him what was happening — a task made all the more painful by the realization that his brother had instigated the crime:

> I don't know what has happened to [George]. He isn't like my brother any more […]. I think them both (GV and LMG) a set of pigs but GV is the cause of it all. Goodstadt does just as Geo says […]. I think you should be on your guard for there is no knowing what they might get up it next […]. I should not let any of them have any thing [*sic*] to do with your affairs next season. Get a good capable man, and one you can trust from England and make a clean start.

Greet turned the matter over to a Manhattan attorney, who started chasing Goodstadt for the ledgers.[63] I have been unable to determine whether he managed to recover any of the monies stolen, nor have I found any evidence that Greet ever learned of the existence of the two Greet-style companies the conspirators also fielded (about which anon), the profits of which they almost certainly pocketed. Greet remained on cordial terms with Percival and Ruth Vivian for years, but had nothing more to do with brother George.

Once again, the companies of Ben Greet Players working the Chautauqua circuits appeared before considerably more people than did the Woodland Players. For eight weeks, Eric Blind's Number 3 company toured *Much Ado about Nothing* through the Northeast, with Blind playing Benedick opposite Mills's Beatrice. Its work that summer is particularly important to our knowledge of Greet's impact in circuit Chautauqua because this was the ensemble studied by one of the pioneers of dramatic instruction in American higher education, Frederick H. Koch, then an instructor at the University of North Dakota. Koch's account of one of its performances being the only detailed, eyewitness description of a tent presentation and the effect it had on a Chautauqua audience I have located, I reproduce it here.

In the essay in which it appears, Koch calls for the creation of a government-endowed municipal theatre system in the United States for the purpose of educating the masses. Several European governments supported theatre because they recognized it was 'a vital educative force in the life of their people'. Koch regretted that American theatre sought merely to entertain, not elevate. Profit-hungry producers were part of the problem, but the uneducated masses that unwittingly believed they wanted only novelty were mainly responsible for the unhealthy state of American dramatic culture. But the educator believed 'popular taste is right at the core, and needs only wise direction and organization to translate it into permanent values. The common people will always accept and cherish the best in art when it is presented to them intelligently'. Cue the Ben Greet Players:

Shakespeare, it may be well to recall, belonged to the common people and wrote his plays primarily for them, keeping his eye fixt [*sic*] mainly on the motley crowd of the pit rather on the curtained ladies of his Globe Theatre, and after all these years his appeal to the masses continues. For several years now, in hundreds of towns from New England to California, Shakespeare has proved a good-money-making attraction for many popular Chautauqua assemblies. I found a unique illustration of this in an impromptu tent-theater of the Redpath System of Chautauquas last summer. I have been privileged to attend a number of such Shakespearean attractions, and desire to cite here an experience in a remarkable audience, which would seem to indicate beyond the question of doubt that Shakespeare — done in the direct, colorful manner of Elizabethan life, with immediate contact between the actor and a really democratic crowd — is not a 'high brow', but is altogether universal in his appeal.

In a crass lumbering-town in the Adirondacks, under a big brown canvas 'top', was assembled one evening last August a happy, unsuspecting concourse, to witness a company of Ben Greet Players in *Much Ado About Nothing*. It was just such a restless crowd one might expect to be gathered in this community made up chiefly of French Canadians and Jews, with a sprin-kling of immigrants of many nationalities — a considerable number of them actually illiterate. I anticipated here a complete failure for Shakespeare's lovely comedy of mingled laughs and sighs; but no sooner was the play well under way than I found such apprehensions entirely uncalled for. For here was an audience genuinely Elizabethan — spontaneous, enthusiastic, versatile in the joyful adventure of life. Surely there was never a more spirited performance on the platform of the old Globe; never had the dialog [*sic*] yielded more bris-tling badinage, nor the poetry more witching charm. The players seemed intoxicated with the unrestrained responses they received. In the scenes of the immortal horse-play between Dogberry and Verges in setting the watch and examining the prisoners, the benches actually rattled approval, and it seemed that the great brown top itself must give way to the uproar of the applause, the unconfined cachinnations, and the robustious guffaws of the delighted mob on the final reiteration of Dogberry's irresistible 'O that I had been writ down an ass!' Nor was the serious side of the story less appreciated. In the Church Scene, especially, a deep emotion was apparent. In the solemn moment when Claudio at the altar refuses to accept the fair Hero as his wife and accuses her before the whole congregation of being unchaste and disloyal to him, the intense silence was suddenly interrupted and made, if possible, more intense by a sharp outburst of rough English from an excited lumber-jack who rose to his feet, eyes flashing and hands clenched: 'It's a lie, you blaggard! It ain't so! That girl's *right!*' The miracle had taken place, the audience had actually become participants with the actors in the play. After the performance I found the players jubilant. They were agreed that this was by all odds the most remarkable audience of the season, the most spontaneous — the most genuinely appreciative hearing they had had all summer. Mr. Eric Blind, a fine Benedick, volunteered that he had not felt himself so completely in the part before: 'Why, that audience saw points in the lines I had never found in them myself before!' and Mr. Braham, who played Claudio, insisted that 'The poetry "got over" extremely well! How closely they listened!' And so they had — the untutored crowd had unwittingly recognized and reclaimed Will Shakespeare as their very own! We may learn somewhat, it might seem, from the elemental, unlettered masses.[64]

The extent to which the eyewitness accounts of Koch and Spectator (partially reproduced in Chapter Four) agree is instructive. Both describe diverse audiences comprising poor, poorly educated non-Protestants, many of whom were non-native speakers or illiterate. Both reporters assumed its lack of education would render it incapable of appreciating Shakespeare, and both were surprised that the audience became so intensely focused on and imaginatively, emotionally, and physically committed to the performance that it grew unruly by contemporary standards of theatrical decorum. Both describe audiences throwing themselves headlong into performances and interacting with actors who exulted that they should do so, stimulating them to achieve a higher level of excellence that in turn magnified audience enthusiasm, thereby creating a dynamic cycle of creativity. The reason the performances generated the powerful results they did — results the actors could not have achieved on their own — was that they wakened an Elizabethan-ness intrinsic to but latent in the audience, which both reporters stated rivalled that at a Globe Theatre each imagined. Blind and his colleagues acknowledged that their performances rarely achieved the effect Koch witnessed. Still, the educator's account points to some of the reasons Greet's companies were so successful in circuit Chautauqua.

It is significant for another, more theoretical reason: Koch's categorical 'Shakespeare [...] is not a "high brow"' disproves part of Lawrence W. Levine's theory to the contrary. Levine asserts that Shakespeare ceased to be popular entertainment by 1890, and that the only Shakespeare lowbrows swallowed after that is what highbrows force-fed them in the name of 'education'.[65] Chautauqua certainly liked to tout the 'improving' nature of its offerings, but one of the reasons the institution grew so rapidly was that the presenters it engaged were uncommonly entertaining. Popular Shakespeare may have vanished from America's cities as Levine asserts, but something virtually indistinguishable from it thrived in the country's vast, rural tent-circuits where heterogeneous farmers, mechanics, and shop-keepers consumed it with as much gusto in the 1910s as their homogenous forebears had before the Civil War.

Under Percival Vivian, the Number 1 company of Ben Greet Players toured *Comedy* and *Twelfth Night* through assemblies in Ohio for nine weeks during the summer of 1915. Veterans Conrey and Hanna joined Vivian on the platforms.

Under William Keighley, the Number 2 company presented *Taming* at assemblies in Pennsylvania and West Virginia for eight weeks. I have been unable to identify any of its members apart from Keighley.

Unsatisfied with what they had stolen, George Vivian and Goodstadt also fielded a Woodland Players-style company to tour a series of high-end venues in the Northeast for four weeks. Its repertory consisted of *Taming* and *Twelfth Night*, and its leading players were Greet alumni Malcolm Dunn and Alma Kruger. Significantly, Vivian and Goodstadt called it 'The Ben Greet Players' — a name licensed to Redpath for its Chautauqua circuits. Because it briefly operated in the territory controlled by the Pittsburgh Redpath Bureau at the same time Keighley's Number 2 company was touring the same plays there, Keighley began advertising his group as 'The Original Ben Greet Players'. Most of the people who saw Vivian and Goodstadt's company were probably unaware they were not hearing a Greet-authorized performance, although the fact that the company presented an abridged version of *Taming* at the University of Pennsylvania in late July was cause for comment; those familiar with Greet's work knew of his strong preference for presenting complete texts at institutions of higher learning.[66] However cut, the performances this company gave were probably based on the actor-manager's productions. Whoever rehearsed it (possibly George Vivian) is likely to have used these at least as a starting point because they were not only the best known and most readily available to the company (ironically, Greet had left his promptbooks with Goodstadt for safe keeping), but also because they were the ones already arranged for open-air presentation.[67]

Incredibly, Vivian and Goodstadt also fielded a circuit Chautauqua company called the Forest Players. That it presented Greet's productions is certain: the cover of its handsome promotional brochure announces 'A Company of Superb Artists properly presenting Shakespeare Plays Produced by the World Famous Ben Greet', while one of its advertisements states 'two of Shakespeare's best plays as arranged by Ben Greet'.[68] That this company, like those of the Coburns and McEntee, invoked Greet's name indicates how ubiquitous it had become in connection with open-air Shakespeare. The Forest Players presented *Taming* and *Twelfth Night* in the Midwest, but I have been unable to determine the duration of its tour or the names of any of its members. That it played assemblies operated by Harrison suggests the Chicago Redpath territory manager did not scruple to harbour this shady band in his circuits. Greet's decision to remain in England was not only starting to prove a costly one, personally, but it had also thrown his American operations into disarray.

The 1915–16 Season and the Shakespeare Tercentenary

In late July, Peffer wrote to Greet to tell him that one of the reasons the upcoming Lyceum season was not coming together as satisfactorily as he had hoped was that local managers were expressing reservations about hosting any company led by Percival Vivian. The young actor-manager had developed a reputation for recklessness and was widely known to be in debt. More than a few stakeholders doubting his trustworthiness, there was a growing consensus that he should be replaced with the more sober and responsible Keighley.[69]

Perhaps at Greet's insistence, Redpath permitted Vivian to lead the company. In September, Vivian began rehearsing it for the new season. (Greet not doing so for the second year in a row, he may have received no compensation from Redpath.) It still included a number of Greet-trained veterans (Irene Bevans, Hanna, Robert Piggott), but many of its members had never worked with Greet, including new leading lady Beatrice Warren. In the shortest Lyceum season it ever played, the company presented *Comedy* and *Much Ado* for ten weeks in the Northeast and Midwest. Brief as it was, the company still drew healthy audiences, including 2,500 people in Louisville and 2,000 in Indianapolis. And this phenomenon was not limited to the larger cities it played; papers from Reading, Pennsylvania to Aberdeen, South Dakota reported it drawing large and occasionally capacity houses.[70]

The managerial picture changed dramatically as winter turned to spring. The announcement that Greet and George Vivian had formally severed all connection was a step in the right direction. More problematic, Percival Vivian decided to strike out on his own. His newly formed Percival Vivian Players would tour Percy MacKaye's *Sanctuary* through Chautauqua circuits from Florida to Michigan that spring and summer.[71]

That a company of Ben Greet Players and two companies of Woodland Players toured that summer was the result of Greet re-establishing a business relationship with Goodstadt.[72] The latter's contract had expired the previous autumn, and his conduct before it did was unlikely to encourage the former to renew their association.

But a curious detail from one of that summer's tours may offer a clue as to why Greet gave Goodstadt another chance.

Blind led the only company of Ben Greet Players to tour circuit Chautauqua that summer. For twelve weeks, it presented *Merchant* at assemblies in the Northeast and Eastern Canada, with Blind playing Shylock opposite Mills's Portia.[73] The programme included a statement from Greet so unusual that a local newspaper published a partial transcription of it. Responding to those seeking to ban the comedy from classrooms on account of its anti-Semitic content, Greet noted that the Jewish characters were not the only ones whose conduct Shakespeare examined and found wanting. The playwright had depicted the majority of the characters in the play

> as citizens of a great universe, struggling, as we do now, in commerce, for the mastery of the market. If one is inclined to take offense, the Christians have more occasion than the Jews, for several of the characters are more than ordinarily human, and certainly very commonplace [i.e. weak and sinful]. Rather, let us look upon the play as the most perfect blending of our [i.e. Christian and Jewish] common natures, and that our earthly desires can only be granted when they bear the imprint of the finger of God.[74]

Did Greet regret preying upon William Poel, and did his awareness of his own transgression inspire him to forgive Goodstadt's?

In April, the Number 1 company of Woodland Players launched another ambitious tour. As in the previous summer, Kearns took the leading female roles and Somnes served as both leading man and company manager. The tour Goodstadt booked was largely patterned on the route the company travelled in 1914 and 1915. Until the end of July, the company presented *As You Like It*, *Comedy of Errors*, *Much Ado*, *Romeo and Juliet*, and *Hamlet* (with Kearns in the title-role à la Sarah Bernhardt) before audiences in the South, South Central, and Midwest. Once again, appearances at institutions of higher learning — including Mississippi State, Louisiana State, the Southwest Louisiana Institute, Baylor, Iowa State Teachers College, Northern Illinois,

Michigan Agricultural, and the universities of Oklahoma, Arkansas, Indiana, Michigan, Virginia, and Pennsylvania — formed the backbone of the tour. Business was satisfactory, and Kearns and Somnes continued to draw strong notices. A simple lack of evidence may account for the unusually high number of gaps in the performance calendar, but demand seems to have begun to wane in the aftermath of the tercentenary celebrations.

As in 1915, the Number 2 company of Woodland Players toured the Northeast. For six weeks, it presented *As You Like It*, *Taming*, and *Twelfth Night*. Malcolm Dunn took the leading male roles, newcomer Violette Kimball the principal female ones, and returning Greet veteran Agnes Elliott Scott acted in support. I have been unable to determine who led it.

Demand for Greet's offerings was declining, but open-air Shakespeare had achieved such a prominent position in American culture that it was singled out for national recognition that spring. Like other periodicals, the country's foremost theatrical monthly, *Theatre*, devoted its April issue to the tercentenary of the playwright's death. It had a universe of images to choose from: portraits of Shakespeare, famous Shakespearean sites in England, English Shakespearean stars, American Shakespearean stars, spectacular ensemble compositions, legendary professional productions, earnest amateur ones, and lavish scene designs and sets. Although it ran pictures of all those things within the issue, the image it selected for the cover was this painting of Edith Wynne Matthison as Rosalind inspired by (if not actually copied from) the 1903 photograph of her reproduced in Chapter Two. The decision suggests the magazine's editor and/or art department regarded open-air performance as the era's most evocative — even representative — Shakespearean mode. The magazine referenced Greet in the brief biography of Matthison it included, but not as the creative force behind the production that brought her to national prominence as a Shakespearean.

Greet never was and never would be a star, but a few experts acknowledged the cultural importance of his work as America celebrated the tercentenary that spring. In an essay she contributed to one of the tercentenary supplements the *New York Times* published that winter and spring, Matthison thanked Greet for teaching her 'whatever living and illuminative understand of Shakespeare' she possessed. The piece Dr Richard Burton, Professor of English at the University of Minnesota and Vice-President of the Drama League of America, wrote for another discussed Greet's broader significance. Condemning many of the practices Greet had been battling since 1903, Burton declared that the sorry state of performed Shakespeare in the United States was the product of the star system, the poor quality of many of the actors who supported stars, indifference to ensemble playing, younger actors' insistence on attempting to impose Naturalism onto verse, the rampant cutting of texts, and continuing devotion to Spectacular Realism. The return to simplicity and 'the assumption that

30. Ira L. Hill's Studio. *Miss Edith Wynne Matthison as Rosalind.* April 1916.

the spectator's imagination will help stage the play' represented crucial advances: 'The work of Ben Greet and the Coburns in aiding audiences to grasp this fact by their return to something of the Elizabethan manner, whether historically accurate or not, is welcome for this reason', while 'the more careful revivals of [...] William Poel, who has been heard as a lecturer in the United States, are of much value to disseminate the doctrine'. Significantly, Burton also noted that

> Our educational institutions, somewhat tardily, have waked up to the realization that education has obligations in the direction of the theatre, with Shakespeare central in it; that a play is not a thing alone to be dissected (and killed) in the classroom, but a vital, vibrating work of art, at home in the playhouse and nowhere else.[75]

Poel, who had continued to produce and publish, was about to spend twenty-one days working with the students at Carnegie Tech — a visit that scholars continue to regard as a landmark in the history of early drama instruction and performance in American higher education.[76] Clearly, however, the nearly 600 dates upon which more than 200 universities, colleges, and normal schools had already sponsored performances by Greet's companies by the time Poel stepped off the train in Pittsburgh that June had an even greater impact on it. As well, Richard H. Palmer discovered that the Coburns advertised that some 124 institutions had sponsored them by 1917.[77] Franklin J. Hildy has shown how Stevens, Payne, and Angus L. Bowmer reached millions while they worked to bring Elizabethan performance and architecture into greater harmony in North America during the 1920s and '30s, but we should bear in mind that Greet and the Coburns had already converted millions to the cause of bare stages, full (or significantly full-er) texts, swift pace, rapid delivery, and Elizabethan dress by 1916.[78] By so doing, Greet, followed into the market he created by his rivals, the Coburns, laid the foundation upon which North American Academic Shakespeare rests.

At least one American dramatic critic agreed with Burton that bare-stage, full-text, fast-paced Shakespeare was an important advance that was here to stay. In a New York *Sun* feature about how the staging and performance of Shakespeare's plays had changed since the seventeenth century, Lawrence Reamer stated that, although Greet's method was the product of inadequate resources and inexact Elizabethan archaeology, it was the one 'destined to prevail ultimately'. The following month, the same paper published an essay by Greet in which he recounted a few anecdotes about presenting Shakespeare out of doors. Possibly influenced by the theories of John Corbin, Reamer judged Greet's indoor staging to have been insufficiently Elizabethan, but a comment the actor-manager made about playing on campuses is worth noting:

> The open air actor touring the States must necessarily be one whose diction will pass the criticism of university faculties. Every inflection of the lines is watched with keen interest by our audiences of the summer schools, and often have I looked out upon hundreds of books of the text in which those present were following every word and studying ever inflection and every interpretation. It puts the actor on his mettle to have his work studied with such determination.

Greet's goal was to recreate the atmosphere of Elizabethan performance, not Elizabethan theatre archaeology, and his presentations were considered so authentic, evocative, complete, and correct that, for nearly a generation, scores of America's centres of higher learning routinely opened their coffers so their students and faculty could experience — and learn from — them.[79]

That is not to suggest that Elizabethan Manner had won the day, as the various offerings for the tercentenary celebrations in New York demonstrated. Sir Herbert Beerbohm Tree and Robert B. Mantell were among those who mounted Spectacular Realism productions for the many who still preferred that method, the former presenting the rarely staged *King Henry VIII*, the latter the equally uncommon *King John*. The *Hamlet* Forbes-Robertson staged illustrated the abstract, stylized turn production design was taking: an almost bare stage, coloured draperies, artistic lighting effects, and nearly three hours' worth of text. The full-text *Tempest* the Drama Society mounted, which featured an elaborate Elizabethan public playhouse fit-up designed by John Corbin, demonstrated that a few Americans were still interested in Sargent-Baker-Warren-style archaeology. But the culmination of the nationwide tercentenary celebrations was a pageant: Percy MacKaye's *Caliban by the Yellow Sands* featured a cast of forty-seven professionals (including Matthison and Blind) supported by more than 1,600 actors, dancers, and singers. An estimated 75,000 people attended the five performances of the Shakespeare-inspired spectacular the company presented in City College's stadium.[80]

1917–21

Shattuck attributes the notable decline in commercial productions of Shakespeare's plays after the tercentenary to audiences being surfeited with them — a state of affairs America's entry into the First World War (1917) and the great influenza pandemic (1918–19) did nothing to improve.[81] That drop off, coupled with Percival Vivian's decision to strike out on his own, may be why no company of Ben Greet Players toured the Lyceum circuits during the 1916–17 season. Moreover, Blind's death from pneumonia (contracted while touring the Northeast with Cyril Maude's company) cast in doubt future Chautauqua tours.[82] If a company bearing Greet's name was to appear on the tent circuits, someone else would have to lead it.

Grace Halsey Mills stepped into the breach. For the first time, a woman ran one of Greet's companies, and she attracted a number of Greet veterans to her side. *As You Like It* was its offering, with Mills playing Rosalind, Dallas Anderson Orlando, Scott Audrey, and Sydney Greenstreet Touchstone.[83] It toured assemblies in the Northeast and Eastern Canada for at least eight weeks during the summer of 1917.

The same season saw Kearns and Somnes forming their own

open-air company, the Elsie Herndon Kearns Players, which serviced the old Woodland Players' market. It presented *Much Ado*, *Taming*, and *Winter's Tale* that spring and summer at educational institutions in the South, South Central, and Midwest.

Just as Burton had credited Greet's production method for making professors reconsider how they should teach Shakespeare, another educator now acknowledged that the actor-manager had been the one to convince institutions of higher learning to formally support theatrical ventures on their campuses. In his influential *The Insurgent Theatre*, one of the pioneers of the teaching of Dramatic Arts, Thomas H. Dickinson of the University of Wisconsin's Department of English, stated that

> Ben Greet had a large share in showing us that we are not absolutely dependent either upon theatres or the machinery of theatrical publicity [...]. When [he] came out of England with 'Everyman' he proceeded to throw its support on the shoulders of new institutions. He recognized the interest this play had for students of literature and so he appealed to colleges to support it and they did so [...]. And with this play he first definitely aligned the universities of this country with the machinery of guarantee and support of theatrical enterprises. The significance of this innovation cannot be overestimated. His next step after creating the college support was to leave the established theatres and play Shakespeare and the old comedies on the campuses of the colleges. Thus was the new system of circuit introduced.[84]

As we have seen, Greet presented *Everyman* on only a few campuses before switching to Shakespeare, and he did not abandon commercial theatres as quickly (or blithely) as the professor implied. But Dickinson was certainly correct when he credited Greet with introducing professional drama to the varsity, inspiring a few faculty members and administrators to bring more theatrical initiatives onto their campuses, and forging a lasting alliance between higher education and performed classical drama. North American institutions of higher learning have remained bastions of Shakespearean production ever since.

The Board of Regents of the University of the State of New York burnished Greet's reputation as an educator that spring when it mandated that state-of-the-art technology be employed in the instruction of English, which subject included not only literature, but also formal recitation and extemporaneous speaking. Specifically, the regents added a requirement that high school students listen to phonographic recordings of speeches from Shakespearean plays in preparation for that year's Regents Examinations. Although several prominent actors made Shakespearean records before 1918, the ones Greet recorded for Victor in 1912 were the ones the regents specified.[85]

Fresh from her success in Chautauqua, actor-manager Mills led the Ben Greet Players during the 1917–18 Lyceum season. The fourteen-member company she fielded included several Greet veterans, including Hare, Sanford (whose Shylock was much praised), and Scott. From September to February, it presented *Merchant* and *Palace of Truth* on a transcontinental tour that encompassed the West, Midwest, and Northeast and was the subject of a full-page photospread in *Theatre*. Mills, who was also an accomplished singer, liked to perform 'The Star-Spangled Banner' before presentations; audiences joined in, and nobody questioned the company's patriotism. By all accounts, the twenty-one week tour was a critical and commercial success.[86]

Mills struck out on her own as soon as the 1917–18 Lyceum season ended. The company she formed, the Grace Halsey Mills Players, toured Israel Zangwill's *The Melting Pot* through Chautauqua assemblies in the Northeast and Eastern Canada that spring and summer.

The Elsie Herndon Kearns Company was also active, presenting Shakespeare plays and Molière's *The Blue Stockings* (*Les Femmes savantes*) in the South, South Central, and Midwest that summer. Kearns and Somnes had made a formal and amicable break with Greet, but they, like others before them, had a tendency to invoke his name in their advertisements. That phrases such as 'including the stars of the Ben Greet Players' and 'the successors of the Ben Greet Company' featured in the company's promotional materials indi-

[17] 'The Ben Greet Players', Redpath-Slayton Lyceum Bureau Brochure, n. d. [1913], p.4, Iowa. In point of fact, Greet and the Woodland Players did appear at a handful of tent Chautauquas that summer.

[18] BG to Harry Harrison, 7 March 1913, Iowa; Crawford Peffer to BG, 22 May 1913, Iowa.

[19] Professional productions of Greet alumnus Charles Rann Kennedy's *The Servant of the House* and Jerome K. Jerome's *The Passing of the Third Floor Back* were also mounted in tent Chautauqua that summer, but Greet's *The Comedy of Errors* was universally considered and advertised as the first play in circuit Chautauqua.

[20] Percival Vivian to Harry Harrison, 13 June 1913, Iowa.

[21] George Seybolt to Harry Harrison, 7 July 1913, Iowa.

[22] According to 'Ben Greet Players Prove Good Number on Chautauqua Bill', *Logansport (Indiana) Journal Tribune*, 22 July 1913, p.1, some 1,800 people attended the company's performance of *Comedy of Errors* in Logansport, IN on 21 July 1913.

[23] 'Redpath Chautauquas', *Lyceum Magazine*, December 1913, p.30.

[24] 'Shakespeare Day', *NYDM*, 30 April 1913, p.13; '"Twelfth Night" at City College', *NYT*, 23 April 1913, p.11.

[25] 'Cincinnati', *NYDM*, 2 July 1913, p.15.

[26] Harry Harrison to BG, 26 June 1913, Iowa; BG to Crawford Peffer, n. d. [late June or early July, 1913], Iowa; BG to George Weiscoff, 1 July 1913, Iowa; 'Chautauqua Engagements for Ben Greet Woodland Players', Ms. List, n. d. [summer 1913], Iowa.

[27] BG to Lucy Love, 1 August 1913, Michigan Love.

[28] 'Cincinnati', *NYDM*, 6 August 1913, p.22.

[29] '6,000 See Ben Greet Players', *Decatur (Illinois) Review*, 20 August 1913, p.9. Auditorium details from <http://findinglincolnillinois.com/lincolnmem-parkandcem.html> [accessed 31 May 2016].

[30] 1913 Redpath Booking Ledger, Iowa. Tickets costing 50¢ for adults and 25¢ for children, if we assume an audience comprising 4,500 adults and 1,500 children, the performances would have grossed $2,625, of which Greet's share would have been $1,462.50.

[31] Weekly operating expense from BG to Crawford Peffer, July 1913, Iowa.

[32] 'Gossip', *NYDM*, 17 September 1913, p.13; 'Goodstadt Gets Greet Players', *New York Clipper*, 4 October 1913, p.1; 'Goodstadt with Greet Players', *Billboard*, 11 October 1913, p.58; 'Ben Greet Spring-Summer Tours', *NYDM*, 5 November 1913, p.7; n. t., *New York Clipper*, 8 November 1913, p.6.

[33] 'Comedy of Errors', *Oswego (New York) Palladium*, 15 October 1913, p.3; The Ben Greet Players, *The Comedy of Errors* and *The Merchant of Venice* Play Programme, 1913–14 Lyceum Tour, University of Michigan Library (Special Collections Library).

[34] 'U.S. Flag Insulted by English Actors', *St Louis Globe-Democrat*, 11 November 1913, p.4; 'Actors Took Down Flag', *Kansas City Star*, 11 November 1913, p.3; 'Greets', *Bedford (Indiana) Mail*, 22 November 1913, p.1; 'Eagle Shrieks at Bard', *NYTr.*, 16 November 1913, p.7; 'Greet Denies Insult to Flag', *NYS*, 16 November

1913, p.16; 'On the Rialto', *NYDM*, 19 November 1913, p.7; 'Good Program', *Danville (Indiana) Gazette*, 16 July 1914, p.1; 'Engaged for 1914–1915', *Auburn (New York) Citizen*, 20 February 1914, p.10.

35 'Thinks Stage is Safe', *NYTr.,* 17 January 1914, p.5.

36 'Ready to Build Booth Memorial', *NYT*, 23 November 1913, section C, p.7. For additional details, see 'Edwin Booth Theatre on Broadway', *NYDM*, 9 July 1913, p.7.

37 'A Taste for Shakespeare', *NYTr.,* 24 January 1914, p.6.

38 BG to Henry Clay Folger, 8 January 1914; BG to Henry Clay Folger, 3 March 1914; Henry Clay Folger to BG, 6 March 1914, Folger Papers, Box 21, Folger Shakespeare Library, Washington, DC; Alman, p.112–13.

39 'Dinner to Greet', *NYDM*, 4 February 1914, p.14.

40 'Ben Greet Denounces Brieux', *NYS*, 2 February 1914, n. p.

41 For details, see 'Sunday Performances', *NYDM*, 11 March 1914, p.8; 'No Performances on Sunday?' *NYDM*, 1 April 1914, p.8.

42 'Tech Students See Ben Greet Players', *Pittsburgh Post-Gazette*, 27 March 1914, p.3; Payne, pp.120–24 and 150–93; 'Next Week Shakespearean Dramas Will Be Given', *New York Call*, 22 March 1914, p.6; 'Shakespearean Plays in Schools', *NYDM*, 25 March 1914, p.7.

42 'The Anderson Chautauqua Will Give Variety of Program', *Anderson (South Carolina) Intelligencer*, 27 May 1914, p.2. 'This Season 3,046 Chautauquas', *Lyceumite Magazine*, July 1914, p.16.

44 Trewin, pp. 202–07.

45 'Chautauqua Dates Have Been Made Up', *Augusta (Georgia) Chronicle*, 14 April 1914, p.7; 'Ben Greet Player, in Hospital Result of Accident', *Muskegon (Michigan) Chronicle*, 15 June 1914, p.12; 'Kellerman Today', *Augusta (Georgia) Chronicle*, 14 May 1914, p.10; 'Americus Chautauqua Success in Every Way', *Macon (Georgia) Telegraph*, 22 May 1914, p.6; 'Grows Bigger and Better', *Athens (Georgia) Banner*, 30 April 1914, p.1; 'Chautauqua Season Nears Climacteric', *The (South Carolina) State*, 16 May 1914, p.6; '"Twelfth Night" Was Presented at Chautauqua', *Columbus (Georgia) Enquirer*, 22 May 1914, p.6; 'Friday Program Quite up to Mark', *Montgomery (Alabama) Advertiser*, 23 May 1914, p.2.

46 'Always Welcome to Geneva', *Geneva (New York) Times*, 9 September 1914, p.7; n. t., *Lyceum Magazine*, August 1914, p.38.

47 Sperdakos.

48 'At White Sulphur Springs', *NYT*, 26 July 1914, p.41; 'Hear Greet Players', *Charleston (West Virginia) Mail*, 30 July 1914, p.5.

49 BG to Lucy Love, 26 April 1914, Yale Love; L. M. Goodtsadt to BG, 31 July 1914, NYPL.

50 'Ben Greet Writes', *New York Clipper*, 2 January 1915, p.1.

51 Elizabeth Schafer, *Lilian Baylis: A Biography* (Hatfield: University of Hertfordshire Press and Society for Theatre Research, 2006), p.133.

52 Henry George Hibbert, 'Our London Letter', *New York Clipper*, 5 December 1914, p.2. For accounts of Greet's seasons at the Old Vic, see Schafer, pp.133–38;

George Rowell, *The Old Vic Theatre: A History* (Cambridge: Cambridge University Press, 1993), pp.97–104; and Isaac, pp.126–93.

[53] William Carter to BG, 27 November 1914, NYPL. For details of the bureau's plans, see 'A Picture Service for Church and Schools', *Independent*, October–December 1914, p.411.

[54] 'Ben Greet Announces Plans', *NYDM*, 2 December 1914, p.11; 'Ben Greet Writes', *New York Clipper*, 2 January 1915, p.1.

[55] Crawford Peffer to BG, 24 December 1914, NYPL.

[56] 'Ben Greet Players in Salt Lake', *NYDM*, 20 January 1915, p.9; 'Ben Greet Players Here Friday Night', *Salt Lake Telegram*, 7 January 1915, p.3. Seating capacity from *Proceedings of the Third Annual Live Stock Association* (Denver: Denver Chamber of Commerce, 1900), p.425.

[57] Percival Chubb to BG, 13 January 1915, NYPL; 'A Country-Wide Shakespearean Festival', *Theatre*, May 1915, p.274.

[58] Crawford Peffer to BG, 11 January 1915, NYPL.

[59] L. M. Goodstadt to BG, 6 April 1915, NYPL.

[60] 'Shakespeare Humanized by Greet Players', *San Antonio (Texas) Light*, 2 May 1915, p.8; 'The Ben Greet Plays', *(University of) Indiana Student*, 9 July 1915, p.2.

[61] 'Notes', *New York Clipper*, 5 May 1915, p.5.

[62] 'Inez Buck Joins Ben Greet Players', *NYT*, 5 May 1915, p.13.

[63] Percival Vivian to BG, 8 July 1915, NYPL; Samuel Wandell to BG, 30 July 1915, NYPL; Samuel Wandell to Greet, 23 August 1915, NYPL; L. M. Goodstadt to BG, 4 October 1915, NYPL.

[64] Frederick Henry Koch, 'Toward a Municipal Theatre', *Quarterly Journal of the University of North Dakota*, 6 (1915–16), 104–121 (pp.116–17).

[65] Levine, p.31.

[66] 'Ben Greet Players at Penn', *PI*, 31 July 1915, p.4.

[67] L. M. Goodstadt to BG, 4 October 1915, NYPL.

[68] The Forest Players, promotional brochure, n. d. [Summer 1915], Iowa; 'Converse Chautauqua', *Swayzee (Indiana) Free Press*, 13 August 1915, p.4.

[69] Crawford Peffer to BG, 30 July 1915, NYPL.

[70] 'Ben Greet Players at the Academy', *Reading (Pennsylvania) News-Times*, 26 October 1915, p.11; 'Greet Players Give Rendition of Shakespeare's Play', *Sandusky (Ohio) Register*, 3 November 1915, p.9; 'Shakespeare Comedy Given by the Ben Greet Company', *Indianapolis Star*, 16 November 1915, p.9; 'The Ben Greet Players', *Aberdeen (South Dakota) News*, 30 November 1915, p.3.

[71] 'Plays and Players', *New York Evening Telegram*, 18 March 1916, p.6; 'Drama Invades the Chautauquas', *NYDM*, 29 July 1916, p.7.

[72] 'Ben Greet Players', *Geneva (New York) Times*, 12 July 1916, p.7; 'Seats for As You Like It', *Richfield Springs (New York) Daily*, 12 August 1916, p.1; 'Personal Paragraphs', *Richfield Springs (New York) Daily*, 16 August 1916, p.1.

[73] 'Drama Invades the Chautauquas', *NYDM*, 29 July 1916, p.7; 'The Redpath Chautauqua System Presents the Ben Greet Players "The Merchant of Venice"', Cast-List, n. d. [Summer 1916], Iowa.

[74] 'Ben Greet Players', *Geneva (New York) Times*, 12 July 1916, p.7.

[75] Edith Wynne Matthison, 'Great Enough to be Rightly Interpreted in Many Different Ways', *NYT*, 12 March 1916, Shakespeare supplement, [n. p.]; Richard Burton, 'And Not Properly Presented, Even Today', *NYT*, 2 April 1916, Shakespeare supplement, [n. p.].

[76] Rosemary Kegl, 'Outdistancing the Past' in Kahn, Nathans, and Godfrey, 247–75 (pp.257–58).

[77] Palmer, 'America', p.16.

[78] Hildy, pp.108–13.

[79] Lawrence Reamer, 'Setting Has Played a More Important Part in the Impression on Public than Either Actors or Managers Have Imagined', *NYS*, 16 April 1916, p.12; Ben Greet, 'Taking Shakespeare Back to Arden in the Theatre without Walls', *NYS*, 14 May 1916, p.4.

[80] 'Forbes-Robertson Again Acts Hamlet', *NYT*, 11 April 1916, p.11; 'At the Theatres', *(Brooklyn) Standard Union*, 11 April 1916, p.6; 'Mantell's King John a Fine Achievement', *BE*, 15 April 1916, p.8; 'In Shakespearean Style', *(Brooklyn) Standard Union*, 25 April 1916, p.11; Shattuck, *Shakespeare*, II (1987), pp.302–08.

[81] Shattuck, *Shakespeare*, II (1987), p.242. I am grateful to Franklin J. Hildy for calling to my attention the dampening effect the war and influenza epidemic had on Shakespearean productions in America.

[82] 'Died', *NYDM*, 6 January 1917, p.11.

[83] 'The Ben Players Greeted', *Cortland (New York) Standard*, 11 July 1917, p.2.

[84] Dickinson, pp.190–91.

[85] 'High Schoolers Study English with Victrola', *Auburn (New York) Citizen*, 4 January 1918, p.6.

[86] 'Ben Greet Players in "The Merchant of Venice" at Santa Barbara, Cal.', *Theatre*, May 1918, p.295; 'Greet Players Give Fine Show', *(San Diego) Evening Tribune*, 15 November 1917, p.6; Clarence Urmy, 'Ben Greet Players in "Merchant of Venice"', *San Jose (California) Mercury*, 24 November 1917, p.2; 'Ben Greet Players Win', *(Portland) Morning Oregonian*, 28 November 1917, p.5.

[87] 'Coit-Alber', *Lyceum Magazine*, May 1918, p.26; 'Coit-Alber Chautauquas', *Lyceum Magazine*, August 1918, pp.21–22.

[88] '"As You Like It" Seen Last Night', *Columbia (South Carolina) State*, 28 April 1921, p.2; 'Record Crowd Sees Ben Greet Players', *High Point (North Carolina) Enterprise*, 9 May 1921, p.1; 'Crime Caused by the Desertion of Christ's Religion', *Augusta (Georgia) Chronicle*, 14 May 1921, p.6; H. C. Smith, 'As You Like It Well Presented', *Fort Wayne (Indiana) Journal-Gazette*, 24 July 1921, p.27; 'Play Presented at Chautauqua Pleases Crowd', *Logansport (Indiana) Morning Press*, 27 August 1921, p.1; '1921 Chautauqua Committee Reports', *Billboard*, 9 July 1921, p.42; '1921 Chautauqua Committee Reports', *Billboard*, 18 February 1922, p.82.

Chapter Eight

A Secret Mission for Shakespeare, 1914–36

Work in Europe, 1914–29

Greet achieved his greatest success as a Shakespearean popularizer in Great Britain during the period 1915–21.[1] Between 1914 and 1918, he directed twenty-four of the Elizabethan's plays and fifteen other 'worth while' favourites (*Everyman*, *She Stoops to Conquer*, etc.) for Lilian Baylis at the Royal Victoria Theatre — seasons that laid the groundwork for its transformation from a variously purposed hall into London's preeminent Shakespearean venue. That Baylis and Greet put up Shakespeare season after season, literally as Zeppelins dropped bombs on nearby Waterloo station, made these years the stuff of theatrical legend.

Greet's mastery of bare-stage presentation, skill as a teacher, and zeal for bringing Shakespeare to schoolchildren were vital not only to the Vic's transformation, but to its very survival. As Akin notes, Baylis's resources had been meagre before 1914, and the additional burdens the war imposed might well have put her out of business had the creative economy the actor-manager perfected during his years in North America not enabled the pair to mount productions that delighted audiences far beyond what might reasonably be expected from their paltry budgets.[2] As Elizabeth Schafer discovered, one way Greet managed costs was by declining to receive a salary for the 1914–15 season, which act he regarded as a contribution to a war he was too old to fight. The three seasons that followed found him accepting expenses only.

Greet was able to recruit a number of able journeymen, including Robert Atkins, Duncan Yarrow, Florence Saunders, Sybil Thorndike, and Andrew Leigh (who also stage-managed). But with so many men at the front, the company he formed comprised mainly prentice-quality young women and old men, with a few boys and military-aged men unfit for service filling up the cry. His recruitment of the Foote sisters, the Keys twins (who later became his landladies at 160 Lambeth Road, Lambeth), and Geoffrey and Stella Wilkinson demonstrated his continuing belief that siblings made for happier, more cohesive companies. The number of sibling-groups increased in 1916 when another former protégé, Russell Thorndike, joined after he was invalided out of the army. The Vic Company lacked stars, but the standard of its principal players was respectably professional. Greet drilled them into a unit capable of breathing life into his productions (their texts now heavily cut to make them more accessible to their new audience), and, like virtually every company he led, its effectiveness as an ensemble was greater than the sum of the skills of the individuals it contained. And Greet's extraordinary vigour and constitution enabled it to maintain a gruelling schedule.

His prominence as a Shakespearean interpreter and the Vic's growing importance as a Shakespearean venue were acknowledged in the summer of 1916. The Shakespeare Tercentenary Summer Festival at Stratford-upon-Avon had been fixed for August. In June, the man who was supposed to have produced it, actor-manager Frank Benson, announced his departure for France with the Red Cross immediately upon hearing of the death of his son at the front. Understandably anxious, the governors invited Baylis and Greet to bring the Vic Company (which had just mounted its own tercentenary celebrations in grand style) to their theatre, where Greet would produce the festival. Knowing they had but four weeks to assemble and rehearse the massive company that would be required, Baylis and Greet accepted. The month-long festival they mounted comprised ten Shakespearean plays and two eighteenth-century comedies. Some of the productions were decidedly rough, but the robust simplicity of

Greet's approach enabled an underprepared company to deliver the plays creditably, even admirably — a point the grateful governors underscored in their closing-night remarks to the considerable applause of the festival attendees.[3]

As Isaac identifies, Greet's devotion to the cause of Shakespeare for schoolchildren is what enabled the Vic to remain in business during the war. The actor-manager's long-time spiritual advisor and sometime collaborator, the Rev. J. Stewart Headlam, had maintained his educational influence through the years. He persuaded the London County Council's Board of Education (successor to the London School Board) to officially endorse bringing schoolchildren to performances at the Vic, which in 1915 began offering specially priced matinees to accommodate them. Like their forebears and North American counterparts, the students enthusiastically embraced Greet's Shakespearean offerings. Hundreds of thousands of schoolchildren from hundreds of schools (many located in the city's poorest neighbourhoods) heard the words of their national poet spoken for the first time on the stage of the Old Vic.

Greet took part in other patriotic activities. In 1918, he played the role of the Mayor of Castleton in Herbert Brenon's propaganda film, *Victory and Peace*, which seems to have been his only cinematic appearance. He also joined long-time friend, American expatriate Mary Anderson, as well as his former American competitor, E. H. Sothern, at a private hospital in Evesham to present scenes from *Macbeth* for wounded doughboys — a visit that became the subject of a feature Sothern wrote for *Scribner's Magazine*.[4]

Determining that paying for the schoolchildren under its supervision to travel to the theatre was too expensive, the LCC decided to begin laying on the shows instead, directly hiring a company and the venues. The board invited Greet to form a company for the purpose of bringing Shakespeare's plays to the schools of greater London. Accepting, Greet left the Vic and re-established the Ben Greet Players in 1918. For the next three seasons, he took his school standards — *As You Like It, Henry V, Julius Caesar, Merchant of Venice,*

Midsummer Night's Dream, Tempest — to students in urban and suburban auditoriums, music halls, and theatres as well as in the open air. By the time the LCC's auditor disallowed the programme in 1921, Greet had, between his years at the Vic and his work for the LCC, presented his Shakespearean productions to a million school-children in greater London.

That more than an estimated 2.6 million American Lyceumites and Chautauquans and English schoolchildren attended perform-ances of Greet's productions between the fall of 1912 and the fall of 1921 is therefore likely. That tally excluding the unknown hundreds of thousands of American undergraduates, Cincinnatians, and ordinary Vic patrons who also attended during that period, it significantly under-represents the actor-manager's actual cultural impact. Greet's Shakespearean productions influenced a generation on both sides of the Atlantic.

Off and on, Greet continued presenting Shakespeare in schools until 1928. The LCC had ceased underwriting Greet's work, but other funding sources enabled him to continue performing in London schools into 1922. And any school that wished to hire the company at its own expense was still free to do so, and the actor-manager persuaded many to do just that. As Ivor Brown and George Fearon found,

> Greet built up a regular touring system of big schools, little schools, schools in towns, schools in the country, schools for the deaf, schools for the dumb, schools for the blind; in fact, every conceivable kind of school became, in the course of time, a playing centre for the Ben Greet Shakespearean Company.[5]

Between these engagements, appearances in provincial theatres, the occasional performance in London, open-air touring, and the limited reinstitution of LCC-sponsored presentations between 1925 and 1928, the actor-manager managed to cobble together a living for himself and his players.

Greet and William Poel were on good enough terms in 1921 to collaborate on another revival of *Everyman*, this time at Poel's originally intended venue: Westminster Abbey. An amateur company comprising clergymen and parishioners gave a dozen performances, the proceeds of which went to the abbey's restoration fund. Greet's name was the only one to appear in the story *The Times* published, but a draft of a promotional notice in his hand indicates that Poel rehearsed the actors, staged the production, and may have been credited in the programme. The paper reported that the Bishop of London mounted the platform after the first performance to declare the Morality the best sermon preached in the city that Lent. He then thanked Greet, whom he described as 'the strongest link there was between the Church and the Stage'.[6]

The Ben Greet Academy of Acting operated for at least some of the 1920s. Of the performers who trained there that decade, Jessica Tandy would go on to achieve the greatest renown. (Although not one of the actor-manager's students, Tandy's future husband, Jack Hawkins, appeared in the all-male *Twelfth Night* Greet mounted in London's Rudolf Steiner Hall to commemorate Shakespeare's birthday in 1927.) That Greet allowed Poel to use the academy as the query- and ticket-sales-point in 1924 for his famous production of *Fratricide Punished* suggests the two were on civil terms, at least that year.[7]

Greet made several extended visits to France between 1922 and 1926. As the headlining performer in W. Edward Stirling's English Players, he assisted Stirling to produce Shakespearean and other English plays with an eye toward establishing a permanent English theatre in Paris. The six-week season they presented at Théâtre Albert 1er in 1925 was co-sponsored by the French Ministry of Public Instruction, the British ambassador, and the American ambassador.[8] Their work was warmly received, and in 1926 the French government presented them with gold medals in recognition of their efforts. But the pair fell out when Stirling insisted on producing Leon Gordon's *White Cargo*, a play Greet considered indecent.

In 1929, King George V conferred a knighthood upon Greet for his services to drama and education — the crowning accolade of the actor-manager's career, now in its fiftieth year. He may have become 'Sir Philip', but the name 'Ben Greet' was impressed so strongly upon the minds of so many Shakespearean enthusiasts on both sides of the Atlantic that one risked failing to draw the largest audience possible if one did not prominently advertise it.

Return to the USA: the 1929–30 Season

Cinema, the automobile, and a new technological marvel — radio — had utterly transformed the entertainment industry. The dramatic urge continued to find ways, old and new, to express itself, but by 1929 American commercial theatre was but a shadow of its former self.[9]

Although almost all the Shakespearean stars of the 1900s had taken up other interests or retired by 1925, star-driven productions of Shakespeare's works continued to be mounted in the largest cities thanks to the three uncommonly talented artists who had emerged in the 1910s to interpret the playwright's works for a new generation: John Barrymore, Walter Hampden, and Fritz Leiber. (That the 1918 production of *Hamlet* that elevated Hampden into the top-tier of American actors was directed by Frank McEntee, staged in the Elizabethan Manner, sponsored by Julius Hopp's Wage Earners' Theatre League and Theatre Center for Schools for poor New York schoolchildren and adults (who paid 'popular prices'), and featured Alma Kruger and Percival Vivian in its cast gives evidence to Greet's continuing influence. And of course Leiber trained under Greet.[10]) The last of the old-school tragedians, Robert B. Mantell, continued to tour his ever-more-antiquated Spectacular Realism productions through the country's secondary cities (appearances on Broadway grew rare after 1917) until his collapse in 1928. His death on 27 June of that year left Hampden and Leiber as America's preeminent Shakespeareans, Barrymore having quit the stage for Hollywood in 1925.[11] Hampden mounted some excellent productions of the play-wright's works in the 1920s, but he was a multi-talented realist.

Recognizing that audiences preferred modern fare to Shakespeare (his Cyrano was much-admired), his repertory grew increasingly contemporary after 1925.[12] More single-minded, actor-manager Leiber toured his Shakespeare Repertory Company through America's larger cities for most of the 1920s. In 1929, he became the co-director and leading player of the newly formed Chicago Civic Shakespeare Society, which promoted itself as America's first permanent, endowed home for the exclusive presentation of the Elizabethan's plays. Based at the Chicago Civic Theater, its company also toured.[13]

Other Shakespeare-focused ensembles could be found on what remained of the road. One of these, the Stratford Players, was formed when some Mantell and Leiber veterans combined to tour what one newspaper called a 'Ben Greet or Coburn'-style production of *Julius Caesar* through a circuit of colleges and high schools during the 1928–29 season.[14] The considerably more famous (and royally patronized) Stratford-upon-Avon Shakespeare Festival Players of the Shakespeare Memorial Theatre made its first tour of select North American cities during the same season. The modest and healthy successes those companies enjoyed, respectively, may have encouraged Redpath to renew its association with Greet. Crawford Peffer and Harry P. Harrison were convinced that American theatregoers wanted to hear professional performances of Shakespeare's plays once more.

Unceasing industry in the pursuit of one's art not necessarily ensuring financial security, and Greet still being in fine health (as this photograph taken that year illustrates), he was happy to accept the salary of $250 a week plus a third of the profits Redpath offered him to lead and perform in a company of Ben Greet Players under the bureau's management during the 1929–30 theatrical season. For booking, promoting, and managing the tour, Harrison and Peffer paid themselves identical salaries and shares.[15]

The company's repertory would comprise two staples (*Everyman*, *Twelfth Night*), one of Greet's less-famous Shakespearean offerings (*Much Ado about Nothing*), and an abstruse version of the playwright's

31. Alec Brook. *Mr. Ben Greet.* 1929.

greatest work that had yet to be staged in the United States. Discovered only in 1823, the First Quarto *Hamlet* was generally regarded a pirated, crudely cut version of Shakespeare's original (the nearly twice-as-long Second Quarto), but Poel's stagings of it (1881 and 1900) had demonstrated its theatrical viability. Sir Donald Wolfit later commended Greet for championing the minority opinion that it was the playwright's first draft that his company had presented at the universities and in the provinces. Having mounted his own production (1928–29), Greet was eager to bring it to the universities, colleges, and high schools upon which the new American tour would be founded — audiences educated enough to appreciate the work's unfamiliar scene-order, altered lines ('To be, or not to be, I there's the point'), and omissions of hundreds more. He had lavish Elizabethan costumes run up as well as rich velvet hangings for which he devised simple lighting effects.[16]

Determined to restore his reputation for quality, he raised a fifteen-member company notable for the number of skilled, experienced players it contained.[17] Its leading man, Russell Thorndike, was supported by Bruno Barnabe (who played Everyman), Stanford Holme, and Kynaston Reeves. Stanford's wife, Thea Holme, who had worked with Greet since 1924, was its leading lady. Other veterans included George Hare and Ruth Vivian, each of whom had been working for Greet, on and off, for nearly three decades. The actor-manager always found a place for a worthy acolyte or two, and that tour was no exception: Edith Mayor would serve her apprenticeship under Greet the way her aunt, Edith Wynne Matthison, had nearly thirty years earlier. In addition to playing minor roles, seventeen-year-old Peter Dearing served as stage manager and directorial assistant to the ageing Greet.[18]

The tour Redpath booked was reminiscent of the Lyceum tours of the 1910s in terms of publicity, financial structure, audiences, and venues. The endorsements of Greet's work included in the handsome promotional booklet the bureau published for the tour — notably from the Rev. Dr S. Parkes Cadman, the English-born president of America's Church and Drama Association, and Dr William Lyon Phelps, Lampson Professor of English at Yale University, who was not only prominent in the same group, but also one of the leading champions of middlebrow culture — underscored the focus on educationally minded, religious theatregoers.[19] Redpath called attention to actor-manager's five decades on the professional stage as well as to the many celebrated performers he had discovered and trained. And of course it made much of his recent knighthood, a distinction 'bestowed in recognition of a life devoted to the cause of drama in education — a life of conscientious service in behalf of the best stage traditions'.[20] As they had been doing for decades, local organizations — notably campus and municipal chapters of the YMCA and YWCA — sponsored the performances. The transcontinental tour would run twenty-three weeks during which two performances per day would be the norm. Audiences would be made up mainly of undergraduates and schoolchildren, most of them from rural America. The collapse of the stock market that October would not affect business for some time.

The company opened with *Hamlet* at Smith College in November. The *Springfield Republican*'s positive review praised the 'masterly' presentation. Thorndike and Greet (playing Corambis [Polonius] and the Gravedigger) were outstanding, and Thea Holme's Ofelia and Reeves's Claudius were both good. Its critic praised the bare-stage presentation for enabling an unusually smooth and rapid performance, as well as the artistic lighting effects for varying the atmosphere and helping signal the scene-changes. The paper also commended *Much Ado* and *Everyman*, which the company presented the following day.[21]

A far more influential notice appeared after it presented *Much Ado* at Columbia University later that week. The *New York Times*'s J. Brooks Atkinson praised Greet's 'able direction' and frolicsome production of the still-rarely staged comedy. The actor-manager's simple method brought the playwright very close and revealed the play for the idiomatic, amusing, affecting, entertaining, keenly pleasurable work it was. That it did not distract attention from the play was to the good because his performers spoke their lines so well: 'Mr. Greet has schooled his actors in the forgotten art of speaking words. You can actually understand the words and the sense of what is spoken'. Atkinson singled out for praise the performances of Thea Holme, Thorndike, and Greet, whose 'infinitely thick-headed' Dogberry was 'a genius of muddled intelligence'. Paradoxically, the stage's obsequious devotion to Shakespeare often amounted to disrespect. Greet revered him intelligently and honestly:

standing on the sunny side of idolatry, he indulges Shakespeare in the elementary prerogatives of the dramatist. Although 'Much Ado About Nothing' is not the best of Shakespeare, Mr. Greet presents it as Shakespeare undefiled, which is enough to hearten the soul of man.[22]

It was an auspicious beginning.

The company remained in the Northeast until early January, touring universities and colleges (Mt Holyoke, Brown, Dartmouth), town halls, and a few preparatory and high schools. Its perform-ances in cities were generally well-received, the only negative review I have found coming during its engagement at the New England Conservatory's 1,000-seat Jordan Hall, where the *Boston Herald* judged *Twelfth Night* marred by dull lighting effects, muddled diction, and overplayed physical comedy. The paper had good things to say about its other offerings. Although only a small audience turned out for *Everyman*, the presentation was effective. *Hamlet* possessed 'a certain freshness, almost modernity [...] that was most pleasing'. Thorndike was 'admirable', and 'the supporting cast was unusually good', particularly Greet and Thea Holme. 'The handsome costumes [...] and very simple staging added greatly to the effect of the play, which ran smoothly, quickly and easily. The audience was most appreciative'. And the easy and polished *Much Ado* 'reflected the experience and skill of every member of the company', Thorndike's Benedick being 'extremely effective'.[23] A near-capacity crowd turned out on 13 December in Brooklyn's 2,200-seat Academy of Music to hear *Hamlet*, which drew much applause and solid notices.[24] An even larger audience packed Philadelphia's 3,100-seat Academy of Music when the company presented *Twelfth Night* there on 1 January. The *Philadelphia Inquirer*'s critic praised the production's smooth rapidity, the performers' impeccable diction, and the general excellence of the comedy before concluding, 'It was the sort of evening which makes one realize that the theatre has its intellectual features after all'.[25] Critically and commercially, the Northeast leg of the tour had been a success.

After playing a few colleges in Virginia, the company made its way to Richmond, where large and boisterous audiences packed the Lyric Theatre to welcome the return of classical drama to a city whose once 'vigorous and brilliant' stage was 'now feeble and too often dark'. The *Richmond Times-Dispatch*'s Clarence Boykin, whose memories of hearing the company as an undergraduate at the University of Virginia were so fond that he had been predisposed to favour the performance, was disappointed by *Hamlet*, which he regarded as inferior to the productions of the New York Theatre Guild and Leiber's company, both of which had presented the tragedy in the city in the last decade. The company's small size required much doubling, which practice the critic found unconvincing (apparently without realizing how Elizabethan it was). Greet, Thea Holme, Reeves, and Arnold Walsh turned in solid performances, but Thorndike's was only competent. Fortunately for the players, 'a good percentage of the audience […] appeared to enjoy the performance and voiced this favor with little reserve'. The company's business manager, Paul Blackwell, recorded audiences of 5,000 and 2,400 at the matinee and evening shows that day, respectively, making Richmond one of the best-attended stops of the tour.[26]

Details regarding the company's activities for the remainder of the season abound thanks to the correspondence between Blackwell, Greet, and Harrison now preserved at the University of Iowa, as well as to the diary actor Stanford Holme kept and later published.[27] The company experienced problems with local members of the Stagehands' Union regarding the number of hands it had to employ to handle its minimal properties. By February, Harrison had persuaded an influential union official to lower the requirements for Greet's minimalist productions, although local hands occasionally disputed this.[28]

From mid-January to early March, the company played engagements in the South and Midwest. As they had in Richmond, schoolchildren typically made up the bulk of matinee audiences. Of the 7,500 tickets the company sold for the two performances it gave in

Columbus, Ohio's 4,200-seat Memorial Hall on 18 January (another high-attendance day), more than half were purchased by pupils.[29] Ten days later, the largest audience for classical drama assembled in Cleveland in many years gathered for a matinee of *Twelfth Night* at the Cleveland Heights High School. As the *Plain Dealer*'s William F. McDermott reported, it comprised schoolchildren who 'constituted a multitude somewhat impressively in excess of that which greets the plays of Shakespeare at the regular theaters'. Greet's low-comedy Malvolio disappointed those who had enjoyed his more nuanced interpretation a generation earlier, but the performance overall was better 'than any Shakespearean representation the town has entertained in at least two seasons'.[30] The company was pleased to welcome a crowd of 3,000 students to the matinee of *Hamlet* it presented in Terre Haute, Indiana's Zorah Temple in February, although Holme described the coughing of the schoolchildren as 'appalling. The greatest restraint had to be placed on BG to prevent him from walking through the audience in the interval with his box of lozenges'.[31] But the tubercular din of the students in Terre Haute was but a minor annoyance compared to the outright wickedness of some their counterparts in Marion, Indiana, who pelted the actors with peanuts and gum during a matinee of *Twelfth Night* a fortnight later. When a wad hit Greet,

> he walked straight off the stage and ordered the curtain to be pulled down. He then walked in front of it and made a speech to the effect that we should only continue if the kids promised to behave. 'Chewing gum is a filthy habit at any time, but throwing it about a theatre is horrible'. We then proceeded with the play with the house lights full up, and all the cast walked sedately through their parts while the audience sulked.[32]

No one was more inured to the challenges of playing for schoolchildren than Greet was, but even he had his limits.

The company was used more gently at the colleges (Ball State, Earlham) and universities (West Virginia, Millikin, Indiana, DePauw, Illinois, Minnesota, Drake, Kansas) that hosted it that winter.

Campus appearances, particularly those organized by student YMCA or YWCA chapters, usually represented excellent business. But these continued to be predicated on presenters' reputations for artistic *and* moral excellence. Lyceum and circuit Chautauqua had always condemned drinking on moral grounds, and a decade of Prohibition had done nothing to endear the practice to the people who continued to compose a key segment of Greet's audience. In February, Thorndike played the Dane at the University of Wisconsin in a state of obvious intoxication, which Harrison later claimed inspired one wag to pen the headline 'Ham-lit!' in a local paper.[33] The company immediately issued a statement explaining that, having just been informed of the death of his mother-in-law, the grief-stricken actor had required fortification in order to fulfil his duty. So eager was Greet to put the incident behind them that he offered to personally refund the university's guarantee. Not-so-clandestine drinking possibly and public drunkenness definitely had the potential to suppress turnout at many of the venues the company played that tour, and yet Thorndike and others continued to imbibe. Blackwell covertly brought this to the attention of Redpath, which repeatedly warned Greet about the financial consequences that might result should the company lose its sober reputation.[34]

Campus performances often drew students from local high schools, but Patrick McGilligan discovered the presence of attendees from a more remote institution that bears mention. One of the schools that organized a field-trip to hear the company's presentation of *Much Ado about Nothing* at the University of Wisconsin was the Todd School for Boys. With a new headmaster who had recently redesigned it along radically progressive lines, the Todd School had already instituted the practice of sending boys to Chicago to hear plays, especially the Shakespearean ones staged by Fritz Leiber. Among the Todd students who made the long bus-ride from Woodstock, Illinois to Madison and back was a precocious fifteen-year-old from Kenosha, Wisconsin. From his parents, Orson Welles had inherited an admiration for the Shakespearean actor-managers of old, and he did not miss the opportunity to witness one of the last of that dying breed practice his art.[35]

That the Southwest and West Coast legs of the tour lost money was the result of them being managed by the Ellison-White bureau, which charged a twenty-five per cent commission for its services. The Ben Greet Players had an especially bad week in the Southwest in March, when it failed to attract respectable audiences in Denver, Albuquerque, El Paso, and Phoenix. It had a decent week playing institutions of higher learning and commercial theatres in and around Los Angeles, but its week in San Francisco's 1,500-seat Columbia Theatre — the only week-long run in a commercial theatre that season — failed to make expenses. The company spent early April playing large venues in Oregon and Washington, where heavy turnout in Portland and Seattle enabled it to begin replenishing its coffers.[36]

Presentations at colleges and high schools in the Midwest made up the tour's final weeks. The company's ability to attract sizable audiences in rural venues demonstrated its continuing viability in increasingly hard times, but the cost of covering the vast distances between engagements swallowed up the profits.[37] It closed the tour with two performances in Indianapolis's Shortridge High School's 1,700-seat Caleb Mills Auditorium on 3 May. A few months later, the *New York Times* estimated attendance that season totalled half a million.[38]

The impressive number of people who heard the company notwithstanding, there were negligible profits for Harrison, Peffer, and Greet to divide. Still, Redpath judged the season successful enough to warrant organizing a 1930–31 tour, a proposal Peffer initially floated in February and that Harrison urged Greet to give his final consent to in April.[39]

Greet was angry not only that the tour had failed to realize its earnings potential, but also that the considerable impact it had on American culture had gone unpublicized, the blame for which he laid squarely on the shoulders of Redpath. The specific criticisms he levelled in a series of testy letters to Harrison indicate that the years had not robbed him of his managerial savvy. The trip to the West Coast had been an ill-conceived stunt, and most of the bookings Ellison-White had secured were not profitable enough to justify the swingeing commission they charged. Redpath had ignored the many excellent suggestions he had proffered for optimizing the company's route; cities like Charlottesville, Rochester, Cincinnati, Montgomery, Lafayette, Chicago, Boulder, and Kalamazoo had always given the company an especially warm welcome and would have been easy to add. The bureau had failed to book a run of *Everyman* in an urban centre for Holy Week as well as a Shakespearean festival in a big city around the playwright's birthday — both of which Greet had specifically instructed it to do. A good press agent was worth his salary; why had Redpath not hired one to tout Atkinson's fine *New York Times* review and the company's triumphs in Brooklyn and Philadelphia? Perhaps most frustrating was the fact that nobody knew so many people were turning out to hear Shakespeare that he had become profitable:

> the pity is, that there are no records of our success + such poor publicity that no one knows that we have been traveling through the country and no means I suppose of stating what our receipts have been and how much money we have made for our auspices [sponsors], etc. I think that these points should be embodied in a sort of glorified balance sheet. This is ugly, but it would make people realize that although we have been on a secret mission for Shakespeare we have been a money maker too.[40]

That Greet had accepted the bureau's offer by the time it began publicizing the 1930–31 tour in May suggests Peffer and Harrison convinced him that they would manage things better, and that the improvements would generate both profit and greater awareness of the cultural impact Greet was having.[41]

The 1930–31 Season

The fifteen-member company Greet fielded that autumn was less experienced than the previous season's ensemble, but it made up in enthusiasm what it lacked in refinement. Besides the actor-manager, it contained five veterans of the previous season's tour: Dearing, Hare, Thorndike, Walsh, and Rex Walters. Thorndike took most of the leading male roles once again. Greet, W. E. Holloway, Vic-veteran Reginald Jarman, Donald Layne-Smith, and Walsh supported him. The company's coequal leading ladies, journeywomen Enid Clark and Muriel Hutchinson, shared the principal female roles.

Redpath and Greet collaborated more fully and intelligently to ensure the season's success. The company would offer a larger repertory (*As You Like It*, *Everyman*, the First Quarto *Hamlet*, *Macbeth*, *Twelfth Night*) in a twenty-four-week season widely advertised as the old knight's farewell tour. Perhaps in response to Greet's plea to monitor overheads more carefully, Redpath decreased the tour's scope. It also booked the company into significantly more colleges and universities than it had the previous year. Indeed, the extraordinary number of appearances at or sponsored by institutions of higher learning, particularly ones that had hosted Greet's companies a generation before, suggests the Englishman may have been directly involved in planning the tour's route, pulling from his impressive memory the names of institutions he had played years earlier. That the papers paid the company considerably more attention suggests the bureau hired a press agent, too.

The ensemble opened its season on 22 October with a performance of *Hamlet* at Miami University of Ohio. It then pushed on to Memphis to kick off a tour of the South Central region that lasted until mid-December. It appeared at a slew of institutions that had previously welcomed Greet's companies, including Louisiana State, the Southwest Louisiana Institute, Texas A & M, Baylor, the universities of Texas and Oklahoma, and Oklahoma State. It also played for several new hosts, including Lamar, Rice, Southern Methodist, and Texas Tech.

It consistently drew large audiences despite the deepening depression. Papers widely reported daily attendances of 8,000 in Houston, 7,000 in San Antonio, 6,000 in Austin, and 5,000 in Kansas City, as well as 'tremendous crowds' in Dallas and Oklahoma City.[42] Figures so high and round should not be accepted uncritically, but the overall impression the coverage conveys is that Redpath and Greet had found a winning formula for profitably bringing full-text Shakespeare to hundreds of thousands of underserved Americans.

Factors other than better management contributed to the tour's critical and commercial success. Everyone knew that Shakespeare was the world's greatest playwright and *Hamlet* his greatest play, but few had heard of the First Quarto, and educational audiences were genuinely excited to hear it. That it would be 'authentically staged' by a celebrated English company led by an eminent (and apparently soon-to-be-retired) dramatic knight only enhanced its appeal. But something more tangible and compelling inspired audiences that season: skilful and passionate acting. As the Baton Rouge *Advocate*'s Edward L. Desobry commented after hearing the company at Louisiana State

> It is so often that a professionally famed musical or dramatic company comes to Baton Rouge for a performance, hastens perfunctorily and impersonally through it, and leaves to repeat the process in other cities, that it was a relief last night to view the genuine enthusiasm of the Ben Greet players of England in 'Hamlet'. Perhaps this personal interest in every performance is what distinguishes the world-famous group. With them it is not a matter of presenting a professional half-hearted performance; it is a superb achievement to match the genius of the 'Bard of Avon'.[43]

Struggling to maintain commercial viability in an increasingly bleak economy and aware that the man who had discovered, trained, and employed so many of them might soon be taking his last bow, Greet's actors played like never before.

Of all the states that hosted the company that fall, Texas extended the warmest welcome. Indeed, the hospitality of its citizens was so overwhelming that Greet was moved to write letters of appreciation he sent to a number of the state's newspapers:

> Before leaving Texas may I be permitted to thank all those kind friends who have helped to make our three weeks' visit so pleasant, and not least our enthusiastic audiences numbering over 50,000. The drama and Shakespeare are certainly alive in this wonderful state. I am, dear sir, yours faithfully, Philip Ben Greet.[44]

The company played a series of short engagements in the Midwest before the Christmas break.

Returning to the road in early January, it spent the next seven weeks touring the Northeast. It played several institutions of higher learning that had hosted it on previous outings (Princeton, Mt Holyoke, Smith), and a few that did so for the first time (Temple, Susquehanna). Sizeable and attentive audiences turned out for the performances of *Hamlet* and *As You Like It* given in Sanders Theatre sponsored by Harvard's Department of English — Greet's first return to the university since 1903. The latter drew the most praise and applause, the *Boston Herald* hailing it as 'a triumph of imagination over realism and of Shakespeare over the scene painters' before noting that, 'while these younger players lack a certain polish, they do invest their actions with a freshness that suits excellently well with the gay spirit of the play. An enthusiastic and responsible audience showed every evidence of enjoying their efforts'.[45]

The Northeast leg also included the greatest number of performances at high schools that season, which amounted to some three weeks' worth of engagements. Strong high and prep school turnout helped produce the largest houses indicated that winter. On 6 January, a gratifying 4,600 attended the company's presentations of *Macbeth* and *Everyman* in Hartford's Bushnell

Memorial Hall sponsored by Trinity College. In early February, 8,000 people — 'the record crowd in the east' — heard it one day in Rochester.[46]

Leaving the Northeast, it stopped off one last time at old host West Virginia University on its way to the Midwest, which it toured for a month. Reverting to a college- and university-intensive schedule, it appeared at the likes of Ohio Wesleyan, Wooster, Toledo, Iowa, and Minnesota State. In early March, it played its final engagement at the University of Michigan.

Heading into the South, the company played a month-long string of engagements at educational institutions such as Jacksonville State, Hollins, the Alabama Polytechnic Institute, and the universities of Alabama, Georgia, South Carolina, and Tennessee. Attendance at the two performances it gave at the North Carolina College for Women on 13 April exceeded 2,500. After commending the work of Greet, Thorndike, and Clark, the *Greensboro Daily News*'s critic reconsidered the value of doing so:

> But perhaps these Shakespearians should not be singled out. The performances were not of two, three or four actors. They were offered by well rounded casts of men and women of ability and training who seemed to love their work, and, loving it, they made others love their art.

The company's presentation of *Hamlet* before a large audience the following night sponsored by Frederick H. Koch's Carolina Playmakers elicited a similar response in the University of North Carolina's newspaper.[47]

Turning north, the company stopped off at Bryn Mawr and Swarthmore on its way to Manhattan, where Columbia University welcomed Greet back for a festival commencing on the playwright's birthday. Between laying a wreath at John Quincy Adams Ward's statue of Shakespeare in Central Park with the members of the New York Shakespeare Club, delivering a fifteen-minute radio address on Shakespeare, and presenting *Hamlet*, no one in the United States honoured Shakespeare more than Ben Greet did that 23 April.[48] The *New York Times* described the gathering that evening:

> Reliable Ben Greet and his reliable players, who will — and do — go anywhere in the service of the Bard, paid him high honors on his anniversary and made a holiday for his more scholarly admirers […]. An auditorium well filled with the devout awaited him there, textbooks clutched firmly in their hands, to make what they could of this *Hamlet*.

'Thoroughly at home' in the academic surroundings, Greet's actors demonstrated 'the sturdy competence long celebrated by their leader, keeping the emphasis always on the play'. Matthison, who had joined the faculty of Mt Holyoke earlier that year, made a special appearance as Rosalind at the last day's presentation of *As You Like It*. The two performances the company gave on 28 April in Troy, New York, sponsored by Russell Sage College and three area high schools, closed the season.[49]

By booking the company into more Greet-friendly cities and towns more proximate to one another, organizing a festival in a major metropolitan centre for Shakespeare's birthday, restricting operations to regions where it paid no or low commissions, ensuring that the company sold many more undergraduate- and full-priced tickets than children's tickets, and more effectively publicizing the tour, Harrison, Peffer, and Greet found a way to turn a profit with educational Shakespeare during the second year of the Great Depression. Critically, the tour was slightly less successful than that of 1929–30. Artistically, the young, enthusiastic company of 1930–31 reminded Americans why Greet was famous. Redpath was already putting together the 1931–32 tour by the time the actors sailed for England in late April.

Shakespeare's success in the provinces stood in stark contrast to his presence on Broadway. In a detailed post-mortem of the New York Shakespearean season published in the *New York Evening Post*, John Mason Brown struggled to recall a time when the playwright's fortunes in Manhattan had been at a lower ebb. Only two genuinely worthy productions had been mounted: *Twelfth Night* with Jane Cowl and *Romeo and Juliet* with Eva Le Gallienne, and the production of the tragedy was old. Maurice Moscovitch's *Merchant of Venice* had been 'a decidedly unhappy excursion into the classics'. The second visit of the Chicago Civic Shakespeare Society company had been distinctly less gratifying than the first; the quality of its actors and productions had dropped off appreciably, and, for all Leiber's 'manifest bardolatry', his 'Shakespeare was something at once so hopeless and so dull, so poor in diction and so muddled in execution that no one with a conscience could recommend it even to the most untutored beginner'. The New York Theatre Guild had abandoned its production of *Much Ado* with Lynn Fontanne and Alfred Lunt after the dress rehearsal. The Paul Robeson-Peggy Ashcroft *Othello* that had drawn mixed notices (and lost money) in London never even made it into rehearsals in Manhattan. Meanwhile, fine actors suited to Shakespeare such as Katherine Cornell and Leslie Howard were steering clear of him. Shakespeare's plays might soon survive only in the classroom and in revivals staged by 'well-meaning mediocrities from whom he should be protected' unless skilled performers of some prominence started mounting mainstream productions of them.[50]

Upon learning of the death of Henry Folger that June, Greet sent a letter of condolence to Emily Folger that led to the limited renewal of their correspondence. In one letter, the Englishman thanked the Folgers for their interest and encouragement. He regretted that he had failed to accomplish everything he 'hoped to do for our Shakespeare in America', but was pleased to report that his company had appeared before a million Americans since 1929 (a barefaced exaggeration) and that, God permitting, they would return in October to play for more. He closed with: 'They do love Shakespeare these young people do and that is the Victory. Dr Parkes Cadman was right when he said so beautifully that Shakespeare was there to lead your good man and thank God for Henry Clay Folger'.[51]

The 1931–32 Season

The eighteen-member company Greet brought to America that October included several veterans of the previous season's tour, including Clark, Dearing, Hare, Holloway, Thorndike, and Walters. Gwen Llewellyn took over for Muriel Hutchinson, and Vera French and Edith Mayor appeared in support. Mark Dignam and Frederick Sargent had worked with Greet in England for years, but had never accompanied him to North America as they now did. The young son of the newly created Dame Sybil Thorndike, Christopher Casson, rounded out the ensemble. Its repertory comprised *As You Like It*, *Comedy of Errors*, the First Quarto *Hamlet*, *Julius Caesar*, *Macbeth*, and *Twelfth Night*.

The company opened the season on 20 October with *Julius Caesar* in Trenton sponsored by the New Jersey State Teachers College, which supplied a sixty-piece orchestra to liven the festivities.[52] For a fortnight it played a number of normal schools, colleges, and universities, including Towson, Penn State, and the universities of Kentucky and Purdue. *Variety* reported that it grossed an impressive $6,000 at the two performances it gave in Louisville on 29 October.[53] Heading into the South, it fulfilled engagements at a number of institutions such as the University of Mississippi, Mississippi State, and the Southwest Louisiana Institute. The largest venue it played during this period was Memphis's 12,000-seat Ellis Auditorium, where it presented *Twelfth Night* and *Macbeth* on 4 November.[54]

Arriving in Texas for a three-week tour, it played another notable string of appearances sponsored by universities and colleges, including Rice, the University of Texas, Southern Methodist, Texas Tech, and several teachers colleges. It drew healthy audiences once more, but it faced a little competition in Dallas, which was well supplied with Shakespeare that season. The Oak Cliff Little Theatre had staged a modern-dress *Taming of the Shrew* in October, and William Thornton's newly formed Shakespeare Guild of America company presented three of the playwright's works at the State Fair Auditorium a week before Greet's company arrived. Leiber's Chicago Civic Shakespeare Society company was due in January, as was the *Merchant of Venice* of old stagers Maude Adams and Otis Skinner.[55] The word was out: there was money to be made touring Shakespeare through the Lone Star State.

Something ominous happened while Greet's company was concluding its stay in Texas. Leiber's troupe had struggled to find audiences in most of the cities it visited that autumn. It was playing Manhattan in late November when its management not only cancelled the remainder of the season, but also disbanded the company.[56] Fritz Leiber was out of the theatre business. With a few movie credits already under his belt, he returned to Hollywood.

Heading north in December, Greet's company toured the West and Midwest for a fortnight, during which it appeared at the universities of Colorado and Wyoming, the Colorado State Teachers College, the Western Branch of the Kansas State Normal School, and the Kansas State College of Agriculture. Its best-attended date may have been 5 December when, under the auspices of the Colorado Women's College, it presented *Twelfth Night* and *Hamlet* in the 12,000-seat Denver Municipal Auditorium for the students of local colleges and high schools. Its two performances in the more intimate (3,000-seat) Ararat Shrine Temple in Kansas City on 15 December sponsored by the Kansas City Teacher's College concluded that leg of the tour.[57] The company returned to New York for Christmas and a two-week break.

Although I have found no direct statement to the effect, the fact that Redpath was able to secure only a scattering of bookings in the Northeast suggest that the Great Depression, now entering its third year, had finally killed off demand. Seen in that light, the dissolution of Leiber's company might better be interpreted as symptomatic of general economic collapse than of audiences abandoning a specific ensemble. Even at 'popular prices', many Americans could no longer afford live drama.

Scrappy as they were, Redpath's bookings enabled Greet to hold on for two more months. The week-long run in the Westchester County Center Auditorium in White Plains took the company into 1932, at which point it reverted to playing high schools and institutions of higher learning, including its last new collegiate host: Massachusetts State.

All told, Greet's companies played more than 265 North American institutions of higher learning on more than 780 dates during the periods 1902–21 and 1929–32, which activities I summarize in an appendix. Readers will recall that the theatrical season comprised forty weeks, or 240 dates. Reckoned in those terms, Greet's companies spent more than three full seasons playing nothing but universities, colleges, and normal schools. To state the matter baldly, no theatrical professional performed more Shakespeare for more undergraduates and faculty. One of the reasons Greet had so much influence on how Americans perform Shakespeare — an influence that continues today — is that he had such a profound impact on the generation that began creating departments of Drama and Theatre all over the United States in the 1910s, 1920s, and 1930s.

On 19 January 1932, the company made its final appearance in the New England Conservatory's Jordan Hall, this time sponsored by the Harvard Dramatic Club. The *Boston Herald*'s critic was impressed by *Julius Caesar*, which it presented to a large matinee audience comprising mainly schoolchildren:

> Sir Philip Ben Greet and his players performed wonders. With little but curtains and a raised dais for scenery, they succeeded admirably in recreating the intensely moving drama of personalities and character [...]. Highly intelligent direction made the most of the small group of actors available for the crowd scenes: the behavior of the mob swayed successively in opposite directions by the orations [...] had been worked out with remarkable care and had as much verisimilitude and dramatic force as might reasonably be demanded.

The critic praised the performances of Dignam, Thorndike, Holloway, Greet, and Sargent, and remarked that, all told, the presentation achieved 'remarkable heights of emotional suggestion, of powerful suspense, of dramatic force, to which more elaborate productions often fail to attain'. That night's *Comedy of Errors* drew a moderate house and a cooler notice. The reason the play was so seldom produced was that it was a messy curiosity. The situations were frequently more amusing than the lines, which were sometimes smutty, and many of the characters the young playwright had drawn were poorly developed. Greet's bare stage helped audience members observe the play for what it was: a neo-classically inspired Elizabethan farce of dubious literary value. Regrettably, most of the actors were given more to declamation than character portrayal, Mayor being a notable exception.[58]

In early February, *Variety* announced that Greet had been forced to abandon the tour because so many institutions found themselves unable to pay the guaranteed minimums they had contracted. The last performance by the company I have confirmed took place in Augusta, Maine, on 26 February. Two months later, the *New York Times* estimated that a million Americans heard the Ben Greet Players between November 1929 and March 1932.[59]

The actor-manager had a few commitments to fulfil before heading home. He had accepted an invitation from Emily Folger to formally represent the English stage at the signal Shakespearean event held in the United States that year. On 23 April, Greet gathered with her, President and Mrs Hoover, the ambassadors of Great Britain, France, and Germany, Dr Joseph Quincy Adams, Cadman, Matthison, and others to dedicate the Folger Shakespeare Library in Washington, DC. Stephen H. Grant notes that one contemporary writer attributed Greet's participation to his having 'probably spoken more lines of Shakespeare than anyone alive'.[60] The actor-manager may have achieved that distinction by 1932 (Sir Frank Benson could have been his only rival), but the invitation may have had more to do with his longstanding acquaintanceship with the Folgers, the high regard Mrs Folger, Cadman, and Matthison had for him, and his unusually strong connection to the United States. As Alman correctly identifies, the telegram Greet sent on behalf of the company thanking Mr Folger for his 'wonderful gift to his countrymen' demonstrates that the actor-manager was one of very few contemporary practitioners to recognize the significance of the library and the Elizabethan theatre it contains.[61]

On 8 May, Greet attended the second annual Shakespeare Association of America dinner, at which he and Matthison presented a scene from *Twelfth Night*. Interestingly, Ivah M. and Charles D. Coburn were among the 150 distinguished actors, authors, and playwrights also present. Any competitive feelings that lingered between the erstwhile open-air rivals was probably mollified by Charles Rann Kennedy's keynote speech, the subject of which was the ignorance and petty-mindedness of art, music, and drama critics. Greet's final North American appearance took place the next day at the American Women's Association Clubhouse. Eighteen veterans of his companies, including Dallas Anderson, Charles Hanna, George Hare, Grace Halsey Mills, Percival Vivian, and Ruth Vivian, joined him for the *Dream* (with some of Mendelssohn's music) for the benefit of the Actors' Dinner Club. Naturally, Greet played Bottom.[62] The Englishman sailed home.

True to form, one of those erstwhile protégés used his name to draw audiences a few more times. In July, Percival Vivian, 'through arrangement with Sir Philip Ben Greet', led a company of Ben Greet Players that included a number of veterans in two performances of the hybrid *Dream* in George Washington Stadium. As it had a generation before, the company presented the comedy in collaboration with the New York Symphony Orchestra under Modest Altschuler, which played the complete Mendelssohn score. The following month, the two groups reunited to present a musically enhanced *Comedy of Errors* at the same venue.[63]

Final Seasons
Back in England, Greet's company immediately returned to work, presenting eight of the actor-manager's open-air Shakespearean standards in the usual manner. The addition of Sybil and Russell

Thorndike's sister, Eileen Thorndike, and Sybil's daughter, Mary Casson, to the ensemble may have boosted its appeal.[64] Week-long Shakespearean festivals at the Kingsway Theatre, London, and the Theatre Royal, Bournemouth, were its most prominent engagements that spring and summer.

Greet produced Alice Mary Buckton's *Eager Heart* at Sadler's Wells with a group of amateurs early in 1933. He spent Shakespeare's birthday in the company of Baylis and John Dover Wilson: the three were the featured speakers at the official celebrations at Stratford-upon-Avon, where they delivered luncheon addresses that were broadcast by the BBC. A few days later, Greet directed the First Quarto *Hamlet*, the cast of which included Wolfit as the prince, Thea Holme as Ofelia, and Greet as Corambis.[65]

A year earlier, two of Greet's former associates, director Robert Atkins and producer Sydney Carroll, had revived one of Greet's old ideas: they transferred their famous 'black and white' *Twelfth Night* to Regent's Park for four performances. Intent on launching something more permanent there and with the support of its superintendent, Duncan Campbell, Carroll put together the financing to pay for the construction and landscaping necessary to build the Open Air Theatre. In 1933, Atkins and Carroll established the annual festival that continues to this day. That at least one contemporary newspaper identified Greet as one of its producers suggests he may have provided backing as well as guidance. He took smaller roles, but was prominent as the Master of the Greensward, the duties of which included introducing each performance, prognosticating on the weather, and generally serving as host and *éminence grise*. He made himself useful in other ways. The production of the *Dream* the Regent's Park company brought to Eastbourne's Manor House Grounds for a week in June 1934 may have been based on his night-time and hybrid productions updated by the use of electric lighting and sound amplification. When his friend, Sir Nigel Playfair, collapsed during a presentation of *As You Like It* the following month, Greet stepped into his role and saved the performance. (Sadly, Playfair died three weeks later.) Isaac provides a detailed list of the productions mounted in the park during the three seasons (1933, 1934, 1935) Greet worked there.[66]

Greet also fielded his own open-air company in the summer of 1933 to undertake a limited tour of *As You Like It*, *Macbeth*, and *Twelfth Night*. He did not appear at every performance, and the company he led included no noteworthy names.[67]

Emily Folger sent him a copy of the first annual report describing the activities at the Folger Shakespeare Library as the year drew to a close. In the last letter Greet ever wrote her, he expressed his admiration for all the goings-on at the library and wished he 'could have been there to teach and talk Shakespeare'. After apologizing for allowing their correspondence to lapse during the war, he told her 'it is lovely to know the memory and the work is there — in Washington'.[68]

Religion remained an important part of Greet's life. He contributed a chapter about his old curate and friend, the radical Anglo-Catholic the Rev. Arthur Henry Stanton, to R. S. Forman's *Great Christians* published that autumn. On 25 February 1934, he delivered the most famous broadcast of his career: reassembling many performers who had recently followed him to America — Darch, Dearing, Dignam, French, Jarman, Mayor — he presented *Everyman* as an hour-long radio play for the BBC.[69]

To celebrate Shakespeare's birthday, Greet directed the Second Quarto *Hamlet* at Sadler's Wells with Ernest Milton playing the title-role, Sybil Thorndike Gertrude, and Wolfit Claudius. Alarmingly, he took the first curtain call — an act so rude that Wolfit recalled it in a letter he penned to Milton decades later. In addition to working at Regent's Park that spring and summer, Greet led his own company in a limited open-air tour, presenting *Love's Labour's Lost* and *Twelfth Night* a few times in the provinces. The presence of veterans Thea Holme and Stanley Drewitt in the company suggests the quality of its offerings may have been higher than it had been in 1933.[70]

In October, Greet was one of the speakers invited to address the opening meeting of the Plymouth Playgoers' Circle. The keynote speaker, Penelope Wheeler, opened the session's topic: 'The Study of

Epic Drama'. Greet went next. The person who spoke after him was a young director named Tyrone Guthrie. Guthrie having worked as Baylis's artistic director at the Old Vic during the 1933–34 season, he and Greet may already have been acquainted.[71] One wonders whether the two men shared the journey back to London, and, if so, whether the topics of Canada, Dorothy Mavor Moore, or Shakespeare under canvas arose. In late November, Greet's company presented a week-long Shakespearean festival at the Theatre Royal, Brighton.[72]

Greet slowed appreciably in 1935. He played the Messenger when Atkins and Carroll revived *Everyman* at London's Ambassador's Theatre for Lent.[73] In late March, the Old Players's Club held a dinner for him to celebrate his completion of fifty-five years on the professional stage. As Isaac, who was there, records, a number of prominent theatrical professionals attended, including Atkins, Baylis, Carroll, Lewis Casson and several members of his family (wife Dame Sybil Thorndike was off touring North America), John Drinkwater, Gabrielle Enthovern, Elsie Fogerty, J. Bannister Howard, Irene Rooke, Phyllis Neilson Terry, Dame May Whitty, and Wolfit. Lady Keeble, who had once been known as Lillah McCarthy, presided and proposed the toast 'To our beloved father and great master'. She also presented a cheque to the man who had given her her first professional opportunity four decades earlier — a gracious way to put some money into the hands of the increasingly needy artist.[74] Greet continued to eke out a living by playing the Patriarch in Seymour Hicks's production of George M. Cohan's *Miracle Man* (his last new role) at London's Victoria Palace, mastering the greensward at Regent's Park, and teaching.[75] He booked but six performances for his own company outside the capital that summer. Two of them, *Henry V* and *Comedy of Errors*, were presented at Tunbridge Wells on 2 July.[76] As few as they were, the performances marked fifty consecutive summers Greet had professionally presented Shakespeare in the open air — an accomplishment that went unnoticed, perhaps because Greet no longer possessed the resources to promote it.[77] That November, the actor-

15   Crawford Peffer and Harry Harrison and Ben Greet, Copy of Memorandum of Agreement, n. d. [early 1929], Iowa.

16   Speaight, pp.48–54; Crawford Peffer to Harry Harrison, 21 August 1929, Iowa; Ronald Harwood, *Sir Donald Wolfit, C. B. E.: His Life and Work on the Unfashionable Stage* (New York: St. Martin's, 1971), pp.114–15; 'Old "Hamlet" Given at Smith College', *Springfield (Massachusetts) Republican*, 12 November 1929, p.11.

17   BG to Crawford Peffer, 15 March 1929, Iowa.

18   Ben Greet Players Programmes and 23 December 1929 Salary List, Iowa; 'Americans and Europeans about the Same, Ben Greet Director and Actor Tells School Reporter in Interview', *Lubbock (Texas) Avalanche-Journal*, 6 December 1931, p.19.

19   For an overview of Phelps's career, see Joan Shelley Rubin, *The Making of Middlebow Culture* (Chapel Hill and London: University of North Carolina Press, 1992), pp.281–90.

20   Ben Greet Players, 'Announcement of the Return American Tour of the Ben Greet Players with Ben Greet Himself in the Cast', Publicity Brochure, n. d. [early 1929], Iowa; Ben Greet Players, 'Announcing the Famous English Actor and Producer Sir Philip Ben Greet', Publicity Brochure, n. d. [late 1929], Iowa.

21   'Old "Hamlet" Given at Smith College', *Springfield (Massachusetts) Republican*, 12 November 1929, p.11; 'Ben Greet Players in Two Presentations', *Springfield (Massachusetts) Republican*, 13 November 1929, p.7.

22   J. Brooks Atkinson, 'The Play', *NYT*, 17 November 1929, p.30.

23   'Jordan Hall', *Boston Herald*, 11 December 1929, p.23; 'Ben Greet Players Stage "Everyman"', *Boston Herald*, 9 December 1929, p.13; 'Jordan Hall', *Boston Herald*, 10 December 1929, p.20; 'Jordan Hall', *Boston Herald*, 11 December 1929, p.23.

24   'Ben Greet Players Stage Hamlet History', *BE*, 14 December 1929, p.24; 'Ben Greet Players Present "Hamlet" at Academy of Music', *(Brooklyn) Standard Union*, 14 December 1929, p.9.

25   '"Twelfth Night" at the Academy', *PI*, 2 January 1930, p.6.

26   Clarence Boykin, 'The Theatre', *Richmond Times-Dispatch*, 10 January 1930, p.18; Paul Blackwell to Redpath, 22 February 1930, Iowa.

27   Holme published the diary in instalments in *Repertory*, a theatre journal he founded in 1931 and edited until it folded in 1933. I am grateful to Ian Gadd for obtaining copies of these diary instalments for me from the Bodleian Library, which possesses the only volumes known to exist of this obscure, short-lived periodical.

28   BG to Harry Harrison, 6 January 1930, Iowa; BG to Harry Harrison, 8 January 1930, Iowa; Harry Harrison to BG, 16 January 1930, Iowa; BG to Harry Harrison, 19 January 1930, Iowa; BG to Harry Harrison, 29 January 1930, Iowa; Harry Harrison to Paul Blackwell, 4 February 1930, Iowa; Paul Blackwell to Redpath, 18 February 1930, Iowa; BG to Harry Harrison, 24 April 1930, Iowa.

29   Stanford Holme, 'Across America as a Member of a Theatrical Company', *Repertory*, 25 April 1931, p.4; '"Hamlet" Presented', *Kokomo (Indiana) Tribune*, 3 May 1930, p.9.

30   William F. McDermott, 'More Shakespeare, This Time by Ben Greet', (*Cleveland*) *Plain Dealer*, 29 January 1930, p.25.

31   Holme, 'Across America', *Repertory*, 9 May 1931, p.14.

32   Holme, 'Across America'. *Repertory*, 23 May 1931, p.14.

33   Harrison, p.204.

34   Holme, 'Across America', *Repertory*, 6 June 1931, p.10; Holme, 'Across America', *Repertory*, 30 November 1931, p.14; BG to Harry Harrison, 27 February 1930, Iowa; Paul Blackwell to Redpath, 27 February 1930, Iowa; Harry Harrison to BG, 5 March 1930, Iowa; Harry Harrison to BG, 10 April 1930, Iowa.

35   Patrick McGilligan, *Young Orson: The Years of Luck and Genius on the Path to Citizen Kane* (New York: Harper, 2015), pp.61 and 164–65.

36   Paul Blackwell to Redpath, 4 March 1930, Iowa; 'Ben Greet Players Revenue', 2 April 1930, Iowa; 'Ben Greet Players Revenue', 9 April 1930, Iowa; BG to Harry Harrison, 24 April 1930, Iowa. Seating capacity from *C-L(1913)*, p.88.

37   '2,300 Persons See Greet Performances', *(Huron, South Dakota) Evening Huronite*, 17 April 1930, p.1; 'Crowd Thrills to "Twelfth Night"', *Lincoln (Nebraska) Star*, 20 April 1930, p.30; 'Le Dernier Cri', *Omaha World-Herald*, 20 April 1930, p.39; BG to Harry Harrison, 24 April 1930, Iowa.

38   'Ben Greet to the Road', *NYT*, 26 October 1930, section 8, p.3.

39   BG to Harry Harrison, 20 April 20 1930, Iowa; BG to Harry Harrison, 22 February 1930, Iowa; Harry Harrison to BG, 10 April 1930, Iowa; Harry Harrison to BG, 22 April 1930, Iowa.

40   BG to Harry Harrison, 11 April 1930, Iowa; BG to Harry Harrison, 18 April 1930, Iowa; BG to Harry Harrison, 20 April 1930, Iowa; BG to Harry Harrison, 22 April 1930, Iowa. Quote from BG to Harry Harrison, 24 April 1930, Iowa.

41   '"Hamlet" Presented', *Kokomo (Indiana) Tribune*, 3 May 1930, p.9.

42   'Famous Play by Ben Greet', *Hattiesburg (Mississippi) American*, 29 October 1931, p.3; 'Ben Greet Players to Give Two Plays in the Auditorium', *Denver Post*, 25 November 1931, p.11.

43   Edward L. Desobry, '"Hamlet" is Presented with Feeling before Audience at New University', *(Baton Rouge) Advocate*, 31 October 1930, p.2.

44   'Drama Alive in Texas Says Sir Philip Ben Greet', *Dallas Morning News*, 25 November 1930, section 2, p.16; 'From Ben Greet', *Wichita (Texas) Daily Times*, 25 November 1930, p.8.

45   'Sanders Theatre', *Boston Herald*, 14 January 1931, p.17.

46   'Ben Greet Players are Well Received', *(Trinity College) Tripod*, 13 January 1931, p.1; 'Famous Play by Ben Greet', *Hattiesburg (Mississippi) American*, 29 October 1931, p.3; 'Ben Greet Players to Give Two Plays in the Auditorium', *Denver Post*, 25 November 1931, p.11.

47   'Ben Greet Players Give 2 Performances', *Greensboro (North Carolina) News*, 14 April 1931, p.5; 'Greet Players Well Received', *(University of North Carolina) Tar Heel*, 15 April 1931, p.1.

48   John Mason Brown, 'Many Years Later: Shakespeare as He Survives on Broadway', *New York Evening Post*, section 4, p.1; 'Tonight's Radio Programs', *NYS*, 23 April 1931, p.24.

49   J. Brooks Atkinson, 'The Play', *NYT*, 24 April 1931, p.29; 'Shakespeare Club', *(Brooklyn) Standard Union*, 25 April 1931, p.6; 'Ben Greet at Mount Holyoke', *NYT*, 3 February 1931, p.27; 'Joins Ben Greet Players', *NYT*, 22 April 1931, p.28; 'Schools Sponsor Presentation by Ben Greet Group', *Troy (New York) Times*, 31 March 1931, p.5.
50   John Mason Brown, 'Many Years Later: Shakespeare as He Survives on Broadway', *New York Evening Post*, 25 April 1931, section 4, p.1.
51   BG to Emily Folger, 12 July 1931, Folger Papers, Box 26, Folger Shakespeare Library.
52   'English Players to Appear Here', *Trenton (New Jersey) Evening Times*, 19 October 1931, p.2.
53   'Louisville Grosses Encouraging', *Variety*, 13 November 1931, p.51.
54   Seating capacity from <http://historic-memphis.com/memphis-historic/ellis/ellis.html> [accessed 31 May 2016].
55   'Students Throng to See Performances of Greet Players', *Dallas Morning News*, 24 November 1931, p.10; 'Sir Philip Ben Greet and His Company Capture Two Large Audiences at their Shakespeare Presentations at C. I. A.', *Denton, Texas, Record-Chronicle*, 1 December 1931, p.8; 'Sigma Tau Delta Scores Success in Ben Greet Players', *Commerce (Texas) Journal*, 11 December 1931, p.12; 'Veteran Actor Brings More Bard to Dallas', *Dallas Morning News*, 3 November 1931, p.10.
56   'Audience Cools to Shakespeare', *New York Evening Post*, 1 December 1931, p.14.
57   'Two Shakespeare Plays Given by Ben Greet Company', *Denver Post*, 7 December 1931, p.23. Seating capacities from 'Convention Plans Near Completion', *Macon City (Iowa) Globe-Gazette*, 8 May 1930, p.7 and <www.dnr.mo.gov/shpo/nps-nr/82003148> [accessed 19 June 2014].
58   'Jordan Hall: "Julius Caesar"' and 'Jordan Hall: "A Comedy of Errors"', *Boston Herald*, 20 January 1930, p.8.
59   'News from the Dailies', *Variety*, 9 February 1932, p.36; 'Sir Philip Lights a Candle', *NYT*, 24 April 1932, p.X2.
60   'Folger Memorial Opened by Widow', *NYT*, 24 April 1932, p.3; Stephen H. Grant, *Collecting Shakespeare: The Story of Henry and Emily Folger* (Baltimore: Johns Hopkins University Press, 2014), p.178.
61   Ben Greet Players to Henry Clay Folger, Cablegram n. d. [April 1932], Folger Collection, Box 21, Folger Shakespeare Library; Alman, p.114.
62   'Scores "Ignorance" of Critics of Arts', *NYT*, 9 May 1932, p.18; 'Theatrical Notes', *NYT*, 9 May 1932, p.19; 'Shakespearean Comedy', *New York Evening Post*, 9 May 1932, p.17; 'Ben Greet in Benefit', *NYT*, 10 May 1932, p.25.
63   'Shakespeare Given Musical Setting', *NYT*, 13 July 1932, p.15; 'To Give "The Comedy of Errors"', *NYT*, 7 August 1932, p.23.
64   'Thorndike Pluck', *Derby Daily Telegraph*, 21 April 1932, p.4; 'Shakespeare Festival', *Hastings and St Leonards Observer*, 28 May 1932, p.9; Advertisement, *Dover Express*, 3 June 1932, p.6.
65   'Eager Heart', *Grantham Journal*, 7 January 1933, p.6; 'Stratford Gala Day', *Aberdeen Journal*, 25 April 1933, p.6; 'Week-End on the Air', *Burnley Express*, 22 April 1933, p.1; Harwood, pp.114–15.

[66] For details, see Conville, pp.15–16; 'Play in a Dell', *Hull Daily Mail*, 5 June 1933, p.4; 'Eastbourne's Unique Attraction', *Sussex Agricultural Express*, 22 June 1934, p.3; 'Sir Nigel Playfair Dead', *Western Daily Press*, 20 August 1934, p.8; Isaac, pp.220–29.

[67] 'Ben Greet Players', *(Kent & Sussex) Courier*, 14 July 1933, p.9.

[68] BG to Emily Folger, 20 December 1933, Folger Papers, Box 26, Folger Shakespeare Library.

[69] 'Great Christians', *Gloucestershire Echo*, 27 October 1933, p.6; 'Sunday', *Edinburgh Evening News*, 24 February 1933, p.8.

[70] Sir Donald Wolfit to Ernest Milton, 15 February 1968, qtd in Harwood, pp. 271–72; 'Love's Labour's Lost', *(Kent & Sussex) Courier*, 22 June 1934, p.11.

[71] 'Plymouth Playgoers' Circle', *Western Morning News*, 4 October 1934, p.1; Schafer, p.148.

[72] 'Entertainments', *Sussex Agricultural Express*, 23 November 1934, p.3.

[73] 'Courageous West End Production', *Yorkshire Post*, 28 March 1935, p.3.

[74] 'Tribute to Sir Ben Greet', *(Kent & Sussex) Courier*, 5 April 1935, p.10; Isaac, pp.22–23.

[75] 'Mr. Hicks' New Adventure', *Yorkshire Post*, 14 May 1935, p.5; 'Taking a Day's Leave', *Yorkshire Post*, 6 August 1935, p.7.

[76] 'Ben Greet Players at Tunbridge Wells', *(Kent & Sussex) Courier*, 24 June 1935, p.10.

[77] Greet's obituary, 'Sir Philip Ben Greet, Actor and Producer of Shakespeare', *The Times*, 18 May 1936, p.19, erroneously states that he professionally produced Shakespeare's plays in the open air for forty-nine consecutive summers.

[78] '"All Star" Shakespeare', *Yorkshire Post*, 8 November 1935, p.10.

[79] 'Dame Madge Kendal's Funeral', *Gloucestershire Echo*, 17 September 1935, p.1; 'Colonel Robert Loraine', *Hull Daily Mail*, 28 December 1935, p.1.

[80] Daisy Ross to Lucy Love, 15 May 1936, Author; Isaac, pp.23, 25, and 234; 'Lady Watson Decides to Emigrate with Her Daughters', *Western Daily Press*, 14 July 1936, p.8.

[81] 'Sir Philip Ben Greet, Actor and Producer of Shakespeare', *The Times*, 18 May 1936, p.19.

[82] 'Ben Greet Dies, 78; Famous as Actor', *NYT*, 18 May 1936, p.17.

[82] 'Ben Greet', *NYT*, 19 May 1936, p.22.

[84] 'Sir Ben Greet's £127', *(Gloucester) Citizen*, 8 October 1936, p.8.

EPILOGUE

Tyrone Guthrie once remarked that all directors 'learn, borrow, steal, if you like, from one another'. More recently, Michael Dobson concludes that Ben Greet's performances inspired hundreds of amateur ones and brought Shakespeare to the audience that has supported open-air Shakespeare ever since.[1] With these observations in mind, I would like to close by examining a few practitioners who employed Greet's methods at the tercentenary and after in order to demonstrate his continuing influence.

Victor H. Hoppe and Angus L. Bowmer

As its offering in 1916, the dramatic society of the Washington State Normal School at Bellingham mounted an open-air production of *A Midsummer Night's Dream*. Its director, the newly appointed Victor Hugo Hoppe of the Department of Expression, assured readers of the *Bellingham Herald* 'that in every essential the play will duplicate the "under-the-sky" productions of the Ben Greets'. Hoppe's claim of authenticity may have been founded on something more vivid and substantial than access to the edition Greet prepared for Doubleday. A native of Akron, Ohio, Hoppe attended Denison University, but in 1908 he also attended the University of Chicago's summer school, where he had immediate access to the two-week Shakespearean festival Greet mounted in Scammon Gardens that July. After graduating from Denison (B. A., 1909), Hoppe enrolled as a postgraduate student at the non-degree-granting Boston School of Oratory, from which he earned a Teacher's Diploma in 1910. Returning to Denison, he worked as an instructor until taking up the professorship at Washington Normal in 1915. He kept his promise to the people of Bellingham the following spring: his production was staged at night on the campus knoll, omitted the play's non-woodland scenes, and featured music, dances, special lighting effects, and local children playing fairies.[2]

In 1921, the *Bellingham Herald* announced the society's second Shakespearean offering: 'Ben Greet's version of Shakespeare's "As You Like It" will be presented on the knoll at the Normal campus under the direction of Professor Victor H. Hoppe'. Its writer noted that the Greenwood Theatre — the name Hoppe had chosen for the purpose-built, 800-seat, open-air venue starting to go up in the knoll — would be completed by 1924 before observing that strong attendance would 'encourage the staging of Shakespearean plays [there] in the future by amateurs, chiefly, through whom, it seems likely, the great poet's traditions and artistry will be handed down in the coming years'.[3] In Chapter Seven, we saw Richard Burton of the University of Minnesota expressing satisfaction in 1916 that 'educational institutions [...] have waked up to the realization that education has obligations in the direction of the theatre, with Shakespeare central in it'. By 1921, a reporter for a paper in rural Washington (possibly coached by Hoppe) clearly recognized that amateurs at academic institutions would be the ones to shelter the playwright whose works the rapidly shrinking world of commercial theatre desired less and less.

Hoppe and the drama club mounted a Shakespearean production every summer from 1921 to 1926, all but one of which they staged in the open air: *As You Like It* (twice), *The Merchant of Venice* (indoors), *Dream*, *Twelfth Night*, and *Romeo and Juliet*. Significantly, one advertisement proclaimed the club's 'Fourth Annual Shakespearean Festival', and notices for the fifth and sixth editions employed similar phrasing. Establishing a reputation for permanency and continuity seems to have been important.[4]

This was the state of performed Shakespeare on campus when the person who would go on to become Hoppe's most famous protégé, Angus L. Bowmer, matriculated in 1924. As a high school student, Bowmer had attended Hoppe's *Merchant* as well as carried a spear in the Hoppe-written and -directed, 150-participant *Coronation of the Tulip Queen* pageant of 1923.[5] As an undergraduate at Bellingham Normal, Bowmer began learning the rudiments of Shakespearean performance and production by acting in Hoppe's second production of *As You Like It* and by acting in and stage managing Hoppe's *Romeo and Juliet*. The former experience was so memorable that Bowmer entitled the autobiography of the festival he went on to found *As I Remember, Adam*, and Hoppe was such a powerful personal inspiration that Bowmer fixed his sights on becoming an instructor at a normal school.

Bowmer got the opportunity to work with a much more renowned Shakespearean interpreter, Ben Iden Payne, while studying for his M. A. at the University of Washington. Bowmer played Boyet in *Love's Labour's Lost* when Payne produced it and *Cymbeline* on the big proscenium stage in Meany Hall in 1930, both of which employed a fit-up of an Elizabethan public theatre designed by that institution's John Conway. The experience taught Bowmer many things about thrusts, shadows, and inners above and below. More important, they demonstrated the value of 'smooth rapidity of tempo', encouraging the 'actors to encounter the audience directly', limited intermissions (Payne allowed two), understanding the meanings of Shakespeare's words, and eliminating every vestige of eighteenth- and nineteenth-century interpretations 'in order to discover and put to use in a twentieth century production what must have been seen and heard in the original sixteenth and seventeenth century productions'.

The Department of English at the Southern Oregon Normal School hired Bowmer as an instructor in 1931. The amateur Shakespearean festival he and his colleagues famously mounted in Ashland four years later successfully synthesized elements attributable to Payne and Hoppe. Payne's influence is apparent in the Elizabethan-style, *frons-scaenae*-like structure Bowmer built as well as in the newspaper notices Bowmer reproduces testifying to the vigorous rapidity of action and the performers' laudable comprehension of the lines they spoke. Hoppes's is evident in Bowmer's decision to mount Shakespearean plays out of doors, in his selection of at least one of the two plays he staged (Bowmer specifically credited Hoppe's Shylock for inspiring his own production of *Merchant*), and perhaps in his choice to have the words 'First Annual Shakespearean Festival' printed on the first programme to create a sense of permanence. Bowmer may have been unaware that he was using and adapting practices Greet brought to America more than thirty years earlier, but there is no doubt that Greet was the one who introduced them to the continent and that his influence extended even to Bowmer's audience. For when Bowmer and his colleagues initially discussed the idea of mounting a theatrical festival in the foundation of the largest of Ashland's abandoned permanent Chautauqua auditoriums, they gave some thought to who might attend such an event. They correctly identified that people still drawn to the idea of Chautauqua, which they regarded as a festival of sorts, might make up an important segment of their audience:

> The Chautauqua had died out all over the country many years before I came to the Rogue River Valley in 1931. But Ashland is a very conservative town. Conservatives tend to hang on to the past. Perhaps this conservatism would be an advantage to reviving the festival idea; especially so if the festival were staged within the same walls which housed the old tradition.

The open-air Shakespeare festivals Greet inaugurated at the universities of Toronto, Chicago, and Columbia as well as the Cincinnati Zoo all petered out after a few years. Thanks in part to the Greet-induced love for Shakespeare shared by old Chautauquans, the one Bowmer founded did not.[6]

Frederick H. Koch

Few institutions celebrated the tercentenary as impressively as the University of North Dakota. Its Sock and Buskin Society, the gown-town drama club founded and led by Frederick Henry Koch of the Department of English, mounted a production of *Much Ado about Nothing* in April as well as well as scenes from *As You Like It* and *Macbeth* later that spring, all in Grand Forks's 875-seat Metropolitan Theatre. The *Grand Forks Herald* attributed the success of the rarely produced *Much Ado* to fine acting and its 'Elizabethan manner' staging. On his own, Koch presented a series of five public lectures on Shakespeare that March and April that attracted sizable audiences from Grand Forks and the surrounding communities. The festivities culminated during commencement week, when Sock and Buskin presented the Koch-directed *Shakespeare, the Playmaker*, a pageant collaboratively composed by twenty students under Koch's supervision. The society performed it twice that June at the Bankside Theatre, an open-air venue Koch designed (with input from Percy MacKaye, Percival Chubb, and Frank Chouteau Brown) and laid out in 1914. Shakespeare certainly did not lack for admirers at the University of North Dakota.[7]

Because Koch is such a major figure in the history of early twentieth-century American play-writing, folk drama, educational theatre, and community theatre, the mature decades of his career are well-documented. However, because the members of his celebrated Carolina Playmakers were the ones to tell his story, little attention has been paid to what he did before moving to the University of North Carolina in 1918.[8] And a study of his early years reveals something as startling as it is significant: Greet's method and repertory exerted a demonstrable influence on Koch — far greater than even the professor's fervent description of the *Much Ado* performance by Eric Blind's company of Ben Greet Players he witnessed in 1915 indicates. Indeed, the man best remembered for pioneering the instruction of the writing of American folk plays in American universities may have been the academic most inspired by and familiar with Greet's work.

A native of Peoria, Illinois, Koch attended Ohio Wesleyan University, where he made a particular study of English literature with an emphasis on early drama, Shakespeare, and Victorian poetry. Following his graduation (B. A., 1901), he enrolled as a postgraduate student at the non-degree-granting Emerson College of Oratory in Boston, where he took the two-year Artistic Course that included classes in Oratory, Gesture, Expression, Dramatic Interpretation, English Literature, and Rhetoric. Upon completing it, Koch began working as a Lyceum presenter; J. W. Pratt booked fifty appearances for him on a minor New England circuit between May 1903 and April 1904. Earning a living as a dramatic reader was an undertaking expressly approved by Koch's supportive father, August Wilhelm Koch, from whom Koch inherited his strong faith, dedication to the Lyceum movement, and reverence for Shakespeare. Although the work paid decently and Koch was skilful enough to secure an audition with the prestigious Boston Redpath Bureau in 1904, he ultimately decided to pursue the academic career he had begun contemplating in 1903. In 1904, he applied to and was accepted at Harvard University to pursue an M. A. in English. Commentators have rightly noted that he became a protégé of George Pierce Baker during the required one-year residence at Harvard, but no one has considered the other theatrical influences he was exposed to during the four years he lived in Boston. While at Emerson, Koch definitely studied with Henry Lawrence Southwick and probably with William James Rolfe, the importance of the latter's work Nan Johnson has begun to recover. More relevant to the present study, he resided in the city at the same time Greet enjoyed his greatest successes there and had direct and immediate access to every one of the Englishman's production described in Chapters Two and Three. That Koch attended one or more performances is probable given his avowed literary interests and the fact that the highly successful six-week engagement the Ben Greet Players played in Boston during the 1903–04 season took place at Chickering Hall — the same building that housed the Emerson College of Oratory.[9]

The University of North Dakota hired Koch as an instructor in 1905. Until the spring of 1910, his drama-related offerings there consisted of 'monodramatic recitations', both on campus (*Everyman, She Stoops to Conquer, A Christmas Carol*) and at Lyceum assemblies (those works as well as *Don Caesar de Basan, The Taming of the Shrew*, and unspecified 'Shakespearean readings') where he established some regional popularity. The only productions he was involved with were a pair of senior-class plays he directed that were presented at the Metropolitan Theatre during commencement weeks: *The Rivals* (1906) and *Tom Pinch* (1907).[10]

The foundation of the Sock and Buskin Society in January 1910 was a landmark event for Koch and the university. According to its charter, it was dedicated to 'the study of the literature of the drama', to 'the promotion of the art of the theatre by the discussion and presentation of good plays', to stimulating and developing 'higher ideals for the drama in America', and to initiating 'a movement to establish as soon as possible a university theatre in the University of North Dakota'.[11] That spring, the *Herald* noted that, eager to take part in the theatrical movement then sweeping America, the society's inaugural offering would be an open-air production. Although the movement traced its origins to ancient Greece, it owed its recent popularity to 'the success of the Ben Greet Players, who have put on many high class open air plays throughout America'. As this grainy photograph of a dress rehearsal illustrates, Koch staged the play he selected, *Twelfth Night*, in textbook Greet fashion, right down to the greenery-adorned platform and canvas screens. The scaffold's dimensions even look right.

The paper reported that the performance on 13 June convinced many of the four hundred people who attended of the value of Koch's plan to build an open-air theatre on campus that might 'become a permanent feature of the dramatic work of the university'. It also generated so much enthusiasm that the society's next meeting was packed.[12]

32. Anonymous. TWELFTH NIGHT. Dir. Frederick Henry Koch,
University of North Dakota, Grand Forks, ND, June 1910.

Sock and Buskin mounted its second production the following
April: an indoor *Everyman* at the Metropolitan for Lent. Koch
directed, played the title-role, and commissioned costumes and
scenery from professional suppliers in Minneapolis. Significantly,
the *Herald* reprinted the seven-character *Everyman* photograph taken
in Mendelssohn Hall (reproduced in Chapter Two) to catch the
attention of readers. It erroneously stated that Sock and Buskin's
production would be the first in which the title-role would be played
by a man. A character called 'Adonai' was listed in the Cast of
Characters it printed, and it even ran the oft-publicized endorsement
from Archbishop Elder of Cincinnati (quoted in Chapter Three)
'congratulating Ben Greet, the eminent English actor, on his
successful revival of this play not long ago'.[13]

A production of *Twelfth Night* employing Greet's exact open-air
staging method followed by an indoor, Lenten *Everyman* extremely

reminiscent of Greet's — the coverage of both of which explicitly reference Greet — suggest Koch strategically employed the actor-manager's methods, repertory, and reputation to launch Sock and Buskin. Koch had ample opportunity to see the Englishman's indoor and outdoor productions during the years he lived in Boston. Greet was one of the most prominent figures in the Education Theatre Movement in 1910, widely known to have performed on the campuses of scores of the nation's most prestigious institutions on hundreds of occasions. Conspicuously imitating and referencing him would have been a canny way for Koch to demonstrate to administrators and other stakeholders the educational value and moral soundness of his work. Appropriating Greet's reputation helped Koch establish a formal place for drama at the University of North Dakota. Koch-supervised, student-written American folk pageants would soon follow.

Whatever exposure Koch had to Greet's work in Boston, he received direct and extended exposure to it while working as a Chautauqua presenter — a facet of his career Charlotte M. Canning discovered.[14] In the summer of 1913, he began touring a five-talk Shakespearean lecture series on Keith Vawter's North Dakota-Minnesota-Iowa-Missouri Redpath circuit. When Koch returned the following summer, he found himself sharing big-tops with George Vivian's Number 2 company of Ben Greet Players, then presenting *The Comedy of Errors*. The reason he attended so many performances by Eric Blind's Number 3 company in 1915 was that he transferred his lectures to Crawford Peffer's New York-New-England-Eastern Canada circuit.[15]

One attribute that distinguishes Koch among the pioneering figures in the history of Drama and Theatre instruction in American higher education is that his abilities as a thinker, writer, and teacher were backed by a high degree of competence as a theatrical practitioner. The foundation of those skills was laid at Emerson, but observing the Ben Greet Players for twenty-four weeks in circuit Chautauqua during the summers of 1914 and 1915 can only have enhanced them. The American members of Greet's companies and a handful of Chautauqua employees excluded, no American I am aware of had more exposure to Greet's methods and productions than Koch. And as his eyewitness account (reproduced in Chapter Seven) makes clear, what he witnessed revealed more than a method. The company's performance had a transformative effect on the professor, awakening him — seemingly as never before — to performed drama's potential to delight, educate, and inspire rural American communities.

Some of the scholarship Koch published after moving to the University of North Carolina further evidences his esteem for Greet's work. As Dobson discovered, Koch and collaborator Elizabeth A. Lay 'highly recommended' one of Greet's acting editions in their 1920 bibliography of plays well-suited to performance by community players. But Dobson significantly underreports how much Shakespeare — and Greet — Koch and Lay endorsed. He states that they recommended four Shakespearean plays, one of which was Greet's 1912 Doubleday edition of the *Dream*. In fact, the pair endorsed fourteen Shakespearean plays, four of them — *As You Like It*, *Comedy of Errors*, *Julius Caesar*, *Dream* — in the 'highly recommended' Greet editions.[16] The actor-manager's name does not appear in Koch and Lay's *Everyman* entry, but the fact that the scholars specify that the play should be performed by three men and four women indicates the extent to which the Poel-Greet production continued to influence how the Morality was staged.

The last place Greet's influence on Koch is apparent is in the activities of the Carolina Playmakers on the campus of the University of North Carolina during the summer months. To celebrate the tercentenary, UNC students under the direction of faculty had staged a Shakespearean pageant containing scenes from *As You Like It*, *The Winter's Tale*, *1 Henry IV*, *A Midsummer Night's Dream*, *Hamlet*, and *The Tempest* at an open-air site in the campus arboretum selected by William C. Coker of the Department of Botany.[17] The spot was so well-suited to outdoor performance that Koch started staging plays there during his first full summer in Chapel Hill. He called it the Forest Theatre, and the only productions his Carolina Playmakers staged in it from 1919 to 1923 were written by Shakespeare: *The Taming of the Shrew* (twice), *Twelfth Night*, *Much Ado*, *As You Like It*, and *Comedy of Errors*. Of the twenty-two plays they presented in it from 1924 to 1944 (the year Koch died), seven were written by Shakespeare.[18] Most of Koch's energies were devoted to fostering the impressive output of original plays and pageants written and produced by the generations of UNC students he painstakingly taught, supervised, and nurtured. But as busy as the Carolina Playmakers kept him and as thrilled as he was in 1925 when he persuaded the administration to let him convert the old Law School into the first state-supported theatre in the United States, Koch scrupulously maintained the open-air tradition at UNC. Thanks at least in part to Ben Greet, Koch regarded outdoor performance in general, and outdoor Shakespeare in particular, as a fundamental component of his work as an educator of the Dramatic Arts.

Koch's debt to Greet was not lost on one of the professor's most celebrated students. The protagonist of Thomas Wolfe's semi-auto-biographical *Look Homeward, Angel* (1929), Eugene Gant, plays Prince Hal in a Shakespearean tercentenary pageant almost identical to the one the citizens of Asheville, North Carolina, mounted in 1916. Fact and fiction diverge, however, when Wolfe describes the pageants' producers. The one in Asheville was produced by a committee, while the one in the novel is produced by a solitary expert, a great pageant-maker whose expertise assures its success: 'The machinery of the pageant was beautiful and simple. Its author — Dr. George B. Rockham, at one time, it was whispered, a trouper with the Ben Greet players — had seen to that'. Wolfe being known for conflating characters, Rockham may be a cross between Koch and Dr E. Reid Russell, the teacher who led Wolfe (who played the prince) and the other students of the North State Fitting School that day in Asheville. The identification by this important author in his breakthrough novel of Greet as the ultimate source and foremost practitioner of open-air Shakespeare is another testimony to the Englishman's American legacy.[19]

Undergraduate Dramatic Societies

As these accounts suggest, the group Greet inspired that continued to exert the greatest cultural influence was undergraduate dramatic societies. The production method he demonstrated at more than 265 institutions on more than 780 dates, coupled with the six acting editions he prepared for Doubleday, armed students with the basic tools they needed to imitate him. And did they ever do so. A casual search of the newspaper databases I used to prepare this book leads me to conclude that compiling a passably comprehensive list of the Greet-inspired or -influenced undergraduate Shakespearean productions mounted at those institutions prior to the actor-manager's death in 1936 would be a considerable undertaking in its own right. That the cumulative effect of all this activity was to establish North American Academic Shakespeare is now evident.

We have seen how the first interest in the United States in Original Practices expressed itself through a handful of archaeological reconstructions featuring elaborate, Poel-style fit-ups and simulated Elizabethan audiences presented in Manhattan, Cambridge, New Haven, and Palo Alto between 1895 and 1908. But mounting fit-up-focused productions was unlikely to catch on, not only because doing so was expensive and required facilities most institutions lacked, but also because these performances seem to have generated little in the way of real enthusiasm.

In contrast, the production method Greet perfected as a professional outdoor/indoor Shakespearean practitioner during the 1880s and 1890s created an Elizabethan atmosphere that thrilled and inspired audiences. Coupled with the moral and highbrow reputation he also acquired during those years, that method enabled him to create the North American academic market in 1903. His success at the continent's elite educational institutions established the scholarly importance of both himself and his method. The offer of a professorship from the University of California in 1905 called international attention to his eminence as an educator-practitioner as it bolstered the scholarly legitimacy of the Dramatic Arts. The educational value of Greet's productions appealed to faculty and administrators, while their ability to delight and instruct appealed to students. Undergraduate dramatic societies across the country gradually began to realize that Greet's method freed them from the constraints imposed by limited budgets and facilities while conferring upon their work a degree of scholarly respectability. John Corbin briefly revived archaeological reconstruction in New York for the tercentenary, but as far as American undergraduate dramatic societies and their faculty sponsors were concerned, staging Shakespearean productions that were as authentic as they could make them as regards text, costumes, performance style, and atmosphere was a better and far more attainable goal. Greet demonstrated what the professional version of that looked and sounded like to hundreds of thousands of undergraduates on hundreds of North American campuses. He even showed students the best places on their campuses to do it. The rest was up to them. Lawrence Reamer's comments in 1916 (discussed in Chapter Seven) make clear that contemporaries regarded Greet as having introduced and popularized the practical, robust production method 'destined to prevail ultimately'. Richard Burton's contemporaneous remarks indicated that the successful introduction of that method into higher education is what inspired not only universities to consider establishing departments of Theatre, but also professors to seek out William Poel's essays and books. While the scholars were reading Poel, thousands of their students were grabbing copies of Greet's Doubleday editions, donning Elizabethan costumes, and stepping onto the greensward and scaffold.

By presenting so much Shakespeare to so many students on so many campuses, Greet gave undergraduates both the cultural authority and the practical means to stage more and better Shakespeare than ever before. Students with halls could mount indoor, Elizabethan Manner productions during the academic year. Those without could mount outdoor, bare-stage productions in the spring, summer, and early autumn. And, thanks to the protracted and very public battle Greet fought against Spectacular Realism on Broadway and elsewhere, students in the know had a dragon to slay in the form of in-authentically staged Shakespeare. Greet first started preaching the virtues of staging practicably authentic Shakespeare in the United States in 1903 — eleven years before Payne started doing so at Carnegie Tech, and twenty-seven years before Payne showed Bowmer the principles of doing so at the University of Washington. That Greet and the Coburns popularized bare-stage Shakespeare years before Payne arrived in the United States cannot be disputed.

In 1909, the founders of the New Theatre incorrectly prophesied that their magnificent building would soon establish itself as Shakespeare's home in the United States. That the playwright would increasingly be found slumming it on college campuses and in Chautauqua tents as the commercial theatre business violently contracted in the 1910s and 1920s is probably not a notion they would have credited. It is, I hope, one that seems plausible in light of the evidence I have presented.

From eBay, I acquired a number of seemingly relevant real photographic postcards manufactured in the United States between 1904 and 1930, four of which I reproduce here. All depict college-aged people dressed in Elizabethan costumes for the purpose of performing *As You Like It* (all-male), *Julius Caesar* (all-male), *Much Ado* (co-ed), and *As You Like It* (all female), respectively. The photographs may have been taken in the open air to save on the (negligible) cost of flashes, but I am inclined to think the reason they were was because that is where these young people mounted their productions.

More specifically, the pictures reveal that *As You Like*, possibly staged using the 'highly recommended' Greet edition, was once beloved of dramatic societies. What they tell us more generally is that college-aged Americans mounted a lot of open-air Shakespeare, and that they valued the experiences so highly that they created and kept mementos of them. (Readers curious to see the cast of Hoppe's second open-air *As You Like It* are encouraged to consult Bowmer's book, which reproduces the yearbook photo that Bowmer himself carefully preserved.[20])

Amateurs, not professionals, became increasingly responsible for sustaining the Shakespearean performance tradition in America after 1916. A great many of them were students at universities, colleges, normal schools, and high schools, and their preferred staging method was — and still is — founded on the one Ben Greet began establishing in 1903. These realities are worth bearing in mind as we continue to study Shakespeare's place in twentieth-century American culture.

33. Anonymous. AS YOU LIKE IT. c. 1904–18.

34. Anonymous. JULIUS CAESAR. c. 1904–18.

35. Anonymous. MUCH ADO ABOUT NOTHING. c. 1904–20.

36. Anonymous. AS YOU LIKE IT. c. 1918–30.

NOTES

[1] Tyrone Guthrie, *A Life in the Theatre* (New York: McGraw-Hill, 1959), p.76; Dobson, pp.172–73.

[2] 'Normal Seniors to Honor Shakespeare', *Bellingham (Washington) Herald*, 22 May 1916, p.6; 'Shakespeare out of Town', *Bellingham (Washington) Herald*, 25 May 1916, p.7; 'Normal Seniors are Capable Actors', *Bellingham (Washington) Herald*, 30 May 1916, p.5. Hoppe's summer at the University of Chicago from *The (Denison University) Adytum* (Granville, OH: Denison University, 1911), p.16.

[3] 'Normal Gives Play', *Bellingham (Washington) Herald*, 18 August 1921, p.12.

[4] 'Play to be Given', *Bellingham (Washington) Herald*, 4 August 1923, p.10; 'Play Opens Tonight [*sic*]', *Bellingham (Washington) Herald*, 6 August 1924, p.16; 'Comedy Presented', *Bellingham (Washington) Herald*, 4 August 1925, p.10; '"Romeo and Juliet" Repeated at Normal; 700 Applaud Players', *Bellingham (Washington) Herald*, 13 August 1926, p.17.

[5] '150 Persons to Take Part in Coronation Pageant of the Tulip Queen', *Bellingham (Washington) Herald*, 8 May 1923, p.8.

[6] Angus Bowmer, *As I Remember, Adam: An Autobiography of a Festival* (Ashland: Oregon Shakespearean Festival Association, 1975), pp. 11, 25–37, and 71–76. For Payne's recollection of his interaction with Bowmer in 1930, see Payne, pp.177–78.

[7] 'Koch Speaks Next Sunday', *Grand Forks (North Dakota) Herald*, 9 March 1916, p.5; 'Thespians of U. N. D. Score in Shakespeare', *Grand Forks (North Dakota) Herald*, 19 April 1916, p.10; 'Elizabethan England is Graphically Portrayed in Sock and Buskin Pageant', *Grand Forks (North Dakota) Herald*, 26 May 1916, p.10; Frederick H. Koch, *The Book of Shakespeare, the Playmaker* (Grand Forks: University of North Dakota Press, 1916), [p. 64]. Seating capacity from *JC(1909)*, p.626.

[8] For a study of Koch's years at the University of North Dakota, see John P. Hagan, 'Frederick H. Koch in North Dakota: Theatre in the Wilderness', *North Dakota Quarterly*, 38.1 (1970), 75–87.

[9] A. H. Koch to FHK, 9 November 1903; A. H. Koch to FHK, 23 November 1903; A. H. Koch to FHK, 7 December 1903; A. H. Koch to FHK, 6 January 1904; Ida Law to FHK, 10 February 1904; J. W. Pratt to FHK, 7 April 1904; R. T. Stevenson, Letter of Reference for FHK, 29 April 1904; A. H. Koch to FHK, 17 May 1904; Letter of Reference from Henry L. Southwick, 31 May 1904. All from Frederick H. Koch Papers, Louis Round Wilson Special Collections Library, the University of North Carolina at Chapel Hill. For a discussion of Rolfe, see Nan Johnson, 'Shakespeare in American Rhetorical Education, 1870–1920', in Kahn, Nathans, and Godfrey, pp.112–30.

[10] 'Everyman', *Grand Forks (North Dakota) Herald*, 4 March 1906, part 1, p.7; 'She Stoops to Conquer', *Grand Forks (North Dakota) Herald*, 7 December 1906, p.5;

'Heard Christmas Carols', *(Grand Forks North Dakota) Evening Times*, 13 December 1909, p.6; 'The Rivals, Senior Play', *Grand Forks (North Dakota) Herald*, 10 June 1906, part 1, p.5; 'University Senior Play will be Given in Several Towns in State', *Grand Forks (North Dakota) Herald*, 31 May 1907, p.5; 'Senior Play', *Grand Forks (North Dakota) Herald*, 5 June 1907, p.7.

[11] 'Dramatic Club is Organized at U.', *Grand Forks (North Dakota) Herald*, 6 February 1910, p.8.

[12] 'Shakespeare's Twelfth Night', *Grand Forks (North Dakota) Herald*, 5 June 1910, p.5; 'Twelfth Night Well Presented', *Grand Forks (North Dakota) Herald*, 14 June 1910, p.13; 'Soc [*sic*] and Buskin Laying Plans', *Grand Forks (North Dakota) Herald*, 25 October 1910, p.6.

[13] 'Production of "Everyman" Will be Notable Affair', *Grand Forks (North Dakota) Herald*, 29 March 1911, part 2, p.13; 'Professor Koch Returned: Was in the Twin Cities to Secure Costumes for "Everyman"', *Grand Forks (North Dakota) Herald*, 2 April 1911, p.2.

[14] Canning, p.197.

[15] 'Koch to Tour Chautauquas', *Grand Forks (North Dakota) Herald*, 25 May 1913, p.8; 'Prof. Koch Had Busy Lecture Trip', *Grand Forks (North Dakota) Herald*, 23 September 1914, p.8; 'In Society', *Grand Forks (North Dakota) Herald*, 20 June 1915, p.9.

[16] Frederick Henry Koch and Elizabeth A. Lay, *Plays for Amateurs, University of North Carolina Record*, 172 (January 1920), 1–67; Dobson, p.181.

[17] 'Beautiful Costumes and Effective Acting Make Pageant a Great Success', *(University of North Carolina) Tar Heel*, 6 May 1916, p.1; <http://ncbg.unc.edu/forest-theatre/> [accessed 31 May 2016].

[18] For a chronology of the productions the Carolina Playmakers staged in the Forest Theatre, see *Pioneering a People's Theatre*, ed. by Archibald Henderson (Chapel Hill, NC: University of North Carolina Press, 1945), pp.100–01.

[19] 'Society and Personals', *Asheville (North Carolina) Citizen*, 16 May 1916, p.6; Thomas Wolfe, *Look Homeward, Angel: A Story of the Buried Life* (New York: Charles Scriber's Sons, 1929), p.302. My thanks to Robert W. Trogdon for calling to my attention Wolfe's reference to Greet and to Park Bucker for supplying the biographical particulars and pointing out Wolfe's tendency to conflate.

[20] Bowmer, between pp.8 and 9.

APPENDIX

North American Institutions of Higher Learning that Hosted Performances by Ben Greet's Companies, 1902–18, 1929–32

Alabama

Auburn U (Alabama Polytechnic Inst.) — 3 April 1931	=1
Huntingdon C (Woman's C of Alabama) — 22 April 1914	=1
Judson C — 21 April 1915, 8 April 1916	=2
U of Alabama — 23 April 1914, 31 March 1931	=2
U of Montevallo (Alabama C, State C for Women) — 8 February 1930	=1

Arizona

Arizona State U (Tempe NS) — 27 March 1913, 8 October 1917	=2
Northern Arizona U (Northern Arizona NS) — 13 October 1917a	=1
U of Arizona — 5 October 1917	=1

Arkansas

Hendrix C (Hendrix-Henderson C) — 25 October 1930	=1
U of Arkansas — 22 May 1914, 23 May 1914, 21 May 1915, 22 May 1915, 24 May 1916, 25 May 1916	=6

California

Mills C — 22 October 1904	=1
Pasadena City C (Pasadena Junior C) — 19 March 1930	=1
Pomona C — 17 November 1917, 22 March 1930	=2
San José State U (San José NS) — 22 April 1913	=1
Stanford U — 21 September 1903, 22 September 1903, 21 October 1904, 19 November 1904, 19 April 1913, 21 April 1913	=6
U of California, Berkeley — 1 September 1903, 26 September 1903, 1 October 1904, 16 November 1904, 18 November 1904, 10 February 1905, 11 February 1905, 1 May 1909, 8 May 1909	=9
U of the Pacific (C of the Pacific) — 23 November 1917	=1
U of Redlands — 18 March 1930	=1

Colorado

Colorado C — 29 March 1913, 7 December 1931a	=2
U of Colorado, Boulder — 8 December 1931	=1
U of Denver (Colorado Women's C†) — 5 December 1931a	=1
U of Northern Colorado (Colorado State Teachers C) — 10 December 1931a	=1

Connecticut

Trinity C — 28 May 1908, 14 June 1911, 6 January 1931a =3
U of Connecticut — 13 October 1915 =1
Wesleyan U — 18 June 1915, 16 June 1916 =2
Yale U — 25 May 1903a, 1 June 1904a, 1 June 1906a =3

District of Columbia

George Washington University — 30 April 1907 =1

Florida

Florida State U (Florida State C for Women) — 20 April 1914, 21 April 1914,
 9 April 1915 =3
Jacksonville State U (Jacksonville State Teachers C) — 26 March 1931, 27 March 1931 =2
Stetson U (Columbia C) — 15 April 1915 =1
U of Florida — 18 April 1914, 7 April 1915 =2

Georgia

Agnes Scott C — 5 April 1916 =1
Brenau U (Brenau C) — 30 April 1909 =1
Cox C* — 3 May 1909, 4 May 1909, 6 April 1916 =3
Georgia Inst. of Technology — 19 April 1915, 6 April 1916 =2
U of Georgia — 9 May 1907, 29 April 1909, 24 March 1931 =3

Idaho

Lewis-Clark State C (Lewiston State NS) — 26 October 1917, 27 October 1917 =2

Illinois

Eastern Illinois U (Eastern Illinois NS) — 17 July 1914, 8 July 1915 =2
Illinois State U (Illinois State Normal U) — 2 July 1909, 2 July 1915, 3 July 1915,
 11 August 1915 =4
Illinois Wesleyan U — 27 August 1913, 4 March 1930a =2
Knox C — 8 July 1913, 28 July 1913, 3 June 1914 =3
Millikin U — 23 May 1905, 30 March 1908, 10 February 1930 =3
Monmouth C — 18 August 1913 =1
Northern Illinois U (Northern Illinois State NS) — 4 April 1908, 29 July 1908,
 8 July 1909, 9 July 1913, 9 July 1914, 8 July 1916 =6
Northwestern U — 16 May 1905a, 4 July 1907 =2
Rockford U (Rockford C) — 6 April 1908a =1
Shimer C (Frances Shimer School and Junior C) — 29 October 1913, 4 June 1915 =2
U of Chicago — 12 July 1905, 13 July 1905, 14 July 1905, 15 July 1905, 19 July 1905,
 21 July 1905, 22 July 1905, 1 July 1907, 3 July 1907, 4 July 1907, 6 July 1907,
 8 July 1907, 10 July 1907, 11 July 1907, 12 July 1907, 13 July 1907, 6 July 1908,
 8 July 1908, 9 July 1908, 11 July 1908, 13 July 1908, 15 July 1908, 16 July 1908,
 17 July 1908, 18 July 1908, 12 July 1909, 13 July 1909, 14 July 1909, 15 July 1909,
 19 July 1909, 21 July 1909, 22 July 1909, 24 July 1909 =33
U of Illinois at Urbana-Champaign — 24 May 1905, 16 March 1906, 13 June 1907,
 27 March 1908, 28 March 1908, 28 June 1912, 29 June 1912, 16 February 1913,
 11 July 1913, 12 July 1913, 9 January 1914, 10 January 1914, 18 July 1914,
 27 January 1915, 23 January 1918, 19 February 1930 =16
Western Illinois U (Western Illinois NS) — 30 June 1915, 1 July 1915 =2
William and Vashti C* — 2 June 1914 =1

Appendix

Indiana

Asbury Female C* — 18 July 1913, 19 July 1913 ..... =2
Ball State U (Ball State Teachers C) — 13 February 1930 ..... =1
Butler U (Butler C) — 20 June 1905, 21 June 1905, 8 June 1916, 9 June 1916,
10 June 1916 ..... =5
DePauw U — 15 February 1930 ..... =1
Concordia Theological Seminary (Concordia C) — 1 May 1930 ..... =1
Earlham C — 21 June 1907, 22 June 1907, 14 February 1930 ..... =3
Indiana U Bloomington — 19 April 1906, 20 April 1906, 18 February 1907,
8 June 1907, 15 July 1911, 17 June 1912, 2 July 1912, 17 June 1913,
1 July 1914, 2 July 1914, 5 July 1915, 6 July 1915, 26 June 1916,
27 June 1916, 12 February 1930 ..... =15
Indiana U-Purdue U Fort Wayne (Fort Wayne Art School†) — 19 June 1905a ..... =1
Indiana U-Purdue U Indianapolis (John Herron Art Inst.) — 28 June 1907,
29 June 1907, 1 August 1913, 2 August 1913 ..... =4
Indiana State U (Indiana State NS) — 1 July 1912, 29 July 1913, 7 June 1916 ..... =3
Manchester U (Manchester C) — 13 March 1931 ..... =1
Purdue U — 12 May 1905, 13 May 1905, 10 June 1907, 26 March 1908,
30 October 1931 ..... =5

Iowa

Coe C — 5 March 1931 ..... =1
Cornell C — 3 December 1914 ..... =1
Drake U — 13 July 1914, 14 July 1914, 13 July 1915, 14 July 1915, 7 March 1930 ..... =5
Iowa State U of Science and Technology (Iowa State C of A & M Arts) —
12 July 1915, 22 April 1930 ..... =2
Loras C (Columbia C) — 20 February 1930 ..... =2
Morningside C — 16 April 1930, 17 April 1930 ..... =1
Parsons C* — 14 June 1914 ..... =1
U of Iowa — 23 November 1915a, 3 March 1931 ..... =2
U of Northern Iowa (Iowa State Teachers C) — 5 February 1913, 10 July 1914,
11 July 1914, 9 July 1915, 10 July 1915, 30 June 1916, 1 July 1916, 7 January 1918 ..... =8
Upper Iowa U — 5 December 1913 ..... =1
William Penn U (Penn C) — 15 June 1914 ..... =1

Kansas

Baker U — 9 December 1913 ..... =1
Emporia State U (Kansas State NS) — 20 January 1913, 10 December 1913,
18 June 1914, 19 June 1914 ..... =4
Fort Hays State U (Western Branch of Kansas State NS) — 20 June 1914,
27 May 1915, 12 December 1931 ..... =3
Kansas State U (Kansas State Agricultural C) — 25 May 1914, 29 May 1915,
14 December 1931 ..... =3
Ottawa U — 26 May 1914, 25 May 1915 ..... =2
Pittsburg State U (Kansas Teachers C of Pittsburg) — 22 June 1914, 23 June 1914,
24 May 1915 ..... =3
Teachers C of Kansas City* — 15 December 1931a ..... =1
U of Kansas — 31 May 1915, 8 March 1930 ..... =2
Washburn U (Washburn C) — 28 May 1915 ..... =1

Kentucky

Eastern Kentucky U (Eastern Kentucky State Teachers C) — 20 March 1931,
  28 October 1931   =2
Western Kentucky U (Western Kentucky State NS) — 29 June 1914, 30 June 1914   =2
U of Kentucky — 17 April 1906a, 27 October 1931   =2

Louisiana

Centenary C of Louisiana — 27 October 1930   =1
Louisiana State U and A & M C (Louisiana State U) — 29 April 1914, 24 April 1915,
  25 April 1916, 30 October 1930   =4
Northwestern State U of Louisiana (Louisiana State NS) — 22 April 1915,
  28 October 1930   =2
Tulane U (Newcomb C†) — 30 April 1914, 1 May 1914, 26 April 1916, 27 April 1916   =4
U of Louisiana at Lafayette (Southwest Louisiana Inst.) — 2 May 1914a, 26 April 1915,
  28 April 1916, 1 November 1930, 16 November 1931   =5

Maine

Bates C — 17 February 1914a, 25 January 1932a   =2
U of Maine — 16 February 1914a   =1

Maryland

Hood C (Woman's C of Frederick) — 1 May 1911, 31 May 1915, 23 October 1931   =3
St John's C — 5 June 1909   =1
Towson University (Maryland State NS) — 22 October 1931   =1
United States Naval Academy — 14 May 1908   =1

Massachusetts

Harvard U — 1 June 1903, 2 June 1903, 12 January 1931, 13 January 1931,
  19 January 1932a   =5
Mt Holyoke C — 2 June 1904, 31 May 1906, 27 May 1908, 15 June 1915,
  30 November 1929, 4 February 1931   =6
Smith C — 27 May 1903a, 11 November 1929, 12 November 1929, 6 February 1931,
  7 February 1931   =5
U of Massachusetts Amherst (Massachusetts State C) — 8 January 1932   =1
Wellesley C — 29 May 1903   =1
Williams C — 1 June 1908   =1

Michigan

Central Michigan U (Central Michigan NS) — 29 July 1909, 20 July 1915, 21 July 1915 =3
Eastern Michigan U (Michigan State Normal C) — 18 March 1908, 21 June 1909,
  14 June 1912, 30 April 1930   =4
Hope C — 31 January 1918   =1
Michigan State U (Michigan Agricultural C) — 20 July 1916   =1
U of Michigan — 7 November 1903, 26 May 1905, 27 May 1905, 17 June 1905,
  24 February 1906, 15 June 1906, 16 June 1906, 19 January 1907,
  26 January 1907, 18 June 1907, 19 June 1907, 21 March 1908, 22 March 1908,
  23 March 1908, 16 June 1908, 11 March 1909, 27 July 1909, 28 July 1909,
  27 June 1911, 28 June 1911, 2 August 1911, 31 July 1912, 1 August 1912,
  20 June 1913, 21 June 1913, 31 July 1913, 23 July 1914, 24 July 1914, 25 July 1914,
  23 July 1915, 24 July 1915, 21 July 1916, 22 July 1916, 26 January 1930a,
  27 January 1930a, 6 March 1931, 7 March 1931   =37

Western Michigan U (Western Michigan NS) — 18 June 1906, 17 June 1907,
　　15 June 1908, 26 July 1909　　　　　　　　　　　　　　　　　　=4

Minnesota
Carleton C — 26 November 1915　　　　　　　　　　　　　　　　=1
Minnesota State U Mankato (Minnesota State Teachers C) — 25 February 1931　=1
U of St Thomas (St Paul Seminary) — 11 July 1905　　　　　　　　=1
U of Minnesota, Twin Cities Campus — 28 June 1905, 29 June 1905, 10 July 1905,
　　9 June 1914, 10 June 1914a, 7 June 1915, 8 June 1915, 22 February 1930　=8

Mississippi
Delta State U (Delta State TC) — 6 November 1931　　　　　　　　=1
Mississippi U for Women (Mississippi C for Women) — 24 April 1914, 14 April 1916,
　　10 November 1931　　　　　　　　　　　　　　　　　　　　=3
Mississippi State U (Mississippi State A & M C) — 25 April 1914, 13 April 1916,
　　11 November 1931　　　　　　　　　　　　　　　　　　　　=3
U of Southern Mississippi (Mississippi Normal C) — 28 April 1914, 12 November 1931 =2
U of Mississippi — 5 November 1931　　　　　　　　　　　　　　=1

Missouri
Central Methodist U (Central Methodist C) — 10 December 1930　　　=1
Drury U (Drury C) — 26 May 1916, 27 May 1916　　　　　　　　　=2
Missouri State U (Southwest Missouri State Teachers C) — 4 December 1930a　=1
Missouri Valley C — 24 April 1930　　　　　　　　　　　　　　=1
Truman State U (North Missouri NS) — 7 November 1913　　　　　=1
U of Missouri — 14 January 1913, 29 May 1914, 30 May 1914, 25 April 1930　=4

Montana
U of Montana — 22 October 1917　　　　　　　　　　　　　　　=1
The U of Montana Western (Western Montana C) — 19 October 1917　=1

Nevada
U of Nevada, Reno (Nevada State U) — 14 February 1905a　　　　　=1

New Hampshire
Dartmouth C — 8 December 1903, 11 December 1929, 12 December 1929　=3
U of New Hampshire (New Hampshire C) — 11 December 1912　　　=1

New Jersey
C of New Jersey (New Jersey State Teachers C) — 22 January 1931a,
　　20 October 1931a　　　　　　　　　　　　　　　　　　　　=2
Georgian Court U (C of Mt St Mary) — 18 June 1909　　　　　　　=1
Princeton U — 23 March 1903, 23 May 1903, 9 April 1904, 20 May 1904,
　　2 November 1905, 20 November 1905, 8 January 1906, 2 June 1906,
　　15 April 1907, 22 May 1907, 23 May 1907, 28 April 1911, 5 June 1911,
　　6 June 1911, 23 January 1931　　　　　　　　　　　　　　　=15
Rutgers, The State U of New Jersey, New Brunswick (Rutgers U) — 22 January 1906,
　　24 May 1907, 12 June 1915　　　　　　　　　　　　　　　　=3

New Mexico
New Mexico State U (New Mexico State A & M C) — 13 March 1913　=1
U of New Mexico — 12 March 1930a　　　　　　　　　　　　　　=1

New York
City C — 23 April 1913 =1
Columbia U — 14 May 1903, 15 June 1903, 16 June 1903, 17 June 1903,
    12 May 1904a, 3 August 1908, 4 August 1908, 5 August 1908, 7 August 1908,
    8 August 1908, 2 August 1909, 3 August 1909, 4 August 1909, 5 August 1909,
    6 August 1909, 7 August 1909, 9 August 1909, 10 August 1909, 11 August 1909,
    12 August 1909, 13 August 1909, 14 August 1909, 16 November 1929,
    23 April 1931, 24 April 1931, 25 April 1931 =26
Cornell U — 2 February 1909a =1
Elmira C — 7 December 1915a =1
Hobart and William Smith Colleges (William Smith C†) — 12 June 1909,
    8 September 1914 =2
New York U — 2 July 1906, 3 July 1906, 5 August 1914 =3
Russell Sage C — 28 April 1931a =1
SUNY at Fredonia (State NS) — 25 November 1912, 7 March 1914 =2
SUNY at New Paltz (State NS) — 14 November 1929 =1
SUNY at Oswego (Oswego NS) — 14 October 1913, 27 October 1914 =2
SUNY C at Potsdam (Potsdam NS) — 11 October 1912, 19 November 1929,
    27 January 1931 =3
Syracuse U — 5 June 1906, 30 January 1909, 7 June 1910 =3
U at Albany, SUNY (State Teachers C) — 22 November 1929 =1
U at Buffalo, the SUNY (State Teachers C) — 13 February 1931 =1
U of Rochester — 7 June 1904, 8 June 1904 =2
United States Military Academy — 27 June 1906, 20 April 1907, 9 June 1915 =3
Vassar C — 3 December 1902 =1
Wells C — 6 December 1909 =1

North Carolina
Duke U (Trinity C) — 19 May 1910 =1
Elizabeth C* — 13 May 1907, 11 May 1909, 11 May 1910 =3
U of North Carolina at Chapel Hill (U of North Carolina) — 14 May 1910,
    11 May 1911, 14 April 1931 =3
U of North Carolina at Greensboro (State Normal and Industrial C & North
    Carolina C for Women) — 14 May 1907a, 12 May 1911, 13 April 1931 =3

Ohio
Bowling Green State U (Bowling Green State Normal C) — 11 February 1918,
    24 January 1930 =2
Case Western Reserve U (Western Reserve U) — 29 June 1908, 30 June 1908,
    1 July 1908, 2 July 1908, 3 July 1908, 4 July 1908 =6
C of Wooster — 31 July 1908, 1 August 1908, 22 July 1914, 26 July 1915,
    20 February 1931a =5
Denison U — 6 November 1915a =1
Kent State U (Kent State NS) — 21 July 1914, 27 July 1915 =2
Lake Erie C — 12 June 1905 =1
Marietta C — 21 November 1912 =1
Miami U (Oxford C†) — 19 February 1907, 17 July 1913, 23 March 1914,
    22 October 1930 =4
Oberlin C — 13 June 1905, 14 June 1905, 23 February 1906, 21 June 1906,
    4 February 1907, 5 February 1907, 20 June 1907, 16 March 1908, 17 March 1908,

24 June 1908, 25 June 1908, 23 November 1912, 17 April 1913, 17 March 1914,
　31 July 1915 =15
Ohio Northern U (Ohio Normal U) — 20 July 1914, 21 June 1915 =2
Ohio State U — 22 June 1908, 23 June 1908 =2
Ohio U — 1 May 1908, 15 July 1913 =2
Ohio Wesleyan U — 7 November 1914a, 21 January 1930 =2
U of Cincinnati — 23 June 1905a, 24 June 1905a, 26 June 1905, 27 June 1905 =4
U of Toledo (Toledo U) — 9 March 1931, 10 March 1931 =2

Oklahoma

East Central U (Eastern Central State NS) — 16 May 1914, 15 May 1915 =2
Oklahoma State U–Stillwater (Oklahoma A&M C) — 20 May 1914, 19 May 1915,
　20 May 1915, 3 December 1930 =4
U of Oklahoma — 12 December 1913, 18 May 1914, 17 May 1915, 20 May 1916,
　25 November 1930 =5
U of Central Oklahoma (Central State NS) — 15 May 1914, 18 May 1915 =2

Ontario

Queen's U at Kingston — 14 February 1906 =1
U of Toronto — 10 June 1903, 11 June 1903, 9 June 1904, 10 June 1904, 7 June 1905,
　8 June 1905, 9 June 1905, 10 June 1905, 6 June 1906, 8 June 1906, 9 June 1906,
　10 June 1908, 11 June 1908, 13 June 1908 =14

Oregon

Oregon State U (Oregon State Agricultural C) — 31 March 1930a =1
Western Oregon U (Oregon NS) — 2 November 1917 =1

Pennsylvania

Bloomsburg U of Pennsylvania (Bloomsburg State NS) — 8 April 1910, 16 June 1911,
　13 June 1913, 27 March 1914, 3 June 1915, 2 June 1916 =6
Bryn Mawr C — 12 December 1902, 30 May 1904, 1 June 1907, 17 April 1931 =4
Bucknell U — 10 June 1913, 10 June 1915 =2
California U of Pennsylvania (California State NS) — 13 June 1910, 19 March 1914 =2
Carnegie Mellon U (Carnegie Inst. of Technology) — 26 March 1914 =1
Dickinson C — 31 May 1916 =1
Drexel U (Drexel Inst.) — 5 June 1916a =1
Franklin & Marshall C — 30 May 1907, 31 May 1911 =2
Gettysburg C — 12 April 1910 =1
Haverford C — 20 May 1912 =1
Indiana U of Pennsylvania (Indiana NS) — 28 June 1910 =1
Kutztown U of Pennsylvania (Keystone State NS) — 31 January 1914, 23 October 1915 =2
Lafayette C — 25 October 1906, 27 May 1907 =2
Lehigh U (Lehigh C) — 4 June 1906, 28 May 1907, 9 June 1911, 5 June 1913,
　6 June 1913, 6 June 1915 =6
Lock Haven U of Pennsylvania (Central State NS) — 19 June 1911, 2 August 1915 =2
Muncy NS* — 21 June 1910 =1
Penn State U Park (Pennsylvania State C) — 27 February 1909, 28 July 1915,
　24 October 1931 =3
Susquehanna U — 17 January 1931 =1
Swarthmore C — 15 May 1908, 20 May 1913, 18 April 1931 =3
Temple U — 15 January 1931 =1

U of Pennsylvania — 25 May 1904, 26 May 1904, 27 May 1904, 23 May 1906,
    24 May 1906, 25 May 1906, 23 April 1907a, 24 April 1907a, 25 April 1907a,
    26 April 1907a, 27 April 1907a, 2 June 1909, 3 June 1909, 4 June 1909,
    26 June 1910, 1 June 1911, 2 June 1911, 3 June 1911, 3 August 1914,
    4 August 1914, 29 July 1915, 30 July 1915, 27 July 1916, 28 July 1916   =24
Ursinus C — 21 January 1931   =1
Villanova U (Villanova C) — 18 May 1913   =1
West Chester U of Pennsylvania (West Chester NS) — 16 May 1908, 18 May 1912,
    17 May 1913   =3

Quebec
McGill U — 4 June 1903, 5 June 1903, 17 June 1904, 18 June 1904, 5 June 1905,
    6 June 1905   =6

Rhode Island
Brown U — 19 January 1903, 13 June 1903a, 7 December 1903, 7 December 1929   =4

South Carolina
Clemson U (Clemson C) — 16 April 1915, 17 April 1915   =2
C of Charleston — 6 May 1907, 21 April 1910, 22 April 1910, 23 April 1910,
    15 April 1914   =5
Converse C — 12 May 1906, 9 May 1909, 7 May 1910   =3
Furman U — 25 October 1912   =1
U of South Carolina — 7 May 1909, 25 April 1910, 26 April 1910, 13 April 1915,
    14 April 1915, 10 April 1931   =6
Winthrop U (Winthrop C) — 12 May 1909, 12 May 1910   =2

South Dakota
Huron U (Huron C)* — 15 April 1930   =1
Northern State U (Northern Normal and Industrial School) — 2 December 1913,
    14 April 1930   =2

Tennessee
Belmont U (Ward-Belmont C) — 4 May 1906, 4 February 1930a, 5 February 1930a   =3
Sewanee: The U of the South — 3 May 1906, 3 May 1907   =2
U of Memphis (West Tennessee State NS) — 24 October 1930a   =1
U of Tennessee — 2 May 1906, 7 April 1931   =2
U of Tennessee at Chattanooga (U of Chattanooga) — 6 April 1931   =1
Vanderbilt U (Peabody C) — 26 June 1914, 27 June 1914, 3 November 1931   =3

Texas
Amarillo C (Amarillo Junior C) — 22 November 1930a, 3 December 1931a   =2
Baylor U — 12 May 1914, 11 May 1916, 12 May 1916   =3
Howard Payne U (Howard Payne C) — 10 May 1916   =1
Kidd-Key C* — 14 May 1914, 13 May 1915, 14 November 1930   =3
Lamar U (South Park C) — 3 November 1930a   =1
McMurry U (McMurry C) — 20 November 1930a   =1
Midwestern State U (Wichita Falls Junior C) — 18 November 1930   =1
Rice U — 4 November 1930a, 18 November 1931a   =2
Sam Houston State U (Sam Houston NS) — 1 May 1916, 17 November 1931   =2
Southern Methodist U — 15 November 1930, 23 November 1931   =2

Tarleton State U (John Tarleton Agricultural C) — 1 December 1931 =1
Texas A & M U (Texas A & M C) — 6 May 1914, 29 April 1915, 6 November 1930 =3
Texas A & M U–Commerce (East Texas State Teachers C) — 24 November 1931 =1
Texas Christian U — 11 May 1914a, 10 May 1915a, 11 May 1915a, 16 May 1916a =4
Texas State U (Southwest Texas State NS, Southwest Texas State Teachers C) —
    6 May 1916, 20 November 1931 =2
Texas Tech U (Texas Technical C) — 21 November 1930, 2 December 1931a =2
Texas Wesleyan U (Texas Woman's C) — 17 November 1930, 25 November 1931a =2
Texas Woman's U (Texas State C for Women & C of Industrial Arts and Sciences) —
    13 November 1930, 30 November 1931 =2
U of Mary Hardin-Baylor (Baylor Female C) — 6 May 1915, 9 May 1916,
    10 November 1930 =3
U of Texas at Austin — 7 May 1914, 8 May 1914, 3 May 1915, 4 May 1915,
    12 November 1930, 21 November 1931 =6

Utah
Brigham Young C* — 11 January 1915 =1
Brigham Young U — 13 January 1915 =1

Vermont
Middlebury C — 19 June 1915, 20 June 1916, 13 January 1932 =3
U of Vermont — 27 January 1906, 12 January 1932 =2

Virginia
C of William and Mary — 12 May 1908, 24 May 1909, 1 June 1910, 4 May 1915 =4
Hollins U (Hollins Inst.) — 15 May 1907, 3 May 1908, 15 April 1931 =3
Hampden-Sydney C — 6 January 1930 =1
James Madison U (Harrisonburg State Teachers C) — 28 May 1915, 29 May 1915,
    4 January 1930 =3
Radford U (Radford NS) — 24 May 1915 =1
Randolph C (Randolph-Macon Woman's C) — 8 January 1930 =1
U of Mary Washington (State Normal and Industrial School for Women) —
    20 May 1915, 26 May 1916 =2
U of Richmond (Richmond C) — 16 May 1907, 27 May 1911, 15 May 1915 =3
U of Virginia — 15 May 1906, 6 November 1906, 17 May 1907, 9 May 1908,
    23 May 1910, 15 May 1911, 16 May 1911, 7 May 1915, 22 May 1916 =9
Virginia Polytechnic Inst. & State U (Virginia A & M C and Polytechnic Inst.) —
    18 May 1909 =1
Washington and Lee U — 5 May 1908, 19 May 1909, 24 May 1910, 25 May 1910,
    13 May 1911 =5

Washington
Evergreen State C — 3 May 1913 =1
U of Washington — 14 December 1904, 16 April 1913 =2
Washington State U (Washington State C)—25 October 1917 =1

West Virginia
West Virginia U — 19 February 1906, 20 February 1906, 21 February 1907,
    30 July 1914, 13 January 1930, 14 January 1930, 18 February 1931 =7
West Virginia Wesleyan C — 2 February 1916 =1

Wisconsin

Beloit C — 12 March 1906a, 14 January 1907a, 9 April 1908a =3
Lawrence U (Lawrence C) — 11 June 1914, 25 February 1930 =2
Milwaukee-Downer C* — 15 July 1907, 16 July 1907 =2
Ripon C — 14 June 1915 =1
U of Wisconsin–Madison — 17 July 1907, 18 July 1907, 27 July 1908,
    7 July 1913, 8 July 1913, 6 July 1914, 7 July 1914, 5 June 1915,
    26 February 1930, 27 February 1930 =10
U of Wisconsin–Oshkosh (Oshkosh State NS) — 8 July 1914 =1
U of Wisconsin–Stevens Point (Stevens Point NS) — 12 June 1914 =1

Wyoming

U of Wyoming (Wyoming State C) — 3 March 1913, 9 December 1931 =2

Total Institutions = 268   **Total Dates = 781**

Key

a = auspices (an institution or a unit of one (English department, drama club, YMCA
    chapter, sorority, etc.) sponsored an appearance at an off-campus venue)
* = since closed
† = since merged with another institution

INDEX

Page numbers in bold refer to figures and tables.

INDEX

INDEX

INDEX

INDEX

INDEX